Praise for the Sha

"The Shadow Falls series belongs to my favorite YA series. It has every-thing I wish for in a YA paranormal series. A thrilling tale that moves with a great pace, where layers of secrets are revealed in a way that we are never bored. It continues a gripping story about self-discoveries, finding a place in the world, friendship, and love. So if you didn't start this series yet, I can only encourage you to do so."

—*Bewitched Bookworms*

"Starts off with action and never loses momentum. C. C. Hunter takes readers on a supernatural thrill ride, full of suspense, drama, laughter, and intense emotions from page one all the way through the last page, ending in one of the biggest cliffhangers I've read."

—*Guilty Pleasures Book Reviews*

"Ms. Hunter handles this series with such deftness, crafting a wonder-ful tale that speaks to the adolescent in me. I highly recommend this series filled with darkness and light, hope and danger, friendship and romance."

—*Night Owl Reviews* (Top Pick)

"*Taken at Dusk* has even more drama and answers for Kylie. Jam-packed with action and romance from the very beginning, Hunter's lifelike characters and paranormal creatures populate a plot that will keep you guessing till the very end. A perfect mesh of mystery, thriller, and ro-mance. Vampires, weres, and fae, oh my!"

—*RT Book Reviews*

"Fans of the Twilight series will love this series. I cannot wait to see how this all plays out in book three."

—*Fallen Angel Reviews*

"*Awake at Dawn* is the second book in the Shadow Falls series and it is easily as awesome as the first! There is almost always something new or exciting going on . . . and readers will easily connect to Kylie and some of the secondary characters."

—*Live To Read Blog*

"The evolving, not-always-easy relationships among Kylie and her cabin mates Della and Miranda are rendered as engagingly as Kylie's angst over dangerous Lucas and appealing Derek. Just enough plot threads are tied up to make a satisfying stand-alone tale while whetting appetites for sequels to come." —*Publishers Weekly*

"*Born at Midnight* is addicting. Kylie's journey of self-discovery and friendship is so full of honesty, it's impossible not to fall in love with her and Shadow Falls . . . and with two sexy males vying for her attention, the romance is scorching. *Born at Midnight* has me begging for more, and I love, love, love it!" —*Verb Vixen*

"With intricate plotting and characters so vivid you'd swear they are real, *Born at Midnight* is an addictive treat. Funny, poignant, romantic, and downright scary in places, it hits all the right notes. Highly recommended." —*Houston Lifestyles & Homes* magazine

"I laughed and cried so much while reading this . . . I *loved* this book. I read it every chance I could get because I didn't want to put it down. The characters were well developed and I felt like I knew them from the beginning. The story line and mystery that went along with it kept me glued to my couch not wanting to do anything else but find out what the heck was going on." —*Urban Fantasy Investigations*

"This has everything a YA reader would want. . . . I read it over a week ago and I am still thinking about it. I can't get it out of my head. I can't wait to read more. This series is going to be a hit!" —*Awesomesauce Bookclub*

"The newest in the super-popular teen paranormal genre, this book is one of the best. Kylie is funny and vulnerable, struggling to deal with her real-world life and her life in a fantastical world she's not sure she wants to be a part of. Peppered throughout with humor and teen angst, *Born at Midnight* is a laugh-out-loud page-turner. This one is going on the keeper shelf next to my Armstrong and Meyer collections!" —*Fresh Fiction*

"Seriously loved this book! This is definitely a series you will want to watch out for. C. C. Hunter has created a world of hot paranormals that I didn't want to leave." —*Looksie Lovitz*

"*Born at Midnight* has a bit of everything . . . a strong unique voice from a feisty female lead, a myriad of supporting supernatural characters, a fiery romance with two intriguing guys—mixed all together with a bit of mystery—making *Born at Midnight* a surefire hit!" —*A Life Bound By Books*

"Very exciting, taking twists and turns I never expected. The main character grows very well throughout the story, overcoming obstacles and realizing things she never thought possible. And the author masterfully ended it just right." —*Flamingnet*

"I absolutely *loved* it. Wow, it blew me away." —Nina Bangs, author of *Eternal Prey*

Whispers at Moonrise

• a shadow falls novel •

c.c. hunter

ST. MARTIN'S GRIFFIN ❧ NEW YORK

WHISPERS AT MOONRISE. Copyright © 2012 by Christie Craig. All rights reserved. Printed in the United States of America. For information, address St. Martin's Press, 175 Fifth Avenue, New York, N.Y. 10010.

www.stmartins.com

ISBN 978-1-250-01191-6 (trade paperback)
ISBN 978-1-250-01192-3 (e-book)

10 9 8 7 6 5 4 3 2

To my editor, Rose Hilliard, and my agent, Kim Lionetti, for helping me reach my writing goals. To my husband for cooking the dinners, for doing the dishes and the laundry, so I could put in the hours to make deadlines and work toward making those dreams come true.

Acknowledgments

So often in this life, we spend so much time telling people when they do something wrong, from the waitress at the restaurant to the bagger at the grocery store. We forget to tell those people who just get it right. So I'd like to tip my hat to one organization and a bunch of individuals who have gotten it right.

To Romance Writers of America for creating an organization that provided me with the knowledge to move up the ladder in this career. To Rosa Brand for her awesome videos and friendship. To Faye Hughes and Kathleen Adey for assisting me in getting it all done. Thanks for all you two do. To all my writing peeps whose support is essential to making this mostly solitary career into one with a group of peers who are there to laugh and cry with, and keep each other inspired. A special thank you to another writing peep, Susan Muller, for the hour of walking, talking, and laughing we do most every day. To my parents, Pete Hunt and Ginger Curtis. You must have done something right because I didn't turn out too bad. Well, I'm not perfect, but for the most part, you must have raised me right. To my kids, who haven't turned out too bad, either. I'm proud of you both. And because as I write this, it's almost Father's Day, thank you to Jason, my son-in-law, for being a champion daddy to my precious granddaughter. A big thank you to the fans who have recommended my series to others. And my gratitude goes to those fans who have taken the time to e-mail me and tell me that my books have touched them in some way. Those e-mails help keep my joy of writing alive and kicking even when deadlines are kicking me in the butt. Thank you to each and every one of you for getting it right.

Whispers at Moonrise

Chapter One

Kylie Galen stood on the porch outside the Shadow Falls office, panic stabbing at her sanity. A gust of late August wind, still chilled by her father's departing spirit, picked up her long strands of blond hair and scattered them across her face. She didn't brush them away. She didn't breathe. She just stood there, air trapped in her lungs, while she stared through the wisps of hair at the trees swaying in the breeze.

Why does my life have to be so damn hard? The question rolled around her head like a Ping-Pong ball gone wild. The answer spun back just as quick.

Because you're not all human. For the last few months, she'd struggled to identify the type of non-human blood that rushed through her veins. Now she knew.

According to her dear ol' dad, she was . . . a chameleon. As in a lizard, just like the ones she'd seen sunning themselves in her backyard. Okay, so maybe not just like those, but close enough. And here she'd been worried about being a vampire or a werewolf because it would be a little hard to adjust to drinking blood or shape-shifting on full moons. But this . . . this was . . . unfathomable. Her father had to be wrong.

Her heart pounded against her chest as if seeking escape. She finally breathed. In, and then out. Her thoughts shot away from the lizard issue to the other bad stuff.

Yup. In the last five minutes she'd been slapped with not one, not two, not even three, but with four oh-crap eye-opening revelations.

Well, one thing—Derek's confession that he loved her—couldn't completely be called bad. But it sure as hell couldn't be called good. Not now. Not when she considered them history. Not when she'd spent the last few weeks trying to convince herself that they were just friends.

Her mind juggled all four disclosures. She didn't know which to focus on first. Or maybe her mind did know. *I'm a freaking lizard!*

"For real?" she spoke aloud. The Texas wind snatched away her words. She hoped it would take them all the way to her father— wherever the dead who hadn't completely passed over went to wait. "Seriously, Dad?"

Of course, Dad didn't answer. After two months of dealing with one spirit or another, the whole ghost-whispering gift and its limitations still managed to piss her off. "Damn!"

She took another step toward the main office's door to unload on Holiday Brandon, the camp leader, then stopped. Burnett James, the other camp leader and a cold to the touch but hot to look at vampire, was with Holiday. Since Kylie couldn't hear them arguing anymore, she figured that meant they might be doing something else—like sucking face, swapping spit, doing the tongue tango. All phrases her bad-attitude vampire roommate Della would use. Which probably meant Kylie was in a bad mood. But didn't she deserve a little attitude after everything that had happened?

Clenching her fists, she stared at the office's front door. She'd inadvertently interrupted their first kiss and she didn't want to do the same with their second. Especially when Burnett had threatened to resign from Shadow Falls. Surely Holiday could change his mind. Couldn't she?

Besides, maybe Kylie needed to calm down. To think things through before she ran to Holiday in bad-attitude hysterics. Her thoughts shifted to her latest ghost issue. How could a ghost of someone who was alive appear to Kylie? A trick, right? Had to be a trick.

She glanced around to make sure the ghost had really gone. The cold had vanished.

Turning, she shot down the porch steps and headed around to the back of the office. She started running, wanting to experience the sense of freedom she got when she ran, when she ran fast, ran non-human fast.

The wind picked up the black dress she'd worn to Ellie's funeral and sent the hem dancing against her thighs. Her feet moved in rhythm, barely missing the Reeboks she usually wore, but when she arrived at the edge of the woods, she came to an abrupt halt—so abrupt that the heels on her black dress shoes cut deep ruts into the earth.

She couldn't go into the woods. She didn't have a shadow—the mandatory person with her to help ward off the evil Mario and his rogue buddies if they decided to attack.

Attack again.

So far the old man's attempts at ending her life had proved futile, but two of those times had resulted in the death of someone else.

Guilt fluttered through her already tight chest. Fear followed it. Mario had proven how far he'd go to get to her, how evil he was when he'd taken his own grandson's life right in front of her. How could anyone be that wicked?

She stared at the trees and watched as their leaves danced in the breeze. It was a completely normal slice of scenery that should have put her at peace.

But she felt no peace. The woods, or rather something that hid within, dared her to enter. Taunted her to move into the thick line of trees. Confused by the strange feeling, she tried to push it away, but the feeling intensified.

She inhaled the green scent of the forest, and she knew.

Knew with clarity.

Knew with certainty.

Mario wouldn't give up. Sooner or later she would face him again. And it wouldn't be serene, tranquil, or peaceful. Only one of them would walk away.

You will not be alone. The words echoed deep within her as if to offer her peace. No peace came. The shadows between the trees danced on the ground. Calling her, beckoning her. To do what, she didn't know.

Trepidation took another lap around her chest. She dug the heels of her shoes deeper into the hard dirt. The heel of her right shoe cracked—an ominous little sound that seemed to punctuate the silence.

"Crap!" She stared down at her feet. The one word seemed yanked from the air, leaving nothing but a hum of eeriness.

And that's when she heard it.

Someone drew in a raspy breath. While the sound came only at a whisper, she knew that the owner of this breath stood behind her. Stood close. And since no chill of death surrounded her, she knew it wasn't from the spirit world.

The sound came again. Someone fed life-giving air into their lungs. Odd how she now feared the living more than she feared the dead.

Her heart thudded to a stop. Much like the grooves left in the earth by her three-inch heels, her growing dread left ruts in her courage.

She wasn't ready. If it was Mario, she wasn't ready. Whatever it was she needed to do, whatever plan or fate she was destined to follow, she needed more time.

Chapter Two

"Are you . . . okay?"

The voice. Not Mario. Derek's voice.

His familiar tone had her initial panic fading, but only for a second. *I'm in love with you, Kylie.* The words he'd spoken less than fifteen minutes ago flowed through her head, bringing with them another emotional storm that made her mind and heart spin. Derek loved her. But what did she feel?

She shifted slightly, and the heel from her right shoe fell off, making her off balance. That's how her life felt—as if it had lost a heel, and her only choice was to limp along.

"What's wrong?" His voice rang with concern.

I'm fine. The words perched on the tip of her tongue, but she swallowed them. Derek, half-fae, could read her. To lie to him about her emotional state was futile. So she turned around and faced him.

"What are you doing here without a shadow?" Derek asked. "You know you're not supposed to be without a shadow in case that freakish rogue returns."

Meeting Derek's gaze, she spotted the panic brightening his eyes. She knew the panic she saw was her own as well. When she hurt emotionally, he hurt. When she experienced joy, he lived it, too. When she feared something, he feared it for her. Considering her emotional state these last few minutes, he must be in hell.

His chest expanded behind the fitted dusty green t-shirt. He held a hand over his hard stomach as he sucked air into his lungs. His dark brown hair appeared windblown, and his bangs clung to his forehead. A drip of sweat rolled down his brow. For a second, all she could think about was falling into him, letting his calming touch chase away the apprehension inside her.

"Is it . . . what I said?" he asked. "If it is, I'll . . . take it back. I didn't tell you that to tear you apart inside."

One couldn't take back an admission of love, she thought. Not if he really meant it. But she didn't say that. "It's not what you said." Then she realized that, too, was a lie. His confession played havoc with her emotions. "Well, it's other stuff, too."

"What stuff?" His words came out breathlessly. His eyes searched hers and she saw the gold flecks in his irises brighten. "I sense you're terrified and confused, and—"

"But I'm okay." She noticed again his winded state, as if he'd just run a mile to get to her. *Had he?* "Where were you?"

He took in another deep gulp of oxygen. "My cabin."

Over a mile. "You felt my emotions that far away?"

"Yeah." He frowned as if he hoped she didn't blame him. She didn't like that her emotions were an open book for him to read, but she didn't blame him. He'd told her once that if he could stop reading her, he would. She believed him.

"I thought you said it was lessening," she said. "Does it still make you crazy?"

His left shoulder shifted upward a couple of inches. "It's still strong, but it's not overwhelming like before. I can handle it, now that I . . ."

Now that he'd accepted he loved her. That's what he'd told her.

That's why their link had grown so strong. Her chest grew heavy with indecision again. It was a good thing that one of them could handle it. Because she wasn't sure she could deal with this. Not with him loving her. Not with any of the revelations she'd been given. At least right now.

"What's wrong?" He stepped closer. So close she could smell his skin—earthy, honest, real.

The temptation to walk into his arms washed over her. She longed to feel the up and down motion of his chest as he breathed, to let what was in the past be what was in the future. Closing her hands into tight fists, she limped past him with her one broken heel, went to a tree, and lowered herself down to the ground. The earth felt cooler than the heat in the air. The blades of grass tickled the back of her legs, but she ignored it.

He didn't wait for an invitation; he lowered himself beside her. Not close enough that they touched, but close enough that she thought about touching.

"So it's more than one thing?" he asked.

She nodded and the decision to confide in him seemed already made. "My dad appeared to me." She bit down on her lip. "He told me what I am."

Derek looked puzzled. "I thought you wanted to know."

"Yeah, but . . . He said I'm a chameleon. As in, a lizard."

His brows pinched and then he chuckled.

She didn't appreciate his candor. Her panic came back threefold. She'd wanted to know what she was so the others would accept her, so she would fit in, but what if she ended up being something that honestly made her a freak?

"I hate lizards," she blurted out. "They're right up there with snakes—evil little bug-eyed creatures scurrying around in the dirt and eating creepy-crawly things." She stared out at the woods again, imagining a brigade of lizards staring back at her. "I saw a program once that showed a long-tongued lizard eating a spider in slow motion. It was gross!"

Derek shook his head, all shades of humor fading from his eyes. "I've never heard of supernatural lizards. Are you sure?"

"I'm not sure of anything. That's what's so scary. Not knowing." She shivered. "Seriously, devouring blood is preferable to having one of those long tongues and dining on insects."

"Maybe he got it wrong. You said ghosts have a hard time communicating."

"At first, yes, but now my dad makes perfect sense."

Derek didn't look convinced. "But what do you think a chameleon supernatural is, or does? All I think they could do is change colors."

Kylie let his words run around her brain for a second. "Maybe that's it?"

"You can change colors?" Doubt showed on his face.

"No. But maybe I can change my pattern. Like how my grandfather and aunt appeared human. And like how I appear human now."

"Or . . . maybe your father's having a relapse and he's just confused. Because I've never heard of any supernaturals who could change their brain patterns."

"What about me?" she asked. "What about my grandfather and aunt?"

He shrugged. "Holiday said it was probably a wizard who cast a spell for your grandfather and aunt."

"Did he cast it on me, too?" Kylie asked.

"No, but . . . Okay, I don't have the answer." He frowned. "And I know that frustrates you. But didn't you tell me that your real grandfather was coming to visit? I'm sure he'll clear it up."

"Yeah." She bit down on her lower lip.

Derek studied her. "There's something else wrong, too?"

She sighed. "When I asked my dad what it meant about being a chameleon, he said we'd figure it out together."

"And that's bad because . . . ?"

Kylie stated the obvious. "He's dead, and he's limited to earthly visits, so does that mean that I'm going to die soon?"

"No, he didn't mean that." Derek's tone deepened with conviction.

She started to argue that he couldn't say that with certainty, but because she wanted to believe him, she bit back the words. Taking a breath, she stared down at the grass and tried to find peace in knowing that her grandfather was going to come in a couple of days. Tried to find peace in having spilled her troubles. And she did feel slightly better.

"Have you asked Holiday?" He leaned in and his shoulder bumped into hers, his warmth, his soothing touch chasing away some of her angst.

She shook her head. "Not yet. She's still in the office with Burnett." And Kylie still hadn't mulled over the whole ghost issue. If someone's ghost appeared to you when they weren't dead, what did it mean? The possible answers started her heart shaking.

"I think this is kind of important," he said.

"I know, but . . ."

"There's something else, isn't there?"

She glanced up. Was he reading her emotions or her mind? "Ghost problems," she said.

"What kind of problems?"

Of all the campers, Derek was the only one who didn't run away at the mention of ghosts. "This person isn't dead."

"So it's not a ghost." Derek looked confused.

Kylie bit down on her lip. "Yes . . . I mean, at first the spirit had the whole zombie thing going on—hanging flesh, and worms—but then it changed. And when it did, the face turned into someone I know."

"How could that be?" he asked.

She paused. "I don't know. Maybe it's a trick."

"Or not," Derek said. "You don't think someone's going to die?"

Not anyone else, she wanted to scream. "I don't know." She yanked a few blades of grass from the ground.

"Who is it?" he asked. "Not someone here, is it?"

Kylie's chest tightened. She didn't want to say it—afraid that if she said it aloud, it would make it so. "I just need to think it through."

Derek paled. "Oh, crap! Is it me?"

"No." She tossed the blades of grass and watched them whirl in the wind on their descent.

When she looked back at him, she could feel him reading her emotions, deciphering their meaning. "You care a lot about this person." His brows pinched. "Lucas?" She heard the pain in his voice from just saying the name.

"No," she said. "Can we drop it? I don't want to talk about it. Please. "

"So it is Lucas?" Derek asked.

"What's Lucas?" A deep, irate voice suddenly spoke up.

Kylie looked up and saw Lucas step out of the trees. His eyes were an angry orange color. She flinched with guilt for a just a second, then fought it back. She hadn't been doing anything wrong.

"Nothing," Derek bit out when Kylie didn't speak. He stood up and took one step toward the office. Pausing, he looked back at her, and then glanced at Lucas. "We were just talking. Don't go all were on her."

Lucas growled. Derek walked away, appearing unaffected by Lucas's anger. Kylie grabbed another handful of grass and yanked it from the ground.

"I don't like this." Lucas stared down at her.

"We were just talking," she said.

"About me."

"I was telling him about a spirit and that . . . it looked like someone I care about, and he asked if it was you. You should feel good that he knows I care about you."

Lucas's scowl deepened. Was it because of Derek or because she'd mentioned ghosts? Lucas's inability to accept her working with the spirits hurt.

"He has feelings for you," Lucas countered.

I know. "We were just talking."

"It makes me crazy." His eyes glowed a deep, burnt orange color.

"What makes you crazy? Me talking to Derek, or me talking about ghosts?"

"Both." His voice rang with such honesty that she found it hard to condemn him for it. "But mostly it's the thought of you spending time with that fairy."

She flinched at his insult toward Derek. Then, unsure what to say, she stood up. Forgetting about her missing heel, she almost tripped. He caught her by the elbow.

She met his gaze, still marked by his were anger. But his touch was tender and caring, with no hint of the fury she saw in his eyes. She remembered that some of his reactions were instinctual, which meant he shouldn't be held accountable. Another part of her knew that instinctual or not, it didn't make it right.

She sighed. "We've already talked about this."

"Talked about what?" he asked.

"Both things. I help spirits, Lucas. That's probably never going to change."

"Yeah, but they scare the shit out of you. They scare the shit out of me."

Kylie tensed. "You think your shifting into a wolf doesn't scare me?"

"That's not the same. They are ghosts, Kylie. That's not . . . not natural."

"But turning into a wolf is completely natural," she said with sarcasm.

He exhaled. "Okay, coming from someone who's lived their life as a human, I can see your point. And while I'm sure I'm never going to love the ghost whispering part of you, I'm working on accepting it." His tone told her how hard that was for him. "But accepting that you're spending time with Derek isn't easy when I know if he were given the chance, he'd steal you away in a snap."

She swallowed raw emotion and touched his chest. His warmth soaked through his shirt and into her hand. "I know how it feels. Because I feel the same way when I see you with Fredericka. And that's the reason I know I can't tell you to push Fredericka away."

He placed his palm over her hand and a soft pleading filled his gaze. "That's different. Fredericka is part of my pack."

She shook her head. "And Derek's a friend."

"Exactly. That's what makes it different. A friend isn't the same as a pack member."

"It is for me." She shook her head. "Think about it. You're loyal to pack members. You would defend them. You care about them. That's the same way I feel about my friends."

"That's because you're not a were. Or at least not yet." He snaked his free hand around her waist and tugged her a little closer. "Hopefully, soon, it will all make sense to you."

I'll never be a were. She stared up at him. The evidence of his anger had faded from his eyes and she saw affection in their deep blue depths. He cared about her. She knew that with certainty. And maybe for that reason, she wavered about telling what she knew. Instantly, it hit her that she hadn't hesitated to tell Derek. Why could she confide in Derek and not Lucas? Bothered by the thought, she forced herself to say, "I'm not a were."

"You don't know that," he said. "The fact that you developed more before a full moon and had mood swings has to mean something."

She shook her head. "I'm not. I know what I am."

His eyes tightened in confusion. "You . . . How do you know?"

"My father appeared to me again. He said I was a chameleon."

Puzzlement filled his gaze.

She frowned. "I don't know exactly what it means."

"That doesn't make sense." He released her. "There's no such thing. Just because some ghost said—"

"It wasn't just 'some ghost.' It was my father."

"And your father is a ghost." Whether he meant it to or not, it sounded like an insult.

His words and his attitude stung. She pulled her hand from his warm chest. All the emotional havoc from earlier whirled inside her.

"I know he's a ghost," Kylie said. "And I wish he wasn't dead. I wish I knew what he meant. I wish that you could accept me for what I am. But I can't change the fact that my dad died before I was born. I can't help that I don't understand what he meant. For that matter, I don't understand a tenth of what's happening in my life right now. And I have a feeling you will never be able to accept me for what I am."

"That's not true." His expression hardened with denial.

"Yes, it is." She turned and limped away.

She heard him ask her not to go. She ignored his plea. Then, stopping, she reached down to remove her shoes. As she straightened, her gaze caught on the row of trees—on how their leaves stirred even when no wind blew. She felt again the unexplainable sense that she was being lured to enter. As tempting as it was, she walked away. Walked away from the forest. Walked away from Lucas.

And both somehow felt wrong.

Chapter Three

Kylie's bare feet moved quickly against the earth as she ran. She heard the blend of voices coming from the dining hall where everyone had congregated after Ellie's funeral. Ellie, who'd died at the hands of Mario.

Another wave of guilt washed over Kylie. She ran faster. She didn't want to join the crowd. She wanted . . . *needed* . . . to be alone.

She'd almost made it to her cabin when she felt a whoosh of air fly past her. A vampire whoosh. Maybe a vampire on the hunt.

Kylie pushed herself to run faster and mentally prepared herself to fight. Not that she stood a chance of winning a battle with a vampire. Whatever super strength she had only served her when she was helping others.

A *protector*, the other supernaturals called her. But how could they call her that when she hadn't protected Ellie? Even Kylie's healing abilities had failed. How unjust was it that she could save a bird, pull it back from death, and yet couldn't save a friend? She would have paid the price. It wouldn't have mattered how much of her soul she'd had to give to save Ellie.

She felt it again—that flash of air as something swooped past.

This time she saw a curtain of straight black hair billow in the wind. Definitely a vampire.

But not one on the hunt.

Della appeared beside her, running at the same breakneck pace. But being vampire, she moved with ease, as if she were taking a leisurely jog.

"What's wrong?" Della's dark hair, hinting at her Asian bloodline, flew behind her like a flag.

"*You* are what's wrong." Kylie came to a jerky stop. "I hate it when you fly by me like that and I can't tell it's you. I feel threatened. I feel like . . . prey."

"Well, damn," Della said in her everyday bad-attitude voice. "Excuse me for being concerned. I heard you running like hell and thought someone was chasing you."

"Sorry. No one is chasing me." Kylie's gaze shot back to the woods. *They're just taunting me to step into the woods and face them.* But who was it, and for what reason? Earlier she'd assumed it was Mario, but could she have been wrong about that?

"What happened?" Della asked.

Kylie pulled her eyes away from the woods. "Nothing."

Della tilted her head to the side, as if listening to Kylie's heart, listening for signs of deception. Della rolled her eyes. "Liar. Liar. Pants on fire."

Kylie groaned. "Fine. I'm lying. And if I were wearing pants, they'd combust and burn my ass."

"Wow. You are in such a lovely mood. What took a bite out of your attitude?"

"You did." Kylie flinched at the sound of her sharp tone.

Della grinned as if enjoying Kylie's anger. Kylie started walking.

"Who's supposed to be shadowing you?" Della asked.

"I don't know." Kylie's gaze shot to the woods and the sensation

hit stronger than ever. She took off running down the path, pushing herself harder. She didn't stop until she got to her cabin. Her
stomach cramped from running. She dropped down on the edge of
their porch.

"So what happened?" Della, not even breathing hard, plopped
down beside Kylie.

Something in the woods is calling my name. That sounded crazy.
Kylie couldn't say it. She looked at Della. Her roommate's slightly
slanted black eyes appeared genuinely concerned, and that made
Kylie feel like a bitch.

"Sorry. I'm in a bad mood."

"Which is so rare," Della said. "I kind of like it."

Kylie rolled her eyes and pushed back her reservations. "Have
you ever heard of chameleons?"

"Yeah," Della said.

"You have? What do you know about them?"

"They're lizards that change colors. According to Chan, they
don't taste too bad. In Hawaii, the local vampires sell their blood.
It's supposed to be as good as O negative."

"No." Kylie pulled her knees up and hugged them.

"No, what?"

"I mean . . . chameleons as a type of supernatural?"

"A lizard supernatural?" Della laughed.

Kylie jumped up.

"Hey." Della popped up beside her. "What's wrong with you?"

Kylie yanked open the cabin door and looked back at Della.
"Everything is wrong."

"Is this about Ellie?" Della's voice hinted at an emotion that the
vamp kept hidden.

Kylie's heart gripped tighter. "Yes, it's about Ellie. It's about me
being a lizard. It's everything."

"You're a lizard?" The seriousness faded from Della's eyes, and she grinned.

Kylie stormed through the door, then swung around. "Yeah, you're a vampire, and I'm a lizard, so just friggin' get used to it."

Della's smirk faded. "Have you been smoking something? Seriously, I think you're a werewolf. This new snarky attitude is a dead giveaway."

"And vampires aren't snarky?" Kylie rolled her eyes.

"No, we're pissy. Snarky and pissy are two totally different things." Della moved inside. The vamp's attempt at humor was to help, not hurt.

But Kylie wasn't in the mood. "I'm not a werewolf." Tears stung her eyes. "If I were, then Lucas would be happy and all would be right in the world."

Della's mouth dropped open. "You're serious. Who told you that you were a lizard?"

"My dad."

Della's eyes widened. "You're shitting me."

"No shitting."

Della fell into the sofa and her gaze darted around the room. "Is he here now?"

"No."

"Good." She slapped her hands on her thighs. "Maybe he was smoking something."

Kylie rolled her wet eyes. "Would you please stop making wisecracks?"

Della snatched up a sofa pillow and tossed it at Kylie. "See, there's the werewolf attitude coming out again."

Kylie swung around to go into her room, but before she got to the door, Della shot in front of it. It was freaky how fast a vampire could move.

"Fine," Della said. "I'll try to be serious, but . . . it's crazy. I know you don't want to believe this, but someone's pulling a practical joke on you. There's no such thing as a lizard supernatural. Just ask her."

"Ask who?" The cabin's main door slammed as Miranda stepped inside. Her blond hair hung loose, streaked with pink, green, and black. Kylie didn't know if Miranda used her Wiccan powers to color her hair or Nice 'n Easy.

Miranda frowned. "Why did you leave me?" she asked Della.

Della made a face. "Sorry. Kylie's having a crisis. I can only be Superfriend to one of you at a time."

Miranda looked at Kylie. "What kind of a crisis?"

Ordinarily, Kylie shared everything with Miranda and Della, but at this moment she wished she'd kept her mouth shut. All this time she'd longed to know what she was, thinking it would solve everything, and yet here she was, supposedly knowing, and feeling more confused than ever.

"A tasty reptile crisis." Della giggled, put her hand over her mouth, and then looked apologetically at Kylie. "Oops."

"What?" Miranda asked.

Della propped one hand on her hip. "Tell Kylie there's no such thing as lizard supernaturals."

"Perry can change into a lizard." Miranda's eyes brightened with pride. "Yesterday he shifted—"

"Please, not another Perry story." Della pressed both her palms against her stomach. "I swear, I'll hurl."

"You are such a bitch," Miranda snapped.

"I'm not a bitch. I'm just sick of hearing Perry stories. 'Perry's pinky toes are so cute. Perry's got the most charming freckle behind his right ear.' "

"You're just jealous! Because you don't have a boyfriend and Kylie and I do!"

Did. Kylie *had* a boyfriend. She wasn't sure what was going to happen with her and Lucas now. His pleas for her not to run off echoed in her heart.

"Jealous?" Della roared back at Miranda. "Please, I'll chew out my own heart before I become lovesick like you."

Miranda held up her hand and wiggled her pinky—a sure sign a spell was about to spill from her lips. Della's eyes brightened and her canines came out to play.

"Stop!" Kylie looked from one to the other. She couldn't take it anymore. "Oh, hell, don't stop. You two have been threatening to kill each other since I got here, and it's driving me mad. So just kill each other and put me out of my misery." Inside, Kylie flinched again. She didn't mean it. Not even now, when furious, but maybe a little reverse psychology would fix these two.

Miranda and Della stared at Kylie as if she'd lost her mind, and they could be right, but it was partially their fault. Their arguing had caused her to go nuts.

"Come on. What are you waiting for? Kill each other. And make it entertaining." She crossed her arms over her chest and stared daggers at the two of them. Her right foot started tapping, just like her mom's tapped when she was about to blow a gasket.

Della's eyes returned to their black color and her canines disappeared under her top lip. Miranda dropped her threatening pinky. So reverse psychology did work. Ha. Who knew?

"What's wrong with her?" Miranda asked Della as if Kylie were too mentally unstable to ask.

"Nothing's wrong with me," Kylie answered, frustrated beyond her limits. "It's what's wrong with you two."

Della glanced at Miranda and shrugged. "She thinks she's a lizard."

"A chameleon," Kylie corrected.

Miranda rolled her eyes. "Poor thing. She's acting like a werewolf."

Della shot Kylie a smirk. "I told her that. But did she listen to me? Hell, no."

"I'm not a werewolf." It didn't matter what Kylie now wished she was.

"If you are, it's okay," Miranda said. "We've vowed to love you anyway."

Kylie dropped down onto a living room chair while her two best friends stared at her with a mix of pity and leeriness. They thought she was crazy. Heck, maybe she *was* crazy. She thought the woods were calling her name and she believed she was a reptile. She leaned back and stared at the ceiling.

"I'm a chameleon," she said, hoping that saying it would bring some kind of instinctual understanding. She held her breath, waiting for an epiphany—an internal knowledge that would make her right with the world.

Nothing came. And nothing felt right. Not her being a lizard, not seeing a ghost with the face of someone who was alive, not with her dad suggesting she would soon be making a trip into the afterworld, and especially not Derek's confession of love.

Nope. Nothing felt right. She moaned.

"Get her a Diet Coke, Della," Miranda said. "Maybe the sugar will give her some brainpower."

"It's fake sugar," Della answered.

"I know. But haven't you ever heard the saying fake it until you make it?"

"Ugh, forget the soda. I'm going to bed." Kylie popped up from the chair and went into her room, slamming the door so hard it rattled on its hinges.

From behind the door she heard them say in unison, "Definitely werewolf."

• • •

She hadn't gotten to her bed when she heard a loud commotion from the living room. Had Miranda and Della finally decided to really duke it out? Feeling guilty for encouraging them, she went to stop them but stilled when she heard voices.

"Where's Kylie?" Burnett's deep tenor spilled through the walls at the same time that her phone started ringing.

She pulled her phone from her pocket and jerked open the door. Burnett stood there with his hand raised to knock. Both anger and a thread of guilt filled his expression.

"Something wrong?" Kylie's ringing phone hummed in her hand.

"Are you okay?"

"Why wouldn't I be?" Had something else happened? At this point, nothing could surprise her.

Chapter Four

"You left without telling me." Burnett's mouth thinned with his reprimand.

"I did not." Kylie saw Della and Miranda behind Burnett, wearing concerned expressions. No doubt, it wasn't wise to disagree with Burnett.

"You were in the office and then you were gone," Burnett barked. "I was supposed to be shadowing you."

"That was almost an hour ago," she said. Had he just now realized she was gone?

The ringing of her phone drew her attention and she pulled it up to see who was calling. Holiday's name appeared on the tiny screen. Then the camp leader, phone pressed to her ear, stormed into the cabin.

"You found her." Relief filled Holiday's eyes and she folded her arms over her stomach and breathed as if she'd run all the way here.

"You shouldn't have left without telling me," Burnett said to Kylie.

Holiday shut her phone off and silenced Kylie's cell. Kylie stared at the camp leader, recalling the ghost issues that she needed to talk to her about. *How could someone alive appear as a ghost?*

"I was in charge of you." Burnett continued his tirade.

Kylie glanced at Burnett as she set her phone down on the end table. She should probably keep her mouth shut, but her bad mood prevailed. "You can't blame me. I told you I was leaving. Not once, but twice. You two were too busy being pissy with each other to hear me." When her own hostile words rang in her ears, she worried maybe Della and Miranda were on to something about her being werewolf.

Holiday stepped closer. "We weren't arguing."

Really, Kylie thought, noticing that Holiday's shirt was on inside out. Not arguing, huh? So what had they been doing that led to Holiday wearing her shirt inside out? All Kylie's frustration lessened and she almost smiled. Almost.

"Yes, we were arguing," Burnett confessed, as if suddenly remembering.

"We were just discussing things." Holiday sent Burnett a look that said, *Don't disagree with me on this.*

"We were discussing it heatedly." Burnett received another hard stare from the redheaded camp leader.

"I'll say," Della mouthed off. "I heard you all the way in the dining room. And I'm not so sure it was my vampire hearing that caught it."

"Yes, it was," Miranda piped up. "Because I didn't get to hear a thing. Then again, I was probably talking with Perry." She got a faraway look in her eyes. "I love talking with Perry."

Della moaned.

"That said," Miranda continued, "nothing is as fun as a good argument. So if someone would like to fill me in, I'd appreciate it." She rubbed her hands together. "Just the good parts."

Burnett exhaled in frustration. "We were just—"

"What we were doing isn't important," Holiday blurted out, blushing.

"So you weren't arguing?" Miranda looked intrigued.

Kylie almost smiled again. Holiday was right. What they were doing wasn't important. The thing that mattered was that they'd made up. The thing that really mattered was if Holiday had managed to talk Burnett out of resigning his position. Shadow Falls needed him.

Holiday needed him.

Everything inside Kylie told her that the two of them were meant to be together. Unfortunately, Holiday resisted the idea of her and Burnett becoming an item. And while she hadn't completely admitted it, Kylie suspected it had everything to do with Holiday's vampire fiancé who'd broken her heart when he left her at the altar. Kylie also sensed there was more to that story than Holiday let on. Not that being left at the altar wasn't bad, but something told Kylie it had been something even more emotionally damaging. Why else would Holiday reject Burnett's love?

God knew it wasn't easy for a vampire to take rejection. Kylie had told him he needed to be patient. Holiday couldn't continue to hold out. Not when Burnett was practically perfect. Tall, dark, moody enough to be fascinating, and with a good heart. Sure, being vampire, he didn't go around passing out good cheer like Holiday did. But he cared.

Did Holiday finally come to her senses?

"Are you staying on at Shadow Falls?" Kylie asked Burnett, breath held in hope.

Burnett glanced at Holiday and damn if he didn't almost smile. "I'm staying."

"Yes!" Miranda and Della high-fived each other and did a little victory dance.

A sense of rightness filled Kylie's chest. Maybe today wouldn't go down in history as the worst day in her life, after all.

Burnett, being his slightly brooding self, didn't seem to share her roommates' joy, but Kylie spotted relief in his eyes. "Next time you are under my charge, don't walk away without my permission."

Kylie nodded, too happy to care if she wasn't at fault.

"Even if you have to knock me over my head twice to get my attention," he continued, taking most of the blame on himself. Kylie's smile widened. As stern as Burnett could be, he wasn't unfair.

She watched Burnett start for the door, and Holiday turned to go with him. Again, Kylie couldn't help but wonder how far things had gone in their time together. Had their clothes been half off when they suddenly realized she was gone?

Holiday looked back at Kylie. Their gazes met and held.

Just from the quick glance, Kylie knew that Holiday, an empath like Derek, had read the swarm of emotions playing hide and seek in her mind. And not the happy ones.

Kylie seldom got anything past the fae. Not that Kylie attempted to hide a whole heck of a lot from Holiday. The bond they shared had moved past friendship. Holiday was family—not the kind you were born with, but the kind you were lucky enough to choose.

"I need to speak to Kylie." The warmth in Holiday's tone had Kylie's chest tightening and she wondered what she'd ever do without the woman in her life. She hoped she never had to find out. The thought sent a shiver down Kylie's spine.

Burnett acknowledged all of them with a farewell glance, and then left.

As soon as he walked out, Della turned to Holiday. "Maybe *you* can talk some sense into Kylie. She thinks she's a lizard."

Five minutes later, Holiday and Kylie sat on the edge of the porch, their bare legs dangling over the edge. The camp leader had changed from the dark dress she'd worn at Ellie's funeral to a pair of cutoff jeans and the yellow shirt that she wore inside out.

Kylie's black dress flared across her thighs, landing right above her knees. If she stretched out her feet, her toes would brush against the grass. She usually liked how the light tickle felt, but for some reason it now reminded her of sitting with Derek earlier out beside the tree.

Pushing that thought aside, Kylie stared down at their feet. Holiday had on a pair of sandals, and her toenails were painted a soft pink.

"What happened?" Holiday asked, concern deepening her tone.

"I don't know where to start," Kylie said.

"How about with the whole lizard thing? What's Della talking about?"

Kylie bit down on her lip. "Before I get into all that, what happened between you and Burnett?"

Holiday glanced away. "He's staying on."

"I know that." Smiling, Kylie bumped her shoulder with Holiday's. "Did anything good happen?"

Color brightened Holiday's cheeks. "I don't feel comfortable talking about this."

"Wow. It must have been good, then," Kylie teased.

Holiday frowned, which meant whatever happened hadn't changed much. Some clothes might have come off, but Holiday's reservations hadn't.

"We didn't . . ." Holiday dropped her face into her hands. "I'm confused, okay? I need Burnett at Shadow Falls. He's strong in all the areas that I'm lacking. And where he's lacking, I'm strong. But . . ."

"But you're scared to admit you care about him," Kylie said, even when her gut told her she needed to back off.

"You don't understand," Holiday said.

"That's because you haven't told me everything," Kylie accused, and she got that sensation again that there were things, emotional things, Holiday kept bottled up inside her.

Holiday sighed. "This is something I need to work out myself. I know we're close and I love that you care." She put her hand on top of Kylie's. "I feel that you're only trying to help, but I need to go solo on this one. And I'm asking you to accept that."

Kylie nodded, knowing she had to respect Holiday's wishes, but not liking it.

"Now, let's get back to you." She bumped Kylie's shoulder with hers. "Talk to me."

Taking a deep breath, she told Holiday about her dad's visit—both the chameleon stuff and the part about them figuring it out together . . . *soon.*

Concern and confusion filled the camp leader's eyes. "Okay, about your dad saying you will work it out together—I don't think it means what you think. Time doesn't mean the same thing in the spirit world."

Kylie considered what Holiday said. "It's not that I don't believe you, it's just . . . there was something about the way he kept saying 'soon.' And he was happy about it."

Holiday shook her head. "Your dad loves you. And I think if he knew you were going to die too soon, he'd be panicking. And the last thing he would do is share that news with you."

It hurt to say it aloud, but she did it anyway. "If I'm going to die, I should know."

"It doesn't work like that. I mean, there are a few people who are able to know of their death and use the time wisely. But when you start planning for the end, most people instinctually stop living for tomorrow. Living for the day is beautiful—too many of us don't do it enough—but to live fully, we must live for today and tomorrow. Think about it, if you knew you were going to die in six months, would you start a project that you knew you couldn't finish? Would you go to school to learn to be a doctor? Would you have a child, knowing you would leave it alone too soon? People miss out on so much if they stop living for tomorrow."

Holiday's little speech sent Kylie right into the lap of another problem. Her ghost problem. She tried to think about the best way to approach it.

"Now, about the whole lizard thing," Holiday said, taking Kylie's thoughts in another direction. "I've never heard of a chameleon supernatural. And while I'm inclined to tell you that he got it wrong, I wonder . . ."

"Wonder what?" Kylie asked.

"I don't know for sure, I'm just—"

"I know," Kylie said. "You're just speculating, guessing, but since I'm feeling pretty clueless, I'd like to hear it."

"I was going to tell you." Holiday's expression told Kylie she needed to be patient.

She'd grown tired of being patient. And yes, she knew that on Thursday, her grandfather Malcolm Summers was coming, and hopefully he'd make sense of all this for her. But that meant a couple more days of not knowing.

"So just tell me. Please." Kylie softened her tone because being impatient might be understandable, but blaming others for it wasn't.

Holiday inhaled. "Maybe he referred to you as a chameleon because your pattern hasn't matured to what it really should be. It's still changing, like a chameleon changes colors."

"But he said I was a chameleon like he was telling me that I was a vampire or witch. Is it possible that there's another type of supernatural race that no one knows about?"

Holiday paused. "My gut says no. The history of supernaturals is documented in books as old as the Bible. But . . . I admit I'm baffled. It seems that whatever is causing this is probably hereditary because of your real grandfather and great-aunt's ability to change their patterns to human. But even that is completely off the chart weird. I'm still thinking it was Wiccan related but . . ."

"Or . . ." Kylie considered Holiday's words. "Maybe that's what it means, the whole chameleon thing. I was talking about this with Derek earlier. Maybe chameleons can change our species. Like a chameleon can change its colors."

Holiday paused as if thinking. "But DNA doesn't work that way. You can't have more than one string of DNA. It isn't possible, because supernaturals only have the DNA of the dominant parent."

Kylie bit down on her lip. "Then maybe it's not the species that really changes, but just the pattern. And in a way it makes sense because a chameleon doesn't turn into a rock, it just changes its colors so it looks like a rock."

Holiday's brow wrinkled. "But . . ." She shook her head.

"But what?" Kylie wanted to know everything Holiday considered.

"It just doesn't feel right. If this ability to hide your pattern actually exists, why haven't other supernaturals heard about it?"

"Maybe we have heard about it," Kylie said. "Maybe this is exactly why they tested my grandmother. You mentioned once that you'd heard about those tests. Did anyone say what the tests were for?"

"Not specifically," Holiday said. "Something about understanding genetics in some supernaturals. But that they went wrong."

"That's an understatement," Kylie muttered. "They killed people." *Killed my grandmother.* Kylie couldn't understand how someone could do that—take a life. For that matter, how could Mario kill his own grandson? Or kill Ellie, who never did a thing to harm him? Or anyone else for that matter?

"I know." Holiday sighed as if sensing Kylie's grief. "Which is why I refuse to let them test you. I don't think the FRU is evil, Kylie. I just don't trust them to not take too many risks with you to find answers. Whatever is going on, we'll figure it out sooner or later."

Kylie sure as hell hoped so. Because right now, it didn't make a lick of sense to her. She gazed back at Holiday. "Is that why you can't trust Burnett? Because he's part of the FRU?"

Holiday looked perplexed. "I trust Burnett."

Kylie arched a brow in disbelief.

"I trust him with Shadow Falls," Holiday confessed.

Just not with your heart. And how sad was that? Kylie thought.

"I wouldn't have him working here if I thought there was a chance he would betray you or any of my students."

"I know," Kylie said. "And I trust him, too. I mean, the whole FRU thing with my grandmother scares me, but I trust Burnett."

Holiday met Kylie's eyes again. "I know that waiting for answers is hard on you. But hold on to the hope that your grandfather will come on Thursday and—"

"What do you mean 'hold on to the hope'? He told Burnett he was coming, right?" Seeing disappointment flash in Holiday's eyes, Kylie's heart sank. "What happened?"

"Burnett tried to contact him again and . . . your grandfather's phone has been disconnected. But it could mean nothing."

"Or it could mean that he's decided not to communicate with me." A knot rose in Kylie's throat.

"Don't get worked up over it until we know."

Kylie pulled her knees up and dropped her head on them, trying not to cry. Was her hope of discovering the truth now slipping away?

Holiday rested her hand on Kylie's shoulder. A sweet calm came with the touch, and while it soothed Kylie's panic, it didn't change anything. They sat there for several minutes, not talking, Kylie trying not to cry and Holiday doing what she did best—offering emotional comfort.

The soft breeze whispered past and somehow Kylie's mind shifted from one problem to another. "Derek told me he talked to you about . . . things."

Holiday brushed a strand of hair off Kylie's cheek. "I'm sorry. I imagine that came completely out of left field."

Kylie nodded. "What am I supposed to do with that information?"

"I don't think you have to do anything."

Kylie exhaled. "It makes me feel crazy and sad, and I start questioning things. And Lucas is jealous of him and I don't blame him for being jealous because I feel the same way about Fredericka. But . . ."

"But you care about Derek," Holiday finished for her.

"I do. I'm just not sure if what I feel for him is what I feel for Lucas. Does that make sense?"

"Perfect sense," Holiday assured her. "You'll figure it out."

"Will I?" Angst rose inside Kylie again. "Everything in my life is a huge effing question mark. I'm tired of not being sure of *anything*. And then the ghost . . ." Kylie let the words fade.

"You have a problem with a ghost?" Holiday asked. "Is it your grandmother? Have you asked her about what your dad said?"

"No, it's not her." How much should Kylie tell Holiday? "At first, the spirit showed up looking like a zombie, hardly even had a face. I insisted she fix that. But . . . then the face she got was . . . someone who wasn't dead."

Holiday bit down on her lip. "Are you sure she isn't dead?"

"I'm sure." *Extra sure.*

"Well," Holiday continued, "it could be one of two things. The most likely answer is that you have a ghost with an identity crisis."

"Seriously? Ghosts can have an identity crisis?" Kylie asked.

"Afraid so. They may not even know what they looked like. Or they may not have liked how they looked, so they plaster the face of someone else on their ghost bodies. Most of the time, they use the face of the ghost whisperer. And seeing your face on a ghost . . ." Holiday shivered. "Not good."

"I can imagine," Kylie said, but she didn't want to imagine it. She already had too much on her plate. "What's the other thing it could be?"

"It's rare," Holiday said. "But did you see *A Christmas Carol*?"

"Yes." Kylie recalled the plot. "The Scrooge thing, right?"

"And the ghost from the future," Holiday said.

Kylie's breath hitched. "This person could be about to die?" Sure, the thought had crossed her mind, as it had Derek's, but not until Holiday said it did it feel real. No, Kylie refused to accept it. She'd seen too much death already.

"Is this one of the things I can change?" Kylie asked, panic building in her chest.

"Probably not." Holiday frowned. "Is it someone you know well?"

Kylie didn't answer. She couldn't. She just kept reminding herself that Holiday had said it was rare.

"Is it someone from Shadow Falls?" Miranda's voice piped up from behind them.

Kylie turned to see Miranda standing in the doorway behind them.

"Sorry," Miranda said. "I didn't mean to eavesdrop . . . but is it someone from here?"

"No," Kylie lied.

"Oh, good." Miranda did a dramatic swipe of her brow. "Your phone's chirping." She held out the phone. "It's your mom. This is like the third time she's called in the last five minutes."

"You should call her," Holiday said. Then the camp leader's phone rang. She glanced down at the number. "It's Burnett."

Holiday and Kylie stood at the same time. Kylie reached for her phone from Miranda as Holiday answered hers.

"Hello." Holiday paused. The worry wrinkle between her eyes appeared. "About what?" Her tone had Kylie hesitating to make her own call. "Let's talk before you go. I'm on my way." Holiday hung up.

"What's wrong?" Kylie asked.

"I—I'll talk with you when I know something." Holiday took off, but her answer had Kylie suspicious that the call had something to do with her.

"That didn't sound good," Miranda said.

Just great, Kylie thought. How much more could she take?

Chapter Five

"Are you okay?" Holiday's voice stirred Kylie awake about an hour later. After trying to call her mom numerous times and leaving several messages, her mind and heart gave up and she went to bed and took a nap.

She looked at Holiday perched on the end of her bed. Sitting up, Kylie yawned and brushed her hair from her eyes. "I've been better."

"Life can be so hard sometimes."

"Tell me about it." Kylie remembered the call from Burnett. "Is everything okay? What happened?"

Holiday stared at her with a vacant expression. "Who's Burnett?"

The cold in the room sent chills spidering across Kylie's back. She blinked and focused again on the woman's features. There was no doubt about it. She was Holiday.

Anger, fear, and frustration swarmed through Kylie's chest. "Okay, let me make something clear. When I told you to fix your face, I meant for you to get your own face, not borrow one from someone else."

The spirit pressed her palms against her cheeks, and her eyes widened. *"Is this not my face?"*

"No, it's not! It's the face of someone I care a lot about, and, nothing personal, but I don't like seeing you wearing it."

"I'm so confused."

"You have an identity crisis," Kylie offered, wanting more than anything to believe it.

"An identity crisis," the spirit repeated.

"Yeah, and you need to figure out who you are and what it is you need from me, because I can't help you if you don't."

"It's mostly a blur." She pursed her lips in the same manner Holiday did when she was thinking really hard, and damn if the resemblance wasn't uncanny. Even the green color of her eyes matched perfectly.

"Maybe you're right," the spirit said. *"I remember always feeling as if I lived in someone else's shadow."*

"That's good," Kylie said, relief allowing her to breathe deeper.

"Good that I lived in someone else's shadow?" The ghost frowned. *"I don't see it as a good thing."*

"No, I . . . I mean it's good you can remember stuff." And right then, Kylie remembered something, too. One quick and easy way to assure herself that this spirit wasn't Holiday Brandon. Kylie tightened her eyes and focused on the ghost's forehead.

The whimsical pattern, like the face, matched Holiday's to a T. Kylie's chest swelled with concern. "You're a fae?"

The spirit propped one bent knee up across her leg, put her elbow on her knee, and then dropped her chin in the palm of her hand. The gesture was so Holiday that Kylie's heart skipped a beat.

"Yup, that's what I am." She tightened her brows and gazed at Kylie. *"Oh, my, what are you?"*

Kylie hesitated. "I'm a . . . chameleon."

The spirit made a face. *"You're a lizard?"*

Kylie frowned, but her concern wasn't about herself. "Do you remember your name?" Kylie held her breath.

The spirit met Kylie's eyes and her brow tightened in puzzlement. Then she stood up and walked to Kylie's window. Staring out in silence, she finally turned around. *"Someone is looking for you."*

"Do you remember your name?" Kylie repeated her question.

Pulling her red hair over her shoulder, the spirit twirled it into a rope. The exact same way Kylie had watched Holiday do just a little bit ago. The ghost looked back. *"They want you to come to them."*

Kylie's chest tightened a bit. "Let's talk about you right now," Kylie said, making a mental decision to focus on one problem at a time.

"But you are so much more interesting. There's all this mystery around you. A lot of questions to be answered. I can feel your emotions, you know. That's what faes do. We feel what other people feel."

"I know," Kylie said, frustrated and scared about the spirit's real identity, but she fought the angst back so she could learn more. Because if she was Holiday, then maybe Kylie could do something, change something to prevent . . .

"I used to be able to touch people and make them feel better, but that went away."

"Why did it go away?" Kylie asked.

She frowned. *"I'm not completely sure. I think I did something bad."* The ghost's bright green eyes filled with tears. *"I hurt people."*

Kylie sensed the spirit's pain, her remorse, but she couldn't deny feeling a bit of reprieve from the confession. Holiday wouldn't do anything wrong. She was too good-hearted. Cared too much.

"Maybe you didn't mean to hurt them," Kylie said, wanting to help. She wrapped her arms around herself as protection against the chill that accompanied a spiritual being.

"I don't know. I think I was angry." The spirit stared at the wall as if lost in thought and then she reached up and touched her throat.

Kylie noticed the painful-looking bruises around the ghost's neck.

"What happened to you?" Kylie asked, a knot forming in her throat at the thought of being choked to death.

The woman looked back at Kylie, her eyes still wet with emotion. *"I'm dead."*

Kylie nodded. "I know." She waited a second. "What happened?"

The spirit shook her head. *"It's like bits and pieces of a bad nightmare. But I think it has something to do with why I'm here. I mean, I should have left by now . . . We . . . supernaturals don't hang around."* She looked down and her image started to fade. *"I need to go figure this out. I think it's important."*

"I'll help you any way I can," Kylie said, remembering Holiday saying the same thing about very few non-humans hanging around after they died. "If you can tell me your name, I might be able to find something on the computer that will help us."

The spirit moved to the window and touched the pane of glass. A layer of ice appeared on the window, the frost blurring the view outside. *"You'd better start figuring out your own problems, too."*

"I'm trying," Kylie said, again seeing Holiday's personality in the spirit and not liking it. "What's your name?" Kylie insisted.

The spirit's figure faded at the same rate as the ice on the window. Then she spoke. *"I think it's Hannah or Holly. Something like that."*

"No," Kylie said, her own voice little more than a whisper.

She then grabbed a clip and put her hair up, determined to go see Holiday, not even sure what she would or wouldn't tell the camp leader. Kylie just needed to see Holiday alive.

Kylie moved out of her room and found the main room in the cabin empty. She started for the door and stopped. Who was supposed to be shadowing her? Not that Kylie really cared. She was just going to the office, but she'd already gotten in trouble once with Burnett about the shadowing business, and she didn't want to go for two.

"Della?" she called out.

No answer came back. Was something wrong?

"Hey." Miranda popped out of her bedroom a second later. "Della had a meeting with Burnett. I'm on shadowing duty." She said it with pride.

Kylie nodded. "Good. Let's go to the office."

"Why?"

"Because I want to talk to Holiday."

"About what?"

"About something."

"Got a 'tude, do ya?" Miranda made a face as if she'd just had to swallow something really disgusting.

Kylie started to smart back, but caught herself. It was understandable that she was in a bad mood, but it didn't give her the right to take it out on her friends. "I'm sorry. I know I've been cranky today. But I've just got a lot of crap on my plate."

"I know," Miranda said in an apologetic tone. "The funeral put us all in a bad mood. But then with your whole lizard crisis, I mean, I'd be in an extra-bad mood if somebody told me that I was a reptile. Which is why I haven't raised my pinky at you one time."

"And I appreciate it," Kylie said, and then realized what Miranda had said. "What did Burnett want to talk to Della about?"

"Beats me."

"Was she upset?" Kylie couldn't help but worry that it had something to do with whatever Holiday was so upset about when she spoke to Burnett earlier. And Kylie hadn't forgotten that at the time she'd gotten the impression it was about her.

"Not really. Between you and me, I think Della's got a crush on Burnett. She just glows when Burnett asks her to do something."

"No, she doesn't. She knows he's totally into Holiday."

"Then why doesn't she go for Steve? She's jealous of us having boyfriends but won't go after Steve. And lately I noticed the same thing you did. That shape-shifter stares at her all the time. He's hot for her."

Kylie motioned to the door. "She doesn't go for Steve because she's still in love with Lee."

"Yeah, I guess that could be it, too." They walked out and started down the path toward the office. "You know, I could put a hex on him."

"On Steve?" Kylie asked.

"No, on Lee. I could easily give him warts. And I could put them some place it would really scare the piss out of him. If you know what I mean."

Kylie shook her head. "I don't think Della would want you to do that."

"She might if we caught her in the right mood."

"I wouldn't even chance asking, because if she's not in the right mood, it might really tick her off."

"Yeah, I guess." They continued down the trail. "Do I really talk about Perry all the time?"

Kylie looked at Miranda. "Yeah, but it's not as bad as Della makes it sound. I'll bet I talk about Lucas all the time." She remembered she'd walked away from him today. Was he going to be angry at her? Did he have a right to be?

"Actually, you don't. But you used to talk about Derek all the time."

Kylie frowned, not liking how that sounded.

"Oh, that reminds me, he came by to see you when you were sleeping."

"Derek came to see me?"

"No, Lucas."

Embarrassed that she'd misunderstood, Kylie bit down on her lip. "Why didn't he wake me up? Why didn't you guys wake me up?"

"He told us not to. He peeked in on you and said to just tell you he came by. Actually, it was kind of sweet. He stood in the doorway watching you for several minutes. He kind of looked sad. Or sappy. Like he was totally in love with you. Della was waving her hand under her nose as if to say he was emitting all kinds of pheromones." Miranda grinned.

Kylie's heart hurt so much she couldn't grin back. Guilt spiraled through her, both for not talking about him as much as she had talked about Derek and for walking away from him earlier when he tried to talk to her. At the time, she'd felt justified, but hindsight always gave her another viewpoint. Was she being too hard on Lucas?

Probably, she admitted. She'd been crabby lately. Hence why Miranda and Della were accusing her of being were. Something she needed to remedy.

She made up her mind. After she spoke with Holiday, she was going to find Lucas and apologize for leaving him like that. She quickened her pace down the trail. The trees on both sides seemed to grow closer together. And Kylie felt it again—the feeling of someone calling her. Luring her to step out into the woods. She stopped and looked out at the line of trees.

They want you to come to them. She heard the spirit's words whisper in her head.

Who was out there? Was it Mario?

Suddenly, she wasn't so sure. It didn't feel evil. It felt . . . She didn't know how it felt, honestly, only that it wasn't completely evil. However, it still scared her to the point that her breath came short, and a chill ran up her spine and tingled at the base of her neck.

"What?" Miranda asked, a note of fear in her tone. "Your aura is going all sorts of strange colors on me."

"Nothing," Kylie lied. She turned and started jogging to the office. As her feet pounded the path, little clouds of dirt floated up. She blinked the dusty air away and that's when she saw the moon—

half full, but bright. And it looked as if it just suddenly appeared in the sky.

Moonrise, she thought. She felt again the whispers echoing in her mind. Whispers she couldn't understand, whispers that both lured her and frightened her.

"Is it a ghost?" Miranda asked, her feet pounding the path as her multicolored hair danced in the wind. "Is it?"

"No," Kylie said, able to speak without huffing.

"Then can you slow down? Because I'm not like you and Della. I mean, I could cast a spell and maybe I could run faster, but that would take some time. And the last time I tried it, I turned myself into an antelope."

"We're just about there," Kylie said, but, remembering how she hated having to work so hard to keep up with Della, she did slow her pace. Suddenly, a whoosh of air blew past them. Kylie's first thought was vampire, but then Perry, in his huge prehistoric bird form, landed in front of them.

Miranda, even huffing and puffing, squealed with pleasure. Perry took his right wing and wrapped it around the little witch, pulling her into his chest and giving her a warm bird hug. Then he cooed, sounding like a dove. As sappy as it was, and even in her bad mood, Kylie's chest tightened. And the tender smile she spotted in Miranda's expression sealed the deal. Love was a wonderful thing. Kylie wanted it. All of it. Complete devotion. All the sappy, crazy feelings.

Images of both Derek and Lucas filled her head. Oh, hell, could she be in love with both of them? Was that even possible?

Perry released Miranda and stepped back. Sparkles started falling around him like iridescent snow. In seconds, human Perry appeared. His sandy blond hair clung to his forehead as if he'd worked up a sweat. His eyes were blue. Bright blue. He wore a pair of black jeans and a T-shirt that read, WHAT DO YOU WANT ME TO BE?

"I was just coming to get you," Perry said, shifting his gaze from Miranda to Kylie.

"Me?" Kylie asked. "Why?"

He shrugged. "They told me to. Ordered me to."

"Who?" Kylie asked. "Who told you to get me?"

"Duh. Burnett and Holiday. I don't take orders from anyone else. Except maybe Miranda." He grinned at Miranda.

"Is something wrong?" Kylie asked.

He looked back at Kylie. "I don't know. But I know your mom showed up and she's fit to be tied. Giving Holiday hell."

"My mom's here?" Kylie asked, feeling confused.

Perry nodded. "Sorry."

Kylie took off at a heated pace. Worry had her feet hitting the dirt and leaving a cloud of dust in her wake.

Chapter Six

Kylie ran directly into Holiday's office. Her mom stood in front of Holiday's desk, making some declaration. Holiday sat behind the desk, listening to the declaration. Burnett stood stoic, taking it all in. Kylie barely gave him a glance. She focused on her mom, who swung around and . . .

Kylie was engulfed in a quick but desperate hug. Over her mom's shoulder, Kylie's questioning gaze shot to Holiday, who stood up. Her mom backed up.

Kylie continued to stare at Holiday. The briefest of memories of the spirit pulled at Kylie's heart. How could they be so identical and not be the same person? Kylie told herself to deal with one thing at a time. So she refocused on her mom. The look on her face scared the crap out of Kylie. It was the same look her mom had when her grandmother had died.

"What's wrong?" Kylie's mind searched for possibilities and her breath caught as one hit. "Is Dad okay?"

She might still be angry at her stepfather, might not have forgiven him for his infidelity with his young intern, but Kylie loved him. She'd never been surer of that fact than right now. Now, when she imagined the worst—imagined her mother telling her that there had been an accident. That Kylie would never get another long hug from the man or go with him on a father/daughter trip.

"Your dad is fine. It's you that isn't." Her mom's gaze shot over Kylie's shoulder and then back at Kylie. "Why didn't you tell me you were sick?"

"I'm not sick."

"You had some headaches. And those nightmares, remember?" Holiday spoke in a certain tone that Kylie didn't quite understand.

Her mom's gaze flipped from Kylie's face over her shoulder again and for some reason it made Kylie turn around. Sitting on the sofa was a man she didn't know.

"I . . . don't understand," Kylie said, and looked back at her mom.

"It was in my records," Holiday said, again in a tone that seemed to mean something. "I put it in the files and the administrators thought maybe your mom should be contacted. To see if perhaps you needed testing."

Kylie continued to stare at Holiday.

"They called me and asked if they had my permission to test you. Baby, are you okay?"

Test me? Administrators?

Oh, hell, the dots started going together. It wasn't any administrators. It was the FRU. They were trying to get her mom's permission to test her.

"I'm fine," Kylie said. "I don't need to be tested." Fear shot through Kylie. Her gaze shot to Burnett. He looked at her, straight on. No guilt. And she sensed he didn't have any part in this. She remembered the phone call and suspected that this was what it had been all about. Her gaze shot to the man on the sofa. Was he from the FRU? Was this the bastard who wanted to use her as a lab rat like they'd used her grandmother?

"Who are you?" she asked before she could stop herself. Then she tightened her eyes and checked out his pattern. She blinked and did it again when he came up human.

"This is John," her mom said. "We were out having dinner when I got the message from Mr. Edwards that you've been blacking out."

"John?" Who the hell was John? Kylie looked at her mom. And damn if her mom didn't look guilty.

"He's the client that I had lunch with the other day, remember? I told you about him."

Kylie did remember. He was the guy who was going to ruin all the chances of her mother and stepfather getting back together.

"As I've explained," Holiday continued, "Kylie hasn't actually been blacking out. I think I might have just made it sound a bit worse than I intended in my reports. And when someone read them, they interpreted things wrong."

Emotion fluttered around like trapped birds in Kylie's chest. Holiday glanced at her and Kylie got the feeling the camp leader was trying to communicate something to her. But damn, Kylie couldn't read minds. She couldn't even read emotions.

"Didn't Kylie have night terrors at home?" Holiday asked.

Kylie suddenly thought she understood what Holiday wanted. "Yes. They were just night terrors, Mom. I didn't pass out. You remember how out of it I get when I have one of those. I'm not sick. I don't need testing. Besides, you already had me tested, remember?"

"But I didn't think you were having them anymore."

"I've only had a couple. And I'm fine. Look at me, I'm fine." She held her arms out, mentally searching for a way to prove it. "I can touch my toes; I can touch my tongue to my nose." It was a little rhyme she and her mom said when someone asked if they were okay.

"But why would Mr. Edwards want to run tests on you?"

Holiday leaned forward in her chair. "Oh, don't listen to him.

He's just overcautious." She smiled, doing her best to sound convincing. "But if you would like to schedule Kylie for some tests with your own doctor for your peace of mind, I'd completely understand. I mean, nothing against the doctors here, but I would hope you have a good relationship with your own physician."

"Do you think I should?" her mom asked Holiday with her worried maternal look.

"Actually, no, I don't. I think Kylie's fine. With only two occurrences of the night terrors, I think she's doing great."

"I *am* doing great," Kylie persisted. "I'm fine. I promise. Please, Mom. I don't want to go through those tests again."

Her mom ran her palm over Kylie's cheek. "Do you know how scared I was? Oh, Lordie." Her mom looked back at Holiday. "You should consider having a serious talk with Mr. Edwards. I swear, the way his message sounded, you would think Kylie was in serious trouble."

"I'm sorry that scared you." Kylie looked at John over her mom's shoulder.

The man stood up, moved forward, and rested his hand on her mom's shoulder. Kylie had the oddest desire to slap his hand away and tell him he didn't have the right to touch her mom.

"Hello, Kylie," John said.

Kylie took in his suave smile, brown eyes, and matching chocolate-colored hair that was styled to perfection. She so wished she could find something ugly about him, but nope. He wasn't ugly. He wasn't completely older-guy hot like Burnett, maybe because he was a tad older, but he had the whole distinguished-looking thing down pat.

"I wish our first meeting could have been under different circumstances," he continued, "but I've been hoping to meet you. Your mom has told me so much about you."

Funny, Kylie thought, her mom hadn't told her so much about him. Well, she'd told her about having lunch and that he'd said he might call her again, but she'd neglected to say he had called. Prob-ably because she knew Kylie had mixed feelings about her dating. Ahh, but right now, they weren't so mixed.

Kylie didn't like him. However, because she didn't have a reason—except her gut feeling and maybe her wanting her mom and stepdad back together—she was going to have to suck it up. Be nice. What was it Miranda had said? "Fake it until you make it." Could she learn to like this guy?

"It's nice to meet you." Kylie plastered a warm expression on her face. But she worried he could tell it was a sham.

"The pleasure is all mine," he said.

Kylie just smiled. He was completely right about that.

For the next half hour, Kylie sat in the meeting room in the office and visited with her mom and smarmy John and pretended like everything in her life was just peachy. Peachy and Smarmy. Phrases that Nana, who'd passed away about three months ago, would have used.

Weird how Kylie seemed to be channeling her right now. She'd love it if Nana would pop in for a visit. *You there, Nana?* Kylie asked in her head while John rattled on about the years he'd lived in En-gland.

Nana didn't answer. But Kylie got the oddest sensation she was close.

"I've always wanted to see England," her mom said, holding on to every word the man said.

"We can fix that," John added with enthusiasm. "I have a trip scheduled next month. Why don't you take some time off and come with me?"

"Really?" her mom said. And damn if Kylie wasn't thinking the same thing. *Really?* The man wanted her mom to go to England with him. She didn't even know him. And would he expect her mom to share a hotel room with him, too? No way!

"Mom's work schedule is pretty demanding. She won't be able to make it," Kylie declined for her mom, before she realized she shouldn't have a say in the matter.

Her mom's mouth dropped open at Kylie's declaration and she shot Kylie a that-was-rude scowl. "Well, my work is demanding, but I might be able to get a few days off." She cut her eyes back to Kylie, warning her not to speak up.

"Great," John said, as if he missed the silent tension.

"Great," Kylie repeated, her smile so stiff she didn't think her lips moved.

"Speaking of schedules." Her mom looked at her watch. "We should be heading home. It's almost a two-hour drive. And I do have to work tomorrow."

Her mom gave her a quick hug. And for her hug-impaired mom, it was pretty good. When Kylie pulled back, she mouthed the word *sorry*. And she was sorry. She didn't want to hurt her mom's feelings, even if she didn't like this guy.

The look her mother sent her was one of pure understanding. Which only made Kylie feel a little worse.

Leaning in again, her mom whispered, "Love you."

"Love you, too." Kylie went back in for another hug, and this time she held on a little tighter and for a second longer.

When she walked them out and passed by Burnett's office, she saw his six-foot-plus frame seated at his desk. He pretended to do paperwork but no doubt his super-hearing ears had been tuned in the entire time. And that was fine, she didn't have anything to hide, but as soon as Mom and the creepy guy left, Burnett had better be up for more than listening. He had a lot of explaining to do.

She had known the FRU wanted her tested, but she hadn't believed they'd go so far as to contact her mom. And if they would go that far, what was next? Would her mom's refusal to have Kylie tested be the end of it? For some reason, Kylie didn't believe so.

When Kylie returned a few minutes later, Holiday and Burnett were waiting on the cabin porch.

"What's going to happen now?" Kylie asked.

Burnett frowned and led them into Holiday's study. "I don't know. I'm stunned that they did this. They called me to come in and talk about changing your mind. I told them that you'd already declined. Someone said you weren't of legal age and suggested they go through your mom. I pointed out that your mom wasn't supernatural and how that could lead to too many questions. I thought I'd convinced them it wasn't the route to take. But when I got back here, Holiday was on the phone with your mom. They must have called your mom the minute I left the office."

Holiday sat down on the sofa. Kylie joined her. When Holiday reached for her hair and twisted it into a rope, Kylie remembered the reason she'd come to the office in the first place. Her gaze went to Holiday's neck and she remembered the spirit's angry bruises. Fear for her friend took a lap around her heart.

"Lucky for us, your mom bypassed calling the FRU back and came straight to us," Holiday said. She met Kylie's eyes. "It's going to be okay," she said, obviously reading Kylie's concern.

"I hope so." Kylie slumped back against the sofa.

"You're still upset about what happened earlier," Holiday said.

"What happened earlier?" Burnett took a step closer.

"I didn't get a chance to tell you . . ." Holiday explained about Kylie's father telling her she was a chameleon.

Kylie waited for disbelief to appear on the vampire's face, or the *you're a lizard* response everyone else had given her. When Burnett didn't offer up either, suspicion settled in.

"What do you know?" she demanded.

His eyebrows pinched. "The word *chameleon* was mentioned in the documents I found about the test responsible for your grandmother's death."

"What did it say? Did it explain how I can have a human pattern and still be supernatural?" Kylie asked, annoyed he'd kept anything from her. Kylie saw Holiday frown as well.

Burnett's gaze went from Kylie to Holiday and concern pulled at his frown. "They didn't explain anything. One of the doctors used the word *chameleon* in his notes. It didn't make sense; as a matter of fact, I wondered if it was a typo. I didn't have the original documents. Just one doctor's notes made while referring to the other documents."

"But at least this proves it," Kylie said.

"Proves what?" Burnett asked.

Kylie gazed from Burnett to Holiday. "That this is what being a chameleon is. Having a pattern that says you're one thing when you're not. I mean, we know I'm not all human." She pointed to her forehead. "And yet my pattern says I am. Of course, it doesn't tell me squat about what I really am."

"I don't think we've proved anything yet," Burnett said. "Yes, I think somehow these two things mean the same thing. I just don't think we've proven what they mean, yet."

Holiday's expression said she agreed with him. "I've been thinking," Holiday said. "Maybe your . . . pattern issues are somehow linked to you being a protector. I don't think there's ever been a part-human protector that we can compare you to."

"I hadn't thought about that," Burnett said. "That could be it."

"But what about the whole chameleon thing?" Kylie asked.

"I don't know," Holiday said. "I'm just saying it could explain your pattern issues."

Kylie's mind ran around everything that was said. The more she thought about it, the less sense any of it made. "I want to read those files."

"I'm sure by now the few files I was able to pull up have already been hidden."

"They killed my grandmother and got away with it, and now they're trying to do the same to me."

"The people who did that were either let go or have retired." His frown deepened. "I know that's how it looks and I agree you should decline testing, but I don't believe they would intentionally jeopardize your life."

"We don't know that." The firmness in Holiday's tone reminded Kylie of her mom's voice in maternal mode.

"Which is exactly why I've done what I have," he said. "Why I'm basically going against my oath to the FRU. I'm on your side. What else can I do to prove that?"

"Please," Kylie said. "I don't want you two arguing because of me."

"You don't have to prove anything." Holiday blushed with guilt. "I'm sorry. I just get so furious on Kylie's behalf."

"I know. I feel it, too." Burnett glanced at Kylie. "And we weren't arguing." He turned and focused on Holiday for a second. "This time we really were just discussing. Right?"

"Right." The slightest of grins appeared on Holiday's lips when she met his gaze.

Kylie grinned, too, even as emotion filled her chest. She was so lucky to have these people on her side. But her smile only lingered a second. "What will their next move be?"

Burnett exhaled. "Chances are they still may attempt to change your mind. Convince you that it's for a greater good. That's what I thought the plan was when I left."

"And is that when I tell them I know about my grandmother? Threaten to expose them if they don't back off?" Kylie asked.

Burnett had taken it upon himself to move Kylie's grandmother's body just in case someone in the FRU decided to hide the evidence of what had happened. In his own words, this would give Kylie some leverage to use against the FRU if they tried to force her to do something she didn't want to do.

"I would just say no, and then if they push, bring up your grandmother's remains." His expression tightened and concern flickered in his eyes. The same emotion reflected in Holiday's gaze.

"What will happen if they find out you were behind the moving of her body?" Kylie asked.

"They won't find out. I covered my tracks," he said adamantly. Maybe too adamantly, as if saying it with conviction would make it so.

"They'll suspect you because you work here. Because you're close to me," Kylie said.

"They might, but they'll have to prove it. And I haven't left any proof for them to uncover."

Kylie hoped that was the case. She glanced at Holiday again and remembered the ghost.

Holiday reached over and put her hand on Kylie's. "Is something else wrong?"

"No. Just this."

"You sure?"

"Do I need more?" Kylie's gaze shifted to the window. She could see the dusk sky going black, but she could still make out the tops of trees swaying ever so slowly.

Her gaze shot back to Holiday and she suddenly felt the need to come clean. "I feel as if I'm being called to something." She motioned to the window. "Something's out there calling me. But I'm not sure what."

Holiday looked confused. "Like being called to the falls?"

"Yeah," Kylie said. Only it felt a lot bigger than that.

"Then let's make a plan to go." Holiday leaned forward. "Do you think tomorrow's soon enough?"

Kylie started to clarify that she wasn't sure it was the falls calling her, but she didn't know how to explain it. So she just nodded.

"I'll go with you," Burnett said.

"Inside the falls?" Holiday looked back at Burnett.

"If you think I should, I will."

"The thought of going to the falls doesn't bother you?"

He shrugged. "I've been there before."

Holiday looked at Kylie and then back at him. "I know. And I find that baffling. Most supernaturals can't seem to force themselves to enter."

A small grin tightened the corners of his eyes. "Like I've been telling you, I'm special."

Holiday sighed. "But the falls—"

"Are not a problem." He cut her off and focused on Kylie. "Why don't I walk you back to your cabin? Della's on shadow duty. I told her I'd see you back." Burnett's diversion of subject appeared to be a deliberate ploy to avoid talking about the falls. What was Burnett hiding? The same question seemed to brighten Holiday's eyes as well.

"She missed dinner," Holiday said.

"All I want is a sandwich and we've got that at the cabin."

Holiday gave Kylie a long hug with warm calming emotion.

The effects from the hug lingered until she and Burnett started down the dark trail and he asked, "Would you like to explain why you lied to Holiday?"

Chapter Seven

"I didn't lie." As soon as those words were out Kylie recalled she'd indeed lied when Holiday asked if there was something else wrong. Damn, she should have remembered that Burnett could hear her heart racing if she lied.

She continued walking. He glanced down with one brow arched in disbelief. "Try again."

Kylie frowned. "It's a ghost issue. I'm just trying to figure it out myself." No way in hell could she tell Burnett about the ghost looking like Holiday. Burnett would freak. Then again, maybe he wouldn't. Maybe he wasn't so afraid of ghosts as he pretended to be.

"What is it that you're hiding from her about the falls?" she asked.

His arched brow lowered. "I'm not hiding anything."

"You can go into the falls when the others can't."

"It baffles me as well," he said. "Though I don't exactly feel comfortable there."

"You didn't feel called to go there?"

He hesitated. "Maybe a little." They walked in silence for the next four or five steps.

"Why didn't you tell Holiday?" Kylie asked.

He cut her a sly look. "Maybe I'm trying to figure it out for my-self." He used the same words she'd used on him.

"Okay." She rolled her eyes.

In a few minutes, he spoke again. "I thought you could talk to Holiday about the ghost issues."

"I can. But I'd like to handle it on my own if I can." It was the truth, so she didn't worry about what he'd hear beneath her words.

He nodded. As they neared the cabin, Kylie remembered she'd wanted to visit with Lucas. "Can Lucas take over shadowing me for a while this evening? I need to speak to him about something."

Burnett seemed to consider it. For a second, it appeared as if he might refuse. "Okay, but don't go into the woods."

His answer had her wondering. "Is the alarm working?"

"Yes, but in certain weather conditions, someone might be able to get into the forest without being picked up."

She nodded.

"Have you seen anyone?" he asked.

"No."

He stopped. "Are you sure?"

"I'm sure," she said. "Sometimes I just . . . the woods scare me a little."

"Then listen to your fears and avoid them."

"That's my plan." Kylie looked at the line of trees and the dark shadows beyond them. She didn't feel anything. Maybe what she'd felt earlier was just her overactive imagination.

Kylie spotted her cabin nestled in the trees. The lights were on and a golden hue spilled out the windows. She saw Della's shadow pass in front of the window and remembered . . .

"What did you have a meeting about with Della earlier?"

"Just FRU business." He sounded purposely vague.

"Is something wrong?" she asked.

He shook his head. "No."

"Are you having her do something for the FRU?"

"It's possible. Why?"

Kylie frowned. "Considering the FRU is causing me such a headache, I'm not thrilled about you getting my friends involved with them."

He stopped, dropped his hand into his jeans pockets, and shook his head as if in frustration. "The FRU is an organization meant to help the supernatural people, just like the police help humans. There have been dirty cops and even groups of cops that have done bad things, but we don't stop trusting the force as a whole."

"I might if they killed my grandmother," she said honestly.

His expression tightened. "I don't agree with everything the FRU does, but without the FRU, the world would be in chaos. The races would all be against each other, killing and maiming each other. The human race would be viewed as a food source."

Kylie shivered at his description.

"If you can't trust the FRU, at least trust me on this," he said. "The good the FRU does far outweighs the bad."

"I'll try to see it like that." But she didn't promise anything. She couldn't.

"You could have just called him," Della said, moving down the dark path toward Lucas's cabin about an hour after Kylie had returned. Kylie got the feeling that Della was a little annoyed that Kylie wanted to spend the evening with Lucas instead of hanging out with her. Especially when Miranda had run off with Perry. But Kylie's guilt over walking away from Lucas earlier made seeing him feel imperative.

"I kind of wanted to be the one to take the initiative." Kylie noticed the moon, a bright silvery white, a little over half full, hanging overhead. It was a pretty night. The temperature had dropped to the low eighties, making it almost comfortable.

"Why? What did you do wrong?"

"I got mad and walked off earlier."

"Was that why he was so sappy-eyed when he came by while you were asleep?" she asked.

"I guess." Kylie gave the line of trees a good long stare and felt nothing, which felt really good. Then she looked back at Della. "What did Burnett want to talk to you about today?"

"Nothing really."

Kylie looked at her. "You know, when you're friends with someone for a while, you don't have to hear their heartbeat to know they're lying."

Della made a face. "Yeah, but I thought that would be more polite than telling you to bug off."

Kylie frowned. "Are you going to do something for the FRU?"

"How did you know?"

"They already had Lucas and Derek do stuff. It just seemed logical. Not that I like it." She remembered Burnett saying the FRU wasn't all bad, and tried to give herself an attitude adjustment, but she couldn't completely let herself trust them.

"I think it would be kind of cool to work for them," Della said. "It would give me a reason to kick some asses every now and then."

"Do you trust them?" Kylie asked.

"I trust Burnett," Della said, and studied Kylie. "Don't you?"

"Of course I do." She hadn't told Miranda or Della about Burnett moving her grandmother's body. It just seemed like something that she shouldn't tell anyone. "They went to my mom to see about testing me."

"Oh, shit, I remember Miranda saying that your mom was here, but I forgot about it. What did your mom say? God, did they tell her you were supernatural? I'll bet it totally freaked her out."

"No, they told her they were worried because I had headaches and passed out and they advised her to have me tested. Holiday explained it was just the night terrors and advised against it."

"Oh, hell. What did Burnett say?"

"He's not for me getting tested either."

"Good," Della said. "I mean, I wouldn't want anyone probing around my head. Not after hearing what happened to your grandma." Della stopped and looked at Kylie. "Do you not want me to work for them because of this?"

Kylie got the feeling that Della would really give up her chance to work for the FRU because of Kylie's opinion—even when it was clear that Della was excited about the possibility. Her appreciation for Della's devotion swelled in her chest.

"No," Kylie said. "But . . . I do want you to be careful."

"I'll be careful." Della rubbed her hands together. "I'm glad you figured it out. I've been dying to tell someone. It'll be so cool."

They got to Lucas's cabin. The lights were on. Kylie knocked on the door while Della hung back by the porch steps. Steve, the shapeshifter who had a crush on Della, came to the door. With everything happening, Kylie had forgotten he roomed with Lucas. And so had Della, Kylie realized, when she heard the vamp draw in a quick breath.

"Hey," Steve said.

"Is Lucas here?" Kylie asked.

His gaze shifted behind Kylie and his expression changed. Kylie knew he'd spotted Della. "Uh . . . yeah. I mean, no. He left a few minutes ago with Fredericka."

"Oh." Kylie tried not to let it show that the news bothered her as she turned to leave.

Steve called after her, "He'll probably be back shortly."

She turned back. "Do you mind if we wait for a while?"

"No." His eyes lit up as he looked at Della. "Come in if you want."

Della cleared her throat in a sound that said hell no.

"Can we just sit out on the porch?" Kylie asked. "It's a nice night."

"Yeah." He stepped out. His brown hair hung across his brow. Even in the dark, Kylie could make out that his eyes were dark brown, and they were filled with interest as they cut toward Della.

When Kylie turned around, Della didn't look too happy, but she sauntered forward. "We shouldn't wait long." She plopped down on the steps.

"Just a bit." Kylie lowered herself beside the unhappy Della. Steve sat down on the side of the porch. No one said a word.

"I heard some of the new teachers were at dinner tonight." Kylie tossed out the conversation starter, hoping not to slip into angst over Lucas traipsing through the woods with Fredericka.

"Yeah," Steve said. "The English teacher, Ava Kane, seems nice. She's half-witch and half-shape-shifter."

"Why don't you just admit that you like her because she has big tits?" Della said.

Even in the dark, Kylie could see Steve's face redden. "I . . . won't deny she's pretty, but that's not what I meant."

Kylie shifted her foot and kicked Della.

"Ouch!" Della glared at Kylie. "Why did you do that?"

"When are classes supposed to start?" Kylie asked, and no one answered—Steve probably because he was afraid to get in trouble again and Della because she was too busy rubbing her kicked ankle.

Steve finally cratered. "I think next Monday."

"Were there any other teachers there?" Kylie looked at Della to answer.

"Yeah," Della added. "A Hayden Yates. He's half vampire, half fae. I think he's going to teach science. He seems okay."

"And?" Steve asked, his tone deeper, even if it was just above a whisper.

"And what?" Della asked.

He stiffened his shoulders. Which Kylie had to admit were pretty broad. The guy was cute. Why wasn't Della at least being nice?

"Why do you like Mr. Yates?" Steve asked. "His sexy body, or do you pretend it's his mind?"

Damn, Kylie thought. These two were as bad as Della and Miranda. Or Burnett and Holiday.

Della scowled at Steve and then looked at Kylie. "I'm out of here."

Embarrassed, Kylie looked at Steve. "Thanks. Can you tell Lucas that I came by?"

"You could probably find him." Steve stood up. "I think they were going down to the clearing by the stream."

"Oh," Kylie said, and took off after Della. Kylie's chest pinched with jealousy as she remembered her and Lucas going to the stream. She was so fixated on trying not to feel the green emotion ping-ponging in her heart, she hadn't realized they were heading the wrong way.

"Where are we going?" Kylie asked.

Della glared at her. "To the stream, idiot. And don't for one minute pretend that you don't want to know what he's doing down there with that she-wolf. If he was my boyfriend, I'd go grab him by the scruff of his neck and teach that wolf a lesson he wouldn't forget. He'd be whimpering like a pup before I let him go."

Kylie continued to follow Della while holding an out-and-out debate in her head over the wisdom of continuing or turning around. If she went to the stream, would Lucas think she'd come because she was jealous? But if she didn't go and Steve told him she'd dropped by and hadn't come, would he think she'd gone home because she was jealous?

Okay, the only thing that came out of that mental debate was knowing that she didn't want Lucas to think she was jealous.

Even though she was.

But did that mean she was wrong?

Or was Lucas wrong? Wrong for taking off in the dark to spend some time with Fredericka by the creek? Was he right now rolling on the grass with Fredericka, kissing her the way he'd kissed Kylie when he'd taken her to the creek?

Or was it as innocent as her getting caught behind the office with Derek?

Kylie looked up at the moon. The glow seemed extra bright and she felt that odd sting on her skin. Just like she felt on the full moon.

She inhaled deeply and told herself she was imagining things.

"Quit trying to talk yourself out of going," Della said.

"How do you know that's what I'm doing?"

"Because I can see it on your face. And because you couldn't walk any slower if you were a turtle on crutches."

"I just don't want to come off like a psycho girlfriend."

"If he's making out with her—or worse, playing hide the salami—then he deserves you coming off like a psycho. Hell, I'll join you and we'll both go psycho on his ass."

"I don't think he's doing that." As if saying it helped her believe it.

"You didn't want to think Derek did it, either." Della sighed as if she regretted saying the words. "No disrespect to Ellie and all, but it was still wrong."

Kylie's chest tightened at the mention of Ellie's name. "That was different."

"How is it different?" Della asked. A low-hanging limb swung back and Kylie caught it with her arm with complete ease. "I think it adds up to the fact that all guys are scum. Maybe we weren't even supposed to mate with them."

"Derek and I weren't together."

"Maybe you hadn't said you were together. But in your heart, you were together."

Kylie remembered what Miranda had said about her talking about Derek more than she did Lucas. Suddenly she didn't want to talk about her screwed-up love life. So why not talk about Della's screwed-up love life? It seemed like the perfect diversion.

"You could have been nicer to Steve."

Della swung around, attitude in her body posture. "I was nice."

"No, you weren't. You accused him of liking the new teacher's tits."

Della resumed walking. "You should have seen him ogling her, it was embarrassing."

"It kind of sounds like you're jealous, which says you like the guy," Kylie pointed out.

Della started walking faster, her pace matching her mood. "I don't like him. But I'll admit he has a nice butt."

"And you said you were going to try to be more approachable to his nice butt," Kylie reminded her.

"I tried. It didn't work out. I guess his butt isn't that nice."

Another branch came back, and the instant Kylie caught it in her palm, she remembered. She stopped and looked up through the trees at the sky. A few stars twinkled back as if laughing at her.

"Crap," she muttered.

"What?" Della looked back over her shoulder.

Kylie glanced around. The moon's glow cast a silver shine through the trees and shadows danced on ground.

"I just remembered."

"Remembered what?"

"I'm not supposed to go into the woods." Kylie inhaled the verdant scent of the trees and the moist earth. Then she internally searched for that feeling of being lured, beckoned as she had been earlier. It wasn't there. So maybe all those feelings were just her over-active imagination. Oh, yeah, she wanted to believe that.

Nevertheless, she'd disobeyed Burnett's orders. Maybe not on purpose, but she didn't think he'd find that excuse acceptable. "We should go back."

"But we're almost there. And you've got me—a badass vampire— with you. Nothing's going to happen. And don't you want to know if Lucas and Fredericka are doing the hokey pokey?"

Kylie caught another branch coming back at her. "If Burnett finds out, he's going to be pissed."

"Then we won't tell him. Trust me. It's gonna be fine."

Against her better judgment, Kylie continued taking steps with Della. The crickets did their thing and an occasional bird called out. In the background, Kylie could even hear the sounds of the wild animals in the park. Normally when the night sang, it meant all was well. It was in the quiet that things jumped out of the shadows. When evil seemed to appear.

Inhaling the night air, she continued moving, jumping over a few patches of thorny bushes and ducking under low branches.

"Crap," Della hissed, and came to an abrupt stop.

"What is it?" Kylie asked, and that was when the forest went silent. Not dead like in ghost silent, but dead like in threatening.

"The next time I tell you to trust me, don't." Della looked back over her shoulder. Her eyes were bright green and her canines extended. "We've got company."

Chapter Eight

"We should run." Kylie's voice was nothing more than a whisper. Her heart throbbing in her chest sounded louder.

"When things run, they get chased," Della answered. "I'd rather do the chasing."

"Smart girl," a deep voice answered back. And just the sound of it sent chills down Kylie's spine.

Three silent figures stepped out from the shadows. The only noise filtering through the thicket of trees was Della's hiss. Kylie moved to stand next to Della in case they attacked. Her mind still played with the option of running. A good option. But first she had to convince Della.

The slight sound of twigs being snapped under footsteps sounded at their backs. They were surrounded.

Time to find a new option.

Even with only the half moon lighting the path, Kylie was able to check the patterns of the three men fronting them: werewolves. The edges of the patterns were dark, as if their intentions were not good natured. That could only mean one thing: rogues.

The bigger man in the middle stepped closer. Della hissed harder. Kylie felt her blood fizz with the need to protect the little vamp. As badass as Della considered herself, this was no fair match. Not that the rogues would care.

"I will kindly ask you to leave," Kylie said, not sure where her bravado came from, but it was there, and she'd be damned if she wouldn't use it. "You're trespassing. This is Shadow Falls property." She stood with her shoulders back, her chin up. Knowing they could smell fear, she tried not to let the seed of that emotion grow any bigger.

Kylie saw Della, poised to attack, and Kylie touched her elbow, hoping to convince the vamp to wait. Maybe they could talk their way out of this.

"Leave now, or I'll rip your throat out first," Della said to the man facing her.

That wasn't the kind of talk Kylie had in mind.

"We did not come here to do harm," the guy in the middle said to Kylie, and then he cut Della a smirk as if mocking her threat. "But if provoked, that could change."

Della hissed louder.

"Then leave." Kylie's gaze moved over him. She got the feeling the one who spoke was the leader. He didn't look old, but things like the gray at his temple and the fine lines around his dark blue eyes told her he was older than she'd first assumed. Caught by his eyes, her mind tried to place him. She felt him staring, doing the same with her, and then his eyes pinched as he read her pattern.

As sudden as a flicker of light, she knew who he was. She sensed he recognized her as well. That kernel of fear lingering in her gut grew. This man didn't value life. He'd already proven that to Kylie once.

He took another step forward. Della tried to jump in front of him, but Kylie grabbed her.

"Let me handle this." The sizzle in Kylie's blood—the sizzle that came when her need to protect arose—grew stronger.

"I'm not here to spill blood," he insisted.

"Then leave," Kylie demanded.

"Yeah, tuck your tail between your legs and run," Della bit out.

A threatening growl came from behind them. Della swung around, yanking away from Kylie's hold, her eyes glowing brighter. Fear took another lap around Kylie's heart. Not fear for herself, but for what was about to happen. Her blood now buzzed as it moved into her veins. She kept her focus on Della. If anyone put a hand on her, this would not end well.

"Calm down," the leader spoke, and Kylie sensed he spoke to her as well as to his own men. "I just came to speak to my son."

"Then speak to him." A new voice rang out from the trees. "But you and your guards back away right this minute." Lucas's voice, deep and menacing, came from Kylie's right. When she turned, she saw that his eyes glowed burnt orange. She watched him lift his head ever so slightly to pull air in through his nose.

She knew then she'd lost her battle trying to hide her fear. Lucas had smelled it as the others probably had. But she wondered if they picked up on the fact that she hadn't feared the fight. She'd feared the emotional havoc it would've caused. Killing your boyfriend's father couldn't be good for a relationship.

"I said, back off," Lucas ordered.

When the three men didn't back up, Della spoke up again. "You heard him, you jackasses. Back off."

Lucas suddenly stood on the other side of Kylie. His warm forearm brushed against her shoulder, leaving no doubt of his loyalty to her, even over his own father. The thought warmed her heart, even as it thudded with panic.

More werewolf campers stepped out from behind the trees. They didn't appear aggressive, but just their presence spoke of their loyalty to Lucas.

"It appears I'm not the only one who brought his guards," Mr. Parker said.

"If I need them, they'll back me," Lucas said.

A low growl came from one of the weres bracketing Lucas's dad. Mr. Parker glanced over at him. "There will be no trouble tonight."

While still leery, and with the tension so thick it made breathing difficult, Kylie heard the command in the man's voice and sensed his men would not defy him. The surge of adrenaline storming in her veins lessened.

Will, another camper and one of Lucas's friends, moved in closer. Somewhere in the back of Kylie's brain, the realization hit. Lucas hadn't been alone with Fredericka. A thread of guilt over doubting him rose in her chest.

As if thinking of the girl brought her here, Fredericka walked out of the line of trees and into the small clearing.

"Mr. Parker," Fredericka said in a light tone, breaking the tight tension. "What a pleasure to see you again." The she-wolf shot Kylie a slight smirk, as if wanting Kylie to know she was friends with Lucas's dad.

"The same here," the man replied with disinterest. He paid Fredericka no heed. He hadn't stopped studying Kylie's pattern. She felt the slightest bit worried that it was doing something strange.

"So the rumors don't lie," Mr. Parker said, sounding perplexed.

"What rumors?" Kylie asked.

"I can see why my son is intrigued by you. A shame that you are not one of us."

Kylie's chest tightened at the implication. As if her relationship with Lucas was doomed.

"Enough," Lucas said. "I think—"

"You are one strange bird, Kylie Galen." Mr. Parker tightened his brows as if to get a closer look at her pattern.

Kylie tilted her chin up a notch. Not a bird, Kylie thought. A chameleon. And an inexplicable sense of pride filled her chest. For the first time, Kylie accepted that while she knew nothing of what being a chameleon meant, there was value in the little knowledge she had.

Lucas turned to face Della. "Both of you go back to your cabin." His gaze settled on Kylie. "I'll see you later."

Resentment at being told to leave stirred in Kylie's gut, but logic intervened and she sensed his intention came from his need to protect her and not to control her. Then she realized that if she resented his authoritative tone . . . She glanced at Della.

"I'd rather help you send these guys off," Della growled.

Kylie spoke up. "We should go."

Della frowned, but her expression said she'd concede. "Fine. I didn't want to hang out with these dogs anyway." She snarled at the intruders.

One of Mr. Parker's guards took a defensive step forward, and both Kylie and Lucas moved in a step. That one step left little doubt that neither of them would allow the guard to touch Della. Kylie didn't miss the frown that Lucas sent Kylie, as if to say he didn't want her taking the protective role. But that was what she was. A protector. A chameleon protector.

Della scowled at both of them, as if to say she didn't need their protection.

"Go. Please," Lucas said.

Kylie motioned for Della to follow her.

As they walked away, Kylie couldn't resist looking back. She saw Lucas, his posture defensive as if his father brought out the worst in him. Her thoughts went to both her own father and her stepfather. Neither of them put her on the defensive. Yeah, her stepfather had made some bad mistakes, and Kylie might still be working on forgiving him, but deep down she knew he loved her. And with her real father, Daniel, well, he cared so deeply he hadn't even let his death separate them.

Kylie sensed Lucas had never felt any affection from his father. Her heart hurt for him, and her blood heated with the need to defend him.

But defend him against what? What was it that had brought Mr. Parker to camp? Something told her it wasn't just to give Lucas a hug. Was something wrong with Lucas's grandmother? His half sister?

A shame that you are not one of us. His words echoed in her head and heart. Could he be here about her? Protesting the fact that Lucas was . . . intrigued with her?

"Burnett's going to be so pissed about this," Della huffed, her hurried pace matching her angry tone.

Kylie nipped at her lip with worry, before expressing her thoughts. "Which is why you aren't going to tell him."

Della looked at Kylie. The vamp's eyes were still bright with fury. "They are rogues."

"But he's Lucas's father." And the thought of Lucas having to deal with Burnett after already having to deal with his father seemed unfair.

"It's against regulations."

"Just like it was for Chan to show up," Kylie reminded her. "And like Chan, Mr. Parker didn't hurt anyone. He just wanted to talk to his son."

Della let out a breath of frustration. "You know, I really hate it when you do that."

"Do what?" Kylie dodged a vine swinging back.

"Use logic and rub my nose in the fact that you're right."

"I didn't rub your nose in it."

"Maybe not. But I still don't like it."

They walked a few minutes without speaking. "Thanks for not telling," Kylie said, knowing that was what Della meant.

They moved through the dense vegetation with only the night's song whispering through the trees. Finally, Kylie spoke up. "Lucas wasn't alone with Fredericka."

"Yeah, I figured that one out, too," Della said. "But . . ."

"But what?"

"I don't know. I mean, I kind of feel as if I sort of encouraged you to go with Lucas and maybe I was wrong."

"Wrong?" Kylie grabbed Della by the arm. "Do you mean wrong to push me, or wrong for me to go after Lucas?"

Della frowned. "Both."

"Why would you say that?" Kylie asked, hurt that Della would make such a statement—especially when her heart was already so confused.

"It's not that I don't like Lucas, I do. But he's werewolf and you're obviously not. I admit I thought you were before. But tonight when we were surrounded by weres, I could just tell that you weren't like them. And after what his grandmother said and now after what his dad said, I think his family and his pack are going to stand in your way."

"He told me he doesn't care what they say." And she believed it. She did.

Sadness filled Della's eyes and Kylie felt the emotion resonate within herself.

Della exhaled. "That's what Lee said, too. And look what happened with us."

It's not the same thing.

While Kylie waited on her porch for Lucas to show up, she contemplated what Della had said and thought about her day from hell.

She'd spoken to her mom, who needed reassurance that Kylie was okay. She'd spoken to Holiday, who needed the same thing. Then her phone chirped again. Derek, this time, wanting the same thing.

"Hey, I just wanted to check in," he said.

It was funny, really, how well she knew him. She knew what he felt without his ever having to say it and so she knew why he'd called. He'd obviously sensed some of her earlier emotions. "I'm fine."

"If you need to talk or anything, I'm here." He sounded so wistful, she felt her heart grow tighter.

"I know," she answered. "And I appreciate it."

"Did you ever figure out the whole ghost issue?"

"Not yet," Kylie admitted, her tone echoing some of the frustration she felt.

"Did you talk to Holiday about it?" he asked, sounding genuinely concerned.

"A little," she said. "But I wasn't . . . I only skimmed the surface."

"Oh, shit!"

"What?"

"That's who it is, isn't it? That's whose face the ghost has stolen. It's Holiday."

Kylie closed her eyes. "Yes, but please don't say anything. I'm trying to figure it out before I take it to Holiday."

"Is she in danger? Does this mean . . . anything?"

"In a roundabout way, I asked Holiday, and she said it was unlikely. But . . ."

"But what?"

"It's just scary," Kylie admitted. "Seeing her as a ghost when she's not dead."

"Hell yeah, it's scary. And you shouldn't have to figure it out all by yourself. I'm here for you. I don't know how to help solve this, but whatever it takes, I'll do it."

"Thanks." She leaned back against the cabin wall, and right then she was hit by a wash of cold. Dead cold.

"And I don't expect anything in return," he said. "I accept we're just friends."

"Thank you." The spirit, identical to Holiday, stood over her, looking down with a frown on her face. "I should go."

"Something wrong?" he asked, and she couldn't help but wonder if he could feel her now.

"Just . . . got company."

"Lucas?" His tone expressed exactly how he felt about the werewolf.

"No. The ghost."

"Oh. So, I'll let you go. But Kylie . . ."

"Yeah?" She stood because she didn't like having the spirit staring down at her.

"I'm here if you need me." He sounded so genuine.

"I know," she said, feeling the words vibrate in her chest. She hung up and met the woman's green gaze.

"I think you should pick him," the spirit said.

"Say what?"

"Between him and the werewolf. I like him. He's fae."

Kylie bit back the frustration. "I think I'd better decide that."

"Just a little advice," the spirit said.

Kylie studied her. "Did you discover anything?"

"Not really, but I remember some stuff."

"What kind of stuff?"

"Scary stuff."

"Can you tell me about it?"

The spirit studied Kylie with the same kind of concerned look Holiday always did.

"I don't think you need to hear it. You're . . . young."

Kylie rolled her eyes. "You came here for me to help you. I can't help if you don't tell me things."

She blinked. *"I don't know if that's true."*

"What's not true?"

"That I came to you to help me." She stood silent for a long moment. *"I think I came to you to help someone else."*

"Who?"

"I don't know exactly. But I sense it."

"What do you sense?"

"That danger is right around the corner." Her eyes filled with worry.

"Can I stop it from happening?"

She tilted her head to one side and considered the question. *"I think so. I think that's why I came. So you could stop it."*

Kylie's heart filled with hope. Surely, if it wasn't possible to help, the spirit would have known. So even if this was Holiday, maybe Kylie could save her. Maybe the person the spirit was supposed to save was herself and she just didn't realize it. "Have you figured out your name yet?"

She shook her head. *"I just keep getting the same thing. I think it's Hannah."*

"Please tell me what you know. It might be important."

She shook her head. *"I'm not ready to talk about it. And it's not a whole lot. Just . . . flashes of stuff."*

"Why aren't you ready to talk about it?"

The spirit turned and stared at the woods as if she'd heard something.

Kylie followed her gaze. She didn't see anyone, but oddly, the feeling she'd felt earlier had returned. Someone was out there. Calling for her.

Who are you? What do you want? She asked the question in her mind.

"They want to talk to you," the ghost said.

"Who?" Kylie asked. "And you said 'they,' so how do you know there's more than one?"

"I just somehow know there's more than one. But if I don't know my own name, how could I know theirs?"

"Have you seen them? Do you know what they want with me?" She shook her head. *"I just sense them. Calling you."*

"Do they mean to harm me?" she asked.

"I . . . can't say for sure. But they don't feel evil."

"They don't really feel evil to me, either." Or maybe she just wanted to believe it. She moved down the steps. She'd almost reached the woods when someone caught her arm—someone warm, someone alive.

Chapter Nine

Kylie swung around, her heart bouncing off her stomach all the way up to her throat.

"Where are you going?" Lucas asked.

"Nowhere." She swallowed the panic. "I was waiting on you and thought I heard something." It wasn't completely a lie; she'd heard it with her heart.

He pulled her against him. "That's when you go inside the cabin, not into the woods. Even normals know that from watching those phony horror shows."

She rolled her eyes. "I would've gone inside if I thought it was evil."

"But sometimes you don't know." He slid his hand down to her waist.

She agreed with him on that point and probably needed to remember it, too.

Yet remembering anything became harder with him this close. So close she felt him breathe. The soft touch of his palm warmed her skin beneath her clothes. The tenderness and heat created a trail of tingling sensation.

He dipped his head down and gazed into her eyes. "Do you have any idea how I would feel if something happened to you?"

"Probably the same as I'd feel if something happened to you," she said. "What did your father want?"

He frowned. "It's Clara, my half sister. She ran off again. She told him she was coming here, but he suspected she went back to her boyfriend."

"I'm sorry. What are you going to do?"

"I don't know." He sighed. "I've already gone after her twice. She said she wanted to come here. But maybe she lied. If I bring her here against her will, what's going to stop her from running off?"

"Is the boyfriend that bad?"

He grimaced. "He's rogue and heavily into a gang."

"And that automatically makes him bad?" She'd learned that not all supernaturals were registered, and to some people that alone made them rogue, but not all unregistered supernaturals were bad, either. Della didn't consider Chan evil. And Kylie chose to believe her grandfather and great-aunt weren't bad. "Are all gangs bad?"

Her question seemed to give him pause. "Not necessarily, but even the gangs that aren't completely unethical are generally into something illegal."

"Drugs?" Kylie asked.

"And other stuff."

Kylie remembered how badly she'd felt for Lucas when she'd seen him looking so defensive facing his own father. She remembered he'd stood up for her against his own family. Her heart hurt for Lucas. "If your half sister is anything like her half brother, she'll do the right thing." She stepped up on her tiptoes and pressed her lips to his.

It was late. It was dark. But the moment seemed so right. What was meant as a quick kiss lingered and became more. Much more. He deepened the kiss and she leaned into him. She felt his body come closer to hers, hard in all the places she was soft.

She heard the purring sound that a were made when he was close to a potential mate. She became almost hypnotized—lured by the sound, tempted and enticed by all that could follow.

He tasted so good, felt so good. She wanted more. She wanted to feel more. To taste more. To experience more.

Then the magic ended when he pulled away. He brushed his hand over her cheek and while his blue eyes held the heat of passion, she could tell his mind was chewing on something else. "I'm sorry that my dad scared you."

She fought the desire to tell him to just start kissing her again. "It's okay," she said, and tried not to sound disappointed.

"No, it's not." He caught her hand and moved to the porch.

"He stated right away that he wasn't there to cause harm," she said, wanting to soothe Lucas. Wanting to make this easier.

"And you should never believe him," he said.

A whisper of fear settled in her chest. They lowered themselves down on the porch so they could lean against the cabin.

He brushed his thumb over her lips. "I don't want my father anywhere around you."

She looked into Lucas's serious gaze. "He hurt you?" The need to protect him made her blood run faster.

"Not me. I'm his son. But he considers anyone else fair game."

"If he's that bad, why do you go there? Why have anything to do with him?"

"For Clara, mostly. But then . . . I need him right now."

"Why?"

"His approval will go a long way to help me get into the were council."

The council he couldn't get on if he married her. The thought shot a wave of apprehension through her and she remembered what Della had said about things not working out between them because of his family and his pack. She pushed that thought out of the way and tried to understand. "But if that's who they look to for approval, then why would you want to be on that council?"

He closed his eyes for a second as if explaining was difficult. "If I make it on the council, then I can change things."

Kylie recalled his grandmother telling her that he wanted to change how the world viewed children raised by rogues.

"But until then, I have to convince him that I see things his way."

"What things?"

He shook his head slowly. "Things I don't think you even need to know."

Kylie frowned, not liking being shut out of his world, even if she wasn't sure she wanted to belong to it. She'd bet that Fredericka knew everything. "But I do need to know. I want to be a part of your life. I don't want to be shut out." *I don't want your pack or your family keeping us apart.*

His eyes tightened. "I'm not shutting you out. I just prefer that you know this Lucas."

She digested his words. "There can only be one Lucas."

"There is only one. One real one. But I have to play games with my father and the council. I have to convince him that I'm on his side."

She shook her head. "I don't understand."

"And I don't expect you to."

She dropped her hand from his arm. "That's not right. How would you like it if you thought I kept things from you?"

A frown pulled at his lips. "You do keep things from me. Things about your ghosts." His eyes brightened with frustration. "Things you talk to Derek about and not me. And you're right, I don't like it."

She considered his words and knew they were true. "I only keep things from you because you don't want to know about them. They make you crazy."

He nodded, and acceptance filled his eyes, but she could tell it cost him emotionally. "And believe me when I tell you that the things I keep to myself are things you wouldn't want to know either."

She looked deep into his eyes, hating this conversation, but only because she cared so much about him. "Secrets between people can't be good. It can keep them apart. Why don't we just tell each other everything?"

"Sometimes what we don't know protects us. It can't hurt us if we don't know it." He leaned his forehead against hers. "I can promise you this, Kylie Galen. I'll do whatever I have to do, but I won't let this hurt you."

She frowned. "What do you mean by whatever you have to do?"

"Just that. I won't let what's happening in my messed-up life hurt you."

His words scared her. But the fear was more for him than for herself. "I'm not some fragile little girl. I'm not the same girl whose window you peeked into."

The playfulness in his eyes was both sexy and warm. "Oh, I've noticed."

"I'm serious."

"I know. But you're still my girl, and I want to protect you."

She rolled her eyes in frustration. "I'm the protector. That's what I do," Kylie insisted.

"I know. You're amazing and can do amazing things. And you've already saved my life. But as a protector, the one thing you can't do is protect yourself. So please don't try to stop me from doing it."

Kylie woke up before the sun the next morning. The only thing she was aware of was Socks sleeping on her stomach, his pointed skunk nose resting between her breasts. She lifted her head and stared at the little guy. He opened one of his beady eyes and then the other, and stared up at her with adoration. The kind of look one got only from a pet.

The kind that said pure love and acceptance.

The silence in the room was loud. Unsure about what had awakened her, she pulled her arm out from under the thin cover to measure the temperature. No cold. No ghosts.

And then she heard it. Or heard her.

"Kitty, kitty," Miranda called from the slightly opened bedroom door. "Come on, Socks. Don't you want to be turned back into a kitten?"

Socks sprang to his feet, leapt to the floor, and scurried under the bed. Kylie wasn't sure if his annoyance was at Miranda for constantly trying to change him back or if he perhaps didn't want to change. Considering Kylie had changed a whole hell of a lot these past few months, she couldn't blame Socks. Change was scary.

Miranda pushed open the door a bit more. "Come on, don't make it hard on me."

Kylie leaned up on her elbow and yawned. "I think he's scared."

Miranda moved in a little more. "I think I got it figured out. I just need to take him outside and into the first morning light."

"Hmm." Kylie rose up, putting her bare feet on the cold wood floor. Too cold? She did another visual sweep to check for ghosts. Nope. She had a ghost-free zone happening.

"Sorry I woke you up. I thought I could just sneak in and grab him." Miranda seemed wide awake and in a good mood as she plopped down and gave the mattress a little bounce.

"No big deal. I was practically awake anyway," Kylie lied. In truth, it had been a pretty sleepless night. After Lucas had left, Della had retired to her room and Miranda hadn't come home, so Kylie had grabbed Socks and gone to bed. Not to sleep. That would have been too easy. She'd tossed and turned for hours, juggling her problems like balls, and not really solving a single one of them.

However, she had to admit, she'd gotten used to thinking of herself as a chameleon. And was thrilled it was one day closer to Thursday, when her real grandfather would visit.

Or at least she prayed he'd visit her.

Remembering her difficulty falling sleep reminded her that the last time she checked the clock, at around three AM, Miranda still hadn't come back.

"So, are you going to fill me in?" Kylie asked.

"Fill you in on what?" Miranda's smile tightened with mischievousness. Kylie studied her friend closer. She wore the same clothes she'd worn to her date last night. Had Miranda woken her to try to transform Socks back into a kitty, or did she need someone to talk with? Not that Kylie minded. She'd woken Della and Miranda up many nights, mostly with dreams or those scary visions—but if she had just needed to talk, she knew they'd be there for her.

"Just what time did you get home, young lady?" Kylie asked in a teasing voice.

"Early. I swear." Miranda giggled. "Early this morning."

"Details. I want details." Kylie rubbed her hands together, mimicking Miranda.

"Don't get too excited," Miranda said. Then she sighed. "We didn't . . . you know. But we did . . . well, you know."

Kylie let the riddle roll around her sleep-dazed mind and shook her head. "I think I get the first 'you know,' but I'm lost on the second 'you know.'" Still feeling the cold on the bottom of her feet, she pulled her legs up on the mattress. The darkness in the room felt lightened just by Miranda's presence.

"We kissed, we made out." Miranda's grin widened, and then she got that sappy lovestruck look on her face. "We fell asleep in each other's arms down by the swimming hole. He held me all night long, and I think I'm in love for real. It's like I know I belong there. In his arms."

Kylie remembered the times she'd fallen asleep in Lucas's arms. Awesome didn't begin to describe it. But had she woken up knowing for sure that he was the one? She couldn't remember ever feeling that way.

Then, realizing this was Miranda's moment, she pushed her self-indulgence away. "Well, I'm thrilled for you." And Kylie was. Even if she was just a tad envious, too.

"I know *you* are." Miranda's smile faded. "I don't think Della will feel the same way."

"Of course she will," Kylie said. "She just has a hard time showing it. Remember how she kept encouraging you to make up with Perry when you were mad at him?"

"I guess," Miranda said, not sounding convinced. "I mean, I feel as if I can't say anything about Perry around her now. I get that she's hurt about Lee and I don't want to make her feel bad, but I also want to be able to talk to her about what's going on in my life. And right now what's going on in my life is all about Perry. Seriously, I don't want to have to walk on eggshells around her."

"And I think you're just worrying too much. Believe me, in a day or two things will be back to normal and you guys will be threatening to rip each other's limbs off for a reason that has nothing to do with Perry."

Miranda exhaled. "You make it sound like we argue all the time."

"Not all the time," Kylie said. "Just most of the time."

Miranda shrugged. "Anyway, do you think you can help me snag Socks so I can see if I got the spell right? Perry listened to me practice for an hour. I want to fix this." Miranda frowned. "I feel like a screw-up."

"You're not a screw-up." Kylie looked down at the floor. "Come here, Socks. Come here, baby."

Miranda fell back on the mattress. "I feel like one, especially when my Wiccan sisters tease me about it. I suck at being a witch."

"They tease you about Socks?" Kylie asked.

"Yeah, not that I blame them. I messed up."

"Screw them," Kylie said. "You should figure out how to curse them with a dose of dyslexia and see how they deal with it."

"They're really not being mean," Miranda said.

"But it hurts you." Anger for Miranda burned Kylie's chest. She hated bullies. Hated people who put other people down so they could feel better about themselves.

Miranda popped back up. "But they're just teasing." She knelt and tapped her fingers on the floor. "Here, kitty, kitty."

Miranda's words seemed to be sucked up by the shadows in the corners of the room. Kylie lowered her foot from the bed and swiped her heel against the bed ruffle.

She waited to feel Socks attack her ankle. The only thing she felt was an icy cold leaking from beneath the bed skirt. An icy cold that gave Kylie a bad feeling.

She looked at Miranda. "Why don't you go outside and I'll . . . I'll bring him to you. He'll probably come out when you leave." For some reason the room seemed to grow darker. Kylie hoped Socks was all that would come out.

Miranda stood. "I don't know why he doesn't like me," she muttered, and walked out.

Kylie cautiously stood and stared down at the bed ruffle. "Socks? Kitty?"

No little skunk came scampering from beneath the bed. No soft meow whispered from beneath to let her know he was okay.

Taking a deep breath, she got on her hands and knees and stared at the unmoving ruffle. She fought the temptation to breathe on it. For some odd reason, she wanted to see something move; the odd stillness of the material didn't feel right. Nothing felt right.

She reached for the cotton material to peer beneath it, praying all she'd find was one scared skunk. Kylie's fingers almost touched the ruffle when a sound—a moan or a strangled cry—whispered from beneath the bed. She jerked her hand back. Her breath caught. That didn't sound like Socks at all.

An icy and unnatural cold snaked from under the bed. Steam billowed out from the bed skirt. Fear, ugly, raw fear filled her chest. She glanced back at the door. Wished she could leave. Knew she couldn't. Instinct told her Socks wasn't alone under that bed.

Still on her hands and knees, she took one tiny knee shift backward. How many times as a child had she feared a monster under the bed? How many times had her mom promised that monsters didn't exist? That moan sounded again.

Her mom was wrong. A monster, or something equally scary, lurked right under Kylie's bed.

She couldn't blame her mom for the lie. Mom didn't know.

But Kylie did.

Not that it mattered. Unwilling to abandon her pet, trying to settle her pounding heart, she reached again for the bed skirt. Right before her two fingers caught the cotton fabric, a hand shot out.

Her own scream faded into the shadows as the cold, dead hand grasped Kylie's arm and yanked her forward.

She fought for freedom, clawed at the fingers, twisted her arm, anything to pry it loose. Nothing worked.

"Help!" she screamed, but no one answered. The clasp around her wrist tightened, dragging her closer. The last thing she saw was the bed ruffle sliding over her face as she slipped into dark oblivion. Her last thought before her mind went numb was that she was finally going to meet the monster living under her bed.

Chapter Ten

Kylie lay flat on her back, cloaked in darkness. Deep, black darkness. *Just a vision. It's not real. Not real.*

Something on each side of her pressed tight against her forearms. It felt real. She tried to move, but couldn't. Fear swelled inside her. She tasted the bitterness of it on her tongue.

Disoriented, she tried to make sense of it. Inhaling, she smelled the earth. Wet, moist dirt. She wasn't under the bed. Where was she? An answer came and she wished it hadn't. She was buried. Another scream filled her throat, but logic told her this wasn't real. *Just a vision.*

But from who? And what? Holiday?

The sound of Kylie's own breath leaving her lips sounded too loud. Instantly, she realized she wasn't alone. It wasn't the sound of someone else breathing. No one breathed but her. Yet the grip on her wrist hadn't loosened. Whoever had dragged her under here hadn't left—someone still clung to her wrist as if that person's very life depended on it. Unfortunately, Kylie knew it was too late. Only she was alive.

"Why am I here?" She tried to move again but felt somehow constricted.

No answer came.

Blinking, her vision slowly adjusted to the darkness. She saw the pattern of old wood a few inches from her face.

She tried to pull her wrist away from the tight grip, but the hold only tightened.

"Oh, shit. What have you guys done?" A familiar voice echoed in the darkness.

Holiday.

"I'm in here," Kylie called out. Only this time no words left her mouth. She couldn't speak.

"Cara M. said she could help us get out of here," another female voice answered.

Footsteps sounded above. The wood panel creaked. Dust and dirt sifted down on Kylie's face. She blinked the grit from her eyes and tried to hold her breath so she didn't choke.

"He's leaving," someone whispered.

Kylie blinked, and when she opened her eyes, everything had changed. She stood in an old dilapidated cabin, staring down at the creaky wooden boards beneath her feet. Then, as if the floor faded, Kylie saw what lay hidden below.

Three decaying bodies lay positioned shoulder to shoulder. A scream spilled from Kylie's lips. She tried to run, but her feet felt frozen. She tried to look away, but couldn't.

One corpse was a woman with dark hair, probably in her early twenties, wearing a nightgown. The second was a blond around the same age wearing a familiar waitress outfit with a nametag on it that read CARA M. And the third . . . Oh God! Holiday.

Tears filled her eyes. Kylie screamed louder when she realized she once again lay flat on her back. Darkness swallowed her up. Panic tightened when she felt something moving at her side. Adrenaline surged through her veins. She leapt up and banged her head so hard, it rattled her brain. She collapsed on her back again.

"Where the hell are you?" A voice echoed around her. A familiar voice. Della's voice. "Mofo!" Light suddenly filled Kylie's vision. "What are you doing under there?"

Kylie gasped, swallowed her scream, and realized she lay on her bedroom floor with a shivering Socks plastered to her side.

"You are just too friggin' weird." Della, looking half-pissed and half-asleep, stood over Kylie holding the bed up above her head. Yes, the whole twin bed—frame and mattress. Holding it up as if it were nothing more than a lightweight piece of foam.

Socks let out a pathetic meow.

Afraid Della might drop the bed, Kylie snatched up the little skunk and lunged to her feet. Her knees wobbled; the skunk trembled in her arms. She glanced down, praying it would be her bedroom floor and not a grave.

No grave. No dead girls. No dead Holiday.

Kylie inhaled. As much as she wanted to push the gruesome memory from her brain, she couldn't. Something in the vision might help her. Help her figure it out so she could prevent it from happening. Help her save Holiday's life.

"What the hell is going on?" Della asked again. "Or do I not want to know?"

"Sorry. Bad dream." Kylie's voice shook.

Della dropped the bed. It banged and clattered on the floor.

"Is there a ghost here?" Della glanced around, obviously not believing Kylie's bad dream excuse.

Kylie took a second to feel the temperature. "No," she said honestly.

Della studied her, her expression softening. "Are you okay?"

Kylie nodded and watched Della's frown return.

"And you aren't going to explain this?" Della asked.

Kylie shook her head. Della really didn't want to know.

"Then good night!" The little vamp shot out of the room, leaving as quickly as she'd come.

Kylie breathed in. Breathed out. Tried to calm her racing heart.

She tried to see the bright side—the bright side of being in a grave with three decaying bodies.

Not an easy task.

However, at least she had something to go on. But would it help her? Oh, God, it had to, didn't it?

She pulled Socks closer, offering comfort and trying to take comfort in holding something as scared as she was. It might have worked if the loud knock on her window didn't have her heart slamming against her rib cage. Kylie jumped clear across the room.

Another scream rose in her chest, but before she released it, she spotted Miranda peering through, her palm pressed against the glass.

"You coming?" she yelled. "We're going to lose the first light."

The cold filled the room. And so did the spirit. Kylie looked over at the ghost who looked just like Holiday. *I'm so sorry. She shouldn't have done that.*

Kylie tried not to envision Holiday, or God help her, the Holiday lookalike, as she had appeared in the grave. "It's okay," Kylie said, and she meant it. She could do this. If hanging out with dead people would save Holiday, she'd do it. Heck, she'd dance with the dead if it meant saving Holiday.

"I need to know things," Kylie said. "You need to show me things so I can figure out how to help you."

"Show you what?" Miranda asked.

Kylie ignored Miranda.

The spirit shook her head. *I told you, I don't think I'm the one you have to help.*

And wasn't that just like Holiday, Kylie thought, too damn stubborn to accept help. Even in ghost form.

"The only help I need is you to bring out Socks," Miranda called from the window again.

"You should go," Holiday said. *"That little fellow would like to be a cat again."*

Kylie looked at Miranda and then back to the spirit. "How do you know what he wants?"

"It's one of my gifts; I can communicate with animals."

"No, you can't," Kylie said. Or Holiday couldn't communicate with animals. Did supernaturals who passed over change their gifts? Kylie didn't think so. Did that mean this wasn't Holiday? And if so, who was she?

"Fine, you want him to stay a skunk," Miranda said in her irate voice.

Socks chose that moment to put his paw over his eyes and Kylie moaned.

A few minutes later, Kylie walked out behind the cabin with Socks held close to her chest. It was still dark and quiet, as if the world hadn't woken up yet. Unlike her, the world didn't get woken up by witches or visions of dead people.

The air held an early morning chill, one of the first signs that summer had outworn its welcome and fall waited nearby to fill its shoes.

When she took another step, she felt it. The calling. Her gaze shot to the edge of woods. Her heart raced and the temptation to move closer whispered her name like an old friend.

Kylie took one step, almost answering the unexplainable yearning, but Miranda's voice pulled her back. "What took you so long?"

"I had to get him out from under the bed," Kylie said, not in the mood to do this, but she remembered the insecurity in Miranda's voice when they'd talked earlier about the other witches giving her a hard time about the goof. Since the first morning light lasted only a few minutes, it was a small price to pay for Miranda's happiness. Then Kylie would sit down and rehash what she'd gotten from the dream. Something in there had to help her make sense of the visions.

Miranda, holding her little black pouch of magic herbs, led Kylie around to the back. "I haven't mistreated him. I have no idea why he doesn't like me."

"I know." But after a month of Miranda following the skunk around trying different spells, Socks had grown leery of her. Kylie would have grown leery of her, too.

Miranda looked up at the eastern sky and saw the light. "It's time." She did a little happy dance. "Put him down."

Kylie gave Socks's black-and-white fur a soft stroke. As crazy as it sounded, she would miss his skunk side. Savoring the sight of him in skunk form one last time, she set him down and backed up, giving Miranda space to work her magic. Of course, Socks started following her, not wanting to be left behind.

"Stay," Kylie said, and motioned for Miranda to start.

Miranda began chanting. Something about light and your true self. Socks started forward again. Miranda waved at Kylie to catch him. Kylie spoke gently to the skunk and he stopped moving. Then, reaching into her bag, Miranda pulled out a pinch of a strange herb-like substance. She tossed it in the air over Socks; a few pieces popped and sizzled as they rained down around him.

Kylie held her breath, waiting to see her beloved pet transform into a feline. But nope. The little animal with a white stripe down his back remained in his skunk form.

Miranda frowned up at the sky and commenced chanting again. She tossed more herbs in the air. This time, Socks rose up on his short skunk legs and swatted his tiny paws at the sparkles.

Yet even after all the sizzle of crackling herbs, he remained the same black-and-white skunk. Miranda looked back at the sky as if desperate and commenced another chant.

She held up her little black bag over his head and just shook it down on the animal.

Socks spotted the string hanging from the pouch and leapt up in the air to catch it. When Miranda pulled it back, Socks started to leave.

"Stop him!" Miranda's frustration rang loud and extra clear.

Kylie knelt and waved the little guy back. His beady black eyes looked at Kylie with confusion. Empathy for her pet filled her chest.

Miranda started to chant again.

Socks tried to escape again.

Miranda insisted Kylie stop him again.

It continued for several more minutes until Kylie held up her hand. "This isn't going to work."

"It has to," Miranda said. "I only have another few minutes of first sun. Just keep him there."

As if Socks understood, he darted between Miranda's legs.

"No," Miranda said.

Kylie caught the confused animal. "I think he's had enough," she offered in her most sympathetic voice.

"But he's still a skunk. Put him down. I can do this. I *have* to."

Kylie understood Miranda's need to prove herself, but . . . "Can't you try again tomorrow?"

"One more chant. Really quick, please? All he has to do is stand there."

Relenting, Kylie set Socks down and Miranda went back to reciting some fancy spell.

When Miranda stopped and Socks was still a skunk, Kylie gave Miranda a look of condolence. "It's okay. We'll try another time," Kylie said, beginning to lose her patience.

"Wait. I forgot to bless the light and wind." Miranda paused as if recalling the words.

Kylie held her hand out, pinky first, and muttered, "Why can't you just wave your pinky at him and say, 'Change back into a cat'?"

The pieces of herbs left on the ground shot up in the air. They crackled and popped around the little skunk and then started swirling around him like a tiny tornado. Socks, raised up on his hind legs, swatted at the bits of herb.

And then, just like magic—well, it *was* magic—Socks the skunk disappeared and Socks the feline appeared.

Miranda gaped at Kylie. "How did you do that?"

Kylie's gaze shot back to her kitten, still batting at the sparkling herbs floating around him. "I didn't do that!" She stared at Miranda.

"Oh, my gawd!" Miranda squealed.

Someone whisked past them in a blur.

"What the hell is it now?" Della came to a jolting stop by Miranda.

"She's a witch." Miranda pointed at Kylie. "You're a witch."

Kylie shook her head. She was a chameleon. "I didn't do that. It was you. Just . . . a delayed reaction."

"No. You're a witch. Right now, you're a witch."

Della rolled her eyes. "What the hell?"

"I'm telling you, I didn't do that," Kylie insisted.

And she hadn't. Had she?

Della squinted at Kylie.

"Mofo!" Della said.

Miranda slapped her forehead a couple of times. "Your pattern says you are a witch."

"What's wrong?" A deep voice came from behind Kylie.

Kylie turned around. Derek, looking disheveled as if he'd climbed out of bed in a hurry, came running up.

"She's a witch," Miranda screeched.

"No," Kylie said. Swinging around, she stared at Socks, still in feline form. Her father had told her she was a chameleon. Her father would know, right? Sure, she hadn't wanted to be a lizard at first, but she'd accepted it. Besides, why would her father lie?

From the corner of her vision, she saw Derek move in front of her. His brow pinched.

"It's not true, is it?" Kylie waited for Derek to deny it.

Doubt filled her. Had Daniel lied? Had her grandmother just been confused when she told Kylie's father they were chameleons? But why would Burnett have heard of chameleons if they didn't exist? Why did her life have to be so damn difficult?

"Tell me already!" Kylie insisted. "Am I a witch?"

Chapter Eleven

Derek nodded. "It's true. Your pattern says you're a witch."

Miranda folded her arms against her chest. "Don't you want to be a witch?" She sounded offended.

"Of course she doesn't want to be witch," Della mouthed off, still looking pissed at being woken up. "It's boring as hell. You don't do anything but throw herbs around and the only way you can fly is on a broom."

"It's not boring! And I do not fly on a broom! I swear, one witch did that and now we all get stereotyped." Miranda's eyes tightened with anger.

"Admit it," Della said. "If you had the power to change yourself, you'd be a vampire."

Miranda vehemently shook her head. "Who would want to be a bloodsucking, cold bitch with fangs!"

Kylie stared at the two of them verbally sparring, tossing insults so fast she couldn't even keep up. Then, too befuddled to intervene, she grabbed Socks before he wandered off in the woods.

Her gaze shifted back to the trees. The woods still called to her. What the hell was going on?

Her mind whirled as she headed to the cabin. Derek fell in step beside her. His shirt, left unbuttoned, fluttered open, exposing his hard abs. Not that she really noticed. Okay, so she noticed, but it didn't mean anything. Except that she was female and females found shirtless guys appealing.

"You're feeling confused," Derek stated.

"Yup." She didn't slow down. She couldn't. She was too annoyed that she found him so appealing. Too annoyed at the damn woods calling her like an old friend to come out and play. She didn't have any old friends. Not anyone looming in the woods.

"You're feeling betrayed," he said.

"Yup. Well, sort of." She continued to the cabin and snuggled her kitten to her chest. Her heart ached and the beginning of tears stung her eyes.

"And you're scared."

"Three out of three," she said. Yet all she felt now was . . .

"Frustrated." Derek finished her thought for her.

She stopped and looked him dead in the eyes. "You don't have to tell me what I feel. I know what I'm feeling."

"And you're in a pissy mood," he added with a smile. When she didn't respond in kind, his humor faded. "Sorry. I'm just . . . I want to understand."

"You know what I'm feeling; what more do you need to understand?" She stormed up the porch steps with Socks tucked under one arm, and yanked the door open so hard it made a loud banging sound when it hit the wall. Socks flinched. Derek followed her inside.

"I know your emotions, but I can only guess the reasons for them."

She dropped down on the sofa and held Socks in her lap. "Look, I'm in a really bad mood right now, and I suggest you might want to leave."

Derek dropped down beside her. He ignored what she said and continued, "For example, I know you're afraid, but what are you afraid of? Are you frustrated because you're a witch, or because your two best friends can't stop biting each other's heads off? And who are you feeling betrayed by right now? Is it me? Is it about . . ."

"No," she said before he mentioned Ellie and Kylie had to deal with those emotions as well. "It isn't you." Or maybe it was a little, she thought, remembering Miranda's comment about how she'd talked about Derek all the time.

"Is it about Lucas?" he asked. "You can tell me if it is. I want to help you and if it means listening to your issues with him, I'll do it."

She pulled Socks closer. "It isn't Lucas." But then she remembered their meeting last night, when Lucas had admitted to keeping secrets from her.

A long pause filled the room. Derek leaned in, his shoulder touched hers, and his emotional healing abilities flowed over her like a welcome breath of fresh air. Kylie had no doubt that the touch was on purpose, that he'd meant to help her.

She stared at Socks, then at Derek, trying to slow down her emotional overload. Trying not to be a bitch.

"Tell me what you're afraid of. I want to help." He stared at her forehead. "Does being a witch scare you?"

"I'm not a witch," she said before she could stop herself. Even with his warm calm flowing though her, she felt her frustrations build. Then she recalled Socks's magical transformation. Had she done that?

"At least, I don't think I am. It's not that I don't want to be a witch, it's . . . Why would my father tell me I was a chameleon if it wasn't true? I don't think my grandmother would make that up. And why would Burnett have heard about the species, if they didn't exist?"

"Burnett heard about it?" Derek asked.

She nodded. "Nothing concrete, just read it in some of the reports." She touched her forehead. What did all this mean? "Is my pattern really showing that I'm a witch?"

He nodded, as if afraid to disappoint her, then asked, "What's going on? I woke up this morning after a terrible nightmare. I couldn't remember it, but the point of it was that you were in trouble. When I was alert enough, I realized that maybe you really were in trouble and I'd just dreamed what I was reading from you. Then I felt all these other emotions from you. Is this about the ghost? Holiday's ghost?"

The vision she'd had flashed in her head like a bad movie clip. She closed her eyes, trying to shut it off, and searching for what to say to Derek. Tell him, or not tell him?

"I had a vision," she finally said, needing to confide in someone— needing to filter though everything she'd learned from the vision. "There were three bodies in a grave."

"Three? So it's like a serial killer?"

Socks moved from her lap and tucked his face into the curve of her arm, almost as if he understood what Derek had said. Kylie brushed her hand down his soft black feline fur. Feline. Had she done this? Had she changed him back?

"I think so." Kylie bit down on her lip and pushed those questions away to concentrate on something more important. "Holiday, or the one who looks like Holiday, was one of them." She recalled all the things her gut insisted might be important. "They were buried below some kind of an old cabin." Her chest tightened. "Seeing Holiday like that was . . . hard."

"I can imagine," Derek said. "Didn't you tell me that the visions were like puzzles to help you figure things out?"

She nodded. "But it wasn't the one who looked like Holiday that brought me into the vision. It was one of the other girls. I think she wants to be found, so they can leave the makeshift grave. So I'm still not sure if the vision is going to help me. Or maybe it can. I don't know." Her chest clutched. "Why can't they just tell me what they need?"

"Maybe if you tell me about it, I can help figure it out."

She looked at Derek. "How?"

"I worked for a PI. I sort of know how to dig things up. I'm good at it."

Kylie scratched Socks under his kitty chin as she tried to think of anything that might help them understand the vision. "One of the girls had on a waitress uniform. Like from a diner or something. For some reason, the uniform looked familiar. And she had a name tag on that said 'Cara M.' The others even called her Cara M., not just Cara, as if they didn't really know her but were calling her that because of her name tag."

"That's good," Derek said. "Maybe you should make a list of all the dinerlike restaurants you've been to lately. I'll go online and see if I can find what their uniforms look like."

As Kylie's mind tried to latch on to any other details that might help, she recalled the spirit's visit right before she'd gone outside to bring Socks to Miranda.

"What's puzzling you?" he asked, sensing her emotions.

Kylie watched her kitten—still finding it hard to believe that he wasn't a skunk anymore—leap down from the sofa. "The spirit told me that Socks wanted to be changed back into a cat. When I asked how she knew that, she said that she could communicate with animals."

"Holiday can't read animals." Derek's eyes widened. "Wait. She can't, but she knows someone . . . someone close to her that is full fairy and actually had a little of the ability to do so."

"Are you sure?" Kylie asked.

"She told me during one of our counseling sessions."

"Did she say who it was?"

"No, but . . . I got the feeling it was someone close. I also got the feeling that it was someone who'd hurt her, because I felt her emotions when she talked about her. And then she changed the subject."

Kylie nodded. Holiday was good at changing the subject when it came to something personal. "So, if this person was close to Holiday, then it would be understandable why she would take on Holiday's appearance as a ghost." Kylie chewed on that thought for a moment, feeling some relief. And it gave her the first real hope that Holiday wasn't in danger.

Kylie sighed. The early morning sun must have risen higher, because she watched as the first gold rays spilled through the window and cast shadows on the wood floor. "So how do we find out who this person is?"

"I can bring it up again in our next counseling session with Holiday. It's this afternoon. Like I said, she didn't want to talk about it, but maybe I can sneak it into the conversation."

Derek's words pulled Kylie away from the problem at hand. "You get counseling sessions from Holiday?"

He frowned. "Not counseling like my-head's-messed-up counseling. We just chat . . . like you two do."

"I didn't mean it was a bad thing. I just didn't know you met with her regularly."

"I have since I came here."

"I knew you were in the beginning, but I didn't think you still did."

"I didn't for a while. But since I've been back . . . I see her now."

Before Kylie could stop herself, the question slipped out. "Do you talk about me?"

"Some," he admitted, looking guilty.

She almost asked for details, but wisdom slipped in. She didn't need to know. Especially if it was about his feelings for her. The less she heard, or even thought, about his confession of love, the better off she'd be.

Her gaze, as if it had a mind of its own, lowered again to his bare chest. Reprimanding herself, she popped off the sofa. "I think I'll go talk to Holiday now about this whole witch issue."

"Are you going to mention the vision?"

She considered the question, but her heart said no. The message came with such certainty that she wondered if she wasn't getting some divine advice. "Not yet. If I don't get anything in a day or so, I think I should."

He nodded. "I'll get busy later trying to figure out what I can." He stood up. "Let's go." The sun spilling though the window hit his chest, making his bare skin look even more golden.

"That's okay," she sputtered. "You don't have to . . . tag along."

Disappointment flashed in his green eyes. "Yes, I do. I'm your shadow until after breakfast."

Oh, great. Her gaze slipped down to his open shirt again. Was she going to have to look, or try not to look, at his chest all morning? "Then at least button your shirt." The words were out before she realized how that sounded.

The disappointment in his eyes vanished and a sexy twinkle took its place. The twinkle brought out the gold flecks in his irises, which she used to admire so much.

"Why?" he asked. "Does it bother you?"

She glared at him. "Don't go there." Then to make her point even clearer, she held up her pinky at him. "I might have powers you don't want to mess with. And since I don't know how to use them, I could really mess a person up. By accident, of course."

He held up his hands in complete submission. "I won't go there. I swear." But the sexy grin on his lips remained as he started buttoning his shirt.

Freaking great, Kylie thought. He'd probably read her emotions and assumed she still found him attractive. Which she did, but not in the way he thought. Okay, so it was in the way he thought but it didn't mean anything. Or so she tried to tell herself as she took off for the front door.

Derek followed right behind her.

When they walked past her two roommates still tossing threats at each other, Kylie didn't even look back. If they were really going to tear each other's body parts off, they would have done it by now. Right?

"Don't panic," Holiday said after Kylie walked in, pointed to her forehead, and explained she might have pulled off a bit of abracadabra and changed Socks back into a kitten.

"Panicking is never good." But she couldn't stop staring at Kylie's pattern.

It might not be good, but Kylie could see panic in Holiday's eyes. Well, maybe it wasn't so much panic as it was sheer befuddlement. No doubt Kylie shared the same expression. Though hers probably *was* panic. And not all because she'd turned into a witch. It was more about seeing Holiday, and the images of the vision that were now popping up like flash cards in her mind. The vision Kylie still sensed she didn't need to share with the camp leader.

"Okay, exactly what happened?" Holiday asked.

"Just what I said." Kylie plopped down in the chair across her desk. "Miranda was trying to change him back with all these fancy spells, but not having any luck. I was concerned about Socks; he didn't want to be there. So I pointed my pinky at him and blurted out something like, 'Why can't you just say, change back into a kitten.' And it happened."

Holiday nodded and continued to stare at Kylie's pattern as if she expected it to change.

"Am I really a witch?"

The fae's brow puckered. "Yes. But . . . yesterday you were a human and before that you were . . . a pattern no one could recognize."

"So you think it'll go away?"

Holiday looked apologetic before she even spoke. "I don't know for sure but . . . more than likely, you're a witch. I mean, if you really have powers."

"But the powers could go away, too." Kylie sighed.

"But . . . if you have powers then you obviously have the witch DNA. Unlike a pattern, DNA is pretty permanent," Holiday said, but she didn't sound sure of anything. "Then again, witches don't have speed the way you have when you run, or sensitive hearing. Most wouldn't have the type of healing gifts you have, either. And very few of them dreamscape." Now Holiday was thinking out loud more than talking to Kylie. "Of course, it could all be related to you being a protector. Or it might be because of the hybrid mix. Some hybrid mixes have—"

"How about ghost whispering? Do witches have that?" Kylie asked.

"A few have it, but not all." Holiday touched her chin, as though completely puzzled. "But what's really odd is that you're appearing to be a hundred percent witch now. But I guess your being a protector could maybe . . . affect that."

She slumped back in her chair as if stumped. "Have you tried to see if you could do anything else?"

"Do what?" Kylie asked.

"Magic?"

"No," Kylie said. "What if I screw something up? Like Miranda does. I could turn someone into a kangaroo or even something worse."

"I doubt you would do that. Why don't you just try to move something?" Holiday pushed a leather, heart-shaped, sand-filled paperweight to the edge of her desk.

"I don't know." Kylie bit down on her lip. "It's totally freaky."

"Not really. Just try." She made a funny face. "And be prepared to duck if we have to."

"Oh, that makes me feel so much better," Kylie said.

Holiday grinned. "Try it."

Kylie took in a deep breath. Then, pointing her pinky at the red heart, she said, "Move."

Nothing happened. Kylie exhaled and grinned. "See, I'm not a witch."

Then the paperweight started to jiggle . . . or beat. At least that's what it looked like it was doing. Beating, pumping, as if it were a real heart.

"Shit!" Kylie said, and either there was an echo in the room or Holiday spurted out the same word. "Did I make it come alive?"

Holiday didn't answer; she was too busy watching the throbbing heart. Then the thing floated up and shot across the room. "Duck!" Holiday screamed.

Kylie dropped to the floor just as the paperweight whizzed past. Unfortunately, Burnett walked into the room.

The heart went right for him.

Chapter Twelve

The heart paperweight hit him in the chest. Shocked, he tried to catch it, but missed. It bounced off his wide, masculine upper body and whizzed off. It stopped in the middle of the room, hung in the air like something filled with helium, and then it rocketed forward, aiming again for Burnett. And like the first time, it didn't miss.

But this blow was much . . . much worse.

Right in the crotch. Or as Della would say, his "boys" took a direct hit.

"What the hell!" he growled. He doubled over in pain. The heart moved back, and he snatched the leather-covered, sand-filled paperweight from the air, and squeezed it until it burst. Unfortunately, when the sand exploded from his tight fist, it regrouped in the shape of a heart and managed to hover in the air.

"Is Miranda in here?" Burnett growled, still doubled over.

Kylie, realizing the screwed-up witch he sought was her, raised her hand and said, "Stop." When nothing happened, she remembered to extend her pinky. "Stop!"

The sand fell to the floor and scattered like . . . well, like sand.

Holiday sat back up in her chair, looking too stunned to speak.

Burnett, fist still pressed into his thigh, rose up to his full height.

"Damn!" Holiday muttered finally.

"Damn!" Burnett echoed.

Kylie looked from the shocked Holiday to the hurting vampire. Kylie thought his outburst was due to the pain, but nope. He stared at her forehead.

"Interesting," said Holiday.

"Strange," Burnett followed, never taking his eyes off Kylie's forehead.

"Just lovely!" muttered Kylie. Their dumbfounded expressions were a foreshadowing of what was to come at breakfast. Leave it to Kylie to be the mealtime freak-show entertainment.

"You're a witch," Burnett said in disbelief.

"Appears that way," Holiday agreed.

"No. I'm a chameleon." And each time Kylie said it, she believed it a little more. It didn't matter that she could reverse spells and turn animals back into their normal form, or that she'd sent a heart flying around the room and ball-busted a vampire. Her father told her she was a chameleon and she believed him.

"Maybe chameleon means something else," Holiday said. "Maybe it has something to do with you being a protector. For that matter, all the other gifts could be due to that as well." The camp leader's phone rang. As if needing a distraction, she eyed the caller ID. Raising her gaze, she met Kylie's gaze with empathy.

"What now?" Kylie bellowed.

"It's . . . Tom Galen, your stepfather."

Just lovely, Kylie thought. A call this early couldn't be about anything good. So, what new disaster did he want to add to the mix?

"Is everything okay?" Derek shot inside the office door. "I heard a commotion," he muttered.

"No," Kylie said just before Holiday answered the call. "At this particular moment, I can't think of one single thing that's okay."

After breakfast, Kylie and Miranda walked out of the dining hall to head back to the cabin. Della had some kind of meeting with Burnett. Kylie had begged out of Meet Your Campmate hour due to her sucky start of the day. Plus she was supposed to go to the falls with Holiday and Burnett as soon as Burnett talked with Della.

"They like you. They're just surprised," Miranda said, apologizing for the entire witch group, who'd done nothing but gape at Kylie's forehead during breakfast. "I mean, we all thought you were vampire or werewolf. Some people had bets on you being a shapeshifter, but none of us ever thought you'd turn out to be one of us."

"You seriously took bets on what I was?" Kylie asked.

"A couple of warlocks started it." She frowned. "Sorry. If it makes you feel better, I lost five bucks."

Kylie shook her head in disbelief. Not that it was just the Wiccan gals or guys reacting. The entire Shadow Falls breakfast crowd had ignored their runny eggs and raw bacon and had eyes only for Kylie's newly emerged witch brain pattern. Or they had until Della, bless her cold heart, tried to help.

The vampire had vaulted up in the air a good five feet, landing with big thump on top of the table—her black tennis shoes landing half on and half off several campers' trays of food. Then with concern for Kylie, Della announced that Kylie had just whispered a curse and anyone gawking at her forehead would be turned into a flatulent goose.

It was, of course, a bald-faced lie. Since Kylie had sent the heart paperweight zipping around the room, she'd been superconscientious about not moving her pinky. Not an easy feat either when trying to fork up runny eggs. Nevertheless, her two pinky fingers were on time-out until Kylie figured out the witch thing.

Kylie stopped out front of the office and debated popping in and asking Holiday if she'd ever gotten in touch with her stepfather. The two were playing phone tag. Kylie also wanted to check and see if Burnett had heard from Malcolm Summers, her real grandfather.

He'd told Burnett he would be here tomorrow, but what were the chances of that happening now when he'd had his phone disconnected and dropped off the face of the earth? Kylie suspected it was because of Burnett's tie with the FRU. Then again, maybe he just didn't care about her. It wasn't as if he'd even known his own son, her father.

That thought stung until she realized it didn't make sense. If it were true, why would he and her aunt have come to the camp pretending to be her father's adoptive parents? The fact that they'd come disguised as humans reinforced that he didn't trust someone at Shadow Falls. And that someone had to be Burnett because of his connections to the FRU.

"Don't you just love Della?" Miranda asked. "She's a pain in the ass, but when it's about protecting us, she steps up to the plate, or on the plates." She giggled. "I'll bet she stomped on about six breakfast platters this morning."

"I know. She's great." Even if the plan backfired.

"I mean, really? A flatulent goose? Where does she get these ideas?"

"I wouldn't know," Kylie muttered. Frankly, she wasn't even completely sure what flatulent meant. Nevertheless, feeling overwhelmed, she decided to chalk it up to a learning experience. Not only did she have a word definition to look up, but she'd learned another important lesson—that being stared at wasn't any worse than when people refused to look at you. Nope, not one person chanced even giving her a quick peek after Della's warning. Flatulent must be really bad.

"This is still so cool. You are a witch like me!" Miranda rubbed her hands together with complete glee.

Kylie wished she shared Miranda's optimism. "I still don't believe it. I don't care that even Holiday half believes it," Kylie said, and then added, "You do know it could change, right? I was all human and now I'm not." And her dad told her she was a chameleon. She believed him.

"But this is the first time you've shown a real supernatural pattern, so it's probably real." The little witch did a butt-wiggling victory dance. "Aren't you over-the-moon excited?"

For Miranda's sake, Kylie plastered a smile on her face, but the over-the-moon comment repeated in her head, reminding her of a certain werewolf.

"I wonder why Lucas wasn't at breakfast," she said aloud. Not that she was all that eager to tell him the news.

"I don't know," Miranda said, still wearing her toothpaste ad smile. Then her smile faded. "Are you worried he'll be disappointed that you aren't were?"

"No," Kylie said, not sure if it was an out-and-out lie. She wasn't worried he'd be disappointed; she was worried he would be devastated. Her heartstrings gave her a few emotional pulls and a knot tightened in her throat.

"Is there any legendary bad blood between weres and witches?" Kylie asked.

"Nothing that I know of," Miranda said. "I mean, weres don't typically like any race but their own. But they don't dislike witches as badly as they do vampires."

Kylie supposed she should be grateful she hadn't morphed into a vamp.

Then again, she had a feeling nothing other than her turning into a were would make her acceptable to Lucas's family and pack. Could their relationship survive the prejudices?

"Do you want to go to the cabin and try out a few spells?"

"Oh, hell no! I don't want to goof anything up."

"You won't," Miranda said. "I'll be with you. I won't let you mess up."

Right, like you've never messed up. The words shot from Kylie's brain and landed on the tip of her tongue, but she managed to swallow them. Just because she was hurting didn't give her the right to hurt others.

"You're just nervous. You gotta trust me." Miranda's bright smile widened even more. "We witches have to stick together."

"Sorry," Kylie said. "I've already managed to zap Burnett in the balls with a paperweight. I'm taking the day off."

"Seriously? You did that?" Miranda snorted with laughter, causing frowns from the group of weres walking past.

Kylie spotted Will and called out. "Will?"

The dark-haired, brown-eyed teen turned around and appeared annoyed. Was it rude to call a were's name? Or was his expression due to more personal reasons? Were all of Lucas's pack members going to start giving her the cold shoulder?

"Yes?" His tone matched his expression.

Kylie moved a few feet away from Miranda. Standing in front of Will, she tried not to let his discontent intimidate her. "Lucas wasn't at breakfast. I was wondering if you know where he is."

Will glanced at the woods, as if stalling. While Kylie couldn't read minds, it was almost as if he were trying to come up with a lie. Why?

"Is something wrong?" she asked.

He motioned the other weres to go ahead. Then he waited for them to get out of hearing range before he spoke.

That had to mean something was wrong, didn't it?

"Lucas was summoned by the Council," Will finally said.

"Is that a bad thing? Is he in trouble?"

"I . . . don't know. That's between him and the Council."

Concern pricked at Kylie's mind. "Do you know when he'll be back?"

"No." He shuffled his feet against the rocky path, then glanced off at the woods again before facing her. "I'm sorry," he added, and something about the tone in which he offered the apology, even the sincerity in his eyes, told Kylie he meant it—but why? For what was he apologizing?

"What are you not telling me?" she asked. "Please just tell me."

"If you have questions, you should ask Lucas, not me."

"So something is going on?" She stepped closer, feeling her heart beating against her ribs. Without warning, her gaze shifted to the woods, and she felt it again. As if the trees were calling her name. But with her heart stuck on her concern for Lucas, she focused on the problem at hand, and on Will. "Is it about me?"

Will's discontent grew more noticeable in his frowning expression. "I don't know. I have to go." He walked away. She watched him leave, silently, and got a nagging feeling that something was brewing.

Will disappeared down the path. Kylie's heart remained on Lucas, but her gaze shifted back to the woods where the trees slowly stirred in the gentle breeze. It was the oddest feeling, like being really thirsty and seeing a glass of water. This feeling, the calling, was even stronger than the call to the falls.

What the hell was going on?

Miranda cleared her throat, and Kylie glanced back at her roommate. "Are you okay?" Miranda asked, and moved closer.

Kylie rolled her eyes. "Why does everyone ask that question when it's obvious that I'm not?"

"Probably wishful thinking," Miranda answered, bumping Kylie with her shoulder, and smiling in sympathy. "Don't worry. If Lucas likes you enough, things will work out. It did for Perry and me."

Kylie breathed in. Then she breathed out. She started walking again, consciously fighting the temptation to take a flying leap into the woods—to figure out who it was and why they wanted her attention so desperately.

They walked another five minutes without talking. Kylie concentrated on the rhythmic sound of her own footsteps, which created a sense of calm. But the scream, a cry of sheer panic, pretty much shot that calm all to hell.

Kylie stopped so fast she nearly tripped and grabbed Miranda's elbow to steady herself. The sound came from the very place she felt lured—the woods. Deep in the woods.

"What is it?" Miranda asked.

Kylie looked at her. "You don't hear that?"

Miranda tilted her head. "Hear what?"

Kylie stepped a foot or two closer to the woods and tried to identify the voice of the screamer. The high-pitched sound told Kylie it was female, but there were no notes of familiarity to it. None.

It didn't matter. She felt it—the familiar fizz, the telltale buzz in her blood that happened when she moved into protective mode.

Her breath caught in her throat; everything inside her said someone needed her. She had no choice but to answer the cry for help. She bolted toward the woods.

"Kylie!" Miranda screamed out. "Don't run!"

Right before Kylie entered the thicket of trees, she called back for Miranda to go get help.

And fast.

Chapter Thirteen

Kylie ran like the wind.

Nothing slowed her down. Nothing could.

Not the thick underbrush.

Not the overhanging limbs.

Not even the seven-foot barbed-wire fence telling her she was leaving Shadow Falls property. *Don't you dare leave Shadow Falls property.* She heard Burnett's warning ring in her head, but she ignored it. She followed the screams.

She even ignored her fear that she was running full-speed ahead into a trap set by Mario and his friends. It didn't matter. She was a protector. She had to protect.

After several minutes of running on pure adrenaline, her breath heavy, she sensed the scream and the screamer getting closer. Then she saw it.

Not the screamer.

She saw the fog—the thick, low-hanging cloud that moved over the underbrush, as if swallowing the ground up. It moved in a way that said the force behind it was more than Mother Nature. This was some unnatural power.

A power that traveled at breakneck speeds.

Logic told her to run, but the screams grew louder, and instinct kept her feet moving right into the mouth of the fog. Movement to the left caught her eyes. A girl raced to escape the thick mist. Her long black hair stirred around her head, reminding Kylie of the picture of Medusa she'd seen in a Greek mythology book.

Still a distance away, the girl's gaze met Kylie's. Relief sparked in the runner's eyes. Doubt sparked in Kylie.

Was this real, was the girl real, or was this another vision? Was the girl truly running for her life, or was she running from a death that had already claimed her?

Questions bounced around Kylie's mind as her feet hit the earth. Faster, she told herself when she saw the fog almost at the girl's heels. "Run faster," Kylie screamed.

Dead or alive, helping the stranger felt essential. The sound of the girl's rapid footfalls echoed through the trees, until her speed helped her escape the mouth of the fog.

Then, as if in slow motion, the girl tripped, lost her footing, and hit the ground. Hard.

The thud of her fall bounced off the trees.

Kylie watched in horror as the fog moved in. She pushed herself, sensing the need to reach the girl before the strange fog. The fizz in her blood gave her strength.

Coming to a sudden stop beside the lifeless body, Kylie snatched the unconscious girl into her arms. She weighed next to nothing. When Kylie looked up the fog was almost upon her. Running on instinct and perhaps panic, Kylie shot off.

Her feet pounded the underbrush into the ground. She hadn't gotten ten feet when the feeling of being lured hit her again. *Come to us. Come to us.* The wind, the trees, everything whispered the same message.

She stopped running. Her breaths came short, in and out. She swung around. "What do you want? Who are you?"

Her heart slammed against her rib cage. Cradling the girl closer, Kylie stared at the fog.

The thick gray cloud hovered twenty feet back, pulsating as if a heart beat within. The air around it stirred as if it breathed.

That's when she stopped being able to breathe, because . . . because freaking hell, fog wasn't supposed to breathe. Fog wasn't supposed to be alive.

Before Kylie could react, the cloudlike air shifted and separated into two different masses. While she didn't sense an evil presence, she could no more deny the fear biting at her backbone than she could deny her own need for oxygen. Part of her instinct screamed to run, another part screamed to stay.

The fog inched back a few more feet as if it sensed Kylie's dread.

So she waited.

She watched.

She listened.

Listened to her name being called.

Kylie. Kylie.

Listened to the words spoken that came with the wind—whispered softly like a breeze stirring in the leaves. *We mean you no harm.*

"Who are you?" Kylie called out.

The girl in Kylie's arms shifted. The weight that had felt lifeless now stirred with life. Glancing down, she saw that blood oozed from the girl's brow. The need to get her help pulsed through Kylie's veins. She looked up again at the fog. The two different masses had taken shapes. Humanlike shapes.

Don't go.

Kylie's instinct to move the girl to safety swelled in her chest. To face the unknown alone was one thing. To do it with a bleeding girl in her care was another.

"I have to," Kylie answered, and turned to leave. She got only a few feet.

Stay.

There was something about the voice, a male voice. She glanced back over her shoulder; air caught in her chest.

Her grandfather? Was that not him? Then Kylie saw the woman and recognized her as her grandmother's sister. Tears filled Kylie's eyes.

She started to turn back but the girl in Kylie's arms screamed. She looked down. The girl's eyes shot open. Her dark blue irises stared up in bafflement and sent a bolt of familiarity rocketing through Kylie.

But she had no time to ponder. The blood oozing down the face of the girl came down faster. Kylie's instinct to get the girl to safety made her own blood sizzle. How badly was this stranger hurt?

"Release me!" the girl ordered in a low growl, and tried to squirm free. "Release me!" she screamed again, and started to fight this time. Her strength told Kylie this was no human. Without Kylie's protective powers, the girl would have easily won her freedom, but not now.

"In a minute."

Kylie took flight holding the squirming blue-eyed stranger close. *I'm sorry.* Kylie spoke the words in her head and prayed they would be heard by those she'd just left. She'd had no choice but to leave. Her need to protect bit down stronger than her own quest.

Clutching the screaming stranger in her arms, Kylie jumped over the barbed-wire fence. Once on Shadow Falls property, the silence in the woods seemed louder than the girl's protests. Without warning, Kylie felt one, two, and then three whisks of air fly past her.

Then Burnett, Della, and a large bird—Perry—appeared beside her, all three moving at Kylie's pace.

Kylie stopped running. So did the others. Tiny sparkling bubbles appeared beside Perry as he morphed back into human form.

The three of them stared at Kylie, or rather, they stared at the screaming girl in Kylie's arms.

"Who is she?" Burnett asked.

"Don't know." Kylie's breaths came short, her mind on her grandfather and great-aunt. "She was running from—"

"She's a were," Della interrupted. "I could smell her as soon as we passed."

The girl stopped struggling against Kylie's hold. Her voice deepened as she met Kylie's eyes. "Release me now! Or you will regret this with your dying breath." She raised her head and glared at Della and then Burnett. "All of you will regret it!"

Burnett spoke directly to Kylie's package. "Give me your word that you will not run."

She glared at him.

"If you do, I'll catch you and I'll be really pissed off."

"If you're fast enough," the girl quipped.

"Oh, he's fast enough." Perry tossed in his two cents. "When he was fifteen, he chased down a shape-shifter in antelope form and kicked his antelope ass. There wasn't enough of that animal left to make a rug."

"Fine," the stranger bit out. "I won't run."

Della moved in and stared at Perry. "You knew Burnett when he was fifteen and chasing antelopes?"

Releasing the girl, Kylie's gaze collided with the antelope ass kicker himself. His expression prepared her for what came next. "I thought I made it clear you were not to go into the woods."

Kylie nodded, but she refused to be reprimanded for doing what, for her, was as natural as breathing. "Someone was in danger."

"*You* put yourself in danger." His gaze shot back to the girl. "What were you running from?"

"Fog." The girl wiped away the blood that oozed from her forehead. "It chased me."

"Fog chased you?" Della snickered. "You smoking something?"

"She's telling the truth." Kylie almost told them about her grandfather, but something compelled her to think first . . . speak later.

"Who are you?" Burnett asked the girl.

"Who are *you*?" the girl countered.

"Definitely were with that attitude," Della muttered.

Perry laughed, then waved at the girl. "You're bleeding. It's dangerous to bleed in front of vampires."

"Don't worry," Della said. "Were blood is nasty."

The girl shot Della a cold look. Kylie got the feeling again, that something about this stranger was familiar.

Burnett spoke next. "I'm Burnett James, the camp leader of Shadow Falls, and you are trespassing."

"You're . . . Burnett?" The girl showed the first bit of insecurity.

"She wasn't trespassing," Kylie spoke up. "I brought her across the property lines."

The female shot Kylie a look of surprise. "I don't need you to defend me."

"I wasn't. Not really."

Burnett's body posture hardened, but his scowl targeted Kylie. "You left Shadow Falls property?"

"I heard her screaming." The bleeding stranger pinched her brows, trying to read Kylie's pattern. Was she still a witch? Or was her pattern doing something else weird?

"You . . ." The girl shook her head. "You're a witch. How could you . . ."

Well, that answered that question, Kylie thought.

The girl turned her blue eyes back on Burnett. And just like that, Kylie knew who she was. The color of the eyes, the way she tilted her head, even her body language hit the mark.

"I'm—"

"Lucas's sister," Kylie said.

"Yes." She focused on Kylie again. "I'm Clara Parker. Who are you?"

"Kylie Galen," Kylie said.

Surprise widened the girl's eyes. "But you're a witch? I thought . . ." She paused. "And you ran and have strength like you're either a were or . . . a vamp." The last word came out sounding like an insult.

Della growled. Burnett's frown tightened.

The frustration of the whole witch issue came rushing back. "I'm just an evolving piece of art. Just call me the mealtime freak show here at Shadow Falls."

"You're not a freak," mumbled Perry. "I'm the resident freak," he said with pride.

Clara continued to stare at Kylie, and then she said, "Why was that fog chasing me? Did you do that with magic?"

"No, I didn't do it."

Burnett focused on Clara. "Your family is worried about you."

Clara rolled her eyes. "They worry too much. I told them I was coming here."

"You were expected two days ago," Burnett reprimanded. "And just so you know, if you plan on staying on at Shadow Falls, we don't like changes in plans without going through the proper channels."

Clara arched her chin up as if to offer Burnett some lip. Remembering it was Lucas's sister, Kylie intervened. "I'm sure she'll adjust. Lucas will fill her in."

"Where is my brother?" Clara insisted.

"He was called to visit the Council," Burnett answered.

Kylie looked at Burnett and wondered if Lucas had told Burnett. If so, why hadn't Lucas told her?

"Is something wrong between him and the Council?" Clara asked Burnett.

Kylie recalled Will's odd behavior earlier when Kylie asked the same question.

"Not that I know." Burnett stood stoically for a few seconds, and then asked Clara, "How badly are you hurt?"

"Just a scratch," Clara answered.

"She passed out," Kylie said.

"Did not," insisted Clara, as if it would make her look weak.

Kylie started walking back to the clearing. Everyone fell in step with her. The sounds of the woods returned to normal, but Kylie barely noticed. Her mind chewed on what she'd seen when she'd looked back the last time, and tried to decide what if anything to share with Burnett. Glancing briefly over her shoulder, she tried to listen with her heart to see if she still felt her grandfather and aunt calling. Were they still there? Or had they left?

The sensation lacked the earlier power, but she still felt it.

"Perry," Burnett spoke up, "you and Della go ahead and make sure Clara gets to the office to be seen by Holiday." Burnett's demanding voice bounced off the trees and caused another wave of silence. "Kylie, I want a minute with you." His tone left little doubt that the minute wouldn't be pleasant.

Kylie stopped walking. Perry shot Kylie a look of pure sympathy. "She was just trying to help," the shape-shifter offered.

Della spoke up. "And nothing happened. All's well that ends well, right? You can't get mad when—"

"Go," Burnett ordered.

Della grunted, and Perry sent Kylie another look of empathy. She loved both of them for feeling the need to intervene, but she could handle this. She hoped.

"I'll see you," Kylie said when Perry appeared poised to argue.

As they walked away, Kylie inhaled a deep breath of wood-scented air. Burnett stepped beside her. They watched the three others move ahead. Clara glanced back. Her gaze expressed more curiosity than concern.

"Is she in trouble?" Clara asked, her voice getting softer as the distance between them increased.

"Let's just say, I wouldn't want to be her right now," Perry answered.

"And your wolf ass is the reason she's in trouble," Della smarted back.

"I didn't ask her to help me," Clara countered.

Kylie waited before she spoke to Burnett. "I shouldn't be reprimanded for doing what I was supposed to do."

"You could have been killed. It could have been a trick to lure you away from Shadow Falls."

"It wasn't. Clara thought she was in danger. I felt her fear and reacted."

"She thought she was in danger?" he asked, picking up on Kylie's slip of the tongue. "Are you saying she wasn't?"

When Kylie paused, Burnett continued. "Exactly what was it you two were running from?"

A need to tell the truth filled her chest, but another need—the need for answers—kept her quiet. "Like I said before. It was fog," Kylie answered, confident that her response wouldn't read as a lie. Her words were true.

Just not the whole truth.

"Did you sense it was evil?"

"I was scared," she admitted again. A shiver rushed down her spine. Not from fear, but from the cold that came when the dead neared. She glanced around, trying not to let on that they had company. The ghost, Holiday's look-alike, peered at them from behind a tree.

"But . . . ?" Burnett asked, sensing she wasn't finished.

"But I didn't sense it was evil." A whisper of guilt came, but if she told Burnett her grandfather and aunt had attempted to see her without permission, what would Burnett say?

"I'm trying to protect you. I can't do that if you don't follow my rules."

"I don't normally break your rules." The cold grew colder and she cut her eyes to where the ghost had been. She'd disappeared. In a flash, the Holiday look-alike stood beside Burnett, looking at him as if she recognized him. The thought sent a tremor of fear through Kylie's heart.

"It could only take one broken rule and it would be too late."

Kylie bit down on her lips, fighting the cold. "I'm sorry." *For upsetting you, not for going.* "I heard the scream and I felt called to help."

"Next time, before answering that call, get me."

"I'll try." She shivered in spite of her attempt not to.

"I think you could do better than try," he countered, then he looked up as if questioning some higher power. "Explain to me why I wanted to be a part of Shadow Falls."

"I can answer that," Kylie said, feeling bad for making him angry. "Because beneath that crusty exterior of yours, you care about us. And you love the other person who runs this place." Kylie glanced at the ghost, wondering if she would react to the words.

The spirit's gaze widened. *"Do you mean . . . ?"*

Burnett frowned, but he didn't try to deny it.

Kylie would've been happy that he'd come to terms with his feelings for Holiday if she didn't have the ghost staring as if . . . as if the confession of love had affected her.

The spirit looked at Kylie. *"He's in love with the camp leader?"* Panic laced her tone. Did the spirit now know she was Holiday?

What's your name? Kylie asked in her head.

"I told you," the ghost answered.

"I'll never get used to this." Burnett started walking.

"Get used to what?" Kylie caught up with him, her attention

more on the spirit who walked beside the vampire, staring at him with surprise.

"The ghosts," Burnett blurted out as if the words cost him.

Kylie stopped and grabbed him by the elbow. "You can feel them?" she asked. Generally, only when a spirit was trapped in a small room could a non–ghost whisperer feel them.

"No," he said.

Kylie stared at him.

"Fine. Maybe I feel them a little. It's probably more about the look you and Holiday get in your eyes when they're around," he confessed. He looked around. "Is she gone?"

"How did you know she was a female?" Kylie asked, realizing the spirit was gone.

His jaw clenched. "I could smell her," he said, as if it were some kind of a sin.

"You can? I didn't think . . . I mean, I didn't think vampires had ghost-whispering gifts."

"I didn't think so either." And he didn't sound happy about it. He shot off walking again, only faster—his pace reflective of his mood.

Kylie kept up, but barely. "Does Holiday know?"

"Know what?" He didn't even look at Kylie.

"About you detecting ghosts? She was curious as to why you could go into the falls and—"

"No, she doesn't know," he said. "And don't mention it. I'll tell her later." Worry tightened his jaw.

They walked in silence for a second. "I didn't mean to cause trouble by going after Clara. I just reacted to my internal instinct."

"Sometimes our internal instincts can be skewed," he added.

She wondered if he was talking about his ability to smell and sense ghosts as well as her protective instincts. "I'll try to do better next time."

"Thank you," he said, as if conceding to what she offered.

They continued forward. The wind stirred the trees.

"Can you tell me more?" he asked.

"About ghosts?"

"No. About the fog. I'd like to forget about the ghosts."

Kylie remembered how she'd felt when she first learned she could detect the dead. She could relate to his feelings. Sometimes she'd still like to forget about her ability.

"Did you sense it was Mario?"

"No." Kylie went over the details, careful not to leave anything out except the ending. No doubt he would question Clara later. But Kylie was almost certain Clara hadn't seen anything that would give the secret away.

"It has to be Mario and his buddies again." Burnett's fist clenched as he walked.

Kylie hesitated to say anything, knowing if she slipped up and lied, he would know. But neither did she want Burnett to worry too much. "Remember I said it didn't feel evil."

"It has to be them." He looked at her directly, a stern, fixed stare. "You do not go into the woods, with or without a shadow. You understand?"

She nodded. She understood, but she didn't say she would comply.

"It has to be some witch or wizard behind this." His brows pinched. "You don't think that you accidentally caused the fog, do you?"

"No," Kylie insisted.

"You sure? With the other incident—"

"It was different." Her cheeks warmed, remembering the incident.

Their pace slowed. The trees and underbrush seemed to soak up the sound of their footsteps. Kylie's mind returned to Clara, and from Clara, it moved to the girl's brother.

"Can I ask you something?" Kylie asked.

"If I said no, would it stop you?"

"Probably not." She debated on how to word her question.

"If it's about anything concerning Holiday and me, I've been ordered to plead the fifth."

She grinned. "Don't worry, the inside-out shirt the other day pretty much told me what I wanted to know about you and her."

The stern-looking vamp half smiled again. His smile faded. "It's not about ghosts, either, is it?"

"No. It's . . . When a Council calls someone in for a meeting, is it bad news?"

"You're talking about Lucas?" he asked.

She nodded.

He moved a limb out of his way, holding it back so it wouldn't hit Kylie. "It can be, but not always."

"Do you know what it is they want with Lucas?" She pushed another limb away.

"No, I don't." His words rang completely honest.

"Are you concerned?" Kylie asked.

He hesitated. "Yes."

"Why?"

"I respect Lucas's need to become a part of the Council so he can help bridge the problems between the weres and the FRU, but I don't want the Council to have too big of an influence over him."

"You don't trust Lucas?" Kylie asked.

"If I didn't trust him, he wouldn't be here. My problems stem from the fact that the were council and the FRU have issues. In general, the were community is less compliant to work within the FRU's rules. It goes back to the pack mentality."

"But couldn't that be because the FRU considered werewolves lower-class citizens?"

"That has changed," he said. "But I'm sure that plays a big part in their behavior, and I can assure you that the FRU treats all were situations with that in mind. However, prejudices stem from both sides.

One of the reasons they were viewed as outcast was because they viewed others as the same."

"So it's a 'which came first, the chicken or the egg' kind of thing," Kylie said.

"I guess it doesn't matter," he said.

When they arrived at the clearing, Burnett looked at her. "I'll walk you back to your cabin. If Della or Miranda isn't there, I'll get someone else to shadow you for the time being. Holiday and I will be there shortly to go to the falls. But until I investigate this whole fog thing, you're not to leave that cabin without me knowing where you are and who you are with."

She flinched slightly at his tone and new demands. Surely he was exaggerating. "Do you mind if I go back to the office with you?" Kylie asked. "I'd sort of like to check on Clara."

He hesitated, but nodded, and they started down the path to the office. Kylie gave the woods one last glance and felt nothing. Had they already left?

Her gut instinct said they had. Question was, would they come back? And if so, could she find a way to go to them?

Before Kylie stepped up on the porch, she heard Lucas talking. "You can't keep doing this!" His voice carried.

Kylie wasn't sure if it was her sensitive hearing or if he was talking that loudly. Considering how private werewolves were, she suspected the former.

"What did I do?" Clara asked. "I told them I was coming here and I did."

"Where else did you go? Did you go see Jacob?" Lucas's tone came out tight.

"Of all people, I would assume you could understand my need to see who I wanted to see."

"As strange as it is, I think Dad's right about him."

"Really, are you going to let him choose your lifemate? Wasn't that what you two were arguing about when you were back there? Your affection for Kylie?"

Kylie's breath caught. Lucas had argued with his dad about her?

"We're talking about you," Lucas snapped.

"I'm here, isn't that what matters?" Clara asked. "Isn't that what you want?"

"What I want is for you to quit playing games, Clara. I'm trying to help you."

"Games? Please, you are the biggest game player of them all. You play games with the Council, with Dad, with your mom, and with Grandma. You even play them with Fredericka. I'll bet you're even playing games with that witch of yours."

"I'm not playing games, and I don't have a witch."

Kylie hesitated as they moved closer to the cabin's steps, and from the look Burnett sent her, she supposed that he, too, was hearing the conversation.

"I could still walk you to the cabin," Burnett offered, and from his tone, Kylie sensed he understood how this might be hard for her. His concern should've been touching; instead she didn't like knowing everyone knew her business. She preferred her private life to stay private.

"I'll have to face him sooner or later," Kylie said, glancing away.

But even Kylie had to admit, later sounded really tempting. Yet she squared her shoulders and continued walking, her gut tight at the thought of Lucas's response to her being a witch.

Chapter Fourteen

As Kylie and Burnett took the steps up to the office, Kylie suddenly wished she hadn't come.

Behind the door, Clara continued arguing with her brother. "I think she might have been the one who sent the fog after me. She pretended like she rescued me, but maybe the witch was just—"

"You think who sent the fog after you?" Lucas demanded.

"Kylie!" Clara fumed.

Kylie's breath hitched.

"Kylie isn't a witch," Lucas said.

Burnett pushed open the office door; Clara and Lucas, positioned in the entryway, turned around. Kylie prepared herself for his reaction.

"I am for the time being." Kylie decided to expose her cards and worry how the game would be played later.

"You're what for the time being?" Lucas asked, unaware that Kylie had been privy to their conversation.

"A witch," she said.

Lucas stared at her forehead. Shock, confusion, and disappointment flickered in his eyes. "What . . . Witches don't have speed. They can't run . . . like you run."

"Confused the hell out of me, too," Clara said. "That's when I realized she probably cast a spell, and if she cast that spell, maybe she did it all."

"I didn't create the fog," Kylie said. Was Clara really already turning on her?

"So how did you know where to find me? And don't lie again and say you heard me. I wasn't close enough for you to hear my screams."

The accusation stung, but Kylie tried not to take it to heart. Clara had reasons for being suspicious. Witches weren't supposed to be able to run like lightning or have super hearing. Which validated Kylie's belief that she wasn't a witch.

But if her grandfather and aunt could turn themselves into fog, did that mean they belonged to the Wiccan species? She didn't think shape-shifters could change into fog, could they? Doubt pulled at her mind.

"Kylie isn't your normal witch." Burnett came to her defense.

Lucas glanced at Clara, to Burnett, then back at Kylie. An apology replaced the stunned disbelief in his eyes.

He continued to gaze at her, but spoke to his half sister. "If Kylie says she didn't do it, she didn't do it."

"You take her word over mine? Now I see our father's concern." Clara's tone rang heavy with accusation. "How can you call yourself a leader of our people when you stand up for a witch over your own kind, own blood?"

Lucas's jaw tightened. "My belief does not come from her words. I know the facts. Kylie has sensitive hearing. She could hear your screams from miles away."

"Witches don't have—"

"As Burnett pointed out, I'm not a normal witch." Kylie gazed at Lucas. Why couldn't he have simply declared he believed her? Was a were's loyalty to his pack so restrictive that his faith in her held no credibility?

Feeling Clara's stare, Kylie continued. "Apparently, my brain has a bad habit of showing different patterns."

"Then there's something seriously wrong with your brain." Clara's tone made her words even more of an insult.

Kylie waited for Lucas to correct Clara. When his gaze found hers, she could swear she saw an apology flash in his eyes, but he remained silent.

And just like that, she knew why. Because to do so would be putting her before Clara. Because Kylie wasn't a werewolf, she wasn't supposed to matter to Lucas. Or at least not matter as much as one of his own. The realization brought with it a wave of pain that caused her chest to clutch. She told herself she didn't need him to defend her, that she knew he cared, so what did it matter that he remained silent?

"My mind is fine." Kylie met Clara's eyes and then briefly glanced at Lucas. Yup. Kylie's mind would be okay; it was her heart she worried about right now. Because while it shouldn't have mattered, it did.

A lot.

"Why weren't you scared of what you saw?" Clara asked.

Unsure what Clara meant, Kylie paused. Had the girl seen more than Kylie knew? "Who says I wasn't scared?"

"Kylie's a protector," Burnett intervened.

Clara's eyes widened. "No shit?"

Uncomfortable at the girl's stare, Kylie suddenly wanted to escape. "I should go." She turned to leave.

Burnett gently caught her by the arm and, as crazy as it seemed, she felt empathy in his cold touch. He leaned in and whispered, "Not until you have a shadow."

"I'm here." Holiday stepped through the door. "I took a short walk to give Lucas and his sister a few minutes to talk." Her green eyes went to Kylie as if she sensed the emotional storm brewing inside her. Holiday motioned for Kylie to follow her out.

Burnett looked at Holiday. "Stay close. There could still be danger around."

"Exactly what happened?" Worry filled Holiday's green eyes.

"We'll talk later," he said. "I need to chat with Clara while everything is fresh in her mind."

Kylie walked out, her heart breaking at Lucas's behavior and her gut worrying about what Clara remembered. Yet one glance at Holiday and Kylie remembered her vision and Holiday's possible demise. Heck, maybe Clara was right. Maybe something was wrong with her mind. Perhaps the stress of everything had finally driven her loony.

Was becoming a witch the first sign of insanity? Or was it just part of being a chameleon?

Kylie followed Holiday to the dining hall to grab a sandwich. Lunch had come and gone and so they had the place to themselves. They barely talked and the awkwardness didn't feel right. When they walked out of the dining hall, Kylie's gaze went to the woods to see if the feeling had left, or if she sensed her grandfather and great-aunt calling her. But she felt nothing.

Holiday reached over and touched Kylie's shoulders. "Talk to me."

Kylie absorbed the calm that Holiday offered and faced her. "I hate prejudices," Kylie said, knowing that only one of the problems at hand, Lucas, could be discussed with the camp leader. If she told Holiday who was in the woods earlier, she'd tell Burnett. And both of them would refuse to let Kylie go to them if they returned. But she had to, didn't she?

"I hate them, too," Holiday said, as if she knew exactly what prejudices Kylie referred to. "If there was one thing I could change in the world, that would be it."

Closing her palm, Kylie fought the feeling of disappointment Lucas's stance with Clara had given her. "You would think after being the target of prejudice, the were society would know how unjust it is."

"I think—"

"Can I please have a moment with Kylie?" Lucas's voice came from behind them. Just hearing his deep tenor caused another wave of pain to wash over her chest. She couldn't think of anything, or anyone who would have stopped her from standing up for him if the shoe had been on the other foot. And yet . . .

Kylie and Holiday turned around. The camp leader met Kylie's gaze, almost asking if this was what she wanted. She nodded.

"Fine, but don't go far." Holiday walked back to the porch and sat down on one of the rocking chairs.

Lucas took Kylie's hand and led her around to the back of the office. He didn't speak, and neither did she. He stopped by the tree, where they'd been earlier, and turned to face her. Not a word left his lips; he just stared.

What she wouldn't give to be able to read his mind. What was he thinking? Was he upset because she was a witch, was he sorry that he hadn't come to her defense? Was he realizing how hopeless this relationship was?

"Thank you for rescuing my sister," he said. "I'm sorry she's so ungrateful."

Kylie nodded.

He leaned down and pressed his forehead against hers. All she could see was his eyes, the blueness of them, the long dark fringe of lashes surrounding them.

"I hurt you." His voice came out even deeper than before.

She didn't deny it.

She continued to stare into his eyes and he didn't blink. The pain reflecting in his deep blue irises made her breath catch.

He closed his eyes and inhaled before speaking. "Have you ever known the right thing to do, but couldn't do it?"

She pulled back just a few inches. "Depends. What's the right thing to do?"

She posed the question even though she was afraid to ask. It wasn't the question that scared her, though. It was the answer. Because deep down, she sensed it. She had sensed it since his grandmother talked to her. She and Lucas had too many things standing in their way for them to make this work.

"I should let you go," he said. "I should put a stop to this . . . to us. Because until things change, everyone will be against us. And yet . . ." His head dipped down ever so slightly and his lips met hers.

So much emotion came with that brief kiss. And while she didn't think she had any room in her heart for more emotion, she felt it move inside her. His pain was her own. His fear was hers. She closed her eyes, fought the ache radiating in her heart, and just savored his touch.

He pulled back and ran his thumb over her lips. "And yet, how can I let you go when you're the thing that keeps me going? When the main part of the reason I want change is you?"

His finger swept over her chin, a sweet touch that nearly brought tears to her eyes. "I'm begging you. Please be patient with me. Trust me when I say that you have a place here." He took her hand and rested it on his chest. "I have to behave a certain way or it will get back to my father and the Council, but it's not how I feel." He paused a moment. "Please don't give up on me, Kylie Galen."

She could feel his heart beating. She could feel it breaking, too, right alongside her own. "I don't give up easily." It was the truth. If she was a quitter, she wouldn't still be at Shadow Falls.

He wrapped his arms around her, leaned against the tree, and pulled her flush against him. They stood like that for the longest time. Not talking. Not making promises. And Kylie couldn't help but wonder if it was because they both instinctively knew those promises wouldn't hold.

He finally pulled away. "I should go help Clara get situated."

Kylie loosened her hold around his waist. But she didn't want to. She didn't want to give him back to Clara or to Fredericka or to his father. As selfish as it was, she wanted him all to herself. Or maybe it wasn't that she didn't want to share him. Maybe she just didn't want to share him with people who were trying to keep them apart.

"Do you want to come with me?" he asked.

Clara would love that, Kylie thought. Not. "I'll let you two have some time alone."

"Thanks," he said as if he'd hoped she'd refuse. He smiled, but beneath the smile was a touch of disappointment. "So you're a witch. I never would have guessed."

"I'm a witch right now," she said.

He looked confused. "You think it will change?"

"Yes. Maybe." What did she believe? "I changed from that strange pattern to human."

"Yes." He stared at her pattern. "But this is a true supernatural pattern." Lucas's attention shot over his shoulder and he growled. Derek came around the office.

Derek's green gaze met hers. There was no apology in his eyes for interrupting them. Even his posture seemed to say he had a right to be here. "I need to see you, Kylie. It's important."

"About what?" Lucas asked.

Derek didn't look at Lucas. The fae's gaze never left Kylie, and while he answered the question, he spoke to Kylie. "It's about your ghost."

"Since when did you become a ghost expert?" Lucas asked.

Derek looked at the were for the first time. "Since I found out

Kylie needed help with them." His implication hung in the air. He supported her when Lucas didn't.

Lucas heard it as well. His eyes tightened and turned a light orange.

Before trouble started, she placed a hand on his back. "Go help Clara."

He didn't look happy, but his expression told her he wasn't planning on arguing.

Yet his next move surprised her. He leaned down and placed an affectionate kiss on her lips. The kiss seemed more about letting Derek know she was his girl than for her pleasure, but she didn't completely blame him.

There had been a time or two she would have loved to kiss him like that in front of Fredericka.

"What is it?" Kylie asked Derek as soon as Lucas moved around the office and was out of earshot.

Derek stared after Lucas and then back at her. "You're disappointed. What's disappointing you?" he asked, reading her emotions right on the mark.

"Nothing." She refused to talk about this with Derek.

"Is it Lucas?" he asked.

"Let it go," she insisted. "I'm with Lucas now."

Though for how long? The question whispered through her head.

A frown pulled at his lips. "I know. I screwed up and didn't realize that I loved you until it was too late."

She held up her hand. "Don't say—"

He reached out and laced his fingers with hers. The press of his palm against hers came with a soft warmth, a sense of calm, and endearment. She frowned at how tempted she was to just hold on, but knowing her emotions were completely out of whack right now, she pulled her hand from his. He was her friend. Just a friend.

"It's okay." He dropped his hand into his pocket. "I accept that it's my fault. And you don't have to tell me you love me." His gaze met hers. "But I can read you, Kylie, and I know you don't want to admit it, but you care about me, too."

"Stop it," she said. "I care about you like a friend."

"No." He continued to stare. "It's more. But don't worry. I know you care about Lucas, too. And that's my cross to bear because I pushed you right into his arms. And as long as you're happy, I can accept that. But if you're not—"

"Please stop." Kylie wanted to start singing "la la la" and cover her ears. And if it wouldn't have been so childish, she would have done it. Instead, she reminded him of the real matter at hand. "Didn't you say you had information about my ghost issue?"

He stuffed both his hands in his pockets. "Yeah. Good news, at least I think it is. But I guess some of it could be bad news, too."

"What?" She hoped it was more good than bad. She could really use some good news.

"I don't think your ghost is Holiday."

"But . . . how . . . what makes you think that?"

"I did some research on the Internet. Simple stuff." He hesitated. "I found out that Holiday has an identical twin. Her name is Hannah."

I think my name is Hannah or Holly, or something like that. The spirit's words echoed inside Kylie's head. "A twin? Why hasn't she ever mentioned her?"

Derek shrugged. "It seems a little odd, doesn't it? I mean, you would think she'd have said something about having an identical sister."

"Yeah." Kylie couldn't deny it hurt that Holiday didn't feel she could tell Kylie things, when she shared everything with Holiday.

"Do you still think this ghost is from the future?" Derek asked.

Kylie considered it. "No. She's dead." Just as the other girls were in the grave she'd seen in her vision. And just like that, Kylie's angst about Holiday not trusting her faded and Kylie's heart filled with sympathy. Kylie couldn't imagine losing a sister, let alone a twin. Was this why Holiday hadn't ever mentioned her? Did grief over her twin's death keep Holiday from ever talking about her sister?

Derek let out a deep breath. "Okay, here's something else that's weird. I couldn't find any death records on her. None. That's why I said this might be bad news."

"What are you saying?" Kylie asked.

Derek frowned. "Holiday might not know her sister is dead."

A knot of grief formed in Kylie's throat. "So I have to tell her."

"If you want, I could do it," Derek offered. "Or we could do it together."

Genuine concern filled his expression. She appreciated his offer, more than he would ever know, but she couldn't let him do it. As much as she dreaded being the bearer of bad news, Hannah had come to Kylie, and she should be the one to tell Holiday.

Then Kylie remembered something else Hannah had said. *I think I came to you to help someone.*

What exactly did Hannah need Kylie to do? Was telling Holiday about her death enough or did she need more?

Derek ran his hand down her arm. "Have you made a list of all the diners you've gone to recently?"

"Diners?" Kylie asked, unsure of what he was talking about. Unsure of why a simple touch could seem so wrong.

"You said one of the girls in the vision was wearing a diner uniform that looked familiar to you."

"Yes, I mean I remember, but no, I haven't had time to do it."

She took in a deep breath. "I'll get to it as soon as I get back to my cabin. I'll e-mail it to you."

"E-mail me the description of the uniform and the girls, too," he said.

"Hey." The sound of Holiday's voice had the knot in Kylie's throat doubling. She turned to face the camp leader and a chasm of empathy and hurt opened in her heart. And yet Kylie couldn't help but admit the relief of knowing that the dead girl wasn't Holiday.

Holiday's green eyes softened. "Something happen?"

For the life of her, Kylie didn't know how to tell her. "No," she lied, but for a good reason. The last thing Kylie wanted to do was just blurt out the news. Then it hit her, maybe she should talk to Hannah first. Perhaps she needed to know exactly what it was Hannah needed before she moved forward.

Holiday nodded, but disbelief flashed in her eyes. "Burnett got called to the FRU office and he insisted we hold off going to the falls until he comes back. I was hoping you could help me set up a few things in the dining hall. We're having a welcoming reception for the new teachers later this afternoon."

"Sure," Kylie said, and she met Derek's eyes briefly.

"Good luck." He mouthed the words and then he reached out and touched her, sending a much-needed current of calmness through her.

"Thanks," she whispered to Derek before she turned to join Holiday. They took a few steps and Holiday glanced over at Kylie with suspicion.

"Boy trouble?" Holiday asked in a low voice.

"Yeah," Kylie said, and it wasn't even a lie. While her heart was aching for Holiday, Derek's earlier words echoed in her mind and left a trail of uncertainty. *I can read you, Kylie, and I know you don't want to admit it, but you care about me, too.*

And the worst part was, he was right.

Chapter Fifteen

"If you want to talk about it, I'm here," Holiday said as they moved around to the front of the office.

"I know." Kylie gazed briefly at the woods, but the feeling from earlier, the feeling of being called, hadn't returned.

Holiday looked over at her and frowned. "Are you really okay? I mean, I respect your privacy. But lately you've been . . . closed off a bit. And I worry. Because . . . well, you usually trust me." Holiday rested her hand on Kylie's arm. Warmth and concern flowed from the touch.

Usually, I'm not dealing with a ghost who looks just like you, who I just found out is your sister, and I don't know if you even know she's dead.

"I don't mean to be closed off," Kylie said. "I'm just . . . between Lucas and Derek, and my grandfather changing his number, and the FRU trying to do experimental tests on me, and my mom dating, I'm a tad overwhelmed."

"And rightfully so," Holiday said.

Thinking about her mom dating led Kylie to think about her stepdad. "Oh, I almost forgot. Did you ever get in touch with my stepdad and see what he wanted?"

"Yeah, he called a while ago. He found out about the FRU saying you needed some medical tests and was concerned."

"Did the FRU call him, too?" Kylie asked, ready to panic that they hadn't given up their mission to treat her like their very own lab rat. Maybe even give her the same test that had killed her grandmother.

"No, and I asked because it scared me, too," Holiday answered, telling Kylie how accurate the camp leader was at reading her emotions. "He said he'd spoken with your mom."

"My mom? Really?" An unexpected smile spread across her lips. "So they're talking again? That's the best news I've heard all day. Maybe she'll dump the creep who wants to take her to England and give my stepdad another chance."

"Perhaps," Holiday said, as if wary of giving Kylie too much hope.

Kylie remembered that Holiday had dealt with the whole parental divorce thing, too. "How long does it take?"

"How long does what take?" Holiday asked.

"How long before you stop wishing they hadn't split? How long before you stop wanting to tell them to cut out the fighting and go back to the way things used to be?"

"I wouldn't know." Holiday sighed and offered a sympathetic smile. "I'm still waiting. I think when you grow up with them together, you just always assume they will stay together. But I do know I've reached a place where I know my parents are probably better off not being together. Nevertheless, I still have times that I remember how it used to be when we were a family, and . . . I wish things were different now. The sad truth is that we change. Parents. Siblings. And when that happens, people grow apart and—"

"But who we love shouldn't change." Or could it? Kylie's mind went from her parents' divorce to Derek, and then to the ghost issue. Then, suddenly, Kylie realized that this line of conversation might be the opening she needed to ask about Holiday's sister. "Did you go through it alone?"

"Alone?" Holiday looked confused.

"What I mean is, do you have any brothers or sisters?" Kylie asked.

Holiday was looking away so Kylie couldn't see her expression, but if the sudden flinch in the woman's shoulders was any indication, Kylie had hit a nerve. Why? What was Holiday not willing to talk about? Had Hannah and Holiday grown apart?

As another second ticked by, Kylie hesitated, not knowing what to do. Should she push for an answer, or just let the moment pass? After all, this wasn't just about her wanting Holiday to trust her, this was about helping Hannah cross over. Once she solved the whole ghost issue, maybe then she could focus more on solving her other issues.

"Unfortunately," Holiday said, ending the uncomfortable silence, "siblings are not always a help in this matter." She reached for her phone. "I just remembered I need to make another call. Can you head over to the dining hall? I asked Miranda and Della to help me, too. Della's taking over shadowing duty. I have a couple of banners to put up and there's some balloons to blow up. They're in the back of the dining hall, and I just wanted to get some tables set up to hold the appetizers. I should be over there in a few minutes. And hopefully Burnett will be back and we can take a quick run to the falls before the ceremony."

"Sure," Kylie said, disappointed. She sensed Holiday was running away so she could avoid answering any more of Kylie's questions.

Holiday arched another brow, obviously picking up on Kylie's discontent, and shook her head. "I still wish you'd talk to me."

And I wish you'd talk to me. "I'm fine." Kylie watched Holiday head to the office and when she turned around, Della was standing there.

"At your service, Miss Witch." Della grinned and stared at Kylie's forehead. "However, I won't deny that I'm disappointed. I mean . . . you liked the taste of blood, so I figured you'd at least be half-vampire."

Kylie rolled her eyes and pointed to her forehead. "I keep telling you guys, I don't think this is final."

"It looks final to me."

Kylie looked back at the woods and wished she felt that her grandfather was still there. Wished she could meet him face-to-face and finally get the answers she needed. But she didn't feel it. Didn't sense that something out there called to her to join it.

She looked back at Della. "And what was I last week? A human, right? And for how long? A few weeks?"

Della made a face. "Okay, I see your point. But this is the first real supernatural pattern you've shown."

"Yeah, and I'm betting it won't be my last. Let's just say, I think I've got ADD brain patterns. They never sit still. One comes, one goes."

"Damn," Della said. "Miranda's right. You really don't want to be a witch, do you?"

Kylie let out a gulp of frustrated air. "That's not it at all. It's just I was told—"

"That you're a lizard." Della made her sympathy face. Not one she used a whole lot, either. "Look, no hard feelings, but I think I'd believe you're a witch before I'd believe that you're a lizard. And if I may add one little thing, if you keep this not-a-witch front up, you're really going to hurt Miranda's feelings. She's already upset. And you know what she's like when she gets upset."

Kylie closed her eyes and inhaled. "I didn't mean to hurt her feelings. If I hadn't gotten the message from Dad saying I was a chameleon, I'd be ecstatic at the idea of being a witch." If frustration wasn't in the driver's seat of Kylie's emotions, surprise would have been behind the wheel. When had Kylie and Della traded places? Normally, it was Kylie calling Della on this offense. "Look," Kylie said, trying to explain herself. "Witch and fae were my top choices of species, but—"

"You didn't want to be a vampire?" Della sounded insulted.

Oh, crap, now Kylie had offended Della. Nothing was going right today. "Please," Kylie said, her frustration not just sitting in the driver's seat anymore, but revving up the engine. "I didn't say that, I just—"

"It's being cold that bothers you, isn't it?" Della asked, looking more hurt, but not mad. And Kylie guessed she should be thankful about that. A hurt Della was hard to deal with, but dealing with an angry and hurt Della was impossible.

"No, it's not being cold, it's . . ."

"It can't be the blood because you liked the taste of blood."

"I like the taste of it, but I don't necessarily like the idea of having to drink it, or the idea of having French fries taste like toad's butt, because that's exactly how you described it. But if I'm vampire, then I'll be happy." When Della's expression didn't change, Kylie added, "Truthfully, it would be cool to be able to fly like you guys do."

"It's very cool," Della said, her expression softening.

"Anyway," Kylie continued, "I'll be happy with whatever I am. I don't even care anymore. But right now, I trust what my dad said, and he said I'm a chameleon. Doesn't that make sense to anyone?"

"No," Della said matter-of-factly. "Sorry, but the whole 'I'm a lizard' thing sounds crazy. Maybe you should come to grips with the fact that you're going to end up just being like one of us. A normal supernatural."

Kylie's head was spinning. First, *normal* and *supernatural* didn't fit in the same sentence, but . . .

"When have I ever been normal?" she asked. "When has anything connected to me, to my powers and gifts and my forever-changing brain patterns, appeared to be normal?"

Della opened her mouth, to argue no doubt, and then shut it. The pause lasted a whole second. Which for Della was a long time. "Okay, you've made another good point, but . . ."

"No buts," Kylie said. "I'm either a freak, or maybe, just maybe, I'm some other type of supernatural. Something not very many people have heard of."

Della pursed her lips as if in thought. "And that would be totally cool, wouldn't it? To be something very rare. Of course, you're already super rare because you're a protector. Hey . . . maybe that's why your pattern went crazy in the beginning, because you're a protector. And you're the first part-human protector to ever exist. Which, like I said, is cool."

"No, I'm not the first. My dad was a protector." Kylie paused. "And it's not as cool as you think." After a second, Kylie added, "Holiday suggested being a protector could have made my pattern do stupid stuff, but . . ."

"But you want to be a lizard," Della said.

Kylie just rolled her eyes and gave the woods another glance. She didn't feel anything, but maybe if she stood among the trees and surrounded herself with the foliage, she would feel it. Her grandfather and aunt could be waiting for her. Her answers could be out there waiting for her. "Can we take a short walk?"

"I thought we were supposed to be helping Miranda and Holiday set up the dining room."

"Just a short one."

"Where to?" Della asked.

Kylie motioned to the woods.

"Oh, hell no! Burnett was very, very, *very* clear on that. You aren't supposed to go in the woods. He'd have my head on a platter. After he chewed my ass out."

Kylie looked around to see if anyone was within hearing distance. Super hearing distance. She didn't see a soul.

She still dipped her head down and spoke in a whisper. "I know who's out there and I need to talk to them."

"What . . . ? Who's out there?"

The sound of a door shutting filled the warm air. "You guys letting Miranda do all the work?" Holiday's voice came behind them.

Kylie turned around and saw her stepping off the office steps. "Just going in."

Della leaned in. "Don't leave me hanging like this."

"Later," Kylie said when she saw Holiday walking up.

"Later what?" Holiday asked.

Guilt stirred in Kylie's chest, but she forced herself to lie. "Later, I'll tell her my bucket of boyfriend woes." She forced a smile.

"Yeah, boyfriend woes," Della said, as if to add validity to Kylie's lie. "Two guys fighting for her heart." Della cut her eyes to Kylie, and the message in her friend's eyes said she'd be pressing Kylie to finish their conversation about the woods ASAP.

"What a bucket of . . . woe that is!" Della said with drama. But somewhere in Della's voice, Kylie heard something else. A bit of envy.

Holiday chuckled. From the camp leader's expression, Kylie sensed she'd picked up on Della's emotions as well. And that caused Kylie to worry. How much of Kylie's woes did Holiday sense? And how long could Kylie keep things from her? Just long enough, Kylie prayed, to know the right way to approach everything.

Holiday shrugged. "From what I hear, she's not the only one with boy troubles."

"Yeah," Della said with sass. "You and Burnett are filling the air with pheromones." The vamp waved a hand in front of her nose.

Holiday frowned. "I wasn't talking about me." She gave Della a pointed look.

"Me?" Della asked, in total bafflement. "I don't have a boyfriend, so how could I have boyfriend troubles?"

"You could have a boyfriend if you wanted one," Kylie muttered, and that remark got her a sharp jab of Della's elbow in the ribs.

Holiday grinned. "Rumor has it you were the cause of some friction down by the lake."

"What friction?" Della asked.

"Between Steve and Chris," Holiday said, and wiggled her brows. Leave it to Holiday to know what someone needed to hear.

Except in Kylie's case. Kylie needed to know about Holiday's sister, but getting Holiday to talk about it, without just blurting out that her sister was dead, seemed impossible. But if Kylie didn't hear from Hannah soon, or Holiday didn't start talking, then blurting it out might be her only option.

"No." Della shook her head, sending her shoulder-length black hair swinging. "It wasn't over me. You just heard it wrong."

Holiday half grinned and shrugged. "If you say so." She paused and grinned like she knew something no one else did. "Come on. Let's get the dining room whipped into shape for the reception." She draped an arm around each of their shoulders and started walking toward the dining hall.

They took about three steps when Della came to a sudden stop. "Really?" she asked Holiday. "It was over me? Chris and Steve were upset with each other over me?"

"I told you Steve liked you." Kylie almost chuckled at Della's shock.

But Della wasn't listening to Kylie. "You're not shitting me?" Della continued, focusing on Holiday, her head tilted slightly as if listening to see if she was lying.

"I swear." Holiday grinned. "My heart won't lie."

"They were fighting—?"

"I said friction," Holiday corrected.

"They're frictioning over me?" She chuckled and then stopped as if to let that piece of info sink in. "No. Not me. It has to be a mistake." But Della's eyes lit up with a spark of self-confidence.

Kylie grinned—even feeling the weight of all her problems pressing down on her, seeing Della beaming with "boy" pride felt good . . . and right. It hadn't escaped Kylie that Della felt left out with both Miranda and Kylie having boyfriends, but she hadn't sensed how big of a chunk that took out of Della's confidence until now. And after the vampire's heartbreak with Lee, Della deserved to feel "friction worthy."

Not that all friction was a good thing. The friction between Lucas and Derek sure as hell couldn't be chalked up as a positive. But for right now, Kylie just wanted to think about Della.

Five minutes later, Kylie realized Della was right. Miranda was upset. The little witch hardly spoke to her as they whipped the dining hall into shape. Of course, Miranda squealed with glee when Della told her about Chris and Steve having "tension." Feeling like a third wheel, Kylie finally walked up to Miranda and apologized for . . . Well, she wasn't sure what she was apologizing for, but she said the magic words, "I'm sorry," and asked Miranda if she'd go over a few spells with her later.

Miranda's eyes lit up. "I would be delighted. Just decide what spell you want to try. And you can trust me, I can do this."

The look of sheer contentment on the little witch's face told Kylie that Miranda's problem was more about Kylie's initial refusal of her help and the ding against her ego than believing Kylie didn't want to be a witch.

While rearranging the tables in the front, Kylie's phone chimed with an incoming text. It was from Lucas.

Still with Clara. Miss you. I'll probably be busy introducing Clara to the pack until later. I'm not going to be at the reception. I'll stop by and see you tonight before you go to bed. Thanks for understanding.

Kylie stared at the phone and sensed she would be seeing a lot less of Lucas now that Clara was here. Kylie inhaled and tried to tell herself that she did understand. That of course he would have to take time with his sister. But between his pack and now Clara, Kylie wasn't sure where she fit in.

Or *if* she fit in.

Fifteen minutes later, Kylie noticed that Della kept glancing at her. Kylie knew the vamp was chomping at the bit to get Kylie alone so she could finish their conversation about who was in the woods. But frankly, Kylie was having second thoughts about coming clean. Telling Della meant she'd have to tell Miranda. Not that Kylie didn't trust them to keep it a secret, but . . . she just didn't want to get anyone in trouble. Then again, considering that she never went anywhere without a shadow these days, she was going to have to trust someone. And she trusted her two roommates more than she trusted anyone else at Shadow Falls.

They were almost finished setting up for the event when Holiday's phone rang. Holiday stepped away to take the call.

Della came moving over so fast that she bumped into Miranda and nearly knocked her down. "Talk and talk fast," Della sputtered at Kylie.

"Talk about what?" Miranda rubbed her shoulder and frowned at Della.

"Shh!" Della held up a finger to silence Miranda and eyed Kylie with persistence. "Talk."

"Don't you shush me!" Miranda bit out.

Kylie exhaled and reached over and touched Miranda's arm, hoping to calm her, then she answered Della's question. "It's my grandfather and aunt. They were the fog."

"They were . . . the fog?" Miranda asked, her bad attitude with Della dropping along with her mouth.

When Kylie nodded, Miranda continued. "Then that proves it, you are a witch, because they have to be some dang powerful witches to pull that off."

"Wait. Why would they do that?" Della asked.

Kylie frowned, and looked again at Holiday standing across the dining hall. Kylie noted how the camp leader's gaze kept moving to Kylie and she suspected the phone call had to be about her.

Again.

Great. What was it this time?

"Earth to Kylie," Miranda snapped.

Kylie glanced back at her two roommates. "I'm not sure it proves anything at this point."

"But why would they chase Lucas's sister?" Della asked.

"I don't know." Then suddenly Kylie did know. "To get me to enter the woods. They've been calling me for a few days now but I thought . . . I thought it might be Mario and his friends and I didn't go. But I'll bet my grandfather knew if I thought someone was in danger, I'd—"

"Do they even know you're a protector?" Miranda asked.

"I don't know." Kylie's mind raced. "I know that Burnett talked with him, but I don't know what all he told them."

"I'm not buying all that," Della said. "Maybe it is Mario pretending to be your grandfather and aunt. Maybe this is just a trick to get his hands on you."

"I don't think so," Kylie said. "And right now I have to follow my gut. I've got too much going on, and it would be nice to get some answers about something."

"What else is going on?" Concern made Della's brows tighten.

Kylie hesitated. "Ghost issues."

"Which means we're not gonna be any help there," Della countered.

Exactly what Kylie thought, too. When it came to ghost issues, it was either Holiday or she was on her own. She recalled Derek, who'd told her he was willing to help her even though chances were he felt the same way about the spirits as the other supernaturals did.

Della piped up again. "But I thought your grandfather was supposed to come see you tomorrow. Why are they turning themselves into fog and sneaking in to see you if they could just show up tomorrow? And how did you know the fog was them?"

"He was supposed to come," Kylie answered. "But since then he's shut off his phone and hasn't contacted Burnett at all. And right when I left the fog took on human form and . . ." Kylie wasn't sure how to put it. "I recognized my grandfather and my aunt. I'm sure of it."

Della's expression hardened. "But if you're wrong, and if we go out into the woods and shit happens—"

"Go into the woods?" Miranda blurted out. "Oh, crap, no! Burnett said she wasn't to go into the woods. To not let her get close to the woods."

"I know," Kylie said. "But if I want answers to what I am, I'm going to have to go to my grandfather, and I don't think he's going to just walk into the camp, not when the FRU is crawling all over Shadow Falls. And after what the FRU did to my grandmother, I can't say I blame him for not trusting them. Heck, even Holiday doesn't trust them."

Miranda bit into her bottom lip. "But if you're wrong . . ."

"I'm not." And just like that, Kylie realized she couldn't put her two best friends in danger. The guilt she still harbored over Ellie swelled in her chest. "But just in case, I'm going in alone."

"No way!" Della said.

"All I want to do is walk a little ways into the woods. You guys can just stand at the edge. If I don't feel anything, I'll come right back out."

"And if you do feel something?" Miranda asked.

"Then I'll know it's them and I'll meet them."

"Oh, hell no! You are not going in alone," Della declared. "You're a protector. In case you've forgotten, that means you can't protect yourself."

"Della's right," Miranda said. "If you go, we all go."

"I don't think any of us should go!" Della said.

Holiday started walking over and, knowing the fae would be able to read the mood, Kylie looked at her two best friends. "Think happy thoughts. Quick. Before Holiday reads . . ." She let her words fade as Holiday drew near.

"What's up?" Holiday asked.

"Nothing," the three of them answered at the same time.

Kylie smiled and tried envisioning Lucas to instill a happy emotion, but Derek's image and his loyalty to her ghost issues popped into her mind. And instead of being happy, more angst filled her head.

Holiday quirked an eyebrow that read as disbelief, but she appeared to move past it and said, "That was Burnett. He's not going to make it back until right before the event and has insisted we postpone the trip to the falls until tomorrow. Is that okay with you?"

"That's okay," Kylie said.

And it was okay. Maybe now she could take that walk into the woods and get some answers—if they were still there. She just needed to figure out how to do it without Della and Miranda freaking out.

Chapter Sixteen

Kylie stood on the edge of the path, ignoring Della and Miranda as they argued over who was going into the woods with her and who was staying at the path. Little did they know, neither of them were going.

She couldn't put them in danger. Even if there weren't any danger, if Burnett found out, he'd give them hell. And hell from Burnett felt pretty dangerous. Somehow Kylie was going to have to figure out how to sneak away and do this on her own.

Besides, she wasn't even sure her grandfather and aunt were still there. Maybe moving into the woods would tell her, but not now. Still, she closed her eyes and listened with her heart. When she didn't feel even the slightest yearning to enter, she spoke in her mind.

Are you still out there?

"I'm here."

The words sounded at the same time as Kylie felt the cold. Not recognizing the voice, she snapped her eyes open. Standing in front of her was a blond woman, early twenties, wearing a diner uniform with a tag on it that read CARA M. Kylie's heart thudded faster when she realized this was one of the girls from the vision, the vision of being buried with Holiday's sister.

Letting go of a sigh, Kylie's breath turned to cold vapor.

"Damn!" said Della.

"Damn what?" asked Miranda.

"Kylie's got company," Della said. "White misty shit always snakes up from her lips when she's chatting with the dead."

"Oh!" Miranda took a step back and stared at Kylie. "Man, her aura is doing some crazy stuff again. This is so damn freaky. I'm so glad I'm not her."

Trying to shut out Della and Miranda, Kylie focused on Cara M. Kylie recalled Derek asking her to describe the uniform so she studied it for details. She snapped a picture of it in her mind—the V neckline, the checkered pattern around the bottom of the skirt—so she could describe it to him later. But why not just ask?

"Where did you work?" Kylie asked.

"I worked at my aunt's voodoo shop," Miranda answered. "Crazy crap happened there."

"She's not talking to you," Della snapped.

"Sorry." Miranda shrugged. "This is so freaky."

"Do you know the name of the diner?" Kylie continued to stare at the spirit.

"I . . . don't know," Cara M. answered. *"But can you please get us out of there?"*

Kylie frowned. "I want to, but I need to know where you are."

"But you do know. The other girl took you there. Don't you remember?"

How could she forget? "I saw you guys and you were under a building of some sort, like a wood floor, but I don't know where that is. What town are you in? Is there an address? Is it close to here?"

"Yes, it's close. It didn't take much time at all to get here."

Kylie considered what she said and asked, "But how did you get here? I mean . . . did you walk or . . . come spiritually?" Kylie hadn't considered how spirits traveled and she realized how little she knew about the whole ghost-whispering thing.

"I don't know," the spirit answered. *"But I can take you back there if you'd like."*

"No," Kylie blurted out. The thought of being trapped in the grave again was too much. She took a deep breath and remembered to talk mentally. *Can you tell Hannah I need to see her?*

"Who's Hannah?"

One of the girls with you. The one with red hair. Kylie could feel Miranda and Della staring and she purposefully turned her back so she wouldn't be disturbed.

"So her name is Hannah? How do you know her name? She's not wearing a name tag." The spirit glanced down at the name tag attached to her uniform. *"Do you know my name? They call me Cara M., but I don't remember being her. My life is like a vague picture book I once looked at and I can recall flashes of the images on the pages, but they never turn slow enough for me to recognize anything."*

That's not uncommon after death, Kylie assured her, remembering Holiday saying that the more dramatic the death, the less the spirit remembered. The thought of what these girls possibly went through sent real pain skipping through Kylie's limbs. Her heart clutched with the need to help them. To do whatever they needed to help them move on.

"Will I ever remember?" Cara M asked.

The spirit's question came with such sadness that the emotion swelled in Kylie's heart. *I'm not an expert, but from what I've seen, things usually come to you. Spirits generally hang around for a reason and once that's taken care of, they remember things, and then pass over.*

Cara appeared to consider Kylie's words and nodded. *"I think the reason is so we can get our own graves. I've never liked roommates. And it's really cramped in that grave."*

Unfortunately, Kylie could remember just how cramped it was. She shivered, feeling her shoulders pressing against the dead girls' bodies on each side. Pushing the thought aside, Kylie concentrated on the conversation and not the horror of what had happened.

I'm trying to get you guys out. But something told Kylie that while Cara M.'s only need might be to escape the makeshift grave, Hannah wanted something much more. But hopefully while solving Hannah's problem Kylie would help out all three of them.

Cara M. stood there as if deep in thought. *"Is it nice where I'll cross over to?"*

Kylie debated what to say, then went with the truth. *I've never seen it, but I think so.*

The spirit looked around, then slowly floated up a good six or seven feet. She hung in the air, causing a big swirl of fog to appear around her, reminding Kylie of a scary movie. After a few seconds, she glanced down at Kylie with eyes that seemed lost, hurt. *"It's nice here, too."* She floated back down to the ground.

"I think I recognize this place. Are we close to that place with the dinosaur bones?"

Hope stirred in Kylie's tight chest. *So you know about this place? Did you live near here?*

"I . . . think so. I see an image of swimming in a lake. There was a lot of laughter there. It must have been fun."

Yes, there's a lake. Can you see anything more? Where you worked? What town?

The spirit frowned. *"I can't."* Darker shadows started appearing beneath her eyes. Shadows that made her look sadder and somehow deader. *"Please get us out of there."* She started to fade.

Wait. Can you tell Hannah I need to see her?

"I can, but I don't know if she'll come. She's upset."

At what? Was Hannah's memory returning, too? The cold began to ebb away.

The ghost completely vanished and the Texas heat replaced the chill, leaving Kylie with even more questions than before.

"Is the ghost gone?" Miranda asked.

"Yes," Kylie sighed.

"Are we going in?" Miranda asked.

"Where?" Kylie asked, confused.

"The woods. Duh."

"Oh, no," Kylie said.

"Thank Gawd!" Della muttered, and all three of them started walking to the cabin. Kylie looked back one more time and wondered if she'd ever find all the answers she needed. In a way, her life was as much of a mystery as a ghost.

They had one hour before they had to be back at the dining hall for the welcoming reception. While still walking, Della and Miranda jabbered about getting ready for the reception. No doubt Della wanted to spruce up to impress both Chris and Steve. Miranda wanted to wow Perry.

Kylie tried to get into the spruce-up mood with them, but her enthusiasm came up short. Lucas wouldn't even be there, so who would she be trying to impress? A vision of Derek popped into her head and she pushed it back and felt guilty for even thinking it.

Trying not to think about Derek reminded Kylie that she'd told him she'd e-mail him the description of the diner uniform. As Kylie moved to the computer, her mind raced with the details she'd collected about what Cara M. had been wearing.

Kylie opened her web account and saw a whole buttload of e-mails: a few from her mom, a couple from her dad, one from Sara, and some spam, and then a few from accounts she didn't recognize.

Ignoring her incoming mail, she clicked on the button to send a new e-mail, typed in Derek's name, and then started typing the description of the waitress uniform. She recalled all the things she'd learned about Cara M. and found herself wishing she had someone to talk to about them. Then again, she did have someone—the person she was e-mailing. Derek.

Miranda and Della's laughter spilled out of Della's bedroom. Why did hearing them laugh make her feel lonely?

The answer bubbled to the top of her mind. Because they were giddy with the idea of romance, of getting all dolled up to impress guys. Right now, the idea of romance left Kylie feeling befuddled. It felt like Lucas was pulling away and somehow Derek was sneaking closer. And nothing felt right.

But she still felt lonely.

Remembering the e-mail from her mom, Kylie picked up the phone and dialed her number. The phone rang four times before her mom answered.

"Hi, Mom," Kylie said.

"Hey, sweetie," her mom answered, and the sound of her voice had Kylie feeling homesick. "Is everything okay?" her mom asked.

"It's fine. Why do you always assume when I call you that something is wrong?"

"I don't always assume that. Only sometimes. And this is one of those times. I must be psychic. So stop pretending and tell me what's up."

Heck. Maybe her mom was a supernatural.

"Nothing," Kylie said. "I just got an e-mail from you and thought I'd call you. You are always saying I don't call enough."

"True." Her mom paused. "What's the matter, sweetie?"

Giving in because lying sure as hell didn't seem to work, Kylie answered, "Just a bad day."

"You know if you change your mind about staying there for the school year, and want to come home, I could get you enrolled back in school here and—"

"I'm not going to change my mind, Mom. I love it here." *I be-long here.* "I'm allowed to have a bad day, right?"

"Yes, just like I'm allowed to worry about you when you have a bad day."

"Well, don't worry too much." There was a sudden background noise on the line.

"Where are you?" Kylie asked.

"Out to an early dinner."

"Alone?" Kylie asked, hoping her mom wasn't out with Smarmy John, who wanted to drag her mom off to England and get her naked and between the sheets.

As soon as the thought came, Kylie tried to push it away.

"Uh, no." Her mom's answer came out sounding guilty. "Not alone."

"With John?" Kylie attempted to keep her disappointment from her voice, but didn't think she was successful.

The silence lingered a few seconds on the line.

"It's a yes or no answer, Mom. It shouldn't take you that long to reply." Kylie realized she sounded just like her mom, too. But damn, she was certain her mom had used the exact line on her at one time or another.

"Uh . . . yes," her mom's reply came out.

Kylie closed her eyes. As if her brain were on automatic pilot, the question slipped out. "You're not having sex with him, are you?" And even before the last word of the inquiry left her lips, she knew she was going to regret it.

Oh, yeah, regret times ten. Kylie felt her face turn red.

Her mom's breath caught and she started coughing. "Uh . . ." More hacking.

"Hello, Kylie." A male voice came on the line. "I think your mom choked on her wine."

Wine? Her mom was drinking wine at three in the afternoon?

Was he planning on getting her drunk and having his way with her?

"Kylie? You there?"

"Yeah." Kylie heard her mom telling John to give her the phone back. Kylie imagined her mom panicking thinking Kylie might ask John if they were having sex. Not that she would. The fact that she asked her mom was probably going on her most embarrassing moments list.

"Kylie?" Her mom must have snagged the phone back. "We . . . should talk later." Her voice came out squeaky, like a cartoon.

"Yeah. Later." Kylie disconnected and stared at the phone.

Okay, lesson learned. Her mom not only couldn't say the word *sex,* she obviously couldn't hear it, either. Did that mean her mom couldn't have sex? Gawd, Kylie hoped so. Lesson number two. Talking about sex with her mom made her queasy. Could she possibly suffer from the same affliction as her mom?

Resting her phone by the computer, pushing thoughts of her mom having sex from her mind, Kylie refocused on the computer and tried not to listen to her roommates giggling about something—probably something to do with sex, too. Moaning, she dropped her head down on the table, feeling the blood rushing to her cheeks, hoping the coolness of the wood would chase away the heat.

Her phone, placed beside the computer, chimed with an incoming text. Sitting up, she picked it up to get the message. Her heart did a little jolt when she saw it was from Derek.

His message read: *You ok? What's happening?*

Kylie closed her eyes. Could he sense everything she was feeling now? She dropped her head back on the table again, so hard she probably bruised her forehead. She took a few deep breaths and then sat up and started texting him back.

Fine. E-mailing you the description of the diner uniform now. U going to the reception?

She held her breath and waited to see if he'd answer.

I'll be there. U?

Oh goodness, did he think the question was like an invitation to hang out?

Was it an invitation to hang out?

Yes. Bye. Guilt set in. But at least the guilt replaced the embarrassment of asking her mom if she was having sex.

Kylie stared down at her phone. Why did texting Derek feel wrong? She shouldn't feel that way. They were just . . . friends. Heck, Fredericka was with Lucas five times more than Kylie was with Lucas. Ten times more than Kylie was with Derek. And Fredericka and Lucas had been lovers.

Trying to shake off the feeling, she finished the e-mail and hit send.

"Kylie?" Miranda called from the doorway of Della's bedroom. "Did you do it?"

Kylie looked over her shoulder and attempted to focus on Miranda's cheery voice. Frankly, she could use some cheer. Lately, it seemed she'd done nothing but chew on her problems. "Do what?" she asked a smiling Miranda.

"Stuff your bra. Did you do it?" the witch asked.

Kylie bit down on her lip and grinned as the memory filled her head. "Sara talked me into doing it in sixth grade, but I chickened out and hid behind a dumpster and got rid of the tissue before we got to school. She was livid when she saw me and she had super boobs and I didn't."

Miranda chuckled and Kylie could hear Della inside the room laughing as well.

Miranda gazed down at her chest. "I admitted that I did it for a while before I got them for real. But Della swears she never did it, but I can tell she's lying."

"I'm not lying," Della countered, popping out of her room. "Truth is, I might have done it if I hadn't seen Tillie McCoy bump into the locker with her size Cs and then walk down the hall with a square boob without realizing she'd smashed her boob stuffing." Della held her hand out in front of her chest. "Seriously, she had one boob out to here and one squared off to here. Crazy thing was, the guys still couldn't take their eyes off them. I don't think they cared one was square."

Kylie chuckled but what she really felt was embarrassment for a girl named Tillie whom she'd never met. "That would be awful."

"It was," Della said. "I think tissue sales dropped in town due to it, too. Seriously, the next day, all the girls in seventh grade had lost a couple of cup sizes and the boys were depressed for a month. That day I decided that being a member of the itty bitty titty committee wasn't the worst thing."

They all laughed again.

"You know boys stuff, too," Miranda said.

"Stuff what?" Kylie asked.

Della pointed to her pelvic area.

"Seriously?" Kylie asked.

"Seriously," Della and Miranda said in unison.

"They use socks," Della added.

"Socks? Why?" Kylie asked. "It's not as if we . . . check down there."

"They think we do," Della said. "Face it, guys have sex on the brain. Girls have romance on the brain."

"Sometimes I have sex on the brain," Miranda admitted. "Well, I mean, I think about it. Does that make me a slut?"

They laughed harder, Miranda included. Then Kylie shook her head, still trying not to imagine a guy with a sock in his pants. "We all think about it, but . . . that is just so . . . crazy!"

Della frowned at Miranda and pressed her hands on her temples as if she'd suddenly gotten a migraine. "Damn! Why did you have to bring up the sock thing? Now I'm going to be tempted to look at all the guys' zippers tonight to check for sock bulges."

"You're right." Miranda giggled. "It's like an accident on the side of the road. You don't want to look, but your eyes go there anyway." She hit the bottom of her chin with the back of her hand and tilted her head back. "We'll just have to keep our chins and eyes above the waist the whole time. Whatever we do, no bulge checks."

They all laughed even harder.

Best of all, the laughter reached down into Kylie's heart and eased her feeling of impending doom. And for that, she was grateful.

The dining hall smelled like cupcakes, which Holiday had the kitchen staff fix for the event. A group of campers hung out over by the appetizers, probably saying hello to the new teachers and a few of the new campers who'd come on board at Shadow Falls. Kylie had spotted one or two new faces the last few days, but hadn't actually met any of them yet. She had to face it; she didn't excel at meeting new people. But considering the first school year at Shadow Falls started next week, she'd have to meet them soon enough.

Standing beside Miranda, Kylie realized the place wasn't as crowded as she'd expected it to be. Probably because the reception wasn't mandatory. Nevertheless, over half the campers were present. Then Kylie noted that none of the weres were here. They'd obviously gone off to do their own thing. Again.

Another sweep of the room told Kylie that Derek hadn't arrived yet, either. She wondered if he was still doing Internet searches to see if he could find a diner in the area that Cara M. might have worked at before she'd been killed. The fact that he was helping her with a ghost issue filled her chest with something warm and scary.

Scary because she couldn't exactly define the warmth. They were just friends, she told herself again. And she found it harder to believe each time she said it, too.

Helen waved at Kylie from across the room. She had her arm around Jonathon. Kylie admired the relationship the two of them had found with each other. It was sweet and romantic. Kylie grinned and waved back. In spite of knowing her problems were still here, she felt . . . lighter, and the grin felt real, too.

Amazing how a little girlfriend-laughing time could raise your spirits. Though she did have to struggle not to look at guys below the belt to see if she detected any sock wearers. And just thinking about it made Kylie want to giggle. Unfortunately, Miranda spotted Kylie's stifled smile and, as if guessing what had caused it, the witch snorted with laughter. Then meeting Kylie's gaze, she pressed her hand under her chin and mouthed the words *chin up*.

Della, across the room, let out another laugh.

"What's so funny?" Burnett walked up beside Miranda.

"Nothing," Kylie said, then feared Miranda would tell him the truth. Miranda was good at blurting out the wrong thing at the wrong times.

Meeting Burnett's gaze, Kylie recalled he could detect a lie, so she quickly added, "Nothing I can share without . . ."

"Blushing?" he asked, looking from her face to Miranda, who glowed an embarrassed pink. The color almost matched her hair.

Afraid Burnett would want more of an explanation, Kylie added, "It's girl talk."

He held up a hand. "You don't have to explain. I really don't speak girl talk and every time I tried to learn it, I regretted it." He almost smiled and his expression softened with what looked like concern when he met Kylie's eyes. "Sorry I didn't make it back in time to go to the falls."

"It's okay," Kylie answered, and then, call her paranoid, but she asked, "The thing you had to do at the FRU, it didn't have anything to do with me, did it?"

"No," he assured her, sounding honest.

She nodded and then she went for a second question, although she was pretty certain she knew the answer. "No word from my grandfather?"

He shook his head. "I'm sorry." He sighed. "With all the things that have happened lately, I'm glad you're keeping your chin up."

Chin up. The words ran around Kylie's head. Miranda snorted another bit of laughter and faced the opposite direction. Kylie had to bite the inside of her cheek to keep from laughing. Then Della's chuckle sounded from across the room.

Wrinkling his brow, Burnett looked over at Della, who fell quickly back into vampire mode and wiped all signs of humor from her face. Burnett shook his head and focused on Kylie again. "If you can stop giggling, the new teachers are all eager to meet you."

"Me?" Kylie asked, his comment chasing the grin off her face. She shifted her gaze to the side of the room where the teachers congregated. They were indeed staring at her.

"Why would they want to meet me?" Kylie's I-don't-like-to-be-singled-out phobia reared its ugly head.

"They've heard about you," Burnett said as if it was obvious.

Kylie could only imagine what some of the campers had told them. Then an even worse thought hit. "Heard about me from whom? You mean, since they've been here, right? *Right?*"

Burnett looked uncomfortable with the questions. He glanced around, almost as if searching for an out, or perhaps searching for Holiday to answer the questions for him. When he didn't spot her, he looked back at Kylie. "I . . . Well . . . news spreads. People talk."

"People? You mean people outside of the camp? People outside of Shadow Falls are talking about me?"

He looked put on the spot, but he nodded. "Just the super-naturals."

Just the supernaturals? "So, the whole supernatural world knows about me?" The thought made Kylie want to find a hole to climb into. It was bad enough knowing the campers were always on "Kylie alert," waiting to see what her wacky brain pattern was going to do next, but to think she was the subject being discussed everywhere made her supernatural butt extremely uncomfortable.

"Perhaps not the whole supernatural world," he said as if trying to console her, and then hesitated as if reconsidering the wisdom of his answer. "I mean, I couldn't say if everyone—"

"Oh, it probably is everyone," Miranda said. "My mom said they were talking about you at Witch Council last week in Italy. And they didn't even know you were a witch then. You can imagine how they are talking now."

Kylie didn't want to imagine. Her chest suddenly felt hollow. "They were talking about me in Italy? You didn't tell me that." She bit down on her lip. "I'm such a freak that—"

"That's why I didn't tell you," Miranda said. "I knew you'd get all weird about it. And you're not a freak," she added. "You're a pro-tector. And being a protector is huge. Very newsworthy like a natu-ral disaster. Not that you're a disaster. I mean, like good news."

Nothing about this felt good. It felt more like a disaster. Not even a natural one.

"Word of a protector would be something people would talk about. But Miranda's right, it's not a bad thing." Burnett looked at Kylie and obviously read her erratic heartbeat and motioned to the crowd of teachers. "They just want to say hello. Not interrogate you."

Say hello to the camp's natural disaster, aka the freak. Kylie's heart raced.

"It's not a big deal," Burnett said.

Right. Only it felt like a big deal to her. Especially when she looked up and noted all three of the teachers gawking at her. Two were even twitching their brows, checking out her pattern—and their actions had encouraged several of the campers to do the same. She could almost hear the roar of thoughts. *Hey, anyone want a good laugh? Check out Kylie's brain pattern again.*

She heard someone say something about her still being a witch. Kylie supposed she should feel happy she had a pattern to check out—instead of one of those screwball shifting patterns that really freaked people out. But even knowing that didn't make her anxiety subside. She hated being in the spotlight.

Burnett, looking baffled at Kylie's emotional dilemma, leaned closer and whispered, "If you really don't want to meet them—"

"No, I . . . I'll do it." It was crazy not to. And she felt like an idiot for letting her insecurities be known. It wasn't that she completely hated meeting people, she just hated meeting people who already had a preconceived notion about her. And she sure as hell didn't like knowing that people in Italy were talking about her. Probably in Italian, and she couldn't even understand it.

Stiffening her backbone, she plastered a smile on her face, hoping to appear less like a freak than they considered her to be. It was, however, the same fake smile she wore when her mom took her someplace she didn't want to go—like to one of those mother/daughter days at work, or to one of those stuffy volunteer luncheons. What was it that her mom had said about that smile? Oh yeah: *You look like you just swallowed a mosquito.*

Yup, she was going to look like a freak, all right.

Chapter Seventeen

Kylie, practically holding her breath, suffered through Burnett's introduction of all three teachers. First was Hayden Yates, aka Mr. Yates to the students, who gave her a nod and a more than uncomfortable stare. The new half vampire, half fae science teacher shook her hand and held on for a second longer than she'd liked.

Considering his fae half was dominant, she was surprised she didn't feel any emotion-altering warmth from him. And although he didn't strike her as a pervert, something about him gave her just a bit of the creeps. She wasn't sure what it was, but she didn't like it, or him. Odd, because Kylie normally didn't make rash assumptions about people—with the exception of her mom's new boyfriend, of course. But that was a special case. That guy wanted to dirty up the sheets with her mom and that just wasn't okay.

Ava Kane, aka Ms. Kane, wore the title of English teacher. She was half-witch and half-shape-shifter, with shape-shifter being her dominant species. She seemed nice enough, but the way she kept twitching her brows, trying to see something different in Kylie's brain pattern, made Kylie uncomfortable. Exactly what did she think she'd find?

Collin Warren, a half-fae, half-human, was the history teacher and a geologist who came off as the quiet type. Odd, for someone with fae blood, because they usually seemed to have a certain amount of natural charm, but then again, perhaps not all half-fae inherited that talent. Kylie had heard that, on rare occasions, some human supernatural blends tended to be more human than supernatural, so perhaps that was the case with Mr. Warren.

Nevertheless, he smiled, said the proper things—"Nice to meet you"—but Kylie got the feeling he was as uncomfortable being put on the spot as she was. Which made her wonder why he'd want to be a teacher.

After everyone knew everyone's name, Kylie stood there, her smile still spreading her lips tight, and waited for something to end the awkward moment. Burnett finally intervened. "Well, I'm glad you all met."

Kylie spun around, thinking only of escaping. But one step forward, and she found herself surrounded by six or seven teens she'd never met. Obviously the new students. The blunt stares and open curiosity in their expressions made her catch her breath again. It was one thing to be gawked at by the regular campers, but newbies . . . Her heart raced and her palms began to itch. Hives were only a few minutes away.

Her swallowed-a-mosquito smile fell flat. And that mosquito she'd supposedly inhaled buzzed in her stomach. She didn't know if she could handle more brain gaping and uncomfortable introductions.

"Is it true that you didn't even have a pattern at first?" one of the girls, a witch, asked.

Suddenly, an arm fell across her shoulders. Before she looked at the owner of that appendage, she recognized Derek's warm touch. "I'm sorry, but you guys are going to have to meet Kylie later. I need to steal her away."

"Lucky guy," one of the new vampires said.

"Yeah, I am," Derek said, sounding possessive.

He guided her through the circle of new students. Moved her with confidence and with purpose—the purpose being to get her the hell away from the gawkers. But damn, she appreciated Derek being there so much. She leaned against his shoulder and heard him sigh.

"Hang in there," he whispered. "I'll get you out of here."

He glanced over his shoulder and she followed his gaze to see him looking toward Burnett. The vampire nodded as if giving permission for him to take her out.

She didn't breathe again until they walked out the dining hall door.

Derek's arm tightened as they left the building, as if telling her he didn't want to let her go. While she hated admitting it, there was a small part of her that didn't want him to let go either. But knowing what was right, she stepped away from his side. And then she met his soft green eyes.

"I'm sorry," she said.

"For what?" he asked.

For everything. For feeling things I shouldn't. "For needing to be rescued. It's crazy. I should be able to handle it. It's just that people stare at me like I'm . . ."

"Special?" He grinned.

"No, like I'm a freak."

He shook his head. "They don't think you're a freak. They're curious. And that one vamp was totally into you, but I'm sure it's still hard."

"Maybe when I know for sure what I am, then it won't be so hard." But she did know, didn't she? She was a chameleon. Was she starting to doubt her heritage like everyone else?

Derek's eyebrow rose. "You still don't believe you're a witch?"

"Not completely," Kylie said.

He nodded. "Well, that should all be cleared up tomorrow, right? When your grandfather comes."

That's when she remembered she hadn't told Derek about her grandfather cutting off his phone or about him and her great-aunt turning into fog. She started to spill her guts to him when she felt the sudden splash of cold.

The smear of condensation started to materialize next to Derek. The familiar feminine form taking shape told Kylie it was Hannah. But Kylie's breath caught when she saw the spirit had gone back to her zombie look. The beige dress she wore was in shreds and stained with mud. Her hair hung lifelessly around her shoulders. Part of her cheekbone was exposed where the skin had decayed and hung loose. And worms moved in and out of her ears.

Gross. Instinctually, Kylie took a step back.

"Not again." Panic filled Hannah's dead-looking eyes.

"What?" Kylie forced herself not to keep backing up. But the worms were falling off her at a rapid rate.

"Huh?" Derek took a step closer and one of the worms fell onto his chest.

Kylie brushed it off and then shook her head.

"Oh." His eyes widened with understanding. He took a small step back, not so much out of fear, but as if giving her space.

Kylie refocused on Hannah. But the spirit's gaze stay glued over Kylie's shoulder. She heard the dining hall door open behind them, and the sound of the crowd followed the door. Hannah continued to stare over Kylie's shoulder. Then, suddenly, her expression grew more panicked.

"No," Hannah muttered and her hands, more bone than flesh, grabbed Kylie by the shoulders. Worms went everywhere.

"Not again! Not again!" The spirit's touch sent wave after wave of icy tremors coursing through Kylie, who forgot about the worms. Pain shot from every nerve ending and her body stiffened from what felt like a brain freeze to her entire body.

"Is everything okay?" Derek moved in.

The throbbing through Kylie's body locked the air in her lungs. She wanted to scream. But she felt as if someone had her by the throat. Black spots started forming in her vision. She felt her knees start to fold. Derek touched her and just like that, the pain and the dizziness vanished. Blinking, she saw Hannah was still there, standing beside Derek.

Kylie breathed, then forced the words out. "Not again, what?"

Hannah didn't answer, didn't even look at her. Derek did, and he appeared concerned.

"Look, I need to know what it is you need me to do. Please, answer me." But the spirit, her frightened dead gaze locked over Kylie's shoulder, faded into thin air.

Derek brushed his hand down Kylie's arm. "You okay?"

Kylie nodded, savoring the warmth of his touch, and then she turned around to see who'd walked out of the dining hall, wondering if that was what had sent Hannah running. Burnett, the new teachers, and a couple of the new students stood by the door.

"Was that Hannah?" Derek whispered.

"Yeah," Kylie said, still trying to wrap her head around what Holiday's sister had meant by *not again*.

"You really okay?" he asked.

She touched her throat. "Yeah. I just don't know what it is that she needs me to do."

"I don't know if this helps, but I think I know where Cara M. worked."

"Where?" Kylie asked.

"When you told me that she could possibly be from around here, I Googled all the diners and cafés in the area. I found some photos and this old newspaper article about some place called Cookie's Café, right outside of Fallen. Have you ever been there?"

"No, I don't . . . Wait. Yes, my mom took me to this restaurant that was really just an old house. That must have been how I recognized the uniform."

"That's it. The house was built in the eighteen hundreds." He smiled as if proud he'd found the answer to at least part of the puzzle.

Kylie almost smiled herself, but then it hit her. What now? Even if all Kylie needed to do was find the bodies, how was knowing where one of the dead girls worked going to help her? Ordinarily, she could talk to Holiday about this but . . . she couldn't do that until she knew exactly what was going on. It would be unbearably cruel to tell Holiday her sister was dead when there was a chance Kylie was misinterpreting the visions.

Then another realization washed over her. She should probably go to the police. But she didn't have a freaking clue how to explain any of this. Which meant it might be up to her to try to solve the murders.

Not again. Not again. Hannah's words rang in her head. What was Hannah trying to say?

Oh, holy hell, Kylie didn't have a clue how to move forward. She wasn't an investigator. She didn't even enjoy watching TV shows about detectives. She glanced back up at Derek. "What should I do now?"

"I called the diner, just to ask if there had been a Cara M. working there, but it's a tourist place and they're only open on the weekends."

Kylie's mind continued to whirl with what she needed to do. "Oh, hell, I'm so out of my league on this."

"Don't worry," Derek said. "I'll help you. And besides, we have until Saturday to decide what to do next."

She looked up at him with complete appreciation. "How can I thank you?"

He grinned with pure sex appeal, the gold flecks in his eyes brightening. "I could think of a few ways."

She frowned.

He held up a hand. "Fine. Just smile a little more. That'll be payment enough."

Thursday morning, Kylie woke up when Socks bumped her chin with his nose. As she blinked away the fogginess of sleep, she stroked Socks's soft feline fur. The sun spilled through the window and she watched as the day's brightness and shadows flickered on the ceiling, fighting for space—a war of sorts between light and darkness.

As the battle took place, she felt her mood host a similar conflict. Her life seemed to be a mêlée of so many problems and yet so many possibilities. She'd lost Derek, but gained Lucas. She'd lost the bond with her stepdad but found Daniel. She'd lost being human, but was now supernatural.

And today was the day she was supposed to meet her grandfather and discover just what it all meant, but she doubted that would happen. A frown pulled at her lips and the darker side of her mood tried to take over.

Not that she'd let it win. She closed her eyes and tried to think positive thoughts. But her mind went to Hannah and the fact that Kylie shouldn't postpone telling Holiday any longer that her sister was dead. Just thinking about how that conversation would go took another bite out of Kylie's disposition.

Then her heart reminded her that Lucas hadn't shown up last night, despite the fact he'd told her he would. That pretty much made it official. The dark side, the bad mood, had won. Glancing back up at the ceiling, she couldn't help but notice there were indeed more shadows than sunlight.

For some crazy reason, she remembered Nana telling her to enjoy her childhood because soon enough she'd be an adult. Was this adulthood? To wake up every day and know it would bring both good and bad? To do things you had to do, even if you wished you didn't have to do them?

Then she recalled another piece of Nana's advice. *Just remember, sweetie, sometimes we can't change what happens, but we can change how we let those things affect us.*

"Easier said than done, Nana." Kylie inhaled a big gulp of frustration and the sweet smell of roses tickled her senses. Turning her head, she saw the single pink rose on her nightstand. The memory of Lucas having robbed his grandmother's rose garden and filling Kylie's room with roses sent her bad mood on time-out. Then, seeing the note beside the rose, she sat up and reached for the slip of paper.

Kylie,

   Sorry I was late. Something came up and I had to go visit my dad. You were out like a light when I got here. But damn, you are so beautiful when you sleep. If Della hadn't heard me opening your window and poked her head in and shot me the bird for waking her up—she's impossible—I would have climbed in bed with you just to feel you next to me.

   You have no idea how much I'd like that. To feel you against me. All of you.

                                               Sweet dreams,
                                               Lucas

Kylie reached for the rose and placed it to her nose. The sweet scent made her smile. Maybe the bad mood wasn't going to win after all.

• • •

Kylie reconsidered her positive attitude when a couple of hours later, she batted at the bugs swarming around her as she moved into the woods with Holiday and Burnett. But it wasn't the bugs causing the deterioration of her good mood. It was one certain dark-haired, blue-eyed werewolf.

Kylie should have been excited about going to the falls. She always felt better after a visit. But right now, she didn't want to feel better. She wanted to feel . . . mad.

Wait. She didn't *want* to feel it, she did feel mad.

Mad at the rose-leaving, note-writing were.

She'd completely let go of her aggravation about Lucas not showing up last night. She'd tried to set aside the fact that he'd practically told her he had to keep secrets from her. While she didn't like it, she'd even accepted that Fredericka, his one-time sex buddy, would always be within touching distance of him, when Kylie wasn't anywhere close enough to touch him herself. She had worked at overcoming the fact that his grandmother, his father, and even his entire pack, were against their being together.

She'd done a lot of setting aside, overcoming, and accepting. And after this morning, she realized that it might have been too much— because after not showing up last night, after hardly seeing her yesterday, he'd barely acknowledged her this morning in the cafeteria.

Another mosquito buzzed past and she swiped at the air, sending the pest headfirst into a tree. *Bzzz . . . splat!*

Couldn't Lucas have come over and had breakfast with her? She wouldn't have even blamed him if he'd brought Clara with him. But no, all she'd gotten was a smile, and even that smile had seemed somehow purposefully short. Then he'd joined the were table with all his other friends, his pack—people who clearly came before her now and probably always would.

Last night, he'd climbed into her bedroom way after midnight while she'd been asleep. He'd left her a rose and a sweet note, and this morning all she'd gotten from him was a half-assed smile. What was up with that?

She sure as hell didn't know. Who was she kidding? She knew exactly what was up. She wasn't good enough for him, because she wasn't a were.

That stung. Really stung. Then, to make matters worse, when Derek sat beside her, Lucas had the audacity to text her and say he didn't like it.

Right. He didn't like the fact that Derek had sat beside her, but he'd chosen not to sit with her. Instead, his sexy little butt was sandwiched between Fredericka and one of the new female weres, who was all over Lucas to the point that even Fredericka was unhappy about it.

Yeah, Kylie could hear Lucas telling her that he no longer cared about Fredericka. She could hear him saying that he hadn't asked the new girl to sit beside him, and she could hear him saying he had to be loyal to his pack. And maybe Kylie was wrong to feel angry, or maybe she wasn't so much angry as she was just tired of playing second fiddle.

Second fiddle sucked.

Another mosquito bit the dust when she swiped it off her cheek.

"You might want to slow down," Burnett said, moving up beside her with his long-legged strides.

Kylie glanced at him. He studied her briefly, then shifted his gaze back to the terrain as if expecting something to jump out at them. He'd been acting antsy since they walked into the woods, not that Kylie paid too much attention; her heart had been too busy fiddling with her second fiddle matters to care if Burnett had drunk too much caffeine.

"Seriously, slow down," Burnett said.

"Why?" Kylie asked.

He briefly glanced over his shoulder again. "As wonderful as faes are, they're slow."

Kylie sighed. She hadn't realized that she was moving at a fast sprint. A non-human sprint. A non-witch sprint, too. Which meant she wasn't really a witch, right? Glancing back, she saw Holiday power walking to keep up.

"Sorry." Kylie slowed down and noticed how Burnett kept looking around as if he expected something to jump out at them. Had something happened? And if so, did it have anything to do with her?

Holiday's footfalls sounded beside Kylie. She glanced from the nervous vampire to Holiday.

"Thanks for slowing down," Holiday said, sounding a bit breathless. In less than a minute, Burnett lagged behind them, just out of vampire hearing range. Probably at Holiday's insistence. No doubt she wanted to talk with Kylie, and Holiday didn't like knowing he'd listen in.

The verdant smells of the forest filled Kylie's senses. For the first time since she entered the woods she recalled her grandfather and the fog. She immediately tried to listen with her heart to see if she felt the calling sensation from before; it wasn't there. Then she wondered if somehow the whole fog episode was behind Burnett's edginess. Or even worse, had they tried to return and set off the alarms? Would Burnett even tell her about it if they had?

Probably not.

She looked back at Burnett. What did the vamp know?

Moving closer to Holiday, Kylie asked, "Can you tell me something and be honest about it?"

Holiday's footsteps on moist earth made squishy sounds, as if Kylie's question had added a weight to her step. "I don't lie to you."

"By omission you do. Not being up-front about something is as bad as lying." And then there was the issue of how little Holiday shared about herself. As much as Kylie confided in Holiday, it hurt to realize it wasn't a two-way street.

"I don't purposefully keep things from you." The truth in her tone hung in the damp air. They walked without talking for a few moments.

"What is it you want to know?" Holiday asked.

Kylie fought back her frustration with Holiday, knowing her anger with Lucas was affecting her attitude. "What's with Burnett? He seems extra alert. Has he . . . learned something that concerns me? Does he have news about my grandfather? Today was supposed to be the day he showed and yet . . . I don't think there's a chance in hell that he's coming. And no one is even saying anything about it, as if it never happened."

Holiday frowned. "Because we didn't think it would happen, we decided to downplay it. But Burnett and I talked earlier about it and he hasn't heard anything about your grandfather. But . . . I agree about him being . . . let's call it on the defensive. I asked about it. He says he's feeling jittery." Her tone seemed to say that Holiday didn't buy it.

And neither did Kylie. Something was up. But what?

As they continued over the rocky path, an unnatural cold seemed to sweep in with every other breeze. Someone, someone dead, was close by. She gave Burnett another glance over her shoulder and remembered their talk about ghosts.

Was that the issue bothering him?

Holiday slowed down and peered back with concern. A slight huff of air leaked from her lips and her expression shifted from concern to annoyance. Not just any kind of annoyance, but the kind that stemmed from the opposite sex.

The mood must have been contagious because Kylie's own thoughts ventured to her opposite-sex issues and she wondered if men weren't just created to drive women crazy.

A few more minutes down the path, Holiday spoke up. "Now it's your turn. What's up with you? And don't tell me nothing, because you have anger dripping from you like a leaky faucet."

Kylie frowned, too angry to deny her feelings. "Lucas is what's up."

"Boy trouble, huh?"

"Boy catastrophe is more like it. I'm not sure I can do this."

"Do what?" Concern sounded in Holiday's voice.

"Do Lucas," Kylie said.

Holiday made a funny face and raised one eyebrow.

"Not do him as in . . . get naked," Kylie blurted out, realizing what she'd said and thinking this was the cause of Holiday's odd expression.

"I mean, dealing with being the last thing on his to-do list. I mean him treating me as if I'm an afterthought in his life. I mean me feeling as if everyone he knows and cares about thinks I'm not good enough for him because I'm not a were."

Sympathy filled Holiday's eyes. "If it helps, I don't think Lucas shares the old beliefs of the weres. Most of the young weres don't agree with them, but there's pressure from the elders in their society to follow them anyway."

"I know," Kylie said. "And I also know that the only reason he's abiding by the stupid rules is because he needs his father's approval to make the Council so he can change things. But when he won't even smile at me for longer than a second, it hurts!" she seethed. "I guess that makes me a selfish twit for feeling this way." Her words resonated deep inside her and the guilt, like flies on a bad banana, started buzzing around her chest.

"No." Holiday cut her green eyes toward Kylie as they took the bend in the trail. "It doesn't make you selfish. It makes you normal. No one wants to be made to feel as if they aren't good enough."

"But I still feel like a selfish twit," Kylie said. The sound of the falls started playing in her ears, and even from this distance she felt the calming in her mood. "Or I feel selfish when I'm not feeling furious."

Holiday leaned in and brushed shoulders with her. "Your feelings are valid. Don't feel guilty. Sure, Lucas is making these choices for a reason. It's part of his quest, and we all must pay a price for following our own paths. But . . ." She paused in thought. "It's not always fair to ask others to pay that price." She glanced back at Burnett again.

Kylie sensed Holiday's words held a personal significance. In the last few days, Kylie suspected the relationship between Burnett and Holiday had gone backward. And she didn't think it was Burnett doing the backtracking.

"I think he'd be willing to pay it," Kylie said.

Holiday frowned. "I was talking about you and Lucas."

"Right," Kylie said. *But you were thinking about you and Burnett.*

They moved off the path and into the alcove of thick trees as they completed the journey to the falls. The moist smell of wet earth perfumed the air, the sound of rushing water played in the symphony of the woodsy sounds, and the serene ambience grew stronger.

Kylie's anger, her frustrations, all seemed lighter with each step. And when they arrived, it was . . . surreal. Each time, she seemed to forget how good it felt. They stood on the bank of the creek and stared through the misty air at the spray of water cascading downward.

Kylie heard Holiday draw in a deep, calm breath that matched her own.

"What is it about this place?" Kylie asked.

"Magic. Power." Holiday reached down to remove her shoes and Kylie did the same. "Back in the 1960s, there was actually a supernatural doctor in botany science who came here to prove that all this could be explained by some chemical compounds in some plant life. A natural drug of sorts."

"But how could that be when not everyone experiences it?" Kylie unlaced her shoes.

"Ahh, but those not welcome here generally feel the opposite, an uncomfortable sensation that urges them to flee. Which is why this scientist believed it was a chemical reaction. Meaning, the few supernaturals who experience positive emotions were just genetically inclined to react differently to the plant's compounds. Like how some groups of people react differently to drugs."

"And what did he find?" Kylie asked, intrigued by the subject, but no more believing it was a drug than she believed in Santa Claus.

Holiday pulled off her shoes and set them beside a rock and stood up, glancing down at Kylie with a slight smile on her lips. "Not a damn thing. After only a few weeks of working in the area, he and his teams suddenly gave up the grant that was going to pay for the project. Rumor was the Death Angels scared them away."

Kylie moved her gaze around the verdant and beautiful landscape. The mingling of mist and sprays of sunshine beaming down from above the trees spoke of the power and magic that Holiday had mentioned. The ambience that existed here was too reverent to be considered a drug, and the natural splendor too spiritual to be dissected and studied under the microscope.

"I can see how the Death Angels wouldn't like unbelievers digging around. I'm glad they chased them away."

"Ditto," Holiday said.

Standing up, Kylie's bare feet sank into the moss-covered bank. Wiggling her toes, she bent down and rolled up her jeans.

Right then something swooped down in front of her. She swallowed her scream when she saw it was the blue jay. The bird she'd brought back to life that had somehow imprinted on Kylie and kept stopping in for visits. Hovering right in front of her, it sang as if personally performing a ballad just for her.

"I'm not your mama," Kylie said. "Go, find your own way. Do what all birds do. Leave the nest, so to speak. Find a hunky blue jay to flutter after."

"That's sweet." Holiday chuckled.

"Maybe, but it's also weird," Kylie muttered.

With her jeans rolled up, she took a step into the creek. The cool water lapping around her ankles felt heavenly. Her heart that had moments earlier ached with raw emotion now felt lighter. Things, at least for right now, felt right. Her world felt manageable; her problems solvable. She eagerly embraced the feeling.

Yet if she'd learned anything from her visits to this special place, it was that even a manageable life didn't mean things would be perfect. A trip to the falls didn't fix anything. It simply offered one the strength to face the hurdles.

Life could still hurt like a paper cut right across the heart.

And she had a few paper-cut scars to prove it. A vision of Ellie filled her heart. Yet as a breeze carrying the misty coolness brushed Kylie's face, the ache faded into acceptance. Every new day was about opportunities. You couldn't always control life, just your response to it.

Stopping halfway across the creek, she turned to look at Holiday. The camp leader stood gazing back at Burnett, who stood in the trees. The expression on her face held concern, fascination, and something else.

Love. Burnett and Holiday were meant to be together. The feeling came on so strong and with such certainty that there seemed to be a message with it—a message Kylie couldn't quite read. Did it mean she was supposed to help make that happen? Or could she trust that if left alone, love would find a way?

And could she feel the same about her and Lucas?

Not that she was prepared to call it love. Nor had he called it that.

But Derek had. *I'm in love with you, Kylie.*

Kylie closed her eyes and tried not to think about anything other than the calm feeling that the falls provided.

Chapter Eighteen

Time seemed to stop as Kylie and Holiday sat side by side in the alcove of the falls. The wall of water diffused the incoming light; only the briefest rays of yellow sun passed through. And when they did, the light caught in the mist droplets and danced in the air. The water rushed down with a low roar, and tiny molecules of moisture brushed against their faces.

The thought occurred to Kylie that maybe now would be a good time to tell Holiday about her sister. If anything could help curb the sting of the news, it would be the magic of this place. Yet even with the peacefulness embracing her, the idea of telling Holiday about the death of her sister had Kylie's heart hurting.

Then a familiar chill filled the damp air. Hannah materialized, standing in the pool of water. Her green eyes, bright with tears and filled with sadness, focused on Holiday.

Oblivious to her sister's presence, Holiday stared at the wall of water rushing down. She rubbed her arms as though she were chilled, and then turned her head and met Kylie's eyes. "A visitor?"

Kylie nodded, her throat getting tighter with emotion when she glanced again at Hannah's tears.

Holiday shrugged. "That's odd. They normally don't come back here." She leaned back on the rocks and stared up at the cave ceiling, as if giving Kylie space to deal with the spirit.

"She hates me," Hannah said. *"And I don't blame her. What I did was unforgivable."* Shame now entered Hannah's wet eyes.

Kylie almost asked Hannah what she'd done, but decided to let her be the one to initiate the conversation. Kylie sat there in silence, feeling the cold of death that somehow seemed to blend with the calm of the falls.

She studied Hannah's emotion-filled expression and she knew the spirit had found her way through the confusion of death enough to communicate.

Enough to remember. Did she recall the moments before her death? The name of her killer perhaps? But all Kylie saw in Hannah's expression was regret.

Watching Hannah took Kylie back to her own near-death experience, to when Mario and his friends had knocked her off the ledge. She'd thought she was about to die. And she would have if Red, Mario's grandson, hadn't saved her and sacrificed himself in the process.

She remembered the regret that consumed her when she thought it was the end. Probably the same emotions Hannah felt now. Wouldn't everyone feel that way? Living, Kylie supposed, meant making mistakes, as well as garnering karma points.

While Kylie had never really defined her job/gift as a ghost whisperer, she supposed it entailed helping the spirits recall the good they'd done as much as helping them absolve any outstanding mistakes. It seemed that when you were alive, you spent most of your time trying to forgive others; upon death, it was yourself you mostly needed to forgive.

I'll bet you two were close, Kylie said. *I imagine you had a lot of fun as sisters.*

Hannah looked up at Kylie. *"We did. I just wish . . ."*

When Hannah didn't continue, Kylie asked, *What is it that I need to do for you? Is it just telling her about you? Is it getting you and the others out of the mass grave?*

"*No, it's more.*" She paused as if still trying to remember. "*It can't happen again.*" Hannah's whisper echoed against the cave's rock walls and the cold of her presence built.

Kylie pulled one knee closer to her chest. *What can't happen again?*

Hannah stepped closer, looking lost in thought. "*I can't look at her without feeling . . . I was so wrong. So jealous. I got what I deserved. I deserved to die, but the others didn't. It has to stop.*" Even more tears filled her eyes. The sound of rushing water punctuated by the quietness of the mist-filled air added a strange kind of eeriness to the moment.

"*He wants her.*" Hannah took another step forward. Desperation filled her eyes. "*And you have to stop him.*"

Kylie's gaze shifted from the spirit's face and became captured by the still water that didn't even stir as Hannah inched forward. Her sad spirit stopped when she stood directly over Holiday, staring down at her with a mixture of love and regret.

Realizing what Hannah had said, Kylie asked, *Who? Stop who from doing what?*

Holiday's phone rang and Kylie looked over at her. The camp leader sat up, her brows pinched. "Okay, that's odd, too. Phones don't usually work in here." Pulling her phone from her pocket, she eyed the number on the screen.

Kylie heard Holiday's breath catch at the same time as Hannah's. The spirit let out a sound of despair and took off running through the falls. Her footfalls, though quick, fell silent on the rock floor.

Right before Hannah's spirit darted through the wall of water, she glanced back at Holiday, who stared transfixed at the number on the phone. Then she disappeared, taking with her the cold that she'd brought.

"Who is it?" Kylie asked Holiday.

Holiday shook her head. "It's . . . Blake."

"Who's Blake?" Kylie asked, somehow certain he was a clue to all this. Was he the one Kylie had to stop from doing something bad to Holiday?

Was Holiday's life in danger?

The hum of the rushing water was interrupted by the sound of someone running, splashing through the falls. Kylie and Holiday looked up.

Burnett, standing guard outside the falls, shot through the rush of water, his face etched with panic. His clothes were wet, and his dark black hair was scattered across his brow and dripping water down his face. "Where did she go?" He blinked, and then his gaze landed on Holiday. His eyes widened. He shook his head in pure confusion. "You just . . . ran out of here. How could you . . . ?"

"What?" Holiday asked.

Burnett just stood there, his complexion paler than its normal olive color, staring as if he'd seen a ghost.

Kylie suddenly realized that was exactly what had just happened. Burnett had seen Hannah.

Oh, shit, Kylie thought. Burnett not only could smell ghosts, he could see them, too.

"How could I run where?" Holiday asked again, tucking her cell phone back in her pocket. "You're not making any sense."

Kylie didn't know what compelled her to do it, but she glanced at Burnett and shook her head, indicating that he shouldn't tell Holiday about what he'd seen.

He opened his mouth and then closed it and studied Kylie. She shook her head slightly again and she knew he'd understood.

He focused on Holiday again. Then, still looking perplexed, he answered, "I misspoke. I thought I heard you call me."

"No," Holiday said. "I didn't."

"Fine," he blurted out, and in a blink of an eye he shot back through the wall of water.

Holiday stared wide-eyed at the spot where he'd stood a flicker of a second earlier. "I know you told me he'd come back here and it's not as if I didn't believe you, but I guess I had to see it to wrap my head around it. I don't . . . I've never seen anyone be able to come back here who wasn't blessed."

Kylie's mind raced with what to say, but then she remembered Holiday's phone call and the anguish in Hannah's expression when she'd rushed out. Then Kylie recalled the distinct feeling that whoever that caller was had something to do with Hannah and could be the person the spirit seemed to be so worried about.

"Who's Blake?" Kylie asked again.

"Don't you have an appointment with one of the new teachers?" Burnett asked Holiday fifteen minutes later as they came to the clearing of the woods after they walked back from the falls. "Why don't you head back to the office and I'll see Kylie to her cabin?"

Kylie cut her eyes up at Burnett and she knew his game plan. He wanted her alone so he could interrogate her about what had happened at the falls. She could tell by his silence and the color of his eyes that the interrogation wasn't going to go easy.

"I still have half an hour if you have something else to do." Holiday studied Burnett with open curiosity, probably confused about his change in eye color. On the walk back, she'd come out and asked him about his ability to walk into the falls. He'd shrugged and said he hadn't given it much thought.

Which was a huge, honking lie. He'd obviously thought about it a lot. And he'd gone back to thinking about it because he didn't speak again for a while. With silence following them as they made their way through the woods, Kylie had done her own thinking, or worrying. Trying to figure out the mystery of Blake with each step, she'd fretted until she'd chewed her bottom lip sore.

When asked about the caller earlier, Holiday had danced around the truth with her answer: "Someone I used to know."

That hadn't told Kylie squat. She'd been tempted to blurt out a list of questions.

Did Blake also know your twin sister that I'm not supposed to know about?

Do you think this Blake character could have done something to your sister, like kill her?

Do I need to tell Burnett about Blake just in case he is the person that I'm supposed to not let hurt you?

Oh yeah, Kylie had a lot to fret over, including the upcoming interrogation from Burnett.

"Nah," Burnett said. "I'll see Kylie to her cabin. You go relax."

Holiday's brow tightened in a total non-relaxing way and she looked at Kylie as if she might know why the vamp was acting so weird. Kylie shrugged.

"Okay." Holiday walked toward the office.

Kylie started the trek to her cabin and made a bet with herself on how long it would take Burnett to start hitting her with questions. One minute? Two?

"Start talking!" Burnett ground out less than twenty seconds later.

Okay, so maybe she overestimated his patience.

He stopped walking and looked at her, his expression one big scowl. "Who was that at the falls who looked like Holiday? Did you use your witch powers to do that?"

Kylie hesitated, unsure how to answer him. She remembered how she'd felt learning she'd be spending the rest of her life hanging out with dead people.

"I didn't do anything."

"Then who was it?" he demanded. "And why did you feel the need to keep this from Holiday?" When she paused, he added, "Now, Kylie! I want answers. And don't forget that I can tell when you're lying."

She exhaled. Understanding his frustration, but . . . "It's Holiday's twin sister."

His brows pinched in confusion. "Holiday has a twin?"

Kylie nodded.

Burnett looked off for a second, then back at her. "Why wouldn't she have ever mentioned this?" He ran a palm over his face, frustration and disappointment filling his eyes. He blurted out his own answer. "Because she doesn't confide in me about anything."

His gaze shot back to Kylie. "But wait. How could this twin be in the camp without setting off the alarms? I checked my phone when I went back outside the falls. The alarms hadn't been triggered and there was no bad weather to make me believe someone could have fooled the system."

"She didn't fool the system. She . . ." There wasn't an easy way to say this, but she still paused to try and find the right words.

"She must have," Burnett continued. "How else would—?"

"She's dead," Kylie said, feeling the pressure to answer under his intense scowl. "Holiday's sister is a ghost."

Chapter Nineteen

"Her twin is dead?" Burnett's tone rang with empathy. "How? What happened?"

Kylie felt a warmth in knowing that he thought of Holiday first before realizing exactly what this meant—not that she didn't expect him to see the obvious any minute now.

Or maybe less than a minute. His eyes widened with hints of panic and his mouth became slack.

"No! She can't be . . . because I can't . . ." He shook his head. "No."

"It's not much different than smelling them. And you already knew that you could do that," Kylie said, hoping to ease the shock.

"It's a hell of a lot different." He raked a hand through his hair. "How could . . . I'm vampire and we don't . . . We don't see spirits."

"I know. I remember Holiday saying that." Kylie paused. "What's even stranger is that you saw her, and normally only the person connected to the spirit sees them. I don't see Holiday's ghosts and she doesn't see mine. So why would you see Hannah?"

"I'm not supposed to see any of them!" he bellowed. "I'm vampire. Very, very few vampires are given this secondary power."

Kylie twitched her brows at Burnett's pattern. "Maybe you're not a hundred percent vampire. Your great-great-grandma could have been a hybrid, and it just kind of popped up now."

He slapped his forehead. "Does my pattern not look all vampire?"

Kylie shrugged. "Yes." She looked at him with empathy. "But considering what I've been through, I've kind of learned not to put a lot of stock in what someone's pattern shows."

He stared at Kylie as if she'd morphed into something evil. "That only happens to you."

"Yeah. Sometimes it feels that way." She found his comment somewhat humorous. She did another shrug, biting back her smile because she didn't think what little sense of humor Burnett had was functioning right now.

"However," Kylie continued, "we can't deny that something's going on. Your pattern says all vampire, and full-blooded vampires aren't usually ghost whisperers."

"Maybe it's punishment because I went into the falls."

Kylie's first instinct, being a ghost whisperer, was to feel a bit insulted that her gift was viewed as retribution; her second instinct was to remember that in the beginning that's exactly how she'd felt. As if she'd been punished.

"What?" he asked, as if sensing she had something to say.

Put on the spot, she said exactly what came across her mind. "To channel Holiday here, it's a gift, not a punishment."

"It's a punishment to me. Frigging hell!" he muttered.

Kylie still didn't understand how it could happen. Because even Holiday had said that very few vampires had the gift of ghost-whispering. "Seriously, your parents are full-blooded vampires, right?"

He stared at her as if the question required some thought. Looking away, he gazed silently at the sky. After several long seconds he looked back at her. "Okay . . . let's forget about my issues with all this." He ran his palm over his face again as if trying to wipe away his confusion. "Why didn't you want Holiday knowing her sister's spirit was here?"

Kylie bit down on the edge of her bottom lip again, then released it when she found it sore. "I don't think Holiday knows. I wanted to figure out exactly—"

"Wait. You don't think Holiday knows what?" he asked, impatient.

"That her sister's dead."

His eyes widened. "She doesn't know? Shit!" He exhaled. "How did her sister die? How long ago?"

Even before she answered, Kylie suspected his reaction. He wasn't going to like this. "She was murdered. She and two other girls."

Discontent filled his gaze and his posture hardened. Two points for guessing his reaction, Kylie thought, and tried not to be intimidated by his fury.

"Murdered?" he bit out. "How freaking long have you known this, and why in God's name are you just now telling me?"

"I . . . I've been trying to figure it out. Hannah's just now able to tell me things. And I'm still trying to put it all together." A small part of her wondered if maybe he was right, and that she'd been wrong to try to deal with this herself. But she hadn't been doing this alone. She had Derek. Then again, perhaps she should have taken it to Burnett instead of Derek.

Her doubt started to rise and then eased. The calm that lingered from the falls swelled in her chest and somehow she knew she'd been right to follow her instinct. And wasn't that what Holiday told her to always do?

"Damn it. You should have come to me so I could help do the figuring."

Kylie held his gaze. "As if you were receptive to hearing about my ghost issues. Besides, I was following what I felt needed to be done."

Burnett's stance relaxed as if he'd seen reason in her words. "But if it's about Holiday, I'm always receptive."

Kylie saw it in his eyes again. His loyalty to Holiday. Because he loved her, Kylie realized. That realization led her to think about Derek and his willingness to help her with ghosts when no one else would.

Thinking of Derek led her heart back to Lucas. The trip to the falls had lessened her animosity toward him, but not completely. Sooner or later, the two of them needed to talk. She just didn't know how that talk would end. Or even how it would begin. Was she right to feel angry at him for keeping his distance when she knew why he did it—to prevent issues with his dad so he could get voted on the were Council? Shouldn't she be more accepting and understanding?

Burnett reached back and squeezed his neck as if to relieve his tension. "Holiday has to be told."

Kylie dug the toe of her right tennis shoe into the dirt and focused on the problem at hand instead of her Lucas issues. "I know. But I thought maybe if I knew exactly what it was Hannah wanted, then it would be easier."

"You think she wants something?"

Kylie nodded. "They always want something. That's why they haven't crossed over. That's why they come to us."

"Come to you," he said, and then added, "Do you have any idea what she could need?"

Kylie prepared herself for his reaction again. "I'm not completely sure. At first I thought it could be just to get her and the others from the makeshift grave. Maybe to find out who did this to her. But now . . . now I think she feels she has to protect Holiday from something or . . . someone."

His expression darkened, but this time his angst didn't focus on her. His eyes brightened with an instinctual need to protect Holiday.

"Before you ask, I don't know who or exactly what poses a danger to Holiday." Kylie suspected it had to do with a man named Blake, but she wasn't completely sure she should share that with Burnett right now. The last time she shared some personal information about Holiday with Burnett, Holiday had flipped. If Kylie discovered Blake posed a threat, then she'd tell Burnett everything. But she needed more information. Information that neither Holiday nor Hannah seemed willing to give.

He waved his hands out in front of him in frustration. "Then go find Hannah and tell her you need answers."

"It doesn't work that way. You don't go to the ghost. They come to you."

His frown tightened. "I don't like this," he said. "None of it."

On that point, Kylie could agree with him.

He stood there, staring out at the trees as if the answers could be plucked from the limbs. She got the feeling he wasn't accustomed to not being able to get information when he demanded it. If he really was a ghost whisperer, he had a lot to learn about patience. She pitied the poor ghost who showed up first.

Burnett finally looked back at Kylie. "Okay, tell me everything you know. Everything. We'll figure this out."

Even before Kylie started talking she had a distinct feeling that getting Burnett involved was going to be a game changer, and she wasn't sure if that was going to be a good thing . . . or a bad thing.

That afternoon, Kylie stood in front of the open fridge, staring. Listening to the hum of the appliance and savoring the cool air hitting her face while Miranda and Della sat at the table behind her.

Amazing how cool felt so much better when it wasn't coming from death. Not that she wouldn't like Hannah to drop in for a visit just now. She really needed answers. But if she'd learned anything, it was that you couldn't rush ghosts.

Kylie had somehow managed to convince Burnett to give Hannah a little more time before breaking Holiday's heart and telling her that her sister was dead. For some unknown reason, Kylie sensed that knowing exactly what Hannah needed was important. Not that Kylie didn't worry it might be her own desire to postpone hurting Holiday that encouraged this decision.

Burnett also agreed that going to the café to check and see if they could get any information about Cara M. would be a good thing. He was going to arrange for them to go out there Saturday morning with Derek. Burnett wanted Derek to go because when she'd told Burnett about what Derek had uncovered so far, Burnett was impressed at Derek's investigative skills.

Never mind that Lucas was going to have a shit fit when he found out Burnett had asked Derek to join them. But who knew, he might not even find out. With as little face time as she had with Lucas lately, he might never know. Or care.

She closed her eyes. He cared. He just cared more about other things right now.

Nipping at her lip, she remembered she still hadn't answered any of Lucas's texts today. She didn't know how to answer them because she didn't know how she felt anymore. One minute she was mad, the next she was contemplating if being angry with him was fair.

"What's wrong?" Miranda asked.

Kylie opened her eyes, focusing on what was in front of her and not what was going on inside her. "We're out of soda."

"Why don't you just zap us some?"

Kylie looked back at Miranda. "Zap as in . . . ?"

"Zap," Miranda said, and held up her pinky.

"Uh, why don't *you* just zap us some?" Kylie asked, and saw Della's eyes widen.

"Because you need to become a zapper," Miranda said matter-of-factly. "You need to embrace your inner Wiccan spirit."

Kylie had somehow avoided any zapping since the whole paper-weight to Burnett's crotch incident. And she'd like to continue avoiding it, but from the look in Miranda's eyes, she knew that wasn't going to be feasible. Well, not without hurting the witch's feelings.

And Kylie hated hurting anyone's feelings. Especially Miranda's.

"Okay . . . how do I do it?" She shut the fridge and inhaled. "Without endangering any of our lives."

Miranda squealed and wiggled her butt in her chair with excitement.

Della shot Kylie a look of approval as if to say she'd done the right thing. "I like the part about not endangering our lives," Della added with a smile.

"Take some very deep breaths," Miranda said. "Relax. Concentrate. Then envision a frosty six-pack and wiggle your pinky."

A frosty six-pack. Kylie inhaled. She held out her pinky, and right then Della chimed in. "We are talking a six-pack of soda and not a cold guy with good-looking abs, right?"

There was a strange kind of sizzle in the air. And suddenly appearing in front of the refrigerator was a shirtless, shivering guy with great abs. His dark hair hung over his brow and his blue eyes studied the three of them in complete bafflement.

"What the . . . !" he muttered.

Kylie gasped.

Miranda giggled.

Della snorted with laughter.

"Go away!" Kylie screamed, her face blood red as she wiggled her pinky at the hot guy. He was gone as quickly as he appeared. Kylie looked back at her two best friends, who were now in fits of laughter. She slapped her hand over her heart, which was racing.

"Don't ever talk me into doing that again!" she screeched.

"Wasn't that . . . oh, what's his name? Zac something?" Della asked. "The actor, I mean."

"Oh my Gawd, it was!" Miranda said.

"I always thought he looks a little like Steve, don't you think?" Della asked.

"Oh, crap!" Kylie buried her face in her hands. "I didn't hurt him, did I? It won't, like, give him cancer or anything?"

"No," Miranda answered, a giggle still sounding in her voice.

"Good," Della said, rubbing her hands together. "Then bring him back. I want to see if he really looks like Steve."

"Are you freaking nuts?" Kylie asked Della. Then she focused on Miranda. "Will he remember this? Will he think he lost his mind?"

"It happened so fast, he'll probably think he imagined it. Besides, it's not your fault." Miranda giggled again. "It's Della's." Miranda pointed at the accused.

"Oh, right. Blame the vampire!" Della bellowed.

Miranda rolled her eyes. "Della put the image in your thoughts and for some reason you just envisioned Zac." Miranda smiled again. "You are obviously attracted to him."

Kylie started to deny it, but couldn't.

"I'm still not taking the hit on this one," Della said.

Miranda looked at Della. "I guess I should have told you to be quiet. Sorry." She covered her mouth when she snickered again. Then she sat up straighter. "But . . . wow. I have to tell you I'm shocked. Only the most powerful witches can transport human beings. Even my mom can't do that."

"Don't you guys think he looks like Steve?" Della asked again.

Kylie dropped into the chair. "I don't care who he looks like. I'm not doing it again. I have no control and no knowledge. I'm sure to screw up."

"That's why you need practice. Besides, nothing bad happened," Miranda said.

"Seriously? I brought a half-naked movie star into our cabin!"

"And what part of that is bad?" Della asked. "I mean . . . I hate to say this, but for the first time I'm seeing that it might be cool to be a witch."

"Thank you!" Miranda sat up straighter.

"I mean, can you just zap yourself anything you want? A hot guy? A cup of O-negative blood? A new pair of jeans?" Della asked.

"Please, you can't do that," Miranda said. "It's totally against the rules."

"But . . ." Kylie stared at Miranda. "You just had me do it."

"Yeah, but you're a newbie. It doesn't count." Miranda looked back at Della. "That's not to say I can't do anything. If it's for a greater good, it'll be okay. If it's for one's own benefit, well, it has to be within reason. If I'm given a tuna sandwich and want turkey, that's not a big deal. It's swapping one meat for another. But if I even do it too much, I'd get called on it."

"By who?" Della asked. "The meat gods?"

Miranda frowned as if to say this was serious and Kylie couldn't agree more. "By the Wicca society."

"Wait," Kylie said. "You mean, they know what I do?"

Della cleared her throat as if in warning, but Kylie didn't understand the warning. She was too concerned about the Wicca society knowing her stupid mistakes to pay attention.

"Yeah," Miranda said. "They're like Santa Claus with their magic crystal balls. They know if you've been naughty or good."

"Great! So someone's looking into a magic ball right now and knows I conjured up a half-naked hot actor? " Kylie asked.

"You did what?" the deep male voice asked from behind Kylie.

Kylie froze, worried that Zac had returned. The fact that she wasn't even the least bit happy about it said a lot about her disposition, too. Then she ran the voice through her head again and recognized the dark tenor.

Crap. She was in trouble now.

Chapter Twenty

Kylie turned in her chair and faced a puzzled-looking Lucas. He wore a pair of black jeans and a solid light blue T-shirt. The shirt fit just tight enough that she knew his abs could compete with Zac's.

He continued to stare. "Did you just say—?"

"It was . . . a spell gone bad. I zapped a guy here for a couple of seconds." Normally, she'd be blushing, but her emotional dilemma with him chased away the embarrassment.

She stood. She felt antsy just sitting there. Her chest swelled with both joy at seeing him, and angst over her unresolved anger toward him. She wanted to kiss him, but she also wanted to let it all out and cry.

"Oh." He looked pointedly at Della and Miranda. Before he put the question into words, they got up—Miranda moved nonchalantly, Della's stance exuded a bad attitude.

"We'll be on the porch." The vamp's tone matched her body language.

"Thanks." While Kylie hadn't confided her most recent misgivings about Lucas to them, she knew they suspected. Just like she knew what went on in their lives. She watched as her two best friends left to give her privacy.

Kylie's gaze stayed fixed on Lucas and his deep blue eyes stayed on her until the door closed. She turned and faced the refrigerator and tried to decide how she felt . . . besides hurt. Just to give herself something to do, she opened the appliance.

"You want something to drink?" she asked, not that there was anything but pickle juice in an otherwise empty jar of pickles and a bottle of Della's blood.

"I texted you three times and e-mailed and you haven't responded." He sounded hurt.

Closing her eyes, she tried to push away the wiggle of guilt tightening her stomach. "I haven't checked my e-mail." She shut the fridge and moved over to the computer desk.

"What are you doing?" he asked.

"Checking my e-mail. You said you e-mailed me." It sounded stupid. Okay, it didn't just sound stupid, it was stupid, but she needed a few minutes to think.

Was she wrong to be angry?

Or right?

She dropped into the chair. With the computer on, it took one mouse click to land on her e-mail. One downward scan of her eyes to see Lucas's name.

The subject on all three of his e-mails was the same: *miss you.*

A knot formed in her throat.

"Are you mad at me for something?" he asked.

"Yes." Her gaze moved back to the screen and it felt as if her heart started swelling—big, then bigger—until it felt as if it was outgrowing her chest. The ache was real and made it hard to breathe.

She swallowed. "No."

"Is it yes or no? Are you mad or not?" He sounded hurt. Or angry. Maybe both.

She closed her eyes and while she didn't hear him, she sensed he'd moved closer. His scent, a wonderfully earthy smell, seemed to take up residence in her cabin.

She inhaled. "Maybe."

"Hmm." He did indeed sound closer. Too close. Right behind her close. Touchable close.

As tempting as it was to turn around, she didn't. She stared at the screen and held her breath.

"Is this what they mean by a woman having the prerogative to change her mind?" A slight sound of humor rang in his voice.

"It could be," she muttered.

"Is this about me not showing up last night? I left a note. You were asleep."

"It's not about that." Her gaze stayed fixed on the computer screen. She spotted three e-mails from her dad. Another emotionally hard thing she needed to deal with. Knowing her mom was dating, knowing that her stepdad and mom probably would never get back together, would make seeing him even harder.

She blinked.

"Then what's it about?" His hand pressed down softly on her shoulder. Warm sensations flowed from his palm. "Because right now, I'd really like to kiss you and I don't know if that's possible. If you really are mad at me, I mean."

Inhaling, her heart raced at the thought of him kissing her. Of feeling his chest against hers.

"It's about you avoiding me," she said. "You're pulling away."

His other hand breezed across her shoulder. "Just until my father gives his approval for me to join the Council. I know it's hard, and yes, being together is going to be even harder with Clara here, but . . . I need his approval. I don't think it will be much longer."

She blinked again, and that's when she saw it. Four . . . no, five e-mails all with the word *fog* in the subject line. Could it be . . . ?

"Oh, shit!" She saw another e-mail from the same address with a subject line that read *talk*.

"Oh, shit what?" he asked.

She opened her mouth to tell him, but shut it at the same time she shut off her e-mail. She hadn't told him her grandfather had been what chased his sister—hadn't told him because it didn't feel right. Telling him now felt even less right.

If she decided to meet her grandfather without Burnett, Lucas wouldn't approve. He'd be overprotective and insist on telling Burnett.

Kylie couldn't let Lucas tell Burnett, because Burnett would not want her to meet her grandfather without his being present. And it appeared as if her grandfather wasn't keen on meeting with Burnett.

She had to meet her grandfather—with or without Burnett. He had answers, and discovering those answers was her quest. How many times had Holiday told her that following your quest was about listening to your heart? And her heart said this was the right thing to do. Lucas would just have to understand.

And just like that, it hit her. Lucas's quest was to get on that Council. And to do that, he had to pretend in front of his pack and Clara that she wasn't that important to him. How could she be angry with him when . . . she had her own agenda that was equally important to her?

Which meant she had to be more understanding. If his quest meant that they couldn't sit together at meals or he had to pretend they weren't boyfriend and girlfriend, she would accept that. Just like she expected him to accept that she had to follow her own quest.

She stood and turned around and faced him. "I'm sorry. I was overreacting." She placed her hands on his chest.

He stared at her, appearing even more puzzled. "You're not mad?"

She offered him a smile that came from deep within. The thought that her grandfather hadn't given up on seeing her filled her chest with a light bubbly feeling. She cut her gaze toward the computer and then met Lucas's gaze. "It hurt to feel that I came second after everyone else, but—"

"You don't come second. When I get on the Council, I'll have the power to put a stop to all this crap. The younger werewolves are clamoring to have someone on the Council to voice their opinion. I'll get their support and the elders won't be able to tell anyone who they should see or share their lives with. They won't hold anyone responsible for the sins of their parents. Please give me a little time."

"I will. And I'm sorry I was a bitch."

"I never said you were a bitch." He pulled her a bit closer. So close that the warmth of his body sent a wave of pleasure through her.

"I know," Kylie said. "And I get it now." She met his gaze and moistened her lips with her tongue. "Didn't you say something about kissing me?"

His brow wrinkled, but with a smile. "I don't think I'll ever understand girls."

"Then stop trying." She lifted up on her tiptoes. She wanted to kiss Lucas senseless, and then she wanted to send him on his way so she could find out what her grandfather said in his e-mails. But the moment Lucas's lips found hers, when his warm chest pressed against her breasts and his hands slipped up under her shirt to fit against the naked curve of her waist, she decided that the e-mails could wait a little longer.

This . . . this was magic. The kind she could do without screwing up.

That night, Kylie lay in her bed with her clothes on, waiting to hear Miranda come in from her nightly outing with Perry. Their evenings were getting later and later. Not that Kylie could blame them. Pulling away from Lucas after their little make-out session had been hard—even with her grandfather's e-mail waiting for her.

Lucas had been humming with desire, and she'd been humming right along with him. The ability that male weres had to seduce their mate had bitten into her heart and soul. His touch had felt so good, she hadn't wanted to stop. It was getting harder not to give in. And yet . . . she did stop.

Maybe because of the e-mails.

Maybe because she didn't want the hint of any unresolved issues to be involved with her first time. And while she understood that Lucas was following his quest, deep inside, it still stung.

Then again, probably the biggest reason she hadn't given in was because Della and Miranda had been sitting outside on the porch. Yup, that was for certain the biggest reason she'd found the willpower to stop things from going any farther than they had.

The fact that she and Lucas had ended up lying on the sofa, kissing, while her two best friends were on the porch, had her blushing when she'd faced the two of them after Lucas had left. Making it worse was knowing Della could smell the pheromones they'd put out.

However, that blush and those pheromones were, hopefully, going to help make tonight's plan work. The plan Kylie had come up with as soon as she'd read her grandfather's e-mail requesting that she meet him—alone—at Fallen Cemetery.

Had her grandfather learned the truth? That until recently his wife, Kylie's grandmother, had been buried there in a mismarked grave?

Her e-mail back to him had been brief: *I'll do everything possible to be there at 1 AM.* The fact that she hadn't heard back from him bothered her very little. He'd asked. She'd answered. What more was to be said? But it hadn't stopped her from checking her inbox every fifteen minutes.

The biggest downside to this whole thing was the lie she'd have to tell her roommates. A lie that was only going to work if Della wasn't automatically tuned in to hear Kylie's heart beat fast at the white lie. If Kylie could state the untruth and Della automatically believed it, she might not even check Kylie's heartbeat. Or at least Kylie prayed it would work that way.

A few minutes later, Kylie heard Miranda and Perry on the porch. Kylie got out of bed. Quietly, she moved into the living room, waiting for Miranda to come inside. Kylie knew Della was probably already aware that she'd risen from bed.

The door opened. When Miranda saw her she gasped.

"It's just me," Kylie said.

"What are you doing up?"

Not chancing lying twice, she commenced with her plan. "Did you see him?" Kylie asked.

"See who?" Miranda studied her. "Are you having one of those weird vision things again?"

"No. Did you see Lucas? He's supposed to meet me and we're . . . going somewhere to be alone." Shooting to the window, she glanced out. "I see him," Kylie lied, and felt the guilt. "Gotta go."

Miranda grabbed her elbow. "Are you going to . . . ?"

Perhaps it was Kylie's imagination, but she could swear she heard Della getting out of bed.

"Tell Della for me. Tell her I want to be with Lucas. Tell her I said to please let us have this time." If Della was listening now with her sensitive hearing, she'd recognize that as the truth. Kylie did want to be with Lucas.

Knowing it was imperative she leave before Della arrived, Kylie skirted out into the darkness, leaving Miranda standing there with her mouth slightly agape.

The late August air held a hint of coolness as Kylie bolted off the porch and ran as fast as she could away from the cabin.

Please let this work. Please let me make it. She repeated the words like a litany. Her body tingled with the knowledge that she followed her heart.

With each footfall that took her farther away, her confidence built. Even hearing Burnett's warning of never entering the woods alone, she knew that route offered the quickest escape, and she took it. Moving between the trees, she accepted the risk. Mario, or someone on his side, could be waiting.

But it was a risk worth taking, she told herself, and ignored the sensation of being followed. Ignored the wiggle of guilt she felt for lying to her two best friends.

She had to lie. This was her quest. And the risk should belong to her, not one of her friends who felt compelled to join her. She wouldn't put anyone else in Mario's path.

Suddenly, the phone in her pocket dinged with an incoming text. She slowed down enough to check the message.

Derek.

"Damn," she muttered, her voice whispering in the night air.

No doubt Derek had sensed her emotions and was concerned. But if she told him, like Della or Miranda, he'd think he had to come with her. She pocketed her phone and then pushed herself to move faster.

As she dodged limbs and jumped over thorn bushes, she listened to the night noises—finding peace in knowing that the darkness hadn't fallen silent. If Della had followed, she would have been here by now. Kylie could only surmise that her plan had worked. Della had relented to Kylie's wish to be with Lucas.

Aware of how far she'd gone, she knew she drew near the fence where the Shadow Falls property ended. Her heart knotted with fear that this was where her plan would get upended. Burnett could come running.

However, she'd heard rumors that someone was constantly breaking the rules. Perry, who never liked being limited when he transformed himself into some other creature. Then, Lucas and his pack constantly being called to visit their elders, who didn't respect Shadow Falls's rules.

Maybe, just maybe, Burnett wouldn't guess that the person slipping out of the property was Kylie.

The fence became visible. It loomed in front of her, a good eight feet in height. Kylie's breath hitched. She pushed to move faster, praying she could leap over the metal barrier.

Her body felt weightless as she moved into the air, higher. Higher. Her feet cleared the fence and she came down on the other side, avoiding a bad landing—and serious injuries. She hit hard and rolled a good seven feet.

She picked herself up and brushed her hand over her elbow that had found earth before the rest of her. The pain dulled, coming in second to her sense of success. She was doing it. She was going to make it.

The stickiness of blood met her palm. The berry scent filled her nose. Who knew her own blood could smell this good? She continued moving, fast, then faster, putting distance between her and the fence.

The sounds of the night continued to sing around her. No vampires making the night go silent. She was alone.

She crossed the road and moved into the trees lining the road as she continued onward. If she estimated correctly, she was only a few miles from the cemetery.

She was finally going to meet her grandfather and learn the truth. The mystery of just what she was—of what being a chameleon meant—was about to be solved. A smile widened her mouth.

The sensation of victory filled her chest and gave her speed, agility, and courage.

Or it did until a male voice called out, "Where the hell do you think you're going?"

Blood throbbed in her ears and she didn't recognize the voice at first—except that she knew it wasn't Burnett. It didn't matter. She didn't care who it was, because no one was welcome right now. She had a mission and didn't want company. And that was exactly what she planned on telling the intruder, too.

She came to a sudden stop—or as sudden as she could when traveling at a manic, inhuman speed. Her knees buckled. She wrapped her arms around a tree, catching herself from a bad fall.

Still unsure of the identity of the intruder behind her, still clinging to the tree for dear life, another voice, a different one from the first, spoke up. "I was about to ask the same question."

Chapter Twenty-one

Disappointment shot through her limbs. She had two intruders instead of just one. She wanted to scream, but air locked in her lungs and not one sound came out. Angry, she swung around and confronted the owners of the two voices. She could be proud of one thing: she'd been right. There were no vampires in the woods.

Just a smart-mouthed shape-shifter, in bird form, and a very pissed-off werewolf.

She gulped down a mouthful of air. Still unable to catch her breath, she bent at the waist and with her hands on her knees she waited for her lungs to open up. When oxygen finally flowed to her brain, her thoughts came clearer.

And one thought stood out. She wasn't going to let them stop her.

Straightening, she met Perry's gaze with sheer determination. Then she shifted the same glare to Lucas. "I'm following my quest. Leave and let me do what I have to do."

"Have you lost your frigging mind?" Perry asked.

"What's going on, Kylie?" Lucas demanded.

Kylie stared at the were. "Just what I said. I'm following my quest.

I need for you to leave. It's important and I'm not asking you, I'm telling you. Leave me alone!"

She hoped she sounded more confident than she felt. Any minute now she waited for the night to go silent and Burnett to show up. For some reason, she felt capable of standing up to Lucas and Perry, but bucking authority never came easy for her. And Burnett was authority with a badass attitude.

Before she considered how it would sound, she asked, "Does Burnett know?"

Lucas ground his mouth shut and continued to stare at her with anger, and perhaps shock, at her behavior.

"How did you find me?" she asked the shape-shifter as tiny bubbles of electricity started forming around him.

A second later, Perry appeared in human form. "I was flying around after I left Miranda and saw you jump the property fence."

She glared back at Lucas. "And you?"

His eyes brightened with anger, his frown increased, but he started talking. "Burnett thought I was the one who'd set off the alarm. He called me, and I had a strong feeling that I needed to make sure everything was okay. Then I saw Big Bird here flying—"

"Big Bird?" Perry's voice deepened with frustration.

"Whatever," Lucas continued. "I saw him and thought I'd check and see what he was up to."

"You're checking on *me*?" Perry's eyes turned the same orange as Lucas's.

"Not like that." Lucas's posture became less defensive. "I thought you might have spotted someone breaking in." His gaze shot back to Kylie. "To hurt the very person who broke out." His scowl deepened; his focus and his frustration were now directed at Kylie. "But that's not important. What's important is why you're putting yourself at risk. You know better. So let's get back before Burnett figures it out."

That was exactly why Kylie had to stop yakking with them and get a move on. If Burnett discovered she was missing, there would be hell to pay.

She glanced at her watch. Five minutes till one. Time ran out. She didn't envision her grandfather as being someone who appreciated tardiness.

Remembering she wasn't powerless, she wiggled her right pinky against her ring finger. However, the idea of using it didn't sit well with her.

"Okay," she offered. "Short explanation. I have to meet someone. So we can either do this the easy way or the hard way."

"Meet who?" Lucas and Perry asked at the same time.

"My grandfather. He contacted me and—"

"How?" Lucas asked.

"E-mail," Kylie answered, unsure why she thought telling them the truth would work, but her other option didn't feel right—especially considering she really didn't know what she was doing when it came to casting spells. Just ask poor Zac.

"Don't be stupid," Perry said. "How do you know it was really from him?"

"I know," Kylie said with confidence, and pushed back the knowledge that Perry could be right. All this could be a trick. But every instinct she had said differently. If wrong, she might pay the price with her life. If right, she'd find the answers she'd been seeking since the first day she'd arrived at Shadow Falls.

Risky? Maybe. But a risk she was willing to take. "And here's the thing," Kylie continued. "You two can either agree to let me go, or—"

"No." Lucas's shoulders grew tighter. "You are not—"

She didn't wait any longer. She twitched her pinky and envisioned a big net falling from the sky, snaring the two of them together, and preventing them from following her.

She saw it rushing down from above and barely escaped being caught herself. "Sorry," she called out, and took off running. With every ounce of power she owned, she focused on getting away before they got loose.

Kylie ran. No, that wasn't right. Because she realized at some point she wasn't running, she was flying. If she hadn't been in such a hurry, she'd have taken the time to appreciate the new addition to her gifts. Ah, but no time. She needed to get far enough away that Perry and Lucas couldn't follow her.

Finally, she spotted the rusty cemetery gates jutting out from the earth like sharp weapons that could take a life. The night appeared to grow darker as she drew nearer. Her chest tightened as she remembered Perry's question. *How do you know it was really from him?*

She didn't. She'd come on blind faith. Was that enough?

Slowing down, her feet came back to the ground. She came to an abrupt stop a few feet from the old iron gates. She went to step forward but a sudden movement behind the gate stopped her. Her heart stopped, too. Her last breath felt trapped in her lungs as she took in the view.

Faces, dozens upon dozens of faces, peered at her through the creaky bars. Their lifeless gazes soulfully stared at her with eyes that begged her for help. If only she could help them all. If only one sweep of her hand or wiggle of her pinky could take care of whatever issue kept them chained to this life, when another awaited them.

Then another thought hit. Were any of these ghosts hell-bound spirits? Those who wanted to take her to hell with them in an attempt to soften their own sentence? Great! Why did she have to think about that lovely possibility now?

She forced herself to take a step closer. The idea that she was going to have to step through those gates and move past the hundred or more spirits ripped at her courage. She remembered how it felt last time when she'd come here and had been touched by so many ghosts—the pain was similar to a brain freeze, but one that happened to the entire body.

But it would be worth it if her grandfather waited inside because she'd get some answers. Definitely worth it. Besides, it wasn't as if she hadn't done this before; she'd come here twice. But not in the dark or the dead of night. Something about the blackness, with only the moon's silver glow making the spirits' gazes visible, made the place look so much more . . . haunted.

Which it was. As if to prove the fact, the cold from the spirits surrounded her and made her skin crawl. She looked up and saw a couple of spirits had moved outside the gate and were slowly easing toward her. Stiffening her spine, accepting she had to do it, she took another step closer, planning to just walk inside. Sort of like jumping into the deep end of a freezing pool and getting it over with. Yet as her foot shifted one more time, a voice, a close-to-her voice—too close—whispered in her ear. *"I wouldn't go in there."*

She yelped and jumped back six feet before she recognized the voice. Taking a breath to calm her nerves, she moved up beside Hannah. Then Kylie recalled what what the spirit had said. Did Hannah know something Kylie didn't? Was she wrong and it wasn't her grandfather waiting for her inside?

"Why shouldn't I go in?" Kylie asked, her nerves no longer calm.

Hannah leaned in and whispered again. *"There are ghosts in there."*

Kylie looked at her agape. "But—"

"I know I'm dead," Hannah blurted out, reading Kylie's thoughts. *"Just like my grave buddies. But seeing all of them"*—she motioned to the gate—*"it still scares the crap out of me."*

Kylie looked from the gate to her watch again; she had two minutes. She had to go in. But she needed to get Hannah to talk. "Look, someone's waiting on me, but I need to know. What is it that you need me to do?"

Hannah closed her eyes, but not before Kylie saw panic fill her gaze.

"Don't run off," Kylie said in a hurry when she felt the cold begin to ebb. "I need to know. It's why you're here. I know it's hard to talk about things, but sometimes we have to do things that scare us. Sometimes it helps. Sort of like me walking into the cemetery." She glanced back at the gate and the hundred dead faces peering back at her.

Hannah opened her eyes; the panic made her pupils large and black. *"He's close by."* Her voice weakened.

"Who's close? What did he do?" When Hannah didn't continue, Kylie took a guess. "Is it that Blake guy? The one who called Holiday when she was at the falls?"

Hannah looked down at her hands finger-locked in front of her. *"She loved him. She got everything she wanted. I just wanted to know what it would feel like to be that happy. I'd had too much to drink. He'd had too much to drink. It was wrong."*

Kylie started putting the pieces together, but she wasn't completely sure, so she asked, "Was Blake the man Holiday was supposed to marry?"

Hannah nodded, and when she looked up, tears and shame filled her eyes.

"Is he the one who killed you?" Kylie asked.

Hannah put her hand over her mouth as if the thought sickened her.

"Is he?" Kylie asked again.

When she moved her hands from her lips, they were trembling. *"I . . . I don't know if it was Blake."* Her eyes filled with terror and sadness at the same time. *"I guess it could have been. I don't remember how it happened."* She paused. *"I only recall . . . his aura."* Pain filled her eyes. *"Details I can't remember, I can't put a name on him, or a face, but the evilness of him as he took my life . . . that I can't forget. And I've felt it since. He sometimes comes back to where he buried us. I hear him walking on the floor above. The three of us cling to each other in death and pretend our souls are already gone."*

Hannah hugged herself as if the memory was too much. *"He disguises his aura most of the time. He has the power to appear normal. But when he's not pretending, he's evil and dark."*

"When he's pretending, is his aura the same as Blake's?" Kylie asked.

"I don't know. I'm not sure. I guess it could be. I never paid attention to that aura. It's the other that . . . haunts me." She paused as if in thought. *"There seems to be a small part of me that says I knew the man who did it."* She paused as if her thoughts went in another direction, and from her expression, it wasn't a good direction. *"He thinks killing brings him power—that's why he does it. And the day I was at Shadow Falls, I sensed he was close. I felt him and I knew. I knew I went to Shadow Falls because of him. He's not happy with just killing me. He wants Holiday."* Her words seemed to linger in the night air when she snapped her head back and looked up at the dark sky.

"What is it?" Kylie asked, fearing the killer was close again.

"I think it's that strange shape-shifter from the Shadow Falls camp. The blond kid with eyes that change colors all the time."

The fear Kylie had felt for Hannah and from a murdering evil being faded, and Kylie's own concern rose. If Perry had found her, Lucas wouldn't be far behind. And then probably Burnett. Hoping she'd be less visible, she moved closer to the gate. She looked again at the dead faces appearing as guards of the cemetery. She didn't know if they recognized her from before. She wasn't sure if they even knew she could see them yet. But one thing was clear: if she didn't go in now, she might miss her grandfather.

Kylie looked at Hannah still glancing up at the sky. "Did he see us?" Kylie reached for the gate to open it.

"*It's her. I told you it was her,*" one of the spirits behind the gate said. Then the spirits' arms started reaching through the bars to touch her. Kylie's vision filled with nothing but the arms coming out between the rusty bars of the gate. The cold shot through her skin and stung all the way to the bone. She bit down on her lip, fighting the pain and panic as she pushed open the gate.

"*He can't see me. I don't know if he saw you.*" Hannah's voice echoed from behind her. With the gate open, Kylie pulled her hand free. The ghosts scattered, but the moment she moved a few feet inside the cemetery, they surrounded her. The cold of their spirits crowding around her coated her lips with ice. The pain nearly brought her to her knees. She forced herself to move a few feet away; the reprieve was instant, even if she knew it wouldn't last.

She looked back at Hannah. Fear filled her gaze—a gaze that was just as dead as those from the cemetery, who were now growing closer.

"*I can't come in,*" Hannah said. "*One of them might be a death angel. If they want to send me to hell for my sins, they can. I deserve it, but not until I know Holiday is safe.*"

"I don't think they'll send you to . . ." Kylie stopped talking when Hannah started to disappear.

"*Save her for me, Kylie. Please save my sister!*" Hannah's words rang in the dark.

The cold from the spirits drew closer. "Please," Kylie said, her gaze moving from one ashen face to another. "Give me some space."

They scurried back a few feet. Kylie looked over her shoulder, hoping she might see someone who walked in this world. Her hopes were futile. Everywhere she looked, she saw only death.

But then the darkness cloaking the tombstone terrain limited her vision. Kylie knew from the few times she'd been here that the cemetery was immense. Would her grandfather know she was here? The thought that it might not be her grandfather waiting for her, that it hadn't been him sending the e-mails, stirred deep in her chest, but she pushed it back.

She took a few more steps, then, remembering Hannah's concern over Holiday, Kylie grabbed her phone from her pocket and dialed the one person she knew would help her.

"Are you okay?" Derek answered on the first ring.

"I don't have a lot of time, but I need you to do me a favor. Go check on Holiday. Stay there. Don't wake her up. Don't let her know you're watching her, but don't leave her until I get there."

"Shit! What's happening, Kylie?" Derek asked.

"I can't explain right now. Just please. Do it."

"Where are you?" he asked. "I know you aren't at your cabin."

She bit down on her lip so hard she tasted blood. "Please." The word came out with desperation.

He finally answered. "Holiday is fine. Burnett's watching her place."

"Why? How do you know? Did something happen?"

"No, I felt you were in trouble and I was walking to check on you when I came across Burnett standing outside Holiday's cabin. He said because of what we knew about Hannah and the other girls, he wasn't taking any chances."

"Good." She wondered if that was why Burnett had called Lucas and not left to check the gate when the alarm went off.

"I can feel you're scared out of your wits, Kylie. Tell me—"

"I have to go." She cut the phone off. Then she glanced at the crowd of spirits, shifting from foot to foot, reminding her of hungry zombies waiting for the right moment to move in and feed. Pushing that fear-inducing, insane thought away, she remembered they were just people. Lost souls robbed of life, chained to this world by some unfortunate circumstance.

Looking around again, she asked, "Is someone else here?"

"I'm here," one spirit said.

"I'm here." A barrage of the same words spoken by each of the dead filled Kylie's ears like thunder. They all wanted to be counted. To be acknowledged.

Emotion filled Kylie's chest. "Is there anyone alive here, besides me?"

"No one else is here who can see us," one of the spirits spoke up, sounding desperate.

"But someone else is here?" she asked. Again she wondered why her grandfather had chosen the cemetery as a meeting place.

"In the back of the property," the spirit of a young girl answered, and she pointed toward the darkest area in the cemetery. *"I saw them under the oak trees, hiding in the shadows."*

"Thanks," she said, glancing up one more time, hoping she didn't spot a pissed-off shape-shifter circling in the dark sky. The clouds must have blocked out the moon, because only a few stars stared back at her from the heavens. She started moving. With each step she prayed that in the deepest, darkest part of the graveyard under the trees, she'd find her grandfather. And with him she'd find her answers.

Chapter Twenty-two

The rear of the cemetery stood eerily quiet. Even more statues stood guard over the graves. Most were covered in dead vines. Some were dilapidated, others decapitated by vandals or the passage of time, their heads resting on the ground. Still, they all seemed to watch her as her feet crunched upon the gravel path. Suddenly feeling alone, she looked back and realized that the chill of the dead had subsided. She was truly alone.

The spirits hadn't followed. Why? Fear knotted in her throat. Did they know something she didn't? Even as panic built inside her chest, she kept walking, praying that coming here had been the right thing.

She saw the trees ahead of her; beneath the alcove of gnarled limbs hung shadows—black shadows that could hide anything, or anyone.

Moving closer, she could hear herself breathe, and in the distance a few birds called out as if in warning. She stopped a few feet from the trees. Their heavy limbs seemed to be reaching out for the cracked tombstones nearby.

"Hello?" Her voice seemed to be swallowed by the night.

"You came," answered a voice, deep and serious.

Breath held, she saw a figure move out of the shadows. Malcolm Summers, her grandfather. He looked younger than he'd appeared at her camp; obviously he'd dressed to play the part of Mr. Brighten. She recalled Della telling her that supernaturals didn't age as quickly as humans.

His gaze met hers, and even in the darkness his light blue eyes stood out. Kylie realized they were her exact color. She studied his face and saw the features of her dad, features that she, too, exhibited.

She suddenly felt insecure, unsure how to behave around him. Her chest ached. Should she hug him, not hug him?

"I'm sorry," Kylie blurted out.

"For what?" her grandfather asked.

"For . . . not being able to talk to you that day in the forest."

"It wasn't your fault," someone else said. Kylie's great-aunt eased out of the shadows and stood beside Malcolm. The woman smiled. Before Kylie realized it, she'd been caught in an embrace. The strength and warmth in her aunt's touch surprised Kylie—the woman felt hot.

When the hug ended, Kylie realized that, like her grandfather, the fragileness her aunt had displayed on the the day she'd come to Shadow Falls had disappeared. Kylie did a quick calculation in her head. The woman had to be in her seventies or eighties, but she didn't look older than fifty.

Chameleons must have a long life expectancy. She tucked that info away for future contemplation.

"Look at you," her aunt said. "So beautiful." She glanced back at her grandfather. "What's wrong with you, Malcolm? Give your granddaughter a hug."

He moved in hesitantly. "I'm not much of a hugger, but I guess the moment merits it." He embraced her. And like her aunt, he felt hot to the touch. The embrace was short, but sweet, and reflective of the ones she'd savored from Daniel, and even her stepfather before their relationship had gone bad.

"You're good at it," Kylie said.

"What?" he asked.

"Hugging." Tears stung her eyes when she saw emotion in his expression.

A smile welled up inside her. "You look like my father."

"I noticed that, too, in the pictures."

"I have so many questions," Kylie said.

"I'm sure you do."

"We're chameleons, right?" She held her breath, waiting for him to confirm what her father had told her. Or was Holiday right, that chameleon meant something different? Would Kylie be accepting her role as a witch after tonight?

The look on her grandfather's face shifted from tenderness to concern. "Where did you learn this?"

"My father," Kylie said. Doubt filled her. Had her father been wrong? "He said—"

Malcolm stilled. "But he's dead."

"She's a ghost whisperer." Her aunt clutched the man's arm in excitement. "I told you I sensed a spirit present when we were at the camp." Her gaze shifted to Kylie. "Your great-grandmother had that gift. She would be so proud."

"So it's true? We're chameleons?" Kylie asked again.

"Yes," they said at the same time.

Kylie's chest swelled with victory. She finally knew. Knew for certain. But no sooner had the feeling hit than questions started forming. Deep down, she sensed her real victory would come when they answered those questions.

She stood trying to assess everything they'd said so she could learn more. Her great-grandmother had been a ghost whisperer, but the two of them weren't. So one chameleon didn't have the same gifts as another one. How did that work?

"My father, he was a ghost whisperer as well," Kylie said, realizing she hadn't checked out their patterns. She tightened her brows. Surprise filled her when she saw they were both humans. Then again, she'd also worn the human pattern not too long ago. Exactly what did being a chameleon mean?

"So you've seen him?" Sadness rang in her grandfather's tone.

"And my grandmother." She looked at her grandfather's forehead again. "Can I ask you—?"

"Heidi?" He said the name with such love that Kylie's chest tightened.

"Yes. Actually, she was the one to tell my father that we were chameleons. But no one at Shadow Falls knows what it is."

Her aunt and grandfather gazed at each other. Her aunt nodded. "Tell her."

"I will," he said. "But you must come with us."

Kylie hesitated. "Why can't we talk here?"

"Not just to talk." He rested his hand on her shoulder. The warmth from his touch was familiar. And Kylie recognized it to be similar to Holiday's and Derek's touches. Did that mean . . . Her grandfather continued. "You must come and live with your own kind."

"Live?" *Live? Leave Shadow Falls?* Kylie shook her head. "I can't. I'm going to Shadow Falls boarding school."

"You don't understand the danger you are in, child," he said.

"From . . . Mario?" Kylie asked.

His brow wrinkled. "Is Mario part of the FRU?"

"No." Kylie hesitated to get into a conversation about the FRU. "He's part of a rogue organization."

"The organization you need to fear is the FRU. They are affiliated with your camp, but they are not what they seem. I have reasons to believe they are responsible for your grandmother's death."

Unwilling to lie, Kylie nodded. "I know."

His expression hardened. "You know what?" When she didn't immediately answer, he continued, "Did she tell you something about it?" His tone matched his expression—serious, demanding.

Unsure if confiding in him was best, but sensing it would be wrong to keep it from him, she nodded. "She was paralyzed from the operation. The one they did on both of you. They killed her."

His blue eyes filled with rage and his hands tightened into fists. "Murdering bastards! Only over my dead body will you return to that school!"

Kylie tried not to react to his threat. But yes, she saw it as a threat. She inhaled a breath to calm herself. "I understand how you feel. I was outraged myself. But Burnett assures me—"

"Burnett works for them!" her grandfather roared, and even the trees seemed to cringe at his fury.

Kylie's aunt moved in and rested her hand on his arm. Kylie recalled how the woman's touch had been so warm the day they'd shown up, pretending to be the Brightens. Was the woman fae? Part fae, perhaps?

"Yes," Kylie said. "Burnett works for the FRU, but he assures me that the people who did that are no longer with the organization. And—"

"And you trust them knowing what you know? Trust him, knowing who he answers to?"

"I don't trust the FRU, but I trust Burnett," Kylie said. "He's on our side. And even more, I trust Holiday."

"You are naïve and young. You don't know what's best for you."

She tried not to take offense. "Young yes, but not so naïve," Kylie said. "I'm following my heart."

"Your heart will mislead you," he said. "Mine did. I trusted them. I was blinded to what they really were. Heidi knew . . . or she suspected, but I didn't listen to her."

"I'm sorry," Kylie said, "but I can't—"

"You can," he demanded.

"No, Malcolm! The child must make up her own mind." Her

aunt spoke to Kylie's grandfather, but looked at Kylie. The woman didn't look angry, but disappointment gripped her expression. Kylie's chest tightened at the thought of hurting these people, but giving in wasn't an option.

Her grandfather swung around and stared back at the tree. His sorrow, his anger, his loss filled the darkness like a living, breathing thing. Kylie went to him. Even frightened, she needed to offer comfort.

"The last thing I want to do is to hurt you. You have been hurt too much. I'm sorry that I can't do what you want, but I have to follow the path I believe is right." Some slight movement in the sky caught the corner of Kylie's vision; she didn't look up, but she suspected that speck answered to the name of Perry. He'd obviously found her. Her time was running out.

"And what if you are wrong and I'm forced to face another death in my own family? One whom I didn't even get to know?"

"I don't think that'll happen," Kylie pleaded.

He stared at the ground as if in defeat.

Feeling certain her time ran short, Kylie continued. "I still have so many questions. Please help me understand what I am."

He looked up. The fury faded from his eyes. "It is impossible to teach you what you want to know in a few minutes, hours, or even weeks. It could take years."

"Then I will be coming to you for years with my questions," she said. "But please, answer me this. What does it mean that I'm a chameleon?"

Her aunt came forward. "Like the chameleon lizard, we can change how we appear to the world. And for our own protection, we have had to hide ourselves to avoid persecution."

"Hide from the FRU?" Kylie asked.

"Sadly, from everyone," her aunt said. "The few who did not hide were viewed as outcasts, freaks, and not belonging to any one kind. At first they thought we had brain tumors and then they just assumed we were insane."

Kylie couldn't deny that she related. Though like most prejudices, it had probably been worse in earlier years. While sometimes she felt like a freak, for the most part, she was accepted at Shadow Falls.

"The FRU studied us like lab rats," her grandfather added. "The elders and Councils of all the species viewed us as mutants. Some were forced to work as slaves for other supernaturals."

The truth stung, but she needed to know it, know all of it. "But what are we? A new species?"

"Not really," her aunt answered. "Normally when supernaturals produce offspring, the dominant DNA is passed on. The child will generally have weaker powers than those who were born from parents of the same species. Chameleons maintain the DNA of both parents and those of their forefathers. Chameleons carry a blend from all species."

Her grandfather met her eyes. "My father was vampire and were. My mother fae, witch, and shape-shifter."

"Wait," Kylie said. "Are you saying that I have the gifts of all species?"

"When you wear that pattern you do. Except . . ." His expression showed concern. "If the rule of protector is the same with a chameleon as the others, then you wouldn't be able to use any of these powers to protect yourself."

She shook her head, trying to soak it all in. "But your pattern shows human," Kylie said.

"It is safer to pretend to be one of them," her aunt answered.

"But I'm half-human," Kylie said. "So how could I be that special blend?"

"At first, it didn't make sense," her aunt said. "But when we studied your mother's family history, we found that she came from—"

"An American Indian tribe," Kylie finished for her. And suddenly a thought hit. "Does that mean that my mother's supernatural?"

"Not supernatural, just gifted," her aunt said.

"Like how?" Kylie asked.

"She may be psychic. Or an empath," her grandfather said. "It is believed that those from this tribe can distinguish supernaturals from humans—sometimes they aren't even aware of it, but are simply drawn to them. There are more gifted humans married to supernaturals than regular humans, even though they are much less in the world population."

He tightened his brows and stared at Kylie's pattern. "Your brain has developed quickly. Most chameleons aren't able to bring forth one pattern and utilize those powers until they are in their early twenties."

"I may be developed, but I'm clueless. I don't know how to do it—how to change my pattern or how to control it."

"Which is why you must come with us." He frowned.

"I can't, but I still need to understand." She looked up and this time she knew it was Perry. "A while back, I showed a human pattern and then I'm sending paperweights around a room and . . . Well, it's not good. But maybe I developed early because I'm a protector. Or they think I am. The truth is they don't know what to think of me."

Her aunt smiled. "We heard rumors that you were a protector. That is a huge honor."

"I guess." Kylie wasn't sure how any of this was going to work out.

Her grandfather stared at her forehead again. "If you aren't in control of it, then you must be forming patterns instinctually.

Normally, it's a learned talent that can take years to master. I would assume you needed the power of speed and intuitively you initiated the change."

"Speed?" Kylie asked, confused. "It wasn't about speed. My friend kept messing up her spell and—"

"Spell?" he asked.

"I'm a witch right now." Kylie said the obvious.

"Not anymore you're not," he said.

Chapter Twenty-three

"You're vampire," her grandfather said.

Kylie's first impulse was denial. She couldn't be vampire. But why would he lie? She touched her arm to check for the lack of heat. She didn't feel cold, but if her core temperature had changed, she wouldn't feel it. Then she remembered how hot the two of them had felt.

Then came another realization. She'd literally flown to the cemetery after casting a net onto Perry and Lucas.

Lucas!

Her next breath shuddered as it went into her lungs. What would Lucas say about her new pattern? He hadn't been exactly pleased when he thought she was a witch. If he thought she were a vampire . . .

"Is something wrong, dear?" her aunt asked.

Kylie stood frozen, trying to come to terms with being vampire. Trying to imagine, or rather, trying not to imagine how Lucas would react. Then she wondered if she'd have to start drinking blood.

At just that thought, her mouth started watering. The tangy, ripe, sweet flavor was tattooed in her memory.

"Dear?" her aunt asked again. "Maybe you should sit down. You look pale."

"Am I?" Was that another sign of vampirism? Instantly, she ran her tongue across her teeth and nearly cut her tongue on her sharp canines. Oh, crap! She was vampire!

Even as the fear of change tumbled around inside her like tennis shoes in a dryer, she remembered how cool it had been to fly through the forest. She supposed that kind of power could be addictive. But what good was a power if you couldn't control it? It would be like her sensitive hearing—neat to have, but if you couldn't call upon it when you needed it, it was virtually useless.

She didn't want to be useless.

"How do I control this?" Kylie asked. "Explain it to me."

Her grandfather sighed. "It's not that easy. You have to train your mind. It isn't something I can tell you how to do; it's something that must be learned over time. It could take years. And until then, you could be a danger even to yourself."

"I will be okay at Shadow Falls."

A frown brightened his eyes. He lifted his head into the air as if to catch a scent. He made a sound, a low growl. The growl and even the way he sniffed at the air reminded her of Lucas.

"Someone came with you." He sounded disappointed in her.

"They tried to follow me. I lost them, but it's possible they've found me now."

His expression grew concerned. "Come with us. We'll help you understand everything. You need to learn who and what you are, Kylie. You can't do this alone."

She slowly shook her head. "I can't come with you."

"But you are one of us. We share the same blood. A chameleon alone will not survive. Look at your father. His death was so unnecessary. Do you think your father would not want you to come and know who you are?"

She inhaled. "I think my father would tell me to follow my heart. And right now, my heart says that Shadow Falls is the right place for me."

His frown deepened and he looked at her aunt. "We must go. Someone is coming." He turned to Kylie. "Do not speak of being a chameleon. Let them think what they may. The less we are talked about, the less we are persecuted."

"Wait," Kylie said. "How can I get in touch with you? I still have so many questions."

"I'll contact you," her great-aunt said, and joined hands with Malcolm.

"How?" Kylie asked. "How will you—?"

Her aunt never answered. It was like Perry had said the day he'd followed them. They just went *poof.*

Kylie stood there, in both frustration and in awe. How would her aunt contact her? How had they done the *poof* thing? Could she do that? She heard fast footfalls from behind, someone running toward her. She swung around, expecting to see Burnett. But it was even worse.

Lucas slowed down. He exhibited a tightness to his gait, a sense of anger, and an even greater sense of unease.

When he got closer she noticed his eyes shined bright orange. Of course he would be furious at her for tossing a net over him and Perry. She looked behind him, expecting to see Burnett appear. Expecting to get a tongue-lashing from the vamp.

Then she remembered she was also a vampire. She swung away from Lucas, afraid of what he might say, afraid to see distaste for her in his gaze.

"That was foolish," he ground out.

She knew what he meant. "Not so foolish." She kept her gaze away. "It was my grandfather."

"And?" he asked.

"And I got some of the answers I needed." She started walking. He moved beside her.

"Do you distrust me so much that you couldn't tell me you were coming here?" he asked.

She shrugged but didn't meet his gaze. "I trust that you'd have tried to stop me. And you proved me right."

"You could have reasoned with me, instead of casting a stupid net." His words came out with a light growl.

"I didn't have time to reason."

"Which is why you should have told me earlier. The idea that you didn't trust me infuriates me."

Like he didn't trust her. "I know exactly how you feel," she said, letting him figure out what she meant.

"It's different," he answered, his figuring-things-out ability right on target.

"No, it isn't." A knot rose in her throat. She still refused to look at him, afraid he'd check her pattern and be repulsed by what he found. And God help her, but she didn't think she could deal with that.

"You told me you understood. You said you overreacted yesterday when you were mad, or not mad, or maybe a little mad. Aw, hell, you confuse me!"

"I did tell you that," she admitted. "And I do understand, or I'm trying to, but when you can't seem to offer me the same courtesy, I'm reconsidering my understanding."

"So we're back to you being a woman and having the right to change your mind," he bit out.

"Yeah!" Tears stung her eyes and she moved faster.

They passed a couple of dilapidated statues with missing arms. She saw Lucas glance at them. How much had it cost him to come into the cemetery? He, like ninety percent of all supernaturals, hated cemeteries. Was that why her grandfather had asked to meet her here? He knew very few supernaturals would enter this place.

But Lucas had. He cared about her more than he cared about his fear of spirits. Would he have entered if he knew that she was vampire? Would he still care about her if she turned to him right now and let him see her pattern?

The question, or rather the fear of his answer, drove her to move faster. She wanted to be alone. Alone to contemplate every word her grandfather had said.

Alone to revel in the knowledge that she'd finally gotten the truth.

Alone to figure out what it all meant.

She was a chameleon. However, for now, she was vampire. But for how long? How long before she could control this crazy thing that was happening to her?

The spirits waited for her at the front gate. Lucas grew tenser, as if he sensed them. Slowing down only long enough to push open the creaky gate, she offered the dead reaching out for her one promise: *I'll be back.*

As soon as the icy wind blew the gate closed behind her, she picked up her pace, running. One foot hit the earth and then the other. She moved with purpose. She wanted to be home. She wanted to be at Shadow Falls.

You are one of us. We share the same blood. A chameleon alone will not survive. She heard her grandfather's warning ring in her ears, but she refused to believe it. The mere thought of leaving Shadow Falls sent a wave of pain shooting across her heart. She couldn't leave.

Yet even as she ran to the one place in her life that felt right, the place she felt the safest, she knew that the answers she sought were not at Shadow Falls, but with her grandfather.

The knowledge caused a sharp pain in the very center of her

heart. Tears welled up in her eyes and slipped from her lashes. She felt them hot against her cold vampire skin. Air shuddered in her chest from the emotion when she realized that before she could retreat to her cabin, she'd probably have to face Burnett's fury.

"Slow down," Lucas demanded.

She ran faster. Burnett's wrath was nothing compared to facing Lucas. His prejudice against vampires right now would hurt more than she could stand.

The gate to Shadow Falls loomed just ahead. Her heart thumped in her chest. She prayed Burnett's tongue-lashing wouldn't take too long. While her body didn't feel the least bit tired, her heart did.

"Damn it, Kylie," Lucas muttered again. Everything from his breathless tone to the stomp of his feet hitting the earth told her he was pushing himself to his limits.

"I said stop!" He sounded closer this time.

Just when she was about to take the leap over the fence, she felt him grab her around her waist. They went down. Hard. He wrapped his arms around her to protect her from the fall and they rolled several times.

"What's wrong with you?" he asked.

She ended up on top of him, his hot body reminding her that she was vampire. He stared up at her face. She tried to get up.

He caught her.

"What's the matter?" he asked again.

He rolled her over and landed on top of her. Afraid he'd see her brain pattern, she turned her head and stared at the underbrush. Tears stung her eyes again.

"Hey." His voice came out more tender this time. He'd obviously noticed her tears. "Look at me."

She didn't. She couldn't. "I just want to get this over with," she snapped.

"Get what over with?" His chest moved up and down on top of her as he breathed.

"Facing Burnett."

"He doesn't know, but if you leap over the fence right now, he will."

She looked back him. "He doesn't know?"

"No. I got out without being detected. And if you'll listen to me, I think I can get you in without him knowing, too. Or you can jump over the fence and go head-on with his wrath."

Realizing she was facing Lucas again, she turned her head. The underbrush against her back felt like soft moss, but the emotion in her chest was scratchy.

"Is that what this is all about? Damn it, Kylie. I already know."

She looked back at him, unsure what he meant. "Know what?"

He scowled. "That you're vampire. I . . . smelled you when I first walked into the cemetery."

His insult hit hard. Emotion had her lips trembling. "If I smelled that bad, then why did you bother to come in?"

His expression darkened. "I came in because I thought you were in danger." He exhaled loudly. "I'm not going to lie. I don't like it, and it's going to complicate things with my pack even more, but . . ." He looked into her eyes. "But what's important to me isn't what's up here." He touched her forehead. "It's what's in here." He rested his hand on her chest, on the upper swell of her right breast.

She felt her heart race. His touch hadn't been meant to be intimate, but it felt that way.

"You mesmerized me from the moment I first saw you when we were kids. I didn't know what you were, and yes, I hoped you were werewolf, but it didn't matter. You ensnared me."

The dampness of her tears spilled out on her cheeks. Suddenly, the soft verdant scent filled her nose. She knew it was both Lucas's natural scent and that of the woods.

"I'm still ensnared." He wiped a tear from her cheek. "I don't care if you're part witch and part vampire."

"I'm not just that," she said.

He looked a bit confused. "Okay. Then what are you?"

She smiled through her tears. "I'm a chameleon. Which means I have a little of everything in me." She recalled what her grandfather had told her about not telling anyone. But Lucas wasn't just anyone.

"Even werewolf?" he asked.

She nodded. "I just don't yet know how to control the shifts from one thing to another." She sighed. "Does that make me even more of a freak?"

"It makes you freaking amazing," he said. "Even when you're a vampire." He leaned down and pressed his lips against hers. The kiss tasted of innocence. And odd as it was, she suddenly remembered him kissing her like this before, but way before. Like before she'd ever come to Shadow Falls. She touched his cheek, and when he pulled back, she asked, "Did you ever . . . climb into my window when you lived beside me?"

He looked guilty, but not much. "Just once. I swear, you left the window open. And I didn't . . . I just—"

"Kissed me?" she asked. The idea didn't make her angry; it made her feel cherished.

"You were . . . my first kiss," he said.

She grinned, and then his mouth lowered to hers again. She barely felt the warmth from his lips when he pulled back. "But I'm still pissed at you for throwing that net on me." He exhaled. "Not that I can stay mad at you."

He kissed her again. Only this kiss wasn't so innocent. Not that she complained. He tasted like passion, like raw, sweet passion. His weight came against her in all the right places and she felt differences in what made him male and her female. His vibration, his humming seduction, entered her every place his hard body now touched hers.

She met his kiss with desperation, wanting to feel it, wanting to savor how he made her feel. His hand resting at her waist, warm against her naked skin, slipped farther under her shirt, and his palm cupped her breast. She moaned with the sweetness of his touch and ached for more.

His kiss moved from her lips to her neck. The feel of his warm kisses made her feel liquid inside. Need, want, desire, she felt it all.

When his hand moved to her back to unhook her bra, she rose up to make it easier. When his hand came back around to her bare breast, she trembled with the pleasure.

He slipped the tank top over her head, discarding the bra at the same time, and his eyes shifted downward to what he'd uncovered. She'd thought she'd feel embarrassed. But it wasn't embarrassment stirring inside her. She felt . . .

"You're so beautiful," he said hoarsely.

That was it. That's how he made her feel. Beautiful. Cherished.

He inhaled sharply. "We probably shouldn't—"

She pressed a finger to his lips. "I want this." She moved her hand behind his neck, threaded her fingers in his thick black hair, and brought his mouth back to hers. And in seconds, they were both lost in each other.

Chapter Twenty-four

The kiss went from hot to smoldering in a vampire's heartbeat. She wasn't even aware that he'd removed his shirt until she felt the wonder of his bare chest against her breasts. She shivered with pleasure. His kisses moved down to her neck and then lower. The sensation had her arching her back and saying his name.

And then his phone rang.

His growl, deep and low, came against her bare shoulder. He raised his head. His eyes were bright, the blue irises hot with desire. "I hate . . . *hate* modern technology."

She grinned.

He rolled over to his back and reached into his pocket for his phone. As he studied the little screen, a frown chased away the passion from his expression.

"It's Burnett." He closed his eyes, then opened them. "I should . . . take it." He looked at her with an apology in his eyes.

"I know," she said, and then, suddenly aware of her lack of clothes, she crossed her arms.

His gaze lowered briefly to her covered chest. He reached for her bra and shirt beside him and handed them to her.

She clutched them to her front to cover herself. Their gazes met again. There was a sense of rightness at stopping things before they went any further. And while she accepted that letting it go this far had been risky, she knew she'd savor the memory.

"I don't regret it," she said.

"Good." He looked so darn sexy without a shirt, but wearing a kiss-me grin. "Because I don't, either."

"Thank you," she said.

"For what?" He frowned at the ringing phone.

"For going into the cemetery even when . . . you hate spirits." *For not hating me because I'm vampire.*

A seriousness filled his eyes. "I'd go to hell to keep you safe, Kylie Galen."

She believed him, too.

He answered Burnett's call.

Kylie spent the rest of the night mostly tossing and turning, unable to sleep. The call from Burnett had just been to check if Lucas had found anything suspicious when he'd looked around after the alarm had gone off. Then Lucas and Kylie jumped over the gate holding on to each other so it would appear only one person had entered. How he'd figured it out, Kylie didn't know and hadn't asked. However, the idea that Lucas had lied, and that Perry might also have to lie for her, didn't sit well with her.

Fretting, she stared at the ceiling while mentally juggling everything she'd learned. She was a chameleon. A rare type of supernatural. But at the moment she was a vampire. And that explained why, in spite of how hard she'd tried to dreamscape to Lucas, she'd failed. Vampires couldn't dreamscape. Rolling over again, she thought about everyone seeing her new pattern.

Her great-aunt's words flowed through her head. *The few who did not hide were viewed as outcasts, freaks, and not belonging to any one kind.*

She could already imagine the campers whispering behind her back again. *Look at Kylie. You'll never guess what she is now.*

Not that whispering was going to do them any good. Her sensitive hearing was in tip-top shape. She'd not only heard Miranda and Della each time they'd rolled over in their beds, but she heard some baby birds crying for their mama to hurry up and chew up the worms and regurgitate them back into their mouths. Regurgitating worms was not a pretty sound, either.

Her mind did another U-turn and she remembered her and Lucas's time together. She grabbed her extra pillow and hugged it. A smile worked its way to her lips. Not just because of how sinfully good things had been, but because . . . because now she believed he cared for her. And accepted her. That was huge. It changed things. She just didn't know how yet.

Recalling his touches, she felt her face grow warm. Probably not really warm, considering her core body temperature was extra low, vampire low, but she'd bet her cheeks were red.

Her brain did another veering off the subject and landed on words her grandfather had said. *You are one of us. We share the same blood.*

Her need to get to know her grandfather, to learn everything about her heritage, sat heavy on her heart. But to leave Shadow Falls . . . ?

That wasn't an option. Even with some of the campers not completely accepting her, she belonged here.

As the night continued, she tried to decide what, if anything, she was going to tell Holiday and Burnett, and even Della and Miranda and Derek . . . She couldn't lie to them all. Could she?

A chameleon alone will not survive. His warning stirred in her already heavy chest.

Pulling the pillow tighter, she sat up. She wasn't alone. She had Holiday and Burnett, and everyone here in her circle. And she'd just have to play it by ear on what, if anything, she'd tell the people close to her.

The sound of her stomach rumbling with hunger filled the silent room. She got up and went into the kitchen. Opening the fridge, she reached for the orange juice, but her hand stilled when she saw Della's blood.

Della would kill her, but . . .

"Where's my blood?" Della's voice vibrated through the entire cabin.

Kylie cringed, stepped out of the shower, and debated between the red or the white towel. She chose the white, for purity. If Della killed her, she'd at least be wearing white.

"Did you spill it again?" Della bellowed, no doubt screaming at Miranda.

"I didn't do anything with your blood," came Miranda's offended reply. "I wouldn't touch it with a ten-foot pole."

Kylie tightened the towel around herself.

"Fess up, witch!" Della snapped.

"I told the truth," Miranda shot back. "Clean the stinky vamp wax out of your ears and listen to my heartbeat."

Okay, now their insults were getting to the ugly stage.

Hurrying, Kylie stepped out of the misty warm bathroom right into the middle of the warpath.

"My ears aren't dirty," Della said, snarling. "I'm not the one letting some shape-shifter suck on my earlobe."

"That's enough." Kylie held up her hands

"I'm never telling you anything else." Miranda sounded so hurt.

"Thank Gawd!" Della spewed. "You think I want to hear about you having your earlobes sucked?"

"Bitch!" Miranda seethed.

"Stop!" Kylie yelled.

"I never said he sucked them," Miranda spit out. "I said he nib-bled on them." She started walking toward Della, her pinky held out like a weapon.

Della bared her canines and started forward. "Same thing. Equally gross!"

"Cut it out!" Kylie shot between her two best friends.

"She poured out my blood!" Della accused.

"Did not!" Miranda mouthed back.

"She's telling the truth." Kylie looked at Della. "I . . . I did it."

"You poured out my blood?" Della asked.

"No. I . . . drank it. And I'm sorry." Kylie held out her wrist, exposing her vein. "Here, have some of mine."

Della stared at her, her brows creased, and then her mouth dropped open. "Holy shit! You're a vampire!"

"She's a witch," Miranda said proudly, standing at Kylie's back.

"Not anymore," Della said. "Use your eyes, Miss Smarty Pants, and see for yourself. Or did Perry lick them, too?"

Not wanting to draw this out, Kylie faced Miranda. It wasn't as if she could hide it.

"Crap!" Miranda gasped. "What happened? Did having sex with Lucas turn you into a vampire?"

"No," Kylie said.

Della slapped a hand on her hip. "Why would having sex with a werewolf turn someone into a vampire?"

"I don't know," Miranda said. "Maybe it was really bad sex."

Della shot Miranda a bird and then focused on Kylie. "Did you have sex with Lucas?"

"No." Kylie tugged on her drooping towel. "We just . . . made out."

"How far did you get?" Della wiggled her brows.

"Thought you didn't like hearing about it," Miranda said in an angry voice.

"Not about earlobe sucking. That's gross."

"Bitch!" Miranda charged at Della; Della charged back at Miranda.

Kylie caught Miranda by the shirt with one hand and Della by the arm with her other hand. Right then, her towel fell to the floor. Naked as a jaybird, and suddenly furious, she stomped her foot. "I said stop!"

Della and Miranda both giggled. No doubt she looked funny naked and furious.

Kylie released them, and then snatched up her towel. "Look, I have some things to share, but if you don't stop arguing, I'm going to walk away and just let you kill each other."

"You tried that line once before," Della said. "We let you down. We didn't kill each other." She snarled at Miranda. "Of course, it could change this time."

Kylie rolled her eyes. "Are you going to stop arguing or not?"

"Maybe," Miranda said. "Especially if you can explain how the freaking hell you can change your pattern. Oh, and if you give us details about last night with Lucas."

Kylie looked at Della. "Truce?"

"Yeah," Della said. "Besides, it's you I'm pissed at now for drinking my blood. You thieving vamp." She showed her canines, but a smile came with it. "And Miranda's right. We want details on both counts."

An hour later, after Kylie had given all the details—or at least all the details she planned on giving—the three of them walked toward the office. Kylie had confessed about going to the cemetery. She'd known Della would be pissed that she'd been tricked, and

Kylie had been right. But telling them seemed important, and not just to clear her conscience. If she needed to meet her grandfather in the future, she'd need allies. Della and Miranda were her best allies.

As well as her best friends.

And a big part of the reason Kylie couldn't do what her grandfather wanted: to go live with him. A detail Kylie had omitted from the conversation.

"Are you going to tell Burnett and Holiday?" Miranda asked as they neared the office.

"I don't know." Kylie looked up at the porch and listened to someone breathing inside. What if they went berserk and forbid her to see her grandfather and aunt again?

Would Holiday do that?

Probably not. But she could see Burnett doing it. Or trying to do it.

Kylie's heart grew heavy when she remembered she wasn't here to just talk about her grandfather. It was time. Time to tell Holiday about her sister. But first, she hoped to talk to Burnett about what all she'd learned about Hannah. He needed to know so he could look into this Blake character.

But damn, Kylie wasn't looking forward to having either of those chats.

"Shit!" Della caught Kylie's arm. "If you tell Burnett about meeting your grandfather, then I'll get my ass in a sling because I let you go. He won't care that I thought you were going to go get lucky with Lucas."

"He'll blame me, too." Miranda frowned.

"He won't blame you two," Kylie said. "It's all on me."

"Right, like Burnett's reasonable," Della said.

"Well, what do you expect? He's vampire," Miranda smarted off.

Kylie ignored their squabbling this time to stare at the window in Holiday's office. She tuned her ears to see if she could hear Burnett inside.

All Kylie heard was someone punching buttons on Holiday's keyboard.

Kylie moved up on the porch. She hadn't yet gotten to the door when suddenly she recognized the scent and the cadence of breathing coming from Holiday's office. It wasn't Holiday.

Or Burnett.

What was *he* doing in Holiday's office?

She waved at her two friends and moved in to stand by Holiday's door. Derek, completely immersed in whatever it was on the computer screen, hadn't heard her. She studied him and remembered calling him from the cemetery, feeling as if he was the only one she could count on.

Sighing, she also recalled him telling her he loved her. She even remembered when it was with him that she would have shared those hot wonderful kisses. Not anymore.

"Hey." Kylie pushed back her crazy feelings.

He literally jumped out of the chair.

"Damn." He ran a hand over his face. "You . . . startled me." Guilt filled his eyes.

"What were you doing?"

"Something I shouldn't be." A groan spilled from his lips. "Holiday asked me to man the office. When I sat down, her computer woke up. It was on her personal e-mail account, and . . ."

Kylie arched an eyebrow in accusation. "You were reading her personal e-mails?"

"Only because it involved Hannah." He motioned for her to shut the door.

She did and stepped into the room. Suddenly, she felt a little guilty, too, but if the information could help them . . . "What did you find out?"

"The e-mail was from a private investigator. Holiday hired him to find her sister."

"Did he find out anything?" Kylie dropped into the chair facing the desk.

"No. But I didn't know that until I opened it." He pushed a hand over his face again. "Which I shouldn't have done. I saw it and I thought it might answer everything."

"I'd probably have done the same the thing," she said, not sure if it was the truth, but saying it for his benefit. "Where is Holiday?"

"She said something about seeing Burnett."

Kylie heard heavy footsteps, and then the door swung open. "It's not me she's seeing." Burnett's gaze zeroed in on Kylie. "Who's Blake?"

Kylie recalled Hannah saying that it could have been Blake who killed her. Kylie got a bad feeling. "Why?"

"Because that's who Holiday's with."

"That's not good." Kylie popped out of the chair. "Where's she at?"

"Who the hell is Blake?" Burnett asked, blocking Kylie's path.

"He's her ex-fiancé."

Jealously flashed in Burnett's eyes.

"And, he might also be the person who killed her sister and the other girls."

Protectiveness replaced the jealousy in his eyes. His fangs dropped down a quarter of an inch from his top lip. He swung around and in a flash was gone.

It took a fraction of a second before she remembered she could flash just like Burnett. She glanced at Derek, and only when his eyes widened did she realize her own canines were elongated. No time to explain, she lit out of the room and the fizzle that she always felt in her veins when she went into protective mode started to buzz.

Kylie just prayed that the buzz was premature and Holiday wasn't in danger.

Chapter Twenty-five

Kylie caught Burnett's scent and in no time she flew beside him. They didn't stop until they came to a small restaurant on Main Street in downtown Fallen, Texas. Holiday's car was parked in front.

As soon as Burnett had his footing, he twitched his brows to check Kylie's pattern. He didn't say anything, but she saw the shock in his eyes before he turned back to the restaurant.

They rushed to the large front window. "In the back corner," Kylie said, her panic lessening at the sight of Holiday, alive, but not looking happy. Then again, she didn't appear in danger either. The man sitting across from her wore jeans and a light blue shirt. He was tall, dark, and . . .

Kylie almost thought handsome, but stopped herself from going there.

"How did you know she was here?" she asked.

"When I saw she was gone, I called her. She said she was at the café, and when someone walked up, I heard her say his name."

Kylie looked back at the window and tuned her ears to hear Holiday's conversation.

"I just came here to ask you if you've seen her," Holiday said.

"And I came here to try to explain what happened," Blake countered. "I made a mistake. It's been over two years, and I haven't stopped loving you."

Burnett growled and moved for the door. Kylie caught his elbow. Dressed in all black today, he looked fierce.

"Wait," Kylie said.

"For what?" Burnett's nostrils flared.

"We need a plan."

"I've got one." His eyes grew brighter when Blake touched Holiday's arm.

"One that doesn't include murder," Kylie muttered, and then added, "You can't just storm in like a jealous boyfriend."

"I'm not jealous," he said.

Kylie heard his heart skip beats. *Oh, that was so cool.*

"Really?" Kylie arched a knowing brow at him.

"He killed her sister," Burnett defended himself.

"I said he might be the one who killed her."

"That's good enough for me." He reached for the door again. Kylie stopped him again.

"Do you really want this to be the way Holiday finds out her sister is dead? In public?"

He stepped back, his eyes telling her he'd seen reason. "Okay, what's your plan?"

She didn't have one, but said, "We hang back and watch."

He frowned. "He could pull a knife and kill her before I could save her."

"In public?" Kylie asked.

"It's not the smartest move, but this guy screwed up and lost Holiday. That tells me he's an idiot." Burnett never looked away from the window as he spoke. His eyes turned a brighter green. A low growl came from his lips. "He's touching her again."

"That's not why I called you, Blake." Holiday pulled her hand back. Her red hair hung loose and stood out against the pale yellow sundress that she wore. "I just want to find Hannah."

"But she's not letting him touch her," Kylie said. "Let's move before she spots us."

Too late.

Holiday looked up, and her eyes widened at the sight of them standing outside the glass door.

"You got a new plan?" Burnett asked. "Because I'm fresh out of ideas, and she looks pissed."

Kylie almost smiled at the fear she heard in the big, bad vampire's voice. "Don't tell her anything until we get her back to camp," Kylie said quickly.

The door swung open as Holiday stepped out. She looked at Burnett, then Kylie. "What's wrong?"

"I needed to talk to you," Kylie said, improvising.

"About what?" When no one answered, Holiday spoke up again. "What happened?"

Burnett started to answer. Afraid he might tell Holiday the truth, Kylie blurted out, "I happened." She pointed to her forehead.

Holiday tightened her brows and her eyes widened. "Oh, my."

The bell from the restaurant doors chimed behind them and Blake walked out. He stopped beside Holiday. "Is everything okay?" He cut his gaze to Burnett.

Burnett, eyes ablaze, pulled Holiday to his side.

"That depends," said Burnett, "on how quickly you get your ass away from here."

Thankfully, Blake had simply offered Holiday a good-bye nod and left without incident.

Kylie couldn't help but wonder if it was because he was suspicious that they knew the truth. Burnett seemed to share the same thought when he watched Blake walk away. The low growl coming from his chest left no question that Burnett planned on seeing the man again. And probably sooner than later.

Burnett and Kylie rode back with Holiday. Holiday peppered Kylie with questions as she drove. "When did you turn into a vampire? Have you experienced any pain? Have your powers changed?" Then Burnett started in with his line-up of questions about Kylie's newly acquired pattern.

Kylie answered as vaguely as she could, not wanting to talk about her grandfather. She accepted she'd have to come clean, eventually, but considering what other news she had to give Holiday, Kylie didn't want to add anything else for the camp leader to worry about just yet.

Back in the office, Holiday tossed her purse on the sofa and looked at both Burnett and Kylie with her "tell the truth or die" stare. Kylie wondered if her mom hadn't taught it to Holiday, because it sure did look familiar.

"Now, explain to me what's really going on," Holiday snapped. "I can sense there's more."

Kylie bit down on her lip. Burnett took a step forward. He squared his shoulders, empathy filling his eyes. He took a deep, apparently heartfelt breath and looked at Kylie. She nodded at him as if giving him the lead. He looked back at Holiday and, in a deep voice, said, "Kylie has something to tell you."

Kylie's mouth fell open and right then she knew it was official: Men sucked at verbal communication, especially where anything emotional was concerned.

Holiday's gaze shot back to Kylie, and her chest swelled with grief. Grief she knew Holiday was going to feel. An emotion Kylie had personally visited and revisited too often lately. Losing Nana, losing her stepfather—even if it wasn't in death, it still felt that way—losing her real father, Daniel, because his visits had been cut off. Then there was Ellie. Kylie had even found herself grieving over Red, aka Roberto.

Inhaling, Kylie motioned for Holiday to sit down. The camp leader studied Kylie's face and probably read every one of her emotions. Stepping to her desk, she sank in the chair. The cushions sighed from her weight. It seemed to be the only noise in the room.

"What is it?" Holiday asked again.

Emotion lumped in Kylie's throat. "I didn't tell you because you told me that . . . you wouldn't want to know. The whole live for today and tomorrow speech. Because at first I thought it was you."

Holiday leaned forward, gripping the side of her desk. "I don't understand."

"The face of the spirit that I told you I recognized. I thought it was you. But it wasn't . . . you."

Holiday's green eyes filled with tears and Kylie knew that Holiday had already put the pieces together. Burnett, much to his credit, moved behind her and tenderly pressed a hand on her shoulder.

"She's dead?" Holiday's next breath shuddered as she pulled it into her lungs. Tears slipped from her lashes and leaked onto her cheeks. "Why . . . didn't she come to me?"

Kylie wiped her own wet cheeks. "I think because she was ashamed of what happened."

"She told you about . . . that?"

"Yeah." Kylie's voice barely came out as a whisper. Burnett looked at her as if wondering what all she hadn't told him.

Grief filled the room. "What happened?" Holiday finally asked. "Was she mountain climbing? I told her it was dangerous to go alone."

Kylie shook her head. "It wasn't an accident."

Anger tightened Holiday's expression. "She was killed? By whom?"

"We don't know for sure." Burnett sat down on the edge of Holiday's desk. The way he looked at the camp leader warmed Kylie's heart. He cared. She just hoped this whole Blake issue didn't push them farther apart.

"But Blake is the prime suspect," Burnett said.

"Blake?" Holiday breathed in. "No, I don't believe . . ." She stopped as if having second thoughts. She swiped at her face again to clear the tears, and then she looked at Kylie. "Okay, tell me everything you know. And don't leave anything out."

That afternoon, at her cabin, Kylie sat at her kitchen table.

Lunch had been so much fun that day—not—that Kylie had decided to skip dinner. There hadn't been one person who hadn't stared, mouth agape, at her or made some wisecrack about Kylie's new vampire pattern.

Okay, that was a lie. Her close friends hadn't stared—or at least they tried not to. Jonathon and Helen had been taken off guard and before they could stop themselves, they'd done their share of ogling. Of course, then Jonathon had come over and welcomed her to vampire society and suggested she join them at their table.

She had declined. She could tell from a few of the vamps' expressions that she wouldn't be welcomed by all.

When Perry walked into the dining room, he'd checked her out, and then sent her a thumbs-up. Obviously, he'd decided not to be mad at her about the whole net thing. Then Kylie noticed all three of the new teachers eyeballing her. For some reason, she just assumed they'd have better manners, but nope, they found her just as entertaining as the others.

However, there had been one thing that made the whole meal ordeal worthwhile. When a smirking Fredericka pointed her out to Lucas, he'd just shrugged and said, "Yeah, I heard." Then he'd glanced at Kylie, not to stare, but to smile.

That smile, with a devilish twinkle in his eyes, had all sorts of meaning, too. Kylie found herself blushing and caring a little less that she was the freak show while everyone downed their burgers and fries. Of course, that lasted for only a few minutes. Then someone else made some smart-mouthed comment about Kylie's mind being off-the-chart weird.

For all the times she wished her sensitive hearing would stay turned on, she now wished she could cut it off—permanently. One only assumed you wanted to hear what was being whispered behind your back.

Staring at her hands resting on the table, she knew part of her bad mood was due to her hurting for Holiday. Kylie wanted to help her, but Holiday insisted on being alone.

The computer dinged with an incoming e-mail. Kylie rushed over, praying it would be from her grandfather or great-aunt. She'd been checking obsessively, especially since her earlier e-mail had bounced back . . . meaning the address she had for them was no longer active.

She dropped into the desk chair, her breath held, as she opened the screen.

Not from her grandfather or aunt.

She stared at her stepdad's e-mail address and accidentally clicked it open. Then she accidentally read it.

Hey, princess, I'm looking forward to seeing you Saturday. Miss you. Miss your mom.

All the emotions over her mom and dad's divorce came hurtling back. She jumped up so fast the chair slammed against the floor and broke into four different pieces. "Screw it!" she bellowed. Throat tightening with emotion, she stomped over and yanked open the fridge. She waited to feel the cool air hit her face.

It didn't feel cold, because she was too cold. She was a freaking vampire!

She swatted a tear from her cheek and looked back to the

computer. What if her stepdad started asking questions about her mom again? Kylie sure as heck didn't want to be the one to drop the bomb that her mom was dating.

Then again, he was probably going to find out Saturday anyway. She'd already gotten an e-mail from Mom asking Kylie if she minded if Creepy Guy—the one who wanted to take her mom to England and bang her senseless—came to parent day.

Kylie had been a breath away from e-mailing her mom back and saying, *Hell yes, I mind.*

But was it fair to rain on her mom's parade? Shouldn't Kylie be content that her mom was happy? Kylie just wished her mom could be happy back with her stepdad. Wished life could go back to the way things were before.

For a second, she remembered how things had been. Her thinking she was nothing but human, her not knowing things such as vampires and werewolves existed.

Her having never known Derek. Her never reconnecting with Lucas.

Her, without Della or Miranda.

Suddenly, Kylie Galen's world before Shadow Falls didn't seem so desirable. Well, except having her mom and stepdad together.

Kylie heard Della's mattress shift and her footsteps pad against the floor. Kylie did another swipe of her face, hoping to hide the watery evidence. Vampires didn't cry.

"There's some B-positive blood that I brought you behind the milk," Della said.

"Thanks."

"How are you feeling?" Della asked.

"Fine. Why?"

Della moved in some more. "Because usually when someone starts ripping apart furniture, they don't feel so well."

Kylie stared at the broken chair and didn't reply.

"Actually, I'm just surprised that you didn't have any symptoms during the turning stage. I'm glad you didn't, because believe me, it's not fun."

Kylie reached for the blood. "You know, this probably won't last."

"The blood?" Della asked. "I can get more."

"No, me being vampire. I'm not really vampire. I mean, I'm only part vampire."

"You look full-blooded," Della said, and then, "How do you change it?" She moved to the kitchen table.

Kylie opened the bottle and suddenly the idea of drinking the blood turned her stomach. Had she already changed into something else? Oh, great! If so, she couldn't wait until breakfast when everyone would have another field day making fun of her.

Closing the cap, attempting to hide her nausea from Della, she said, "I don't understand how it works. How to make it happen, how to make it *not* happen."

She faced Della. "Am I still vampire?"

Della nodded, and Kylie saw from the girl's expression that she could tell Kylie had been crying.

"Go ahead and say it," Kylie said. "I'm supposed to be a badass now that I'm a vamp."

"I don't care if you're badass," Della said with sincerity.

Frustration welled up inside Kylie because she was being a bitch, because Della was being nice, but mostly because she couldn't go running to Holiday for answers this time.

Holiday didn't have the answers. And the people who did, her grandfather and aunt, didn't want anything to do with Shadow Falls and were now "undeliverable."

A chameleon alone will not survive.

And right now, Kylie felt very alone.

More tears flowed and Kylie swiped at her cheeks. "I hate feeling like a freak," Kylie bellowed out. "I hate feeling as if I have no control over my own body."

Her thoughts went to Hannah. And to Hannah's concern that someone was out to hurt Holiday. *And I'm tired of people dying.*

"Your grandfather didn't tell you how to . . . handle it?"

Kylie let go of a deep sigh. "He said it would take years for me to learn."

"So you're going to go around changing from thing to thing without being able to control it?"

"That's the way he made it sound. I don't know." Kylie dropped into a chair.

After a pregnant pause, Della asked, "What did you think of your grandfather?"

"What do you mean?"

"I mean, did you like him, not like him? Was he some old fart with one foot in the grave?"

"No, he wasn't . . . that old. And he seemed nice. He looked like my dad. But reminded me a little of Burnett, serious and stern."

"But?" Della said, making it sound like a question.

"I didn't say 'but.'"

"Yeah, but you looked like you were thinking it."

Kylie exhaled. "If I tell you something, will you not say anything . . . to anyone?"

"Cross my cold heart," Della said. "And promise not to cry. Especially if I look half as bad as you do when I do it," she said, as if attempting to coax a smile out of Kylie.

Kylie didn't smile. She couldn't. "He wants me to go live with them."

Della's eyes widened and the humor quickly faded. "You're not going to do it, are you?"

"No," Kylie said. "I don't think so."

Right then, she heard her grandfather's voice again. *Come with us. We'll help you understand everything. You need to learn who and what you are, Kylie.*

"Don't think so?" Della repeated Kylie's words. "That sounds like you're considering it."

"No," Kylie said.

And she wasn't, she told herself. She really wasn't.

Although she might not have much of a choice . . .

Chapter Twenty-six

Kylie slipped into bed early that night. Having hardly slept the night before, she'd hoped she'd sleep like the dead. Well, not like the dead, but sleep like a hungry vampire, slightly turned off by the idea of drinking blood, who was mentally frazzled.

No such luck. She lay staring at the ceiling, petting the purring Socks, and worrying about Holiday and wishing Lucas would call. Right then, Socks crawled up on her chest and started giving her kitty kisses on her chin.

Kylie stared at the kitten. "If and when I turn into a werewolf, are you still going to love me? Remember I loved you when you were a skunk."

The kitten meowed with what Kylie hoped was a *yes*.

"Do you think Holiday knows we love her?" Kylie asked.

Talking to Socks did little to ease the worry from her heart. Giving in, she reached for the phone. She wasn't even sure who she was going to call, Lucas or Holiday.

Holiday answered on the third ring. "Hey, is everything okay?"

"Yeah, I'm . . . worried about you, thought maybe I could come over for a while."

The line went silent. "I . . . appreciate it, but I think I need to be alone."

"That's fine," she assured Holiday, although she'd ached to hug Holiday and offer her some comfort.

"Has she come to see you again?" Holiday asked.

"No." Kylie ran her finger under Socks's chin.

"If she does . . . tell her to come see me? Tell her I'm not mad anymore, I just . . . need to see her." There was so much grief in Holiday's voice that tears stung Kylie's eyes.

"I'll do that." Silence, painful silence, filled the line. The only thing Kylie could hear was Holiday's grief. "Holiday . . ."

"Yes?" Holiday's voice shook just a little.

"I love you. I know that sounds sappy, but you and Shadow Falls mean so much to me. I don't know if you understand how much good you do for everyone who comes here."

You are one of us. We share the same blood. A chameleon alone will not survive. Her grandfather's words echoed in her heart again.

"I belong at Shadow Falls," Kylie said, and then flinched when she realized she'd spoken her thought aloud.

"Of course you do." Holiday sounded confused. "Are . . . you okay?"

"Fine," she lied. "Just worried about you."

"Don't worry," Holiday said. "And Kylie, I love you, too. We'll talk tomorrow, okay?"

Holiday hung up. Five minutes later, melancholy still had her in its grips when Burnett called and asked if she'd spoken with Holiday. "I did," Kylie said. "I asked if I could come over, but she said she wanted to be alone."

"She told me the same thing," he muttered.

"Then we should respect her wishes," Kylie said.

Burnett exhaled. "Do you think she still loves him?"

While the question was a complete conversational U-turn, Kylie followed it perfectly. The fact that Burnett trusted her enough to show his vulnerability surprised her. The realization made her feel slightly guilty for keeping things from him. But she didn't have a choice, did she?

"No," she said, certain that Holiday loved Burnett. But it wasn't Kylie's place to say it.

"I'm going to have to bring him in to interview him," Burnett said.

"I know," Kylie said. "But you can't mistreat him or assume he's guilty just because he used to be with Holiday."

"You think I'd do that?" Burnett asked.

"Yeah," she said honestly. "I saw the way you looked at him this morning."

He remained quiet for a second. "Have you spoken with Hannah again?"

"Not yet."

"It would be *helpful* if she could tell us more," he bit out.

As if Kylie didn't realize it. "It's a shame they don't always cooperate."

"If she shows up, ask her to . . . come talk to me."

"Are you sure?" Kylie recalled how he'd reacted to the whole ghost issue.

"Hell, no, but I'll do it if it will help Holiday." The line went silent again. "Before I forget, Derek's going to come to your cabin and walk you to the office at six in the morning. We'll go to the café . . . to see if we can find anything out on Cara M. I've checked and there isn't a Cara M. listed as missing. Do you think maybe you read it wrong?"

"No, I've seen it several times."

"Okay," he said. "We'll go and see what we can find first thing in the morning. Then we'll have to rush back here before the parents start showing up."

Oh, joy, Kylie thought. She had almost forgotten that was tomorrow.

As soon as Kylie hung up with Burnett, she heard a tap at her bedroom window. She expected the blue jay, but was wonderfully surprised when she saw Lucas pushing open her window.

"Why can't you people use a door?" Della called out from the living room.

"'Cause I didn't come to see you," Lucas called out, and smiled at Kylie.

His smile did all kinds of wonderful things to her mood. He moved in, sat on the edge of the bed, and then leaned down and kissed her. It was warm, soft, and, she sensed, purposely short.

"I can't stay long." His gaze lingered on her lips. "No matter how much I want to."

"What's going on?" she asked.

"My dad summoned me again."

She frowned. "I don't like your dad," she said, and then felt bad for having said it. "Sorry, I didn't—"

He put a finger over her lips. "I don't like him very much, either." Then he smiled. "I have to go, but . . . maybe later, you can dream of me." A sexy twinkle filled his eyes.

She frowned. "I tried last night and couldn't. I think it's because I'm vampire."

He frowned. "I knew being a vamp would be the pits."

Kylie rolled her eyes.

"I heard that," Della shouted.

"Can you hear this?" Lucas shot a bird toward the door.

Kylie jerked his hand down. "Don't get her started," she muttered to Lucas, and then called out, "Go to bed, Della."

Lucas exhaled. "I need to go." He leaned down and kissed her again.

The kiss was the last thing Kylie thought about when she drifted off to sleep. She tried again to dreamscape, but nothing happened. So instead, she just dreamed. Dreamed how it could be when she understood everything about who and what she was. Dreamed of when Lucas was free of trying to appease his pack.

Kylie woke up the next morning around 4 AM. The room was cold, so she knew someone else was here, but they never manifested, which was just rude—like playing Peeping Tom. Sitting up, she whispered, "Hannah, is that you?"

No one answered, but the cold somehow felt different.

A shiver ran down Kylie's spine. She pulled the blanket up around her shoulders and sat there, breathing in the cold air. Was this one of the girls buried with Hannah, or was this someone new? It felt new—unfamiliar. Had someone from the graveyard followed her back? As always, when a new spirit appeared, Kylie pretty much went back to feeling anti-ghost.

Kylie listened to her clock mark off two minutes before the cold faded. Socks moved from under the bed and leapt up onto the mattress and curled up into a tight little knot on her lap. "You're a little anti-ghost, too, aren't you?"

The kitten let out a muffled meow that seemed to say, *Hell, yes.*

Kylie pulled Socks closer and then settled back into the pillows, half hoping to fall back asleep, half trying to dreamscape again. No such luck.

Her mind ran from seeing her mom, stepdad, and mom's new boyfriend to Hannah and the trip to the café she'd be making in a few hours. Would they learn who Cara M. was? Would that help them figure out who killed them?

Sitting there, Kylie recalled how Hannah had gone all weird on her when the new teachers had walked into the dining hall yesterday. Did that mean anything? "Hannah, if you can come for a chat, I'd appreciate it. And your sister wants to talk to you and so does Burnett. You're a very popular ghost."

The room remained silent and warm. Realizing if she stayed in bed she'd just let herself get caught up in angst, she tossed back the covers and got up.

Maybe Holiday was already at the office. And hopefully, Della wouldn't bite her head off for wanting to head out early. She'd have to call Derek and let him know she was already at the office.

It was still pitch-dark when Kylie and Della stepped out of the cabin. The temperature was down and there was a fall-like feeling in the black morning air. Della hadn't bitten her head off when she told her she wanted to go see if Holiday was at the office, not literally anyway. But Kylie could tell she wanted to.

No doubt, playing shadow was finally getting to Della. Kylie didn't blame the vamp. Maybe it was time Kylie talked with Burnett about putting a stop to it. Mario hadn't been around in a while. She sensed Mario had backed off and even Miranda said she didn't feel a thing. Kylie could only hope he'd gone forever.

"Too damn early," Della muttered.

"If you don't want to go, I'll be fine."

Della kept walking, but not bitching. "I guess it proves it," Della hissed.

"Proves what?" Kylie asked.

"That you're really not a vampire. I mean, we sleep the best during the AM."

"I told you I wasn't all vampire. I . . ." Kylie went silent when she heard the footfalls coming down the path. Della's eyes widened at the same time, then motioned for them to move into the edge of the woods. They hid behind a bush, waited, and watched—watched as a dark figure moved down the trail.

He wore a dark sweater, one with a hood that partially concealed his face. Kylie didn't recognize his shape or his gait. If it was one of the regular campers, she would have, wouldn't she?

Della sniffed the air. "I don't recognize his scent," she whispered.

"What's the plan?" Kylie asked.

"This?" Della leapt out of the woods, canines showing, eyes a bright green, and landed with a thud in front of the stranger.

Chapter Twenty-seven

Kylie, taken by surprise by Della's aggressive move, stood there a second before she realized Della could be in danger. With the vamp a few feet in front of the man, Kylie bolted out of the woods and stopped about three feet behind him.

Della took a defensive step toward the man. He jumped back and slammed right into Kylie. He swung around, a growl escaping his lips, but the hood still obscured his face and prevented Kylie from knowing who and what she was up against.

"Who are you?" Kylie asked. Feeling the sizzle of protective power, she went to yank off the hood from his head.

He ducked and moved a few feet backward—closer to Della. "Stop this!" he demanded.

"You stop," Della ordered.

He pulled off the hood of his sweater. "Is this the way you treat your teachers?" Hayden Yates asked.

Della, being Della, didn't back down. "If they go sneaking around in the shadows, dressing like some criminal, then yeah, that's the way we treat 'em."

Kylie held up her hand to Della, hoping to calm her, not that

Kylie felt all that calm. Her power was on full alert, her adrenaline set on high.

"Since when is taking a walk sneaking?" He used his teacher's voice.

"Since you sneaked up on us," Della smarted off.

Logic lessened Kylie's adrenaline. "I . . . we . . . You scared us," Kylie said.

"I wasn't scared," Della snapped.

Mr. Yates frowned. "Next time, try saying hello instead of attacking when someone walks up."

"That *was* hello," Della said. "If we'd attacked, you'd be bleeding . . . or dead."

"We overreacted," Kylie intervened, and then remembered that she didn't particularly like this guy. He seemed to be somehow secretive and his dark clothes and concealed face seemed to confirm it. However, Kylie's manners and respect for authority mandated she behave a certain way. "We apologize."

"We do?" Della asked sarcastically.

Kylie motioned for Della to start walking.

Della shot the teacher another frown before turning around. And the moment they were several feet ahead, Della whispered, "I don't like him."

"Me either," Kylie said, yet she couldn't put her finger on why.

"You think he's working with Mario?" Della asked.

"No. I . . . don't know," Kylie said. "Let's not jump to conclusions."

They arrived at the clearing where the office and dining hall stood. Kylie noticed the lights were on in Holiday's office. Then she noticed the dead silence. Not a bird or even the wind dared to make a sound. The fact that Della had stopped walking and her eyes glowed bright green told Kylie she wasn't imagining the sense of danger. Someone was here.

"Everything's fine," a voice, a strange voice, spoke behind them. Both Kylie and Della swung around. The man, in his early thirties, wore a black suit. A quick check of his pattern told Kylie he was vampire. The way he held out his hands, palms exposed, told her he wasn't looking for trouble. Then again, he was a stranger and on Shadow Falls property. Who the hell was he?

"It's okay." His at-peace stance had little effect on Kylie, and even less on Della.

"I'll be the judge of that." The glow from Della's green eyes spotlighted her extended fangs.

The man pulled his suit coat back and flashed the badge attached to his belt. "I'm Agent Houston, FRU, a friend of Burnett's." The way he said "friend" seemed to mean something, though Kylie wasn't really sure what. "Burnett asked me to stand in for him while he went to pick up a suspect."

"Stand in for him for what? Suspect for what?" Della asked, or more like demanded.

The agent's gaze shifted to Kylie, as if he knew she'd understand. And she did. Burnett had brought his man to watch over Holiday, and obviously he'd gone looking for Blake. But understanding didn't make this stranger her ally. Sure she trusted Burnett, but the badge Agent Houston had just proudly flashed did him more harm than good when it came to her.

"I can't go into details," he said, "but you're going to have to trust me. Kylie knows."

Trust? Not likely, Kylie thought, but when his heartbeat didn't appear to be lying, Kylie looked at Della. "He's telling the truth."

"I know," Della said as if annoyed, but the color change in her eyes said she'd backed down. Or she had until she had Kylie alone, and then no doubt she'd verbally bludgeon Kylie for information. Della didn't like to be in the dark.

"I'm going in to see Holiday." Kylie looked at Della.

"She's popular this morning," Agent Houston said.

Kylie looked to the window and saw a male figure. "Who's in there?"

"One of the new teachers," Agent Houston answered.

Kylie tensed. "Hayden Yates?" She looked at Della. How had he gotten ahead of them? Della's expression matched Kylie's.

"No," the man said. "A Collin Warren. He said he was the new history teacher. Is there a problem with him?" The agent's voice deepened as he took a small step toward the office.

"No," Kylie said. "He's fine." But right then, footsteps echoed from down the path.

"You expecting someone?" the agent asked.

"Not really," Kylie said, but she suspected who it might be.

And she was right.

Hayden Yates, his hood back to covering his head, stepped into the clearing. "Good morning." He lifted his chin, his gaze on the tall FRU agent standing defensively.

"You know him?" the agent asked Kylie.

Mr. Yates squared his shoulders as if insulted.

"He's a new teacher," Della said, but her tone said more. It said she didn't like him, and the agent picked up on it. He took another step toward Mr. Yates.

Mr. Yates didn't back away. He held his ground, and she thought they might come to blows. Then Hayden's gaze shifted to her as if reconsidering his stance. "I mean no harm, just taking a walk," he told the agent in a resigned voice.

Kylie still felt something . . . something not right, something not honest about the man.

Hannah's warning rang in Kylie's ears. *And the day I was at Shadow Falls, I sensed he was close. I felt him and I knew. I knew I went to Shadow Falls because of him.*

Could Hayden Yates be Hannah's killer? Could he have applied for the job here just to get to Holiday? It seemed unlikely, but Kylie wasn't taking any chances. And as soon as Burnett got back, she planned on sharing her concerns.

Kylie waited in the office's entrance for Mr. Warren to finish his conversation with Holiday. In a few minutes, both he and Holiday stepped out. Mr. Warren nodded politely and offered her a soft-spoken "Good morning."

"Morning." Kylie sensed again that he was as shy and unsure of himself as she was. Maybe even more. Sort of a male version of Helen. And yet he'd chosen to teach. No doubt his love of history pushed him down this path. For that, she had to admire him.

When he left, Kylie looked at Holiday and instantly went in for a hug.

They held on to each other for a second longer than normal.

"You okay?" Kylie asked.

"I will be in time," Holiday said.

Kylie heard Mr. Warren speaking to the agent outside. "Is this his first year teaching?" She nodded toward the window.

"How did you guess?" Holiday sighed. "He was recommended by a friend of a friend. He's not so bad when it's one on one. I hope you guys don't chew him up and spit him out."

Kylie grinned. "Perry might consider it."

Holiday frowned. "Promise me you'll not let that happen. He really seems like a nice guy and I think he'll make an excellent teacher. I'd appreciate it if you'd sort of take him under your wing."

Kylie chuckled. "Again, Perry might do that."

Holiday's grin, while a little forced, surfaced. She glanced at the clock on the wall. "You're up way early."

"Couldn't sleep," Kylie said.

"Did Hannah come by?" Grief snuck into Holiday's voice and Kylie's own chest swelled with the emotion.

"No. Sorry." There was a pause. "Is that coffee I smell?"

"Yeah, I . . . normally don't drink it, but this morning I figured I could use it. Grab a cup, and then I want to hear how the whole vampire transformation happened."

Oh, crap, Kylie thought as she went to collect her coffee. It was either time to come clean or to get busy burying herself in lies. She could probably come up with a story that Holiday would believe—a story that didn't include her sneaking out of Shadow Falls to meet her grandfather. But lying to Holiday of all people felt wrong.

"You did what?" Holiday asked, setting her coffee on her desk when Kylie started her explanation a few minutes later. "How many times do I have to explain to you that as a protector, you have no powers—zero—to protect yourself? You didn't even know the e-mail was from him."

"I knew," Kylie said.

"How?" Holiday leaned forward.

Kylie bit into her lip. "He was the fog."

"He was what?"

"My grandfather and my great-aunt, they were the fog. They somehow transformed themselves into fog."

"How . . ." She let go of a deep breath and let the confusion settle around her, and then said, "You still can't just disobey rules."

"I was following the main rule. The one you've told me dozens of times." She paused. "To follow my heart."

Holiday stared at Kylie as if debating the issue. "You could have asked someone to go with you."

"They wouldn't have met me."

"You don't know that," Holiday said.

"Yes, I do. They left when Lucas showed up."

"Wait, Lucas went with you? He knew about this?" There was a reprimand to her voice.

"No. He and Perry followed me, but I . . . detained them and took off. When Lucas caught up with me, my grandfather and aunt disappeared. They don't trust anyone here because of the FRU involvement with the camp. Considering everything that's happened, you can't blame them for that."

"I can blame them if they encourage you to put your life in danger." Holiday fell back into her chair with frustration.

"They don't even know about Mario. And look at me. Nothing happened. I had to go. I had to know the truth."

Holiday closed her eyes and kept them closed. When her lids finally fluttered open, Kylie saw most of her frustration had faded. Her shoulders relaxed. "And what's the truth, Kylie? What did they tell you?"

"My dad was right. I'm a chameleon."

"And what, exactly, is that?" Holiday asked.

"I have a blend of all the supernaturals and I maintain the DNA from all."

Holiday shook her head. "But that's not possible. The dominant parent's is the only DNA that passes to the child."

"That's what makes us different."

Holiday leaned back in her chair, her expression one of bafflement. "That's . . . huge." She tweaked her brows at Kylie's forehead. "So what constitutes the pattern you show?"

"I don't know . . . exactly. He said it usually took years before a chameleon learned to control it. That it takes a while to learn to do it. But then he said something that led me to believe that I can change it according to the powers I need."

"So he changed you into a vampire?"

"No, I . . . he said I must have done it instinctively. When I was trying to get away from Lucas and Perry, I just kept telling myself to move faster. So maybe that's how it happened."

"Have you tried to change it again?" Holiday arched a brow in curiosity.

"No." Kylie shook her head. "The last time you had me try to do something that I wasn't sure how to do, Burnett nearly wound up sterile."

Holiday chuckled. Seeing Holiday smile was so good that Kylie smiled back.

"What else did your grandfather say?" Holiday asked.

Kylie's heart gripped. If Holiday was vampire, she'd hear the lie forming on her lips. Telling Holiday that Kylie's grandfather wanted her to leave Shadow Falls seemed like giving Holiday a reason to dislike him—a reason to insist Kylie stay away from him. And she couldn't stay away.

Taking a breath, she fought the guilt swelling inside her, because Holiday might not hear the lie in her heartbeat, but she could read her emotions. Squaring her shoulders, she met Holiday's eyes. "Not much else. Lucas showed up and . . . they left."

"Who left?" Burnett asked.

Kylie inwardly flinched. She'd been so busy trying not to feel guilty, she hadn't heard him approach.

"Did you find him?" Holiday sat up, tension pulling at her shoulders.

Kylie had suspected Burnett had been looking for Blake, but it surprised her that he'd told Holiday. "Find who?" Kylie asked, to be sure she'd been right.

"Blake," Burnett answered. "And no." He looked at Holiday. "I've left messages at both his work and cell that we need to talk."

"Should I call him?" Holiday asked.

"No," Burnett clipped. Shifting his shoulders as if to push off the stress, he looked back at Kylie. "Who were you speaking of when I walked in? Who left?"

Holiday glanced at Kylie and she could see the message in the camp leader's eyes. She left it up to Kylie whether to tell him . . . or not.

She appreciated that, and when she imagined Burnett's reaction to her disregard for the rules, Kylie almost went with the "not." But realizing the position she was putting Holiday in by lying to Burnett, Kylie reconsidered. She didn't want to be the one to cause even a ripple of discontent between them. Not when her goal was to get them together.

"You're going to be upset," Kylie said.

"How upset?" He frowned.

It turned out Burnett had been quite upset. Kylie had been relieved when, an hour later, Derek showed up and the four of them left for the café to see if they could find out anything about Cara M.

When Burnett and Holiday walked into Cookie's Café, Derek held her back and let the door close. "Is everything okay?"

He'd obviously picked up on Burnett's *cheerful* mood. Although Kylie didn't know if it had everything to do with her, or the fact that he'd been unable to run down Blake.

Looking up at the glass door and seeing Burnett staring back at them, she recalled some of their earlier conversation.

"The FRU is not the enemy," he'd insisted, when Kylie reminded him her grandfather had a reason to distrust Shadow Falls.

"You're not the enemy," Kylie had said. "But I'm still not sure about the FRU. And while I know you don't want to admit it, you wouldn't have hidden my grandmother's body and wouldn't be keeping some facts from them if you completely trusted them."

Burnett hadn't argued with that, but Kylie pointing it out hadn't done much to improve his mood. He was obviously torn between his loyalty to Shadow Falls and his loyalty to the FRU. Not that Kylie worried. She trusted him. Getting her grandfather and aunt to trust him was another matter.

Derek cleared his throat to get her attention. He wore his favorite jeans and dusty green T-shirt. "Did something happen?"

"Not really," Kylie whispered to Derek, slightly bothered by how close he leaned into her, brushing her shoulder with his. Or was she bothered by how aware of his touch she was? Pushing that thought aside, she reached for the glass door.

But she got the craziest feeling that someone was watching her. She swung around, but Derek blocked her view of the street.

"Is something wrong?" he asked.

"No." She still shifted to see around him. But the brief sensation she'd gotten was gone. Were her grandfather and aunt close by? She glanced all around, left and right. The old houses lining the street had been turned into gift shops, and an old red caboose now served as a concession stand. What she didn't see was anyone peering back at her. No one. Nothing.

So she turned back and walked inside the café packed with a chattering crowd.

The smell of bacon flavored the air in the old house that served as a café. She didn't find the smell the least bit tempting. The downside of being a vamp. The room held wall-to-wall tables, filled with hungry people who looked like vacationers. The sound of forks clinking against plates echoed with the voices.

Only one table stood empty and Holiday led the way. A server came out of the back, carrying a tray of food that smelled like cinnamon rolls.

"Is that the same uniform?" Derek asked as they sat down.

"Yeah." Kylie's heart lightened with hope that this would lead them to the killer.

Another waitress, Chris G., according to her name tag, stopped in front of their table.

"You guys ready to order?" Before they spoke, she waved at another table. "One minute."

"Actually," Burnett spoke up, "we're here hoping to get some info on a Cara M., a waitress who—"

"Oh." She walked away.

"Oh, what?" Burnett frowned as she took off. She stuck her head through the door and called out, "Hey, Cara, someone wants to talk to you."

Burnett, Holiday, and Derek all turned and looked at Kylie.

"She can't be alive," Kylie said. "Trust me. She's dead."

Then a pretty blond, with a name tag that read CARA M., walked out of the back. "She looks alive to me," Derek said. "And even kind of hot." He blushed.

Chapter Twenty-eight

Kylie opened her mouth to speak, but didn't have a clue what to say. Or do, for that matter.

"Hi, Cara," Derek spoke up, glancing at Burnett as if making sure it was okay to take the lead. Burnett nodded and Derek continued. "We wanted information on a Cara M."

She pointed to her name tag. "I'm Cara M. M for Muller."

Kylie studied the waitress's face and tried to compare it to the spirit. It wasn't her. Was it? Kylie played emergency recall in her memory but could only envision her long blond hair and blue eyes. Which this girl had, but . . .

"I'm sorry," Derek said. "We were under the impression that Cara M. no longer worked here."

"Well, I'm still here. Been here since I was fifteen, over two years. Why?"

"Is there another Cara M. who worked here?" Kylie tried not to stare, but feeling desperate to discover the truth, she couldn't stop herself.

"No." The girl looked at Kylie. "What's this about?"

Kylie noticed that the waitress's name tag had come unpinned and barely clung on the uniform. "What happens if you lose your name tag?"

Cara cut her eyes toward the back of the restaurant. "The manager has a freaking cow."

"And what would you do to prevent him from having a cow?" Kylie leaned forward.

"What do you mean?" Cara asked.

"She means, do you ever loan your name tag to one of the other girls?" Derek asked.

The waitress leaned closer as if afraid someone might hear. "The boss hardly notices. But I don't understand why you want to know this." She smiled at Derek as if . . . well, as if he was some cute guy and she was some cute blonde. Which she was. Which he was. A frown pulled at Kylie's lips.

Holiday touched the girl's arm. No doubt to send her some calming emotion in hopes of encouraging her to answer. "Have any of your waitresses just . . . disappeared?"

Kylie saw Burnett tilt his head, listening for a lie, and Kylie did it as well.

"They quit all the time. The owner can be a real jerk." Cara spoke the truth.

"Has anyone just left? Never officially quit?" Holiday asked.

Cara paused. "Yeah, there was a girl like that. A Cindy something. Can't remember her last name."

"Did Cindy ever borrow your name tag?" Burnett added his voice to the conversation.

"Was Cindy a blonde?" Kylie tossed out her own question.

"Yes," Cara said to Burnett, and then focused on Kylie. "And yes. Why?"

Between Holiday's casual touches on the girl's wrist and Derek's flirty smiles, the girl answered all their questions about Cindy. Before she walked off, Burnett asked if her manager or the owner of the restaurant was here.

Cara grew nervous. "Did I do something wrong?"

"No," Burnett assured her. "But can you let her know I need to talk to her?" He pulled out his wallet and flashed his badge. Kylie wasn't even sure what the badge meant to humans, but it didn't seem to matter.

Cara's color paled. "Oh, shit. Did something happen to Cindy?"

Yeah, Kylie thought. Something happened. Something really bad, too.

Before leaving, Burnett had the name Cindy Shaffer and a copy of the resume she'd filled out with her emergency contacts. When he sent the info to FRU via his phone and asked for the driver's license, they answered within a few minutes. When he showed Kylie the image of a smiling young blonde, tears filled Kylie's eyes. It was her. And Cindy Shaffer would never smile like that again.

While Burnett spouted orders over the phone for someone at the FRU to contact the Shaffer family, Holiday ordered some cinnamon rolls. They arrived, hot and covered with gooey white icing. Derek ate two, Holiday nibbled on one. Kylie and Burnett picked at their pastries with even less enthusiasm. Even with Kylie's stomach grumbling, she couldn't stomach the taste. That, and she kept seeing the image of the smiling Cindy.

"Are you drinking your meals?" Holiday asked Kylie in a low voice.

"Not regularly, but I'll start." She didn't look forward to it.

Burnett paid for the breakfast. As they walked toward the car, Kylie got the feeling again that someone was watching her. She swung around and saw a male figure disappear inside one of the stores. She'd barely gotten a glimpse of a shoulder and arm, but she recognized those appendages.

Kylie shot across the street.

"What is it?" Burnett's feet ate up the pavement right beside her.

Kylie stopped in front of the store. Her gaze flew to the large carved wooden sign that read PALM READER. She reached for the door. "I thought I saw someone."

Burnett grabbed her, his eyes now green in protective mode. "Who?"

Kylie heard Derek call her name from the other side of the street. "Let me find out." She rushed inside the store.

Burnett rushed in with her.

The first thing Kylie noticed was a voodoo doll hanging from the ceiling with pins in it. The second was a foul odor. She slapped her hand over her mouth and nose. Even while wanting to gag, she searched the room for the man she'd seen enter the building. When the place looked empty, she glanced back at Burnett.

"Garlic." He frowned. "Just breathe it in; the reaction will fade. It doesn't kill us."

"Can I help you?" a voice asked from behind a counter in the corner of the room.

Kylie forced herself to pull her hand from her mouth and looked at the woman dressed in a brightly colored, loose-fitting dress that had con-artist-pretending-to-be-a-clairvoyant written all over it. But just to confirm her assessment, Kylie checked her brain pattern. Human—but shady looking. Definitely a con artist.

Kylie tilted her head to the side to hear if anyone else was in the old house. Not a sound. No one breathed inside these walls but the three of them, and Kylie still wished she didn't have to breathe. The smell crawled down her throat. She focused on the door. Where had the man gone that she'd spotted rushing inside?

Noting that the backdoor stood slightly ajar, she tuned her ears to listen for anything outside. If he'd left out the backdoor, he was gone now.

"Uh . . ." Kylie pushed words around her gag reflex, but before the words spilled out, she noted the hand-painted sign hanging over the register.

NO SHOES, NO SHIRT, NO SERVICE. AND UNDER ANY CIRCUM-STANCES, NO COLD-HEARTED VAMPIRES.

She glanced at Burnett and back at the sign.

He frowned.

"You need a reading?" the woman asked.

"No." Kylie ignored her desire to heave. "A man just walked in. I thought I knew him."

"Yeah. The bell rang, but I was in the back; when I got here the person had vanished. Probably a spirit. I get them all the time."

Kylie put out her feelers for ghosts. No deadly cold filled the space. And who could blame them? The stench of garlic probably scared them off, too. She eyed the woman again, who Kylie now had down as a complete nutcase. A stupid nutcase if she thought a sign and some garlic would actually keep vampires away.

The woman noticed Kylie's attention to the sign. "Don't be too quick to judge. I see them around here all the time. They have a different smell about them."

"Seriously?" Burnett asked in mock disbelief. "You believe in vampires?"

"You aren't the only non-believers," she said. "But I have proof. The Native Americans drew pictures of them on the cave walls on my grandmother's property."

"Interesting stuff for fairy tales." Burnett glanced at Kylie. "You ready?"

As soon as they walked out, he bit out, "Who the hell did you think you saw?"

She didn't consider keeping it from him. She'd been going to tell him, she just hadn't had the time. "What do you know about Hayden Yates?"

"The new teacher?"

She nodded.

"I personally did an extensive check on all the new employees. Why? Do you think I missed something?"

"I think he gives me bad vibes."

"Bad vibes?" Burnett asked.

Kylie nodded. "And this morning before the sun came up, Della walked me to Holiday's office and we caught him following us." She stopped talking, realizing that wasn't altogether true. "Maybe not exactly following us, but he was walking around. And Hannah insists whoever killed her is close to the camp."

"And that's who you think you saw?"

She nodded.

He frowned. "But Blake, Holiday's ex, has been in the area, too. Hannah could have meant him."

Burnett wanted Blake to be guilty, and Kylie wasn't sure he wasn't, but . . . "I know, but I'm just . . . Maybe I'm making more out of it than I should."

"Or not." Burnett snatched his phone from his pocket and dialed. "Della," he said into his phone. "Find Hayden Yates at the camp."

"Can I whup his ass, too?" Della's voice echoed from the phone.

"No, don't let him know you're checking on him. I just want to know if he's there. And do it now!"

"I'm already on my way," she smarted back.

The line went silent for a second. "Okay . . . I'm at his place, peering though his window. He's reading the paper, sitting on the sofa. You sure you don't want me to kick his ass? Did Kylie tell you we think he was following us?"

"Yes."

"Is that an affirmative on whupping his ass?" Della chuckled.

"No," Burnett said, missing the humor. "Thanks." He hung up and met Kylie's gaze.

"I don't think he could have made it back to the camp in that time," Burnett said.

"I know," Kylie said. "So maybe it wasn't him."

Burnett frowned. "But to be safe, I'll do another rundown on him."

Kylie appreciated that.

"Where the hell did you guys go?" Derek stopped beside them.

"I thought I saw someone." Kylie spotted Holiday moving across the street.

"What happened?" she asked.

"Kylie thought she recognized someone." Burnett motioned for them to cross the street. "We should get back to the camp before the parents start showing up."

Oh, great! Now Kylie had the whole parent issue to deal with.

Holiday looked at her watch. "We'd better hurry."

They moved across the street to get in the car. All *five* of them. Yes, five.

Burnett hit the clicker to unlock the doors. Holiday popped in the front seat. Kylie stood by the back door when Hannah leaned in and whispered, *"I call window seat."*

Hannah, Derek, and Kylie climbed in. As soon as Burnett got settled behind the wheel, his shoulders stiffened and he swung around. The look, the sheer panic in his gaze, told Kylie she wasn't the only one hearing and, more than likely, seeing Hannah.

Burnett drove in silence, but kept looking back in the rearview mirror. Kylie shivered from the chill of Hannah's presence.

Have you figured out anything else? Kylie spoke in her mind.

Hannah ignored Kylie's question. Instead, she stared at Derek. *"He's cute."*

"Damn, it's cold in this car." Derek draped his arm around Kylie. The warmth of his arm did feel good, and being this close, close enough to get a good whiff of his natural scent to chase away the scent of garlic, didn't feel so bad, either. And for that reason, she shifted away and cut him a warning look that said, "Don't push your luck."

Sometimes she thought he forgot she wasn't really with him anymore. Not that it wasn't easy for him to forget, with Lucas never hanging around her . . .

"You should definitely choose him." Hannah leaned into Kylie's shoulder. The icy feel of her touch caused Kylie's spine to stiffen. *"And speaking of romance, the bozo in the front seat better watch himself. If he hurts my sister—"*

"I won't," Burnett muttered.

"Won't what?" Holiday and Derek asked at the same time.

"Nothing." Burnett slammed his jaw so tight he had to have cracked a few teeth.

Hannah leaned forward and stared at Burnett in the rearview mirror. The mirror frosted over. *"If you break her heart, I swear, I'll neuter you in your sleep."*

Burnett's jaw tightened some more. Holiday gaped at the rearview mirror and then stared wide-eyed at Burnett. A second later, she swung around and gave Kylie the befuddled look. "Is it her? Is Hannah here?"

Kylie froze, literally from Hannah's icy presence, but also from not knowing what to say.

When Kylie didn't answer, Holiday stared back at Burnett. "Can you see her? Can you see ghosts? How can you do that?"

"We've got a ghost in the car?" Derek's voice rang a bit high-pitched.

"Had a ghost in the car," Hannah said. Her teary-eyed gaze stared at Holiday, and then she vanished, leaving the saddest of sad moods to fill the car like smoke.

The moment Kylie spied her mom and John, her mom's creepy new boyfriend, walking into the dining hall, holding on to each other like a couple of horny teenagers, Kylie found herself envying Hannah's ability to vanish. Why did her mom think bringing John was a good idea? And if she had to bring him, couldn't she keep her hands off his butt while she was here?

Yup, Kylie's mom had her right hand tucked into the back of John's jeans pocket. And frankly, the man didn't even have a nice ass!

Surely her mom wasn't getting serious about him and felt these visits were needed for Kylie to get to know him—before . . . before they did something stupid, like get married.

The thought scared the crap out of Kylie. Inhaling, she told herself she was overreacting; as Nana would have said, she was making a mountain out of a molehill.

Then again, her mom hadn't answered Kylie's question about them having sex. And chances were, her mom wasn't about to answer that inquiry today, either.

Kylie's mom turned around and spotted her on the other side of the dining hall and smiled. Kylie waved, hoping her mom would do the same, freeing her hand from John's ass, but nope.

Taking a deep breath, Kylie faked a smile.

Her mom grinned up at John, and the man swooped down and kissed her. Kissed her . . . with tongue, and right there in front of all of Kylie's campmates.

"Just shoot me," Kylie muttered.

"I think they're cute." Holiday leaned into Kylie as if reading her emotional overload.

"And I think I'm going to puke." Kylie swore she was going to have a sit-down, serious chat with her mom and find out exactly what was going on. When the kiss kept going, Kylie decided again that yup, she'd love to vanish. Just up and disappear.

"Take some deep breaths and calm down," Holiday said. "You're exploding with panic."

Kylie looked at Holiday. "My mom's French-kissing a guy in front of everyone," she muttered. "Of course I'm panicking!"

"Shit!" Holiday snapped.

"Shit, what?" Kylie asked, alarmed at the panic in Holiday's voice.

"Oh, Kylie," Holiday murmured. And then she looked across the room and waved down Burnett, her arm motions serious.

"What is it?" Kylie looked to the door, thinking someone unwanted, possibly Mario, had walked in.

No Mario.

"Damn it to hell and back!" Holiday whispered. "Kylie, where did you go?"

"What do you mean? I'm right here. Standing right next to you." Kylie looked down at her feet, but she saw only the floor. No sneakers, no legs. No Kylie.

"Oh, shit!" she muttered, and while she hadn't thought about it in quite a while, she remembered her dad telling her that they would work things out together. Was this it? Was this what dying felt like?

Chapter Twenty-nine

Wait, Kylie thought. If she was dead, wouldn't she be on the floor in a crumpled, lifeless heap?

"Oh, crap!" Kylie muttered when her mom, a dumbfounded look on her face, walked up to Holiday.

"Where's Kylie?" her mom asked.

"She ran to . . . to the bathroom, I think, but . . . I'm not sure." Holiday's voice sounded an octave too high.

Burnett stopped at her mom's side, his serious gaze trying to read Holiday. "Something wrong?" His calm front almost sounded convincing, but Kylie saw the stress tightening his jawline.

"Uh, Kylie . . . she . . . disappeared. I thought maybe you could find her."

Disappeared? So, she'd just disappeared. She wasn't dead.

"Disappeared?" All sorts of questions filled his eyes.

Holiday nodded and didn't break eye contact as if mentally telling him it was serious.

And hell yeah, it was serious. She was freakin' invisible.

"It's crazy." Her mom sounded confused. "She was here and then . . . she vanished."

Vanished? Kylie suddenly remembered wishing she could vanish. Vanish like a ghost.

Damn! Damn! Damn! If there was ever a lesson in the old adage of be careful for what you wish for, this was it.

Questions flashed across her mind. Was she still a vampire? Had she turned back into a witch and accidentally wiggled her pinky when she made the declaration? Or was this completely connected to her being a chameleon? That's when she recalled that her great-aunt and grandfather had gone *poof,* both from the car the first day they'd shown up at Shadow Falls, and at the cemetery. Was *poof* the same thing as vanishing?

Her grandfather's words echoed in her head. *Come with us. We'll help you understand everything. You need to learn who and what you are.*

More than ever, and maybe not even for the first time, Kylie wondered if he was right.

"You've lost her daughter?" John snapped. "What kind of place loses kids?"

"We haven't lost her," Holiday said, but Kylie saw fresh panic flash in her eyes. "I'm sure she'll show up any minute."

Her mom seemed to relax, but Kylie didn't get a warm fuzzy feeling from Holiday's tone. And when Kylie listened closely, she heard the camp leader's heart beating to the tune of a lie.

Crap! Crap! Crap! Kylie tried to think. She had to get herself out of this because . . . well, apparently she'd gotten herself into it.

"I can do this," she said, needing a little encouragement even if it was as fake as a mall Santa.

She tried to rationalize. If she'd gotten this way by wishing it, maybe she could un-wish it. She started un-wishing, if you could call begging to everything holy in her mind to change her back as un-wishing. She closed her eyes and realized that if it worked, she'd magically appear. That would freak everyone out even more. "Go somewhere else," she muttered to herself. "Somewhere private." She dashed toward the bathrooms.

Hurrying into the room, she heard voices but ignored them, and stormed into an empty stall. Breathing in, then breathing out, she closed her eyes, closed them really tight. "I wish . . . I wish I was visible." She opened her eyes. Her gaze shot to her feet. Or to the space where her feet should have been, but weren't.

A knot formed in her throat; fear bounced around her chest like bumper cars. What if she stayed like this? What if . . . No! She'd been in worse situations. Heck, she'd been kidnapped and chained to a chair and survived. She'd been tossed off a cliff and came through it. All of a sudden, she questioned again if this was Wicca related. She wiggled her pinky. "Turn me visible. Turn me visible."

Nothing happened.

"What the hell have I done?" The knot in her throat doubled in size. She started to cry. "Somebody help me, please?" She leaned against the bathroom stall door. "Daniel." She whispered her father's name, even though she knew the likelihood of him showing up was slim to none. "Can you please, please help me?"

"Think yourself there," a voice said.

Her breath caught when she realized it wasn't just any voice, but Daniel's. She pulled away from the door and saw the vague apparition of him, crowded between the toilet and the stall wall. "Think it. Make it so in your head."

"How?"

"Think it. In your heart. You have the power—" He faded.

"No," she begged, but he was gone.

Wiping her tears, she did what he said. She concentrated on being visible. On being there, physically.

Closing her eyes again, with no faith but desperate enough to try, she concentrated. She opened one eye and peered down. Her feet had never looked so beautiful in all her life.

"Thank you! Thank you!"

"For what?" someone asked in the stall beside her, but Kylie barely listened, too excited that she wasn't invisible anymore.

She walked out of the stall and came to an abrupt stop when she saw Steve and Perry both standing in front of urinals, their jeans hanging low on their butts. The sound of urine hitting ceramic filled her ears. It wasn't a pretty sound.

Her face heated to a nice shade of red.

The stall door behind her swished open. "What are you doing in the boy's restroom?" someone asked.

Steve, pants still down, swung around. Completely around. Kylie slapped her hands over her eyes.

"I didn't see a thing. I swear." Okay, maybe she did, which had her face turning hotter.

"What the hell?" Steve growled. Along with Perry's laughter, she heard the sound of zippers being pulled up.

"I'm sorry." Hands over her eyes, she moved in the direction of the door, but she hit a wall instead.

Perry laughed again. "Our friends are all put up. You can open your eyes now."

She did, but refused to look at anyone. *Their friends!* She darted out, wishing she had a minute to get her head together before . . .

Too late.

Holiday spotted her. And so did her mom and John. All three came hurrying over.

Holiday stared at her wide-eyed with questions flashing in her eyes. Questions Kylie didn't have answers to.

"Was that the boy's bathroom you just walked out of?" her mom asked, sounding a bit annoyed, but mostly worried. John moved in and slipped his hand around her waist. Something about the way he touched her had Kylie envisioning them naked together. Oh, Gawd. They were having sex. She knew it.

Then she saw it. Saw it in her head. And it was not pretty!

"Are you okay?" her mom asked. "You're beet red."

"Yeah." Kylie squeaked. She pushed away the image of them naked before she wanted to vanish again.

"You were right there," her mom said in a mildly scolding voice. "I turned my head and you were gone when I looked back."

Kylie opened her mouth to say something, to apologize, or maybe to say something mundane like *beautiful weather isn't it*, but those weren't the words to leave her lips.

"You didn't turn your head. You were sucking face with that idiot." She inhaled, clamping her mouth shut, but it just flew back open. "You're sleeping with him, aren't you? Have you even read the sex pamphlets you gave me all those years?"

Her mom gasped and her face brightened. So that was where Kylie got her ability to blush. Her mom opened her mouth, obviously to scold Kylie, but nothing came out. Not a word.

John cleared his throat in a scolding tone. What in holy hell gave him the right to clear his throat at her? "Now, Kylie, that wasn't nice."

"You mean the kiss?" Kylie asked. "Because, frankly, I didn't say it was nice. It was actually quite embarrassing."

That's when Holiday cleared her throat. Kylie could handle Holiday's intervention, but not this bozo's, who was doing the dirty with her mom.

"I really think we should go outside," Holiday said.

"I think the girl needs a firm talking-to," John said.

Kylie's spine went ramrod straight. And damn if she didn't feel her canine teeth grow a little longer. She had emotions racing through her so fast she couldn't even begin to define how she felt. Except hungry. For blood. How dare he feel he had the right to correct her?

"I hope you're rich, because that's the only reason I can think my mom might like you."

Her mom gasped, and so did Kylie. Why was she saying these things? Oh, shit, she needed to shut up. What was wrong with her? Had going invisible addled her brain? Or was being vampire making her as ballsy as Della?

"You're being quite rude, young lady." John looked at Kylie's mom.

"She's not being rude!" a deep voice sounded behind Kylie.

The voice rang all kinds of familiar bells, but Kylie couldn't think straight to know who it was, so she turned around to put a face to the voice.

Oh, shit! Could this get any worse?

"I happened to witness it as well. And frankly I agree with my daughter. It was inappropriate." Her stepdad shot her mom a stern look.

Her mom's face turned even redder, but Kylie recognized that red-faced expression, and it wasn't embarrassment. She was pissed!

"How dare you tell me what's appropriate!" her mom snapped.

Shame filled her stepdad's expression. He looked at Kylie. "I didn't know Kylie was there. I wouldn't have done it if I had. I've apologized a hundred times. But two wrongs—"

"Let's all take a walk," Holiday said again. But no one took a step.

It took Kylie about a second to realize what her stepdad meant. She opened her mouth to say something, but what? *Don't worry, Dad, Mom doesn't know that I watched your young skank rub herself all over you and practically give you a handjob in the middle of downtown Fallen?*

Nope, that didn't sound like the right thing to say. So she ceremoniously shut her mouth and started praying for a miracle, because it would take one right now to fix this mess.

"You wouldn't have done what?" her mom asked, and when her stepdad didn't answer, her mom's fury focused on Kylie.

"What did you see?" she asked in her speak-or-be-grounded tone. And grounded sounded like the best option.

Guilt fluttered in Kylie's chest. But for what? she asked the unwelcome emotion. Not telling her mom had to be the right thing, didn't it?

"Why don't we walk outside," Holiday piped up again, and put a hand on Kylie's mom's shoulder.

Her mom's expression softened. Thank God for Holiday's emotion-altering touch. The panic blossoming in Kylie's gut lessened. Leave it to Holiday to save the day.

But then Kylie saw the way John stared at her stepdad. And when he opened his mouth, Kylie questioned if Holiday could pull off a miracle.

It didn't help matters when Lucas came to a sudden stop beside Kylie, his eyes glowing a shade of pale protective orange. Not that she didn't love that he cared enough to protect her, but the last thing she wanted to have to do was explain his eye color to her stepdad, her mom, and the man who was having sex with her mom. And thinking about that had Kylie's eyes stinging. Shit! Were they glowing now?

"You have no right to judge her after what *you* did." John took a defensive step toward Kylie's stepdad and her own protective instincts sparked to life.

"No wonder your daughter lacks respect," John quipped.

Lacks respect? Kylie felt her fangs grow a little longer, and she was so mad, she'd missed Derek joining the crowd, but Lucas hadn't missed it, because he growled.

Holiday moved in, and keeping one hand on Kylie's mom, she rested her other palm on John's shoulder. For a second, the tense energy sucking up oxygen diminished.

Kylie sent up a silent prayer of thanks. Then she noted the expression on her stepdad's face. And she immediately recanted her gratitude.

"Who the hell do you think are? Don't you dare insult my daughter," her stepdad said. Holiday looked from her mom to John and back to her stepdad. Poor Holiday had only two hands. Before anyone could stop it, her stepdad's fist made contact with John's nose. Blood poured. All the vampires in the room, including herself, breathed in the sweet scent.

Lucas tried to move her back, but she wasn't budging. Kylie's mom screamed. John started swinging his fists at her stepdad, missed, but knocked Holiday over in the process.

Burnett flew across the room and tossed John to the floor. And everyone . . . everyone in the room, all the campers, all the campers' parents, all the new teachers, especially Hayden Yates, stared at the foolhardy chaos that was her life.

Refocusing on the mess before her, she felt as if she were the star on some new reality show: *Parents Behaving Badly.* She watched in complete mortification as the scene continued.

John rose to his feet and apologized to Holiday.

Her mom seethed.

Her dad tried to talk to her seething mom.

Holiday tried to touch everyone.

Burnett continued to glare green daggers at John, proving how hard it was for a vampire to accept an apology. Not that she blamed him. Kill him. Kill him. She cheered the vampire on.

Lucas hadn't stopped scowling at Derek and Derek hadn't stopped ignoring Lucas.

Everyone reacted in one manner or another. Everyone except Kylie. She didn't move, not even to breathe. She stood frozen in the same spot, and concentrated . . . concentrated really hard on *not* wishing she could vanish—because down deep, that's exactly what she wanted to do.

Chapter Thirty

Burnett ushered everyone involved in the dispute out of the dining hall. Kylie moved with him like a robot, one foot in front of the other, still not wanting to let her emotions rise to the surface for fear of what might happen. Meaning, she'd either start again with the wiseass comments—channeling Della's attitude—or she'd vanish. Both could cause irreparable damage.

Right as she stepped out the door, followed by Lucas and Derek, she heard someone's parent say, "Wouldn't you know, it's always humans causing shit."

Inhaling the sunshine-filled air, trying not to be insulted for her mom and stepdad, and trying to control the mortification of it all, she watched Holiday guide her mom and John into the office building. Burnett waited a second, then in an unsympathetic voice, he ordered her stepdad to follow him inside—obviously into different rooms. Kylie sensed they were all going to get a stern talking-to. Not that they didn't deserve it, but . . . she felt odd being the one watching her parents getting pulled into the "principal's office" instead of the other way around.

Remembering some of the things she'd said to her mom and

John, Kylie suspected her stern talking-to was probably just around the corner.

Once the office door closed behind Burnett and her stepdad, Kylie swung around with the intention of throwing herself into Lucas's arms. She needed a little TLC—someone to lean on. But Lucas wasn't there. She looked back at the dining hall and saw him moving inside, no doubt heading back to his pack. God forbid his pack believe his assistance in stopping the disruption was anything more than a good deed, or because he actually cared about her.

Right or wrong, her heart broke right then. Derek, however, suddenly appeared beside her. Her eyes stung, her throat knotted, and the next thing she knew she was in his arms. Warm, strong arms that were so good at holding her and offering comfort.

It was wrong. So wrong. She needed to stop this. Stop relying on Derek.

"Quit feeling guilty," Derek whispered in her ear, reading her emotion right on cue. "I'm just a friend, helping out another friend."

No, she thought. He was a friend who used to be more, a friend who'd told her he loved her and wanted to be more again. He was someone that on odd occasions she still thought about having more with, too—someone she knew she could turn to for help. And yet, it wasn't his arms she longed for, it wasn't him she needed to hold her.

A while later, Holiday stepped out onto the office's porch and motioned her over. Great, now it was Kylie's time to get her punishment. Accepting she deserved it, she stiffened her spine and went to face the music.

But the look on Holiday's face wasn't one of reprimand. She immediately embraced Kylie. "Dear Lord, child. Please tell me you're okay."

"I'm okay," Kylie lied.

Holiday exhaled. "You scared the life out of me. What . . . ? What happened?"

When Kylie met the camp leader's green, caring gaze, the air in Kylie's lungs shuddered. "I scared the life out me, too. I . . . just vanished. I could see and hear you, but you didn't know I was there. I . . . I went poof." *Just like my grandfather and aunt had.*

Holiday touched Kylie's forearm to offer calm. "Okay, we need to talk about it, figure it out, but first let's deal with your parents and get them on their way."

Kylie's chest tightened with the realization that as much as Holiday tried, she wouldn't be able to help Kylie figure this out. She needed her grandfather and aunt. *A chameleon alone will not survive. Come with us. You need to learn who and what you are.*

Realizing Holiday was studying her, Kylie blurted out, "I said terrible things. I don't like John."

"Well, if it makes you feel any better, right now, neither do I." Holiday pressed a palm to each of Kylie's shoulders. "Just go talk to them. I think they're all in agreement that they're the ones in the wrong. Your dad's in my office and your mom and John are in the conference room. Can you do this?"

Kylie nodded.

As she walked away, Holiday pulled her back for another hug. "It's going to be fine, okay? There's nothing we can't figure out."

If only that were true.

Kylie stepped into Holiday's office. Her dad, sitting on the sofa, rose and met her face-to-face. And his face showed his emotions. Remorse. Sadness. A lot of sadness.

"I'm so sorry, baby. I behaved like an idiot. It won't happen again, I promise you."

Kylie nodded. "Everything just got out of hand."

He nodded. "But it wasn't all in vain. It forced me to face the truth. I needed that."

Did his voice just shake, or was she imagining it? "What truth?"

"I'm giving your mom her divorce. She wants it; she's got it."

Defeat filled her stepdad's eyes. Defeat, like she could never recall seeing before. One word came to her mind. *Broken*. He was a broken man. Seeing it hurt so damn much!

"Dad, I think Mom's just—"

"No." He held up his hands. "I didn't mean . . . I'm not blaming your mom. I accept I messed up. I don't even understand how I could do it, when I loved her so damn much from the first time I saw her in high school." Tears filled his eyes as he pressed his palm to Kylie's cheek. "Don't ever fall in love, princess. It hurts too damn much."

His words echoed in her head as she recalled the pain she'd felt when she turned for Lucas and he wasn't there. She wondered if her stepdad wasn't too late in offering that piece of advice. But she pushed her own emotions aside to deal with his. He needed her.

He took another deep breath. "Losing her kills me, but I deserve it, and I'll learn to live with it, but what I can't live with is . . . losing you. From the day the doctor dropped you into my arms, I loved you."

Tears filled Kylie's eyes. "You aren't going to lose me."

"Good, because I'm your father and I don't want you to ever forget that."

But he wasn't her father. The words "I won't forget" rested on the tip of her tongue, but she couldn't say them. She looked away. She hadn't meant that cut of her eyes to mean anything.

Yet it had. She heard his sharp intake of air. She glanced back and saw it in his eyes. He knew. He knew that she knew.

"Your mom told you," he said.

Hurt filled his eyes and the same feeling swelled in Kylie's chest.

"No." *My real father came to see me from the grave.* She had to come up with a lie and quick. "I found your original marriage certificate and learned she was already pregnant, and everything else fell into place."

"I couldn't have loved you more if you were mine. I never wanted you to think I didn't love you because of it."

"I know," she said. "And the fact that you loved me when I wasn't yours meant something." She spoke the words to soothe him, because his pain filled the room, but then she realized how true they were. He'd loved her when he didn't have to.

He'd done all the daddy/daughter things with her: sold Girl Scout cookies, helped her build a matchbox car to enter the school race, and gone on all the father/daughter trips. Then there were the hugs, when her mom wasn't good at giving them. She leaned into him, needing a hug now, and thinking he could use one, too.

She savored his embrace. He'd always been good at this. She heard his breath shake, and she cried into his shoulder like she had so many times as a child. That's when she realized she'd forgiven him. He wasn't a bad man; he'd just made some bad mistakes.

He was, after all, just human.

After her dad left, Kylie pulled herself together, and walked into the conference room to face her mom and John. Like it or not, she had some apologizing to do, so the sooner she got it over with, the better.

Kylie's mom shot up from her chair. John followed. "I'm sorry," Kylie said. "I—"

"We're sorry, too. Aren't we, John?" her mom blurted out.

"Yes, I spoke too freely." The apology came from John's lips but didn't appear in his eyes. "It was a mistake that will not repeat itself."

"You're just human," Kylie said, but she didn't say it with all that much confidence. And she studied his face to see if he reacted to the remark. He didn't. She still had to stop herself from checking his brain pattern again.

The scary thought was that if he wasn't human, he was a chameleon. She recalled Red, who'd given his life to save her, telling her that he was the same thing that she was, only not born at midnight. So . . . Mario must be a chameleon, too. And if John was a chameleon, could he be in cahoots with Mario?

She was overreacting, she told herself. Her feelings probably stemmed from the fact that he was the reason her stepdad didn't stand a chance of getting back with her mom. However, she decided to ask Burnett to do a background check on dear ol' John.

Kylie's mom moved closer. "John, can you give Kylie and me some time alone?"

Here comes the scolding. Kylie bit her tongue and told herself she should be happy her mom decided to spare her the embarrassment of scolding her in front of her man toy.

However, the man toy looked unhappy when he turned for the door. Kylie bit her tongue harder. But damn, this guy brought out the worst in her.

The moment John walked out, Kylie blurted out, "I'm sorry. I shouldn't have said those things." And she was sorry, not because she'd said them to John, but because she'd probably hurt her mom. That had never been her intention.

"No, Holiday was right. Showing up here with him wasn't the best idea. I just . . ." She blushed. "He makes me happy, Kylie. I can't even explain it, but it's almost the feeling I got with your real dad."

Kylie recalled something her grandfather said, that the humans who were blessed found themselves attracted to supernaturals. Her suspicions rose about John.

"I wanted you to get to know him, because . . . because he's important to me. And—"

Dear Lord, this was hard to hear. Before she knew what she planned to say, she'd started talking. "Dad's sorry about all this, too, Mom. If you brought John here to make Dad jealous, it worked. I know Dad hurt you, but if you still love him . . . he loves you."

Her mom closed her eyes as if searching for the right words. When she looked up, raw emotion shined in her eyes. "I did want your dad to see me and John, but I can't . . . Your dad and I won't be getting back together." She took Kylie's hand. "I'm sorry, baby. I can't . . ."

Kylie squeezed her mom's palm. "I understand."

Her mom sighed. "Do you?"

Kylie nodded. It still hurt like the devil, but she understood.

Her mom sighed as if she was about to say something difficult. "Please try to see the good in John. He's not the reason your dad and I broke up."

"I know." That was all Kylie managed to say. She wasn't sure she could ever see any good in John.

Her mom bit her lip and made a funny face. "Now, about the question you asked. If John and I were . . . If we . . ."

"Are having sex?" Kylie finished for her, because God knew her mom would be here all day trying to say it.

Her mom blushed. "I'm an adult and I'm capable of making that kind of decision. You're young and . . ." Her eyes widened. "You aren't . . . you haven't . . . ?"

"No, Mom. I haven't," Kylie said. "But I will someday, and I don't want you to have an aneurism when you find out."

Her mom looked horrified. "I won't. As long as you're thirty."

Kylie rolled her eyes. "Mom."

"Okay, twenty-nine." She paused. "You know, it hurts to see you grow up."

"I know; it hurts to see you grow up, too."

Her mom's brow wrinkled with confusion. "What?"

"I could say it hurt to know you're having sex, but I thought you'd prefer the euphemism."

Her mom chuckled at the same time a cold entered the room, a familiar cold. Daniel? A quick glance around the room told her he couldn't manifest. But she knew he'd tried.

Her mom smiled. Then she reached over and hugged her. "I swear, sometimes when I'm with you, I can almost feel your father here."

"Me too," Kylie said, and wondered how much her mom could really feel.

The chill in the room grew colder, but oddly it came with a hint of anger and frustration. Had her dad overheard the conversation and was making his opinion known about the whole sex-with-John issue?

I know, Dad, Kylie spoke in her head. *I don't like him, either.*

Even before her mom and John pulled out of the parking lot, Holiday and Burnett had Kylie by her elbows. "Let's talk," Holiday said.

Kylie gazed back at the dining hall. "Shouldn't ya'll be in there?"

"First things first," Holiday said as Burnett led them to the office.

"How the hell did you disappear like that?" Leave it to Burnett to cut to the chase.

"I don't know." Kylie walked into the office. "I wished I could vanish like a ghost when I saw my mom and John kissing, and then . . . I did."

"You wished yourself invisible?" Holiday asked.

"I guess," Kylie said.

"Then how did you come back?" Burnett closed the door.

"I un-wished it." Knowing how crazy it sounded, she glanced at Holiday and dropped down on Holiday's sofa. "Sort of like how you tried to teach me to shut off a ghost."

"Visualization." Holiday arched her brows as if impressed.

Not that Kylie shared her viewpoint. "It was scarier than hell. I remembered what my dad said about us working things out together and I thought I was dead." She paused. "How am I going to stop it from happening again?"

Holiday looked at Burnett as if expecting some wisdom from him.

"What?" He held up his arms in defeat. "I ain't got shit. I'm just now learning to deal with ghosts."

Holiday rolled her eyes. "You read the reports at the FRU. Did it say anything, or lead you to assume anything, about a chameleon's gifts?"

"No. The only thing it stated was some of the case studies considered themselves chameleons." He frowned. "There could have been more in the other reports, but they conveniently disappeared."

Right then, Kylie couldn't help but remember her grandfather's warning about the FRU.

"We need to read the other files," Holiday said. Her eyes stayed on Burnett. "How can we do that?"

Kylie closed her eyes. She didn't know what they were going to do, but she knew what she was doing. First, she was going to find a way to get back in touch with her grandfather, and then . . .

A wash of pain spilled over her. Could her grandfather be right? Did she have to leave Shadow Falls and go with him in order to get the information she needed?

After a few minutes of both Burnett and Holiday trying to come up with a solution, they finally concluded that Kylie should be careful about what she wished for.

Right! As if she hadn't come up with that one by herself.

Burnett's phone rang. He answered the call. "Yeah," he said. "How long has she been missing?" Both Holiday and Kylie tried to pretend they weren't listening, but how could they not when the call was obviously about Cindy, the waitress at the diner, the once-smiling young woman in her driver's license who was now in the grave with Holiday's sister?

"Okay," Burnett said. "Get me the file. Did you get anything back on the other matter?" Burnett's eyes shifted to Kylie, telling her that the "other matter" involved her, as well.

Burnett listened and suddenly that's when it hit Kylie. She couldn't hear the conversation on the line. What happen to her . . . "Hey," Kylie screeched at Holiday. "Am I still vampire?"

Holiday tightened her brows. Shock filled her eyes. "No."

"What am I now?" Kylie asked.

"Welcome to my world," Holiday said.

"I'm fae?" Oh, great. More "Kylie's a freak" moments from the other campers were predicted to arrive soon. As if the parental chaos wasn't enough to get them talking about her.

Her aunt's words echoed in her mind. *The few who did not hide were viewed as outcasts, freaks, and not belonging to any one kind.*

Holiday nodded and smiled a smile that came with a lot of empathy. And Kylie not only saw it, but felt it.

Burnett must have heard the conversation, because as soon as he pulled the phone from his ear, he stared at her forehead and said, "Damn."

"What did you learn?" Holiday asked, as if sensing Kylie didn't want to discuss her ever-evolving brain pattern.

"Cindy Shaffer disappeared about six months ago."

"So after Hannah disappeared," Holiday said.

"Do we know for sure that Hannah didn't just leave for a while and then . . ." He paused and sympathy flowed out of him in waves.

"And then was killed," Holiday said, and the words no more left her lips than the grief floated off her and filled Kylie's chest. Kylie had always been empathetic to others, but this was so much more intense.

Not a cakewalk, Kylie thought. Being fae would take some getting used to, but at least she could go back to eating food again. Then she thought about Derek and how he'd said her emotions had felt supersized. That must have been so hard on him.

Burnett moved in. "The police are investigating her disappearance. They have a suspect—old boyfriend—but they couldn't prove anything. I'll go over their files, but considering what we know, I don't think this is tied to her personally."

"What else did you learn?" Kylie asked, remembering Burnett's glance at her during the call.

"I had another check done on Hayden Yates."

"And?" Kylie asked, but even before he spoke she felt his discontent at having to tell her.

"He's clean. There's nothing in his background that points to him being anything other than what he says he is."

Kylie exhaled, not sure she believed it. She'd been so sure there was something hinky about him. Then she remembered . . . "Can you check out my mom's boyfriend?"

"You think *he's* behind Hannah's murder?" Burnett asked, confused.

"No, nothing to do with Hannah. I just . . . don't like him."

"I don't, either," Burnett clipped, "but that doesn't mean he's a criminal. There's a lot of people out there that I don't like."

Kylie frowned. "He gives me the creeps and I'd feel better if—"

"I'll do it," Burnett said, but she felt his emotions and knew he believed it was a waste of time.

"There's something else I want to talk about," Kylie said.

"Why do I have the feeling I'm not going to like this?" Burnett asked.

Kylie glanced at Holiday, who looked equally concerned. "I think it's time to call a halt to the whole shadow thing," Kylie said.

"No!" Burnett's expression grew grim.

Kylie sat up straighter and felt her backbone stiffen. "I'm tired of never being alone."

"You're alone in your room when you go to your cabin," he countered.

"Della's listening to every move I make. I can't do it anymore. I want my life back. Mario hasn't tried anything else for weeks now. Miranda said she doesn't feel any unwelcomed presence. I don't feel his presence. Maybe he's given up."

"People like him don't give up. He's waiting for the opportunity to strike."

"I promise to be careful, and if I feel anything, you'll be the first person I tell."

"No!" he said again.

Kylie felt an odd kind of energy building in her gut. Everything inside her said she was right, that they couldn't force this on her. She didn't understand the ball of vigor, or her lack of fear at standing up to them right now. If she wasn't so mad at his out-and-out refusal, she might have been more afraid that something else weird was happening to her.

"I'm not a prisoner here," she said. "I have a say in this."

"A say in if you get yourself killed or not?" he asked in anger.

"I'm not going to get killed." She tilted her chin back and looked at Holiday, hoping she'd see reason in the camp leader's eyes.

"This is because you want to see your grandfather again, isn't it?" Holiday asked, and while she saw Holiday's disapproval, Kylie also felt Holiday's compassion.

"Partly." Kylie didn't even consider lying. There was just a sense of rightness to her request. "But that's not all it's about. I'm tired of being babysat."

Burnett went to speak again, but Holiday intervened. "Would you promise to stay out of the woods?"

"She's already broken that promise," Burnett said.

"I promise." Kylie ignored Burnett.

Holiday leaned forward. "Will you promise to confirm with us when you meet your grandfather?"

"Will you promise not to stop me?" Kylie asked.

"I promise we will assess the situation and only stop you if we feel your life's in jeopardy."

"By whose judgment?" Kylie asked. "Some people's idea of safety is not reasonable." She didn't even flinch when she looked at Burnett—who, by the way, looked even more furious. And she felt every bit of his anger.

"This is insane. My job is to protect you," Burnett snarled.

"No," Holiday corrected him. "Our job as school administrators is to teach Kylie how to survive in the human world. Like it or not"—she glanced at Kylie—"she has the right to leave. And that is the last thing we want to happen right now."

Somehow, Kylie knew that the ball of energy in her gut had been about projecting how serious she was on this issue. Was that a fae talent, or was that from her chameleon abilities? Kylie didn't know. But it was pretty damn cool, even if it scared her.

"Do I have a choice in the matter?" Burnett bit out.

"No," both Kylie and Holiday said at the same time.

Burnett's phone beeped in an odd kind of way. He grabbed his device and pushed a few buttons. "Someone just jumped the front gate." He turned to leave, but stopped when a figure flashed in the doorway.

Blake, Holiday's ex-fiancé and the suspected murderer, stood there. "I heard you were looking for me."

Kylie jumped to her feet and stood beside Burnett, ready to defend Holiday.

But Holiday acted as though she didn't need protecting. She jumped up and met Blake's glare. "Did you do it?" she asked, fury pouring out of her.

"Did I do what?" he asked.

"Did you kill Hannah?"

Chapter Thirty-one

"What?" His gaze cut to Burnett and Kylie and then back to Holiday. Disbelief filled his eyes and rolled off of him in waves. "Hannah's dead?"

Kylie tried to listen to his heartbeat, but not being vampire anymore, all she could do was read his emotions. They came off sincere, but could she trust that?

"Answer me, damn it!" Holiday slammed her palms down on his chest. Her emotions were a whole bag of raw pain, betrayal at its worst.

Burnett moved to Holiday's side and gently pulled her back, but his eyes were bright green and on Blake with warning.

Blake exhaled, his frustration sounding in the released air. "You are so biting on the wrong vampire! This is meritless."

"Not so meritless," Holiday said. "She told me you were furious with her when she told you that she planned on telling me the truth."

"Of course I was furious. We were getting married. I loved you. She told me if I showed up at my own wedding, she'd stop the ceremony."

"Did you kill her?" Holiday demanded, her anguish filling the air Kylie breathed.

Blake stared at Holiday, hurt radiating from him. "Of all the people in the world, you know me better than that. Do you really think I could murder Hannah?"

"What I think doesn't mean shit," Holiday seethed. "I didn't think you'd sleep with my sister, but you did."

"We were drunk and . . . I'd just started dating you. It was a damn mistake. And then the next thing I know, I'm in love with you. I'm still in love with you. And yes, I wanted to tell you then, but I was scared. At first, Hannah acted as if it never happened, so I convinced myself—"

"That you could get away with it?" Tears pooled in Holiday's eyes.

"No, I convinced myself that one mistake wasn't enough to stop two people who loved each other from finding happiness."

"That's enough." Burnett walked over and grabbed Blake by the arm. "You're coming with me."

Blake pulled away and the two men stared each other right in the eyes.

"Not yet." Holiday looked at Burnett. "I want to talk to him."

"You did," Burnett countered.

"Alone. I want to talk to him alone," she said.

Burnett's body turned into one knotted muscle. Jealousy oozed from his pores. "He's a suspected serial killer, Holiday, who illegally entered Shadow Falls. I need to get him to the FRU office."

"Serial killer?" Blake's eyes turned defensive. "I didn't harm Hannah or anyone else."

"That's what they all say," Burnett clipped, and reached for Blake again. The man moved back, his eyes growing hot.

"What's wrong?" Blake baited Burnett. "Worried she might still feel something for me?"

Holiday moved in and rested her hand on Burnett's arm and spoke with honesty. "Burnett has no reason to worry. I want the truth from you, Blake, that's all. And then I want you to climb right back under whatever rock you've been hiding under." She motioned with a firm hand for Burnett and Kylie to leave.

Burnett's body language and emotions said what he thought of that idea. But something told Kylie that Holiday needed this time alone with Blake, and Burnett needed to give it to her.

Kylie touched Burnett's arm, felt the warmth flow from her touch, and saw his expression soften. He looked back at Holiday right before he walked out. Kylie looked at Blake. And right then, her gut told her that he wasn't Hannah's killer.

But if it wasn't him, who was it? Then Kylie again remembered Hannah saying the killer was here. Here at Shadow Falls. Kylie couldn't help but think again of Hayden Yates. It didn't even matter that Burnett's check had come back clean; she didn't trust that guy. And by God, she wasn't going to lower her guard where he was concerned, either.

Burnett didn't move more than a foot away from the door. Kylie figured he was listening to every word spoken in the other room. For Holiday's safety, of course, so it wasn't really an evasion of privacy. At least that's what Kylie wanted to believe.

She couldn't hear the conversation, and as slightly uncomfortable as it made her listening in on private conversations, her own need to protect Holiday had her wishing she could.

"Was Blake telling the truth?" Kylie asked, wondering if the emotions she'd read from Blake were as telling as his heartbeat.

Burnett glanced over at her. "About what?"

"About not killing Hannah?"

"It doesn't matter," he said gruffly, and looked back at the door.

"Doesn't it?" she asked.

He shook his head. "The heart can lie. People, evil people with no conscience, have no problem lying."

Kylie remembered Della telling her that in the beginning. But as much as Kylie wanted to believe Blake was their man, what she'd felt from him wasn't evil. "For what it's worth, his emotions felt real."

"You mean when he said he still loved her?" Burnett's jealousy practically bounded out of him and bounced off the walls.

Kylie swallowed. "I meant his shock about Hannah being dead, but . . . that, too."

Burnett closed his eyes and pressed a hand against the door.

"But just as real were Holiday's sentiments when she said *all* she wanted from him was the truth. She doesn't love him, Burnett."

He looked back at Kylie, sadness radiating from his eyes. "She used to."

"Is that important?"

"It is when that's what stopping her from letting anyone else get close," he said. There was a pause, and then as if to change the subject, he said, "I don't agree with Holiday's decision on removing your shadows."

"I know," Kylie said. "But tell me this—how would you take having someone shadow you all the time?"

She heard him swallow and felt his emotional answer. He wouldn't have accepted being shadowed for a single day.

All of a sudden, the room turned cold. Ghost-visiting cold. Then Hannah appeared beside Burnett; her presence came with a thick swarm of panic. *"He's here! He's here! You've gotta stop him! He's going to try to kill her,"* she screamed at Burnett.

"Who's here?" Kylie asked.

Burnett didn't wait for an answer. He bolted through Holiday's door, without bothering to open it. Ripped off the hinges, the door landed with a loud thud on the floor. He walked across the splintered wood and faced Blake.

Door removed, Kylie watched the scene from the outer room.

Blake, already on his feet, stared at Burnett with fury.

Holiday, still sitting at her desk, wore an expression of shock. She shot up from her desk chair, showing how slow fae reaction time was to that of a vampire.

Burnett, both his hands fisted at his sides, spoke to Blake. "Either you come the easy way, or the hard way." His threat rang with honesty. "I don't care which."

Kylie's gaze shifted to the spirit. Hannah stood frozen, gaping at the scene playing out. An ugly brown aura surrounded her. While deceased, there was plenty of emotion lingering beneath the icy chill of death. Kylie picked up one emotion loud and clear. Shame—big, heaping mounds of shame. Then she felt the spirit's surprise. Oddly, Hannah's initial panic and fear had faded.

Something didn't feel right. It was almost as if Hannah hadn't known Blake was here, and if she hadn't known Blake was here, how could *he* be the one causing her panic? "Did Blake do this?" Kylie asked Hannah in a hurried breath. No answer. "Hannah?" Kylie said her name again. Then the ghost faded.

"What's going on?" Holiday asked Burnett again, and Kylie's gaze locked on the three people in the room.

Blake looked back at Holiday. "I didn't do this. I probably don't deserve another chance with you, but I don't deserve this." He turned to Burnett. "I'll go with you, I'll answer your questions, but if you lay a hand on me, I'll kill you."

And from the man's emotions clouding the air, his threat rang with as much sincerity as Burnett's.

It had been a lazy Sunday afternoon with a lot of frustration floating in the air. Miranda was frustrated because there was a new shapeshifter ogling Perry. Holiday was frustrated because . . . well, as if losing her sister the first time hadn't been bad enough, now her spirit hadn't shown back up. Burnett was frustrated because he couldn't find one thread of evidence against Blake. Therefore he couldn't hold him.

Kylie was frustrated over the whole disaster that was her life.

The only one not in a pissy mood was Della, and Kylie, even being an emotion-reading fae, wasn't sure what mood Della was in, but it felt wrong. The girl was following Kylie around like a lost puppy.

Even now, pulling up her e-mail, Kylie felt Della standing over her shoulder. Kylie turned around and frowned. "What?"

"What, what?" Della asked.

"You're reading over my shoulder. You're not even my shadow now."

"I'm not shadowing you. And I didn't know your e-mail was so private," Della said.

Right then, Kylie got a huge sense of anxiety, coupled with a sense of sadness, and then anger from the vamp. Della's emotions were dancing all over the place.

"What's up with you?" Kylie asked.

"Not a damn thing." Della dropped into a kitchen chair.

Kylie shifted her gaze back to her e-mail and clicked to check mail. No new e-mails. Nothing from . . .

"You're hoping to get something from your grandfather, aren't you?" Della asked.

Kylie looked back again. "Maybe. Why?"

Della frowned. "You're going to go live with him, aren't you? You're gonna leave Shadow Falls."

The question cut like a knife in Kylie's chest. How could she explain to Della that leaving was the last thing she wanted to do? Yet, there was a part of her that said it might be the only way she could learn about who and what she was.

And after seeing the shock on everyone's faces at the camp when her new fae pattern emerged, there was a part of Kylie that longed to be with people who didn't judge her. And the sooner she learned to control this changing-pattern game and the powers that came with it, the sooner she could come back to Shadow Falls and really fit in.

"That's what this is about?" Kylie asked.

"Yeah, that's what it's about. And don't think I didn't notice you didn't deny it, either."

Kylie chose her words carefully. "I don't have plans to do that." That was the truth. She was still praying that it wouldn't prove the only way.

"But your fae ass has thought about it, haven't you?" she asked.

"Yeah, my fae ass has thought about it, but—"

"But nothing! I'm not letting you go, Kylie." Tears filled the vamp's eyes. "I lost Lee, I lost my parents and my sister and all my friends back home. You and Miranda are all I have, and Miss Witch is so obsessed with a certain shape-shifter right now, I hardly even have time to argue with her anymore."

Della stood up and swiped at her cheeks. "I'm freaking tired of losing people I care about."

Kylie stood up. "You're not losing me." Her own eyes stung. Even if she had to go away, she'd be back. She belonged here. Surely Della realized that.

Della huffed. "I'm leaving next weekend to go . . . to go do what I gotta do for Burnett. And all I can think about is that you won't be here when I get back."

"I'll . . ." Kylie finally heard what Della said. "Where are you going?"

Della frowned. "I can't tell you."

"Shit." Kylie shook her head, recalling the anxiety she'd read from Della. Was Della scared? Of course she was scared, Kylie realized, but Della would never admit it. Kylie went and hugged the vamp. Della didn't like it, but she didn't fight it too hard. "Whatever you're doing for Burnett, it damn well better not be too dangerous."

"Group hug! Group hug!" Miranda said, bolting through the door.

"No." Della lurched back. "That one was just for Kylie," she said, trying to sound badass, but Kylie read her embarrassment loud and clear. "Go hug Perry." Della stormed into her bedroom and slammed the door.

"What crawled up her butt and put her in such a sunny disposition?" Miranda asked.

Kylie rolled her eyes. Then the computer dinged with a new e-mail, and she scurried over to see who it was from. Her mom.

The thought crossed Kylie's mind like sandpaper. If she did have to leave Shadow Falls, what in the hell would she tell her parents?

Kylie glanced back at Miranda. "Maybe you should go pick a fight with Della so she'll know you still care."

Dinner that night was supposed to be a celebration to kick off the new school year. Books and class schedules were passed out. Kylie and Della had all the same classes. Miranda was in two of Kylie's five classes. Kylie couldn't help but wonder if this wasn't Burnett's idea of shadowing her without calling it shadowing.

Not that she was going to let that thought ruin her night. Sitting at a table with Della, Miranda, Perry, Jonathon, and Helen, Kylie downed her second piece of pizza. It was good to enjoy food again. Not that her improved mood had anything to do with the thin-crust pepperoni. It wasn't even the party atmosphere, or the party itself; it was what was happening after the party.

She eyed the clock—only two hours to go.

Right then Steve came over to their table and dropped down in an empty chair beside Della. Kylie almost grinned when Della literally blushed.

"What's up?" Steve asked.

"Hi, Steve," Kylie said, wanting him to feel welcome. Before coming to the dinner, Della had confessed that Steve was also supposed to go with her on the mission for the FRU. Della, of course, was pissed. Ahh, but she hadn't been able to hide the excitement in her stream of emotions.

Jonathon and Steve started chatting about some classes. Della seemed to relax and so did Kylie. Miranda nudged Kylie with her elbow and leaned in. "I think he likes her," she whispered in a very low voice. But Della, not missing a word with her sensitive hearing, shot Miranda a scowl.

"Here's to a great year." Someone made a toast across the room. Everyone seemed to be in a festive mood, and for the time being, everyone had stopped staring at Kylie's pattern. Probably another reason Kylie was in a better mood.

But no sooner did she appreciate not being stared at than the hairs on the back of her neck started doing a two-step. When she swerved around, Hayden Yates turned his head. Her heart gripped when she saw Holiday standing next to him in the crowd. Not talking with him, but talking to the shy teacher Collin Warren.

Kylie still didn't like Hayden being that close to Holiday. She zeroed her gaze on him and when he glanced back, obviously feeling his neck hair dancing, their gazes met. *I swear if you hurt her, you'll pay for it.*

He looked away; Kylie kept her gaze locked on him for several moments, and she hoped like hell he understood her message, because it wasn't a threat. It was a promise.

Just thinking about the possibility of anyone hurting Holiday made Kylie's blood thicken and start to fizz—a sure sign that while her pattern might have changed, she was still a protector.

Someday she hoped to be able to say that with a total sense of pride, but right now it seemed to be just one more thing making her different from everyone else.

Kylie had no sooner turned back when she felt another pair of eyes on her, only a different kind of feeling tiptoed up her spine. Even from fifty feet away, Lucas's gaze felt like a caress. He winked. He glanced at the clock and she knew that like her he was counting down the time until they met.

"Damn!" Jonathon yelled, pulling Kylie's gaze from Lucas. "You cut yourself." Jonathon was holding Helen's hand; blood oozed from his grip.

Helen, looking a bit squeamish, had a bloody apple in her other hand and a bloody knife sitting in her lap. "It's okay." Her words lacked confidence. "It's not bad. Is it?"

Jonathon released his hold on her hand to look at it. His eyes grew bright, no doubt because of the blood, but even more apparent was his concern for Helen. "You need stitches," he said.

Helen looked up at Kylie. "Can you just fix it?"

Kylie's breath caught. It had been a while since she'd thought about her healing powers. And the few times she'd thought about them, she remembered those powers had failed Ellie. Kylie had failed Ellie.

"I . . . don't know if I can." She looked into Helen's eyes, saw her pain, but a lump of fear formed in Kylie's stomach right alongside the two slices of pizza. "I couldn't dreamscape when I was vampire; I probably can't heal as a fae."

"But faes are known for their healing," Helen reminded her.

"Oh, yeah." Kylie let go of a breath that shuddered on its escape from her lips. "What if I mess up?" She could still recall how devastated she'd been when she hadn't been able to bring Ellie back from the dead. Looking at her hands, she remembered how her palms had been coated with the girl's blood.

"You won't," Helen said with complete confidence.

Looking up, Kylie remembered how Helen had helped her by checking out her brain to see if she had a tumor the first week she'd been at camp. Helen had helped Kylie, and she couldn't say no.

She stood and moved over to the chair next to Helen. The shy and trusting girl held out her bleeding palm. Breathing in, Kylie recalled that she had to think healing thoughts. Amazingly, her hands suddenly felt hot. She gently ran her fingertip over the wound. Her touch created a tiny wake around the pooled blood on Helen's palm.

Fearing failure, Kylie put her whole palm over the wound. Hesitating to check to see if she'd done it, she suddenly realized that the entire lunch room had gone silent. Not a sound echoed in the large room.

Cutting her eyes up briefly, she realized everyone stared. Everyone! *Freaking great!*

Helen lifted her hand away and brought it in front of her face. Wiping the blood away with her other hand, a shy smile lifted her lips.

"You did it," Helen whispered, sounding as self-conscious as Kylie at all the unwanted attention.

Kylie leaned in. "Why is everyone staring?"

Helen made a funny face and came closer. "Because you're glowing."

"Glowing?" Kylie asked.

Helen nodded.

Kylie noticed that light did seem to emanate from her skin. "Shit!"

"No shit!" said Della. "You look like a firefly. This is so freaking cool!"

More like *not* cool! Kylie thought.

Holiday walked over, eyes rounded, and bafflement coming off her in waves.

Kylie stared up at her, mortified. "Make it stop. Please. Pleee-assse."

Chapter Thirty-two

"Where are you going?" Della asked when Kylie stepped out of her bedroom an hour later with her hair and teeth brushed, and—thank God—no longer glowing.

She almost told Della she didn't have to report to her anymore, but decided she'd probably ask Della the same thing if she were leaving the cabin.

"I'm going to meet Lucas," Kylie said.

Della titled her head to listen to her heartbeat.

"I'm not lying," Kylie said.

"I know. I heard," Della said. "Have fun. And don't do anything I wouldn't do."

"Gosh," Kylie teased, trying not to be grumpy. "That leaves my options wide open."

Della grinned. "But if you come home glowing, I'll know what you did."

"Not funny," Kylie said, and meant it. Then she took off.

Thankfully, she'd stopped glowing about ten minutes after she'd healed Helen. Out of sheer desperation, she'd asked Holiday, "Why did that happen? It never happened before when I healed someone."

Holiday's shrug and "I don't know" didn't surprise Kylie. But it was just one more thing that had Kylie taking her grandfather's warning more seriously. What if these crazy things continued? Right now, it was just the supernaturals who considered her a freak of nature. What would happen if she did something like this in front of regular humans?

Running down the path, hoping the feel of the wind in her hair would take the edge off her mood, she made it to the office in no time. The sound of a few people still lingering in the dining hall filled the night. Before anyone saw her, she cut around to the back of the office. The second she saw Lucas waiting for her by the tree, her frustration vanished.

She ran toward him and he snagged her up and pulled her to him. His arms wrapped around her waist. His thumbs slipped under the hem of her tank top to touch her bare skin. The kiss was sweet and warm. When he pulled back and smiled, she knew what he was thinking.

"Don't mention it," she said, feeling another "glowing" joke coming on.

"I'm just jealous."

"Jealous?" she asked, thinking she'd been wrong. "Of what?"

"I want to be the only thing that makes you glow."

She thumped her hand on his wide chest. "I'm telling you just like I told Della and Miranda. It's not funny."

"You looked beautiful." Honesty flowed from his comment. "Like an angel."

She frowned. "I don't want to be an angel. I want to be a regular supernatural."

"Okay, I won't talk about it anymore. I'll just kiss you instead."

And what a kiss it was. Hotter, sweeter, and more mind-numbing than ever. When he pulled back, she heard his pulse humming, a natural seduction mechanism for weres, and she wasn't above being seduced by it. She was lost in the sound.

"It must be close to the full moon again." She smiled up at the heat in his eyes, knowing her eyes held the same.

"Yeah." He inhaled as if trying to get oxygen into his brain. "You are driving me crazy. Sometimes, I just want . . ." He took a step back. "Let's try talking for a while."

She grinned. "I kind of like driving you crazy."

"That's mean." He pointed a finger in her face, but his tone rang humorous.

Not really mean, Kylie thought. It wasn't as if she'd planned anything to happen tonight. But if it did . . . Right then, she recalled Holiday's words of wisdom about boys, or rather sex. *When you do make that decision, it's a decision you make rationally and not one you just let happen. You understand the difference?*

Kylie did understand the difference. Problem was, it was easier to let it happen than to plan it. Planning it meant talking about it. And that would be embarrassing.

She inhaled sharply with a sudden realization. If she couldn't talk about it, she shouldn't do it—because unless she wanted to go through what Sara did with her pregnancy scare, it was essential that they talk about it.

"What is it?" Lucas asked.

She opened her mouth to answer—to talk about it—but closed her lips just as quickly. They could talk about it later. Later, but, for certain, before anything happened.

"Nothing." Her voice sounded like a frog ready to croak.

He studied her face. "You're almost glowing again."

"Crap!" She held out her arms and studied them in a panic.

He chuckled. "No, you're just blushing. Where did you slip off to in your head?" He tapped a finger to her temple and with her fae gifts, she felt the passion ooze from him.

"Nowhere," she lied. "Let's just . . . talk." *But not about sex.* Because obviously, she wasn't ready to have that conversation.

He studied her as if he didn't believe her, then reached for her hand and laced his fingers into hers. His palm felt warm, but not nearly as warm as it had when she'd been a vampire.

"Okay. Let's talk." They sat down on the soft ground, under the alcove of the tree. "Why don't you tell me how you got out of being shadowed? It doesn't sound like Burnett just to ease up on something like that."

"He didn't want to. But I . . ." She recalled the strange feeling she'd gotten when she'd stood up to Burnett and Holiday. As if the power of persuasion was . . . a real power. Then again, maybe it was. "I persuaded him."

"How? He's not easy to persuade."

"I . . . sort of threatened I might leave."

"Leave?" Concern filled his blue eyes. "You were just bullshitting him, right?"

Mostly, but I'm beginning to worry. She almost told him that, but decided she didn't want to get into that particular conversation with Lucas, not when they had so little time together, so she just nodded. "I agreed not to go into the woods, and to tell them before I went to see my grandfather again."

"What?" His super-charged werewolf protectiveness spilled out of him. "Burnett's going to let you go see your grandfather again? Alone?"

She nodded. "As long as it doesn't appear too dangerous."

"How are you going to know if it's dangerous?" He shook his head, his dark hair scattered across his brow. "Don't go until I come back." He cupped her chin in his hand. "Promise me."

"Come back from where?" she asked.

His frown tightened. "My dad again. This time I'm going to have to spend some time there. A week or more."

She tried to wrap her head around what he said. "But school starts tomorrow."

"Yeah." Sarcasm flowed from him. "But my dad doesn't see getting an education as being important."

"Can't you just tell him no? That you'll come to see him during parent weekend?"

"I wish," he said.

"But why for so long?" Suddenly she couldn't help but wonder if Fredericka planned on going with him.

He touched her cheek. "He's being insistent, Kylie. He gets something in his head and he won't let it go. I'm sorry."

The sincerity in his apology filled her chest. Sincerity and . . . guilt. For what?

He brushed her hair behind her ear. "You know I have to do this to get on the Council. I wouldn't do any of this if it wasn't for that. And . . . when it's over, it's over."

"What's over? What does he want you to do?"

"He just . . . He's crazy and I have to go along with him for now. Please . . . just understand for a little longer. In less than a month, the Council will make their choice. A month is all I need and then I don't have to go along with his plans."

"What plans?" She felt a touch of resentment swell inside her. "I hate your secrets."

"I know," he said. "I hate them, too. But you have to trust me on this."

For some crazy reason, when he said *trust*, she sensed he meant something . . . more. More as in . . . "Is Fredericka going?"

"No," he said. "Just me."

"Not even Clara?" she asked, still confused about the emotions she read in him.

"No. She might come for a while but not stay." He pulled her against him and they just sat there for the longest time not talking. Her heart hurt for him because she sensed how much he really didn't want to go, didn't want to do whatever it was his father had planned.

But he was going and was probably doing it—whatever it was. And he felt guilty about doing it, too. Why?

"Will you call me?" she finally asked.

"I'll try, but if he's monitoring my calls, I can't be caught . . ."

"Talking to me," she finished for him.

He exhaled and she knew it was the truth before he answered. "I don't like it."

Neither did she. Not even a little bit.

A second passed and then he said, "You didn't promise me that you won't go see your grandfather until I get back."

"I can't promise," she said, aggravated that he wanted promises and answers from her, but still held so much back. "I'll do what I have to do." And he'd just have accept it, as she was trying to accept what he'd told her, or rather what he hadn't told her.

Monday morning, the first-day-of-school jitters at Shadow Falls didn't feel any different from all Kylie's first-day jitters. She was both excited and anxious about being forced into a room full of people who seemed to know some secret to life, a secret she didn't have.

In spite of knowing what she was, and being surrounded by other supernaturals, she still felt like the outsider—the floater, floating to one group and then another, and not really belonging anywhere.

No doubt she'd follow Della and Miranda and socialize with whoever they hung out with, and their friends wouldn't reject Kylie, but she wouldn't get that sense of belonging. Just as it had been in her old school. Only difference was that she would have been with Sara, another misfit.

While putting on her makeup, Kylie thought about Sara. They hadn't talked in weeks but Kylie would change that later. While she accepted they had changed and probably didn't have nearly as much in common as they once had, Sara was still . . . Sara. And today, Kylie missed her more than ever.

The morning air had a touch of fall to it. Deciding what to wear, and how to wear her hair, had taken way more time than it should have. She hadn't thought she'd even care, since Lucas wasn't here, but the vibe had been contagious as Miranda and Della had worked to get themselves picture perfect.

Kylie hadn't dressed up for anyone. Yet when Derek looked over from the fae breakfast table, his eyes told her she looked pretty. She found herself smiling and then that smile vanished and she started missing Lucas.

After breakfast, they had Meet Your Campmate hour. Kylie drew Nikki's name, the new shape-shifter, the girl Miranda accused of having a crush on Perry. Kylie had worried that the new camper would pepper her with questions about the glowing episode, but nope. All Nikki wanted to talk about was Perry. Miranda had been right. The girl had a serious thing for Perry. Not that Kylie suspected Perry would play along. Nevertheless, before the hour ended, Kylie had nicely mentioned that Perry was already otherwise committed.

The girl had nicely ignored her, too.

The hour hadn't ended when Kylie debated what, if anything, she'd tell Miranda. Jealousy was an ugly emotion. Kylie was lucky that Fredericka hadn't gone with Lucas to his dad's place, or she'd have been battling the green-eyed emotion herself.

Kylie's first class was English with Della, Miranda, and Derek. Although absent, Lucas was in the class as well. Ava Kane, the new teacher, had an easy teaching style, not that any of the guys noticed anything other than her body. Not a male in the room wasn't mesmerized. Even Derek. Chances were, if Lucas had been there, he'd have been just as taken.

While the boys only had eyes for the teacher, the teacher only had eyes for Kylie's forehead. Was her pattern doing something new? She actually turned to Della and asked. Della assured her that she was still just a regular boring-ass fae.

When the class ended, Miss Kane stood by the door. And when Kylie walked past, Miss Kane leaned down and whispered, "Sorry. I shouldn't have stared, I'm just fascinated by . . . you."

Kylie felt her sincerity. "It's okay," Kylie offered, even though she wished it weren't. At least the woman apologized, which was more than what ninety percent of the campers would do.

History class—next in line—was difficult to sit through. As hard as Collin Warren tried to hide his jitters about teaching, they rang loud and clear. His nervousness filled the room like smoke, yet unlike Miss Kane, not once did the man look Kylie in the eyes. Frankly, she wasn't sure he looked anyone in the eyes.

Yet, because of Holiday's request that Kylie take the nervous teacher under her wing, when the class ended, Kylie hung back to offer a word of support. The students all left the room, except for her. She hoped the man would acknowledge her, but he sat at his desk, head down, shuffling his own papers.

She moved to stand in front of his desk. He still didn't look up. Okay . . . this was weird. She got being shy, but this was over the top—the kind of shyness for which a person might require medicine.

"Hello," she said.

He exhaled as if unhappy, but looked up. "Can I help you?"

Emotions flowed from him—something more than just extreme shyness. Almost fear, mingled with frustration.

"I wanted to say welcome to Shadow Falls. It can be hard—"

"I . . . I need practice." He glanced away. "I'll get better at it."

"I wasn't going to criticize." She sympathized with how he must feel, knowing he'd sucked his first day at teaching. "Practice makes perfect, my Nana used to say."

He looked up. "Do you see her?"

"See who?" Kylie asked.

"Your Nana. Isn't she passed? I hear you have the gift of speaking with the dead."

The question caught Kylie off guard. "Yeah. I mean, she died about four months ago, but I haven't spoken with her."

"But you talk to others, right? The dead?"

Kylie nodded. "Yeah." Unable to read him at the moment, she added, "I know it sounds pretty freaky."

"Not at all. I'd love to be able to ask the dead questions."

Kylie tried to digest what he'd said.

He diverted his eyes. "I mean . . . with my love of history. How great would it be to talk to those who lived before us?"

"That makes sense," Kylie said. And it did, but it was still odd. Most supernaturals would never have wanted to deal with the dead, not even for the love of history. She looked to the door. "I should go before I'm late."

As Kylie walked away, she felt him watching her. Okay, Collin Warren was even stranger than she'd first assumed. She really hoped Holiday knew what she was doing when she hired him.

Kylie had just left that cabin and started down the path to her next class when her phone rang. Glancing at the number, a wave of nostalgia hit.

"I was going to call you, too." Kylie sighed.

"The first day of school doesn't feel right with you not here," Sara said.

"I know." Kylie bit down on her lip.

"How are things?" Sara asked. "You still got two cute boys after you?"

"I pretty much decided on one."

"Derek," Sara said.

"No," Kylie corrected. "Lucas."

"Hmm, for some reason, I thought you'd go with Derek, but Lucas is yummy."

Why did you think that? "How are you doing?" Kylie asked, deciding she didn't want to know Sara's answer to the other question.

"Still cancer free," Sara said. "As you well know."

Kylie ignored the comment. "I'm glad."

"When are you coming home next?" Sara asked.

"I think there's a parent weekend in two or three weeks." If she wasn't still pulling stunts like glowing and vanishing, that was.

"Good, because I need a Kylie fix. Agh, there's the bell. I gotta run. I'll call you in a week or so."

A week? There was a time not so long ago when not a day would go by without them talking.

Kylie pushed away the melancholy at how her life had changed. Then, pocketing her phone, she hurried to class. The thought that it was Hayden Yates's class sent a shiver of dread skittering up and down her backbone.

The second she walked up to the door of Hayden Yates' classroom, Kylie decided that the awkward vibes Collin Warren gave off weren't nearly as unsettling as Mr. Yates's.

The man hadn't even looked at Kylie, yet somehow she knew he'd been keeping tabs on her—that he not only knew she was standing at the door, but he'd been waiting for her.

The question that had weighed on her mind grew heavier. Was he behind Hannah's and the other girls' deaths? If so, did he know Kylie suspected him?

Stepping farther into the classroom, she noticed that everyone was already in their seats. Only one seat remained. Kylie's gut turned into a pretzel.

Fredericka sat right behind the empty seat. The girl smiled, or rather smirked.

Kylie hadn't thought about having to deal with the she-wolf in her classes. Trying not to look at Fredericka, Kylie went and sat down.

As she slipped into the seat, she heard the were say, "Oh, boy. Extra light now the glowworm has shown up."

Kylie gritted her teeth and stared at the book on her desktop.

"Bitch," Della muttered from across the room.

Kylie, suddenly angry with herself for letting Della fight her battles, swung around and faced her nemesis. "In addition to glowing, I've discovered other new talents. Here's one you're going to love—giving smart-ass weres the mange. Especially ones that still slightly reek of skunk."

Chuckles escaped from several of the nearby students. Fredericka rose defensively from her seat, her eyes glowing a shade of pissed-off orange.

Seeing the fury in the wolf-crazed gaze, Kylie questioned the wisdom of spouting off her mouth. No doubt about it, she was about to get her ass whupped by a were—and on the first day of school. How special was that?

Chapter Thirty-three

"Sit down!" Mr. Yates's order echoed through the room. "Kill each other on your own time, not mine."

Kylie turned around, surprised the suspicious teacher hadn't let the she-wolf take her out.

The tension still hung thick when he started teaching. Facing forward, Kylie debated if she would get a pencil stabbed in her back from Fredericka.

But nothing happened. Mr. Yates started talking about how adrenaline can create strength in humans, and how it partly explained how supernaturals received their powers. His teaching skills were above average, and he had everyone hanging onto his every word. Even Kylie found it hard not to be enthralled. Yet everything in Kylie's gut told her he hadn't come here to teach. And considering Hannah's warning that the killer was here, Kylie wasn't about to let down her guard.

Her need to stay on guard shot up a notch when the class ended and she was half out the door and she heard him clear his throat.

"Kylie, stay a few minutes."

Kylie froze, her back still to him. Della, equally wary of the man, leaned in and whispered, "I'll be right outside the door."

Pulling her books closer to her chest, remembering she suspected the tall thirty-something teacher of being a serial killer, she moved back into the room with caution.

"Did I do something wrong?" An image of the three girls, their decomposed bodies in that grave, filled her mind. What kind of evil person did that?

"No—well, yes. As a protector, you shouldn't pick a fight with a were."

"She started it," Kylie said, and frowned at how juvenile that sounded. But this man gave her the creeps and brought out the worst in her.

His concern was touching—not—but she suspected there was more to this little chat. "Is that all?"

"I feel as if we got off on the wrong foot." Sincerity, a heavy dose of it, seemed to flow from him, but Kylie didn't buy it for a second. If an evil person without a conscience could lie to a vampire, he could also fake his emotions.

He continued, "I'd like to believe you would trust me."

Had he told Hannah and the other two girls the same thing? Did he get them to trust him and then wrap his hands around their necks and choke the life out of them? She could swear he looked at her throat.

Chills spread down her spine. She heard the sound of the other campers leaving the area. Was Della still outside the door? If she screamed, would Della be able to get here in time to save her?

"I don't trust very easily," Kylie said.

"I got that feeling." He took a step toward her.

She took a step back, his presence making it hard to breathe. "You know what else I don't do?" Her heartbeat played to the tune of fear, but she fought not to let it show.

He laced his fingers together. She couldn't help wondering if he was remembering how it had felt to use his hands as weapons.

"What's that?" he asked.

"Let anyone hurt someone I love." Kylie listened again, and there wasn't a sound coming from outside. The only noise bouncing off the freshly painted walls was the whishing noise of the ceiling fan.

Had Della left?

He tilted his head to the side. "What are you accusing me of doing?"

"What have you done?" Kylie fed her lungs a mouthful of air and held it.

"Nothing," he said.

Liar! She could feel it, feel him hiding the truth. "Like I said, I don't trust very easily." She turned her back on him, and with each step, she expected to feel him snatch her back, to feel his hands wrap around her throat, choking the life out of her the way he'd done the others.

Three days later, after suffering through yet another Hayden Yates class, unable to think of anything except the threat this man posed to Holiday, Kylie stormed into the office. Burnett and Holiday were arguing again; she heard them before she reached the porch, but she didn't care.

Well, she did care, just not enough to quiet the alarm blaring inside her. Hayden Yates was hiding something. That something was probably murder. And until Kylie could make Burnett and Holiday see this, Holiday's life was in jeopardy.

Walking right into Holiday's office, Kylie slammed the door behind her. "I don't like him."

"Me either," Burnett roared.

Holiday cut her eyes from Kylie to Burnett. "You two aren't even talking about the same person."

Kylie looked at Holiday for an explanation. Holiday obliged.

"Blake has offered to help look into Hannah's disappearance. He was the last person to see her alive, so I think we should accept his help."

"A suspect helping with the investigation, that makes about as much sense as fried ice cream."

Holiday leaned her elbows on her desk. "You can't find one thing that points to his guilt."

"He slept with your sister!" Burnett roared.

"Guilty of murder, not of being a piece of shit."

"And I'm telling both of you," Kylie said, "Hayden is guilty."

"There's no proof of that," they said at the same time.

"He wears a glove over his emotions. Every time he opens his mouth to speak, half truths come out. I feel it."

Burnett shook his head. "I've dug so deep into his background, I can practically tell you when he stopped wearing diapers."

Holiday's chair squeaked. "Kylie, if Hayden was out to hurt me, he's had plenty of opportunity. I interviewed him the first time when I was away taking care of my aunt's funeral. It was just him and me."

Kylie frowned. "I don't care. I still—"

"Both of you are wrong," Holiday insisted. "Blake didn't do this, and neither did Hayden. And if we don't stop focusing on them, we'll never find the killer. And we might never find Hannah's and the other two girls' bodies."

Burnett's eyes brightened and Kylie could read his mind. It wasn't finding the bodies that worried him so much; it was protecting Holiday. Hannah's warning felt imminent and Burnett felt that, too.

"Where the hell is Hannah when we need her?" Burnett bit out. He looked at Kylie. "You haven't seen her, felt her? Nothing?"

Kylie dropped on the sofa. "The last time was when she saw Blake here in the office."

"See," Burnett bellowed. "She probably figures we caught the bastard."

"I don't think so." Kylie almost feared disagreeing with Burnett when he was in this kind of mood, but getting them to see her point felt crucial. "She didn't look as if she thought it was over when she left."

He folded his arms over his wide chest. "Can we have a séance? Hold hands and call her back?"

"A séance?" Holiday rolled her eyes. "You have so much to learn about spirits."

"I don't give a damn about learning about spirits. I just need Hannah to come and tell me once and for all who she thinks is trying to hurt you."

On Friday morning, Kylie had skipped breakfast and Meet Your Campmate hour. She barely made it to English on time.

Obviously, Burnett wasn't the only one who needed to learn more about spirits. Kylie didn't know enough, either, because while she had felt Hannah's presence in the last few days, and again this morning, the spirit wouldn't manifest. Kylie had tried to appeal to her the way Holiday suggested. No luck. Kylie had even resorted to begging. Nothing.

Sitting at her desk, she reached down to make sure she'd brought her phone. The slight bulge in her pocket was reassuring. Maybe she was dreaming, but she hoped Lucas would either call or at least text her. But so far, nothing. That stung.

Looking up at the front of class, Miss Kane started talking about famous authors and the books they would be reading for the first six weeks. Who knew Jane Austen and so many others were supernatural? Kylie sure as hell didn't.

Intrigued by the conversation, Kylie barely noticed the noise when it started. Just a slight knock, as if someone were tapping on a door. The tap became a loud knock. Confused, she looked around, and oddly, no one else reacted.

Inhaling a strange vibe, she stared straight ahead again. As the noise grew louder, a slight movement to the right of the teacher caught Kylie's attention. The closet door behind Miss Kane rattled on its hinges, telling her where the banging originated.

Cutting her eyes left and right, she prayed she'd see someone, anyone, reacting to the obvious disruption.

Nope.

Then the cold of a spirit sent goose bumps racing up her arms. A trail of steam floated up from her lips, impairing her vision. Miss Kane said something, but Kylie couldn't hear over the ear-piercing hammering.

"Kylie? Kylie?" Someone called her name.

Who? Kylie couldn't think.

Forcing herself to look up, she saw the teacher staring at her as if waiting for a response. Kylie tried to talk, just a muttered, "Huh?" but not a word would leave her shivering lips. Then she saw it. Steam, lots of steam, billowing out from under the closet door.

Damn! Damn! This wasn't a normal spirit's visit. It felt more like the beginning of a vision.

That thought had hives popping out all over her chilled skin. Not because visions were scarier than hell, but because visions generally ended up with Kylie unconscious, or even worse, babbling incoherently.

Not here, Kylie pleaded. Not in front of twenty-five other campers.

An icy touch whispered across her shoulder. She looked back. A woman, her skin a pale ashen color, with dark purple circles under her gray eyes, stared at Kylie.

"She needs to see you." The spirit wore a white nightgown and her long brown hair hung around her shoulders. She raised her hand and pointed to the closet in front of the class.

"Who are you?" Kylie asked, and realized she'd forgotten to talk in her head.

All the students were now staring. Kylie could hardly think. So cold. She could barely feel her own skin anymore.

"Who's in there?" she asked.

In the distance, like static noise, Kylie heard others talking. Someone else called her name, maybe it was Della, and then she thought she heard Derek, but nothing sounded right, or felt right.

"She needs to talk to you."

Suddenly, realizing it could be Hannah behind that door, Kylie forced herself to stand up and walk to the closet. Even determined to do it, she hated doing it in front of people. But what choice did she have? Her knees wobbled as she neared the closet door.

She saw Miss Kane backing across the room, fear turning her complexion pale.

Kylie completely understood. She was pretty damn scared herself.

She reached for the closet's doorknob. Before she touched it, a hand ripped through the wood. Bony fingers latched onto the front of her shirt and yanked her through the splintered wood of the closet door. And yet it wasn't the closet.

The dark, dank place smelled of dirt, herbs, and death.

She screamed. Hard. Loud.

"Kylie? Kylie?" The voices echoed in the distance and then faded. Now, the only sound she heard over her own screams was the clanking sound of metal hitting metal.

She lay flat on her back. Gritty dirt rained down on her cheeks from above. The desire to brush it away hit, but her arms were locked at her sides. Even before she opened her eyes, she knew where she was.

The grave—she was in the grave with Hannah and the other girls. And something told her she might never escape.

Chapter Thirty-four

Buried alive.

Panic scraped across Kylie's mind and clawed at her chest. Opening her eyes, she saw only darkness, but felt more particles of dirt sift down. She went to blink and each speck of grit scraped across the top of her lids.

Please, I don't want to be here, she screamed in her mind. Her eyes adjusted to the dark and tears stung her sinuses, but the watery weakness helped wash away some of the grit.

She went to breathe, but her mouth wouldn't open; something held it shut. Her lungs demanded oxygen, so she drew air in through her nose. Her throat knotted at the smell, the smell of death and then a heavy herb scent. She forced herself to turn her head to confirm what she suspected: that this vision had landed her in the grave.

A long strand of red hair rested against the side of her face. As had happened in the other vision, she was the spirit. She was Hannah—only unlike the woman whose body she inhibited, she breathed. The thought that she was in the corpse brought on another wave of nausea. Then another followed when she saw a large black beetle move across her lashes. Its prickly legs inched over her cheek and poked its head up into her left nostril.

She started snorting and struggling to free herself, but nothing worked.

Turning her cheek a little farther to the right, her gaze came upon the face of Cindy Shaffer. A scream rose in Kylie's throat, but stayed bubbled in her mouth that was still forced closed. Her heart thumped against her breastbone at the sight. The girl's facial skin hung loose, exposing some cheekbone. But the girl's mouth was covered with duct tape. Staring down past her own nose, Kylie saw she bore the same tape. And the decomposing body she was in was shackled with chains. Was this supposed to mean something? Or had the killer really done this?

Another loud clank came from above. Kylie's gaze shot up toward the noise. She saw a long iron spike being pushed through a hole in the slats that appeared to be decaying wood flooring. The piece of iron dropped on top of her, and the cold of it sizzled against her forearm, which was pinned at her side. On one end of the metal bar was some kind of ornament, a cross. Kylie recognized the emblem as being like the rusty fence and gate at the cemetery.

Footsteps sounded on the floor above as if someone was walking away, but then he returned, and another piece of rusty fencing was pushed through the hole. This time, Kylie saw the hand of the person shoving the iron inside. As the arm moved almost in front of her face, the cuff of the shirt rose slightly upward, exposing the edge of a silver watchband.

What am I supposed to learn from this? Kylie asked with her mind, and looked at the dead girl at her side. Another wave of panic filled her lungs when a fat snake at least two feet long slithered up her chest and then higher. The cold, damp feel of its underbelly muscles inching across her cheek had a scream building in her throat.

She had to get out of here.

• • •

"You're fine." The calm sound of Holiday's voice had Kylie opening her eyes seconds later. She took a quick look around. She was in Holiday's office. But why was she . . . ?

The vision played in her head like a horror movie in fast forward. Panic flooded her chest. She jackknifed up, jumped off the sofa, and slapped at her arms, legs, and face, hoping to chase away the feel of death and underground creatures moving against her skin.

"It's okay," Holiday said again.

No, it wasn't. She'd been dead and had a snake crawling over her face and a bug playing peekaboo inside her nose. That was so not okay.

Kylie took a deep breath, then bent over and barfed—once, then twice. Barfed all over someone's dark pair of shoes.

"Oh, damn!" a deep voice said.

Kylie recognized the voice and the shoes.

She looked up at the disgusted expression on the badass vampire and started to apologize, but instead barfed again. She missed Burnett's shoes this time, but made a direct hit to the front of his shirt.

"Oh, fu—," Burnett muttered, but never finished the word.

Holiday wrapped her arm around Kylie. "Breathe. Just breathe. It's going to be okay." She guided Kylie back to the sofa. Burnett, holding his arms away from his shirt front, handed Holiday a damp cloth, which was quickly pressed to Kylie's forehead.

Kylie reached for it and wiped her mouth, and then looked at Burnett. "I think you need it worse than me." Tears filled her eyes and her whole body trembled. "Sorry."

He looked down at his shirt and back up at her. "I'm not mad."

She focused on Holiday's face, felt the calm flowing from her touch, and tried to remember exactly what had happened. How had she gotten . . . Her memory started to fall into place one piece at a time.

But it only took a few pieces for her to start panicking again. "Please tell me I didn't go wacko in English class."

Holiday's gaze filled with empathy. "It's not your fault. And Della brought you here as soon as she got you out of the closet."

Kylie flopped back on the sofa and started to wish she could vanish, but stopped herself before it came true. "I hate this. I really, really hate this."

Kylie stared at the ceiling. Burnett left the room, but returned in record time wearing a different shirt. Obviously he didn't keep a new pair of shoes handy in his office because he now stood in his socks.

After a few minutes, Holiday asked Kylie, "Can you talk about it?"

"I was Hannah. But . . . most of the time when I have these types of visions and I'm the spirit, the spirit isn't dead and . . . in a grave with bugs and snakes." Kylie's breath shuddered.

"Hannah's trying to show you something. That's what visions are all about," Holiday said. "Tell me what happened."

Kylie swallowed a tight knot down her throat. "I don't know what she wants me to see. We were in the grave. There were snakes and bugs. I saw plenty of those." She wiped her face, remembering the snake slithering across her cheek.

"Tell me everything," Holiday said. "Everything."

Kylie started recounting it, from the footsteps sounding on top of the rotting wooden planks above her, to the herb smell and the scrap pieces of iron that looked like they came from the cemetery. When Kylie finished, Holiday's expression went white.

"What is it?" Burnett asked, not missing the look on her face.

"Someone knows Hannah is reaching out from the grave."

"How do you know that?" Kylie asked.

"The tape over their mouths and the chains. You said you smelled herbs and that you saw someone adding iron from the graveyard. In the past, it was called cold iron. It's basically iron, but some of it was blessed by practicing Wiccans. It was used to keep spirits from escaping, and . . . the herbs, there are several that are used to silence spirits. That's what she was trying to tell you. That someone is trying to stop her from communicating with us."

"And Blake knows you are a ghost whisperer," Burnett said. "It's logical that Hannah would come to you."

"But if that's the case, why is he just now trying to silence them? He would have done that in the beginning."

"She's right," Kylie said. "It's someone here. Hannah told us that much. And excuse me for sounding like a broken record, but Hayden Yates is bound to have heard I'm a ghost whisperer. *Everyone* here has." And if they hadn't, today sealed the deal.

Holiday twisted her hair in a tight rope and then met Kylie's gaze. "I don't want to suspect someone here," she said, and then met Burnett's gaze. "But Kylie's right. It could be someone from Shadow Falls. And if it was the iron from Fallen Cemetery, then Hannah's and the other's bodies are close by."

"Fine," Burnett growled. "I'll go back and run Hayden Yates through every damn database I can find. Until then, you don't let the man within two feet of you."

"I still don't think it's Hayden," Holiday said.

"And I still do," Kylie insisted.

"Who else could it be?" Burnett asked.

"One of the new students or teachers," Holiday said, "but . . ."

"Most serial killers are men. And I don't see a teen being able to pull this off."

"And Hannah keeps calling the killer a he," Kylie said.

Burnett huffed. "I'm not sure Collin Warren could look at someone long enough to kill them."

"But he's strange," Kylie said. However, Kylie's gut just knew that Hayden Yates was up to no good.

"Being extremely shy doesn't make him a killer," Holiday pointed out. "It just makes him socially awkward."

Burnett shook his head. "But just to be sure, I'll check him out again, too. You stay away from both of them."

Holiday rolled her eyes. "How am I going to run a school and not talk to any of the teachers?"

"I could always lock you in my cabin," Burnett said.

"You wish," Holiday said.

Burnett's eyes brightened and a smile barely tilted his lips up slightly. "That I do."

Kylie smiled for a second, too, completely getting Burnett's underlying message. Then for some reason, Kylie thought about Lucas, and started missing him, wishing he could be here to help her cope. *Don't ever fall in love, princess. It just hurts too much.*

Her stepfather's words echoed in Kylie's head and right then, she knew. She loved Lucas.

As if the epiphany gave her heart and mind a reboot, she suddenly recalled being in Miss Kane's closet and screaming at the top of her lungs. She closed her eyes as embarrassment flooded through her. If any of the other campers hadn't quite made up their minds about whether she was or wasn't a freak, she'd made it easy for them.

Kylie felt Holiday slip her soft hand against her wrist, as if reading some of her emotional angst. The touch had little effect this time. Kylie was in love with Lucas, a guy who couldn't even be seen in public with her, and she'd made a complete idiot out of herself with one of her ghost visions.

"Burnett," Holiday spoke softly, "why don't you go find some shoes and give Kylie and me a few minutes alone."

Something about being alone with Holiday had Kylie letting go and allowing herself to fall apart. She fell against the camp leader's shoulder and started sobbing.

Holiday held her, held her so tight that Kylie cried harder. After a few minutes, Holiday spoke. "I'm so damn sorry. Hannah shouldn't have come to you. You're too young to have to deal with this."

The words brought a sudden halt to Kylie's pity party.

She pulled out of the embrace. "No. I mean, sure, it's hard, but this is what I do. I'd do it for a stranger. And I'd do it for your sister again and again." *And if it meant stopping someone from hurting Holiday, I would do that and more.*

Kylie wiped her face to clear the tears and knew she was all red and blotchy. Not that she cared. This was Holiday. Her mentor, her big sister. Her friend.

"Besides," Kylie added, "it's not just the vision. It's Lucas. I think I love him. No, I'm pretty sure I love him. Oh, shit! I'm in love with a boy who can't love me back."

Holiday brushed her hand over Kylie's cheek. "Oh, hon, he might not supposed to be in love with you, but that doesn't mean he can't, or that he doesn't."

Kylie inhaled deeply, trying not to let herself cry again. "He hasn't told me he loves me. I mean, I haven't told him either, but . . . Derek told me he loved me. And . . ." She closed her eyes, trying to figure out how to put it. "And sometimes I'm confused about what I feel for him, but just now, seeing what you and Burnett have, or what you could have, it made me realize I want that. I'm tired of hiding what I feel and being afraid of it."

The tears Kylie had stopped shedding filled Holiday's eyes. "Love's always scary."

Kylie felt Holiday's emotions blend with her own. "It shouldn't be scary," Kylie said. "Burnett loves you. Even I can see it. And I know you love him. Don't lose out on something wonderful because you're scared."

"I just need some time," Holiday said.

"Time we might not have. Life's fragile. Look at Hannah, and Cindy and the other girl. They don't get the opportunity to love again. We have the chance and we're not doing it. I should have told Lucas how I feel. I should have forced him to be honest with me about what's happening with him. You should tell Burnett how you feel."

Holiday bit down on her lower lip. "I thought I was the one offering advice here."

"Yeah, well, the tables turned," Kylie said. *Things change.* Kylie just hoped with all the things changing, the one constant in her life would be Shadow Falls. The thought of losing Holiday and everyone here, even the ones who considered her a nutcase, was too much. They were her family.

That night, Kylie had tried to dreamscape with Lucas, but it wasn't working. She texted him, called him, and even e-mailed. No answer came back. Then at two in the morning, staring at the ceiling, her phone rang. She grabbed it without checking the caller ID.

"Lucas?" she said his name at the same time she hit the light switch. The cold in the room came on faster than the light.

"Sorry," the voice on the line said. "Just me."

Kylie shivered then frowned when she recognized the voice. "I just tried—"

"It's okay," Derek said, but his tone said it wasn't really okay. "I just woke up and felt you worrying. I tried to call you earlier to see how you were after the vision, but you didn't call me back."

Kylie pulled the blanket up around her neck. The spirit standing by the bed faded, but before she did, Kylie recognized her as the woman from earlier that day. Remembering who was on the phone, Kylie's chest swelled with emotion.

"I . . . It's been crazy." She'd gotten his messages. She just hadn't wanted to talk to him because of the emotional storm she felt about

Lucas right now. It wasn't fair to Derek, because even though she wasn't doing anything wrong, she knew their friendship offered him hope that she would change her mind, and she didn't think that hope had a hell of a lot of merit.

"You're pulling away again," he said.

"Derek, it's—"

"Kylie, you don't have to explain. I know." He paused. "It's okay. And someday I'll even be able to say that and mean it."

"You're a special guy," Kylie said, hurting for him.

"I know," he said, and chuckled. "And that's why I'm not completely giving up. But I'm working on it. I just called to check on you."

"I'm okay," Kylie said.

"Then I'll say good night." Rejection sounded in his voice.

"Derek, I'm really—"

"Just say good night, Kylie," he insisted.

"Good night," she whispered, and nothing was sadder than the sound of that dead line.

Putting her phone down, Kylie looked around. The cold from the spirit had lessened but she could tell she lingered nearby.

"Who are you?" Kylie asked.

The woman didn't answer. And why should she? They never made it easy.

But then, neither did the living.

"Kylie! Kylie!" The voice jolted Kylie from a deep sleep before the sun rose the next morning. She shot up, chills crawling up and down her spine like spiders. Without even knowing why, her blood sizzled with the need to protect. Protect someone.

Still half asleep, she pushed her hair from face and stood in the middle of the room, breathing in and breathing out. Her pulse raced, and panic filled her chest, crowding her lungs. Something was happening. She felt it.

Someone needed her. Someone needed Kylie's protection.

Who?

Her mind raced as she tried to make sense of what she felt. Then Kylie remembered the voice. She let it play in her mind, again and again, until finally she recognized it.

"No!" She grabbed her jeans and T-shirt.

Holiday was in trouble.

Chapter Thirty-five

Right before Kylie lit out of her room, she glanced at the clock on her nightstand. Five AM. Holiday would be at the office already.

Kylie stormed into Della's room, but the girl wasn't there. Probably at an early vampire ceremony. Kylie didn't wait a second longer; she bolted out of the cabin and flew like the wind to the office. The only thing that felt heavy about her was her heart. As if her heart knew Holiday's situation was bad. Really, really bad.

When Kylie got to the office, she found the door ajar. Not a good sign. Even worse, there was glass shattered all over the wet floor of the entrance. The broken handle of the coffee pot lay in the corner, another sign that a struggle had taken place.

"Where are you, Holiday?" Kylie's voice trembled. Tears filled her eyes and she tried to think.

Burnett. She needed to contact Burnett.

She reached into her pocket for her phone, only to realize she hadn't brought it. She ran into Holiday's office. The room looked undisturbed. Whoever had gotten Holiday had done it in the entrance area. He'd probably been waiting for her when she came in this morning, or maybe walked in when she'd been making coffee.

Hands shaking, Kylie grabbed Holiday's office phone. She couldn't remember Burnett's cell number. But damn, she could get to his cabin quicker than find his number.

She tore out, her feet barely touching the ground. She didn't know if she'd morphed into a vampire or if in protective mode she simply had more power. She didn't really care. Only one thing mattered, one thought echoed in her mind. Save Holiday. She had to save Holiday.

She made it to Burnett's cabin, and didn't even knock. She screamed his name when she entered, but no one answered. No one.

She went into his bedroom. The bed stood empty.

Recalling the vampire ritual, she tore out again. Della had told her once where they held it. She shot through the woods, not caring about her promise to not enter. If she ran into trouble, being in protective mode, she could kick ass and ask questions later.

She exited through the line of trees into a clearing. The wind whizzed past as she moved. Coming to a jolting stop, she found herself circled by a half-dozen angry vamps, their eyes glowing at the idea of an intruder disturbing their ceremony.

Lucky for her, the Shadow Falls vamps weren't likely to attack. A good thing, because even in protective mode, she didn't know if she could take on all six of them.

"Where's Burnett?" Kylie snapped. "Or Della?"

"What is it?" Burnett came to a stop beside her.

Kylie never answered. She didn't have to. He saw it in her eyes.

"Holiday?" The sound in his voice had Kylie's chest aching. Her blood pumped faster.

Kylie's breath caught. "He's got her."

"Who?" he demanded as Della stopped at his side.

"I still don't know," Kylie answered, and her eyes spiked with more tears. But they had better find out, and soon, before it was too late.

• • •

Three minutes later, after Kylie had explained everything, Burnett had spouted out orders for all the vamps and her to go search the Shadow Falls property. If Holiday was still here, they'd find her. Burnett headed back to the office to see if he could find clues and to check to see if the alarm was functioning.

Kylie headed to the west side of the property. But when she passed the trail that led to the cabin where Hayden Yates lived, she did a complete U-turn.

She slammed down on his porch. Heard him moving around inside. Heard him talking to someone.

She stormed in without knocking and oops, forgot to open the door. It landed with a loud crack on the floor. Hayden stood by the sofa, his hooded sweater in one hand as if he'd just removed it, and his phone in the other. His dark hair appeared darker, wet with sweat. His skin looked flushed, as if he'd been running. But from what?

Or better yet, from where?

"Where is she?" Her tone came out deep, filled with fury and warning.

He cut off the phone. "Where is who?" he asked in innocence.

"Don't play games with me." Her blood now fizzed in her veins. Her patience, if she'd had any at all, was now gone.

He tossed the hoodie and his phone on the sofa. Beside those two items was a watch. A black-banded watch.

"You're vampire now. Try listening to my heart for the truth."

Kylie had already listened to his heart, but it didn't matter. Didn't matter that he had a different watch from the one she'd seen in the vision. He could have two watches. "That only works with people who have a conscience."

"And you're assuming I don't."

"You've been hiding something ever since you got here." She took a step closer. Her intent was to get answers, and she didn't care how.

He apparently read her mood, because he held out his hands, palms up. "Perhaps, but it isn't what you think. I haven't hurt your precious camp leader."

"I didn't tell you who it was! So how the hell—"

"I'm no fool. Burnett stakes out at her house most nights."

"If you've hurt her, I'll kill you." She didn't flinch at hearing the words. They were true. For Holiday, Kylie would kill.

But what if she'd failed Holiday and it was too late? Anger, fear, and love burned in Kylie's chest. Her hands shook.

"I don't doubt you could kill me," Hayden said, holding his submissive pose. "Your strength right now appears . . . palpable." He inhaled and she could swear he looked sincere, even respectful. "It isn't my place to"—he hesitated again—"speak up." He ran a hand through his hair. "It would probably be beneficial for me to just keep my mouth shut. But unfortunately, unlike you believe, I do have a conscience."

He closed his eyes again and when he opened them, she saw complete honesty. And she saw something else, but she wasn't sure what it was. Something about him that looked . . . familiar in a weird way. "I saw Collin Warren out and about this morning. Something told me he was up to no good."

Kylie listened to Hayden's heart speak the truth. She continued to study his eyes, which held no dishonesty. "Who are you?" she asked.

He brought both hands up and brushed his hair from his brow. "See for yourself."

Kylie did see. His pattern was the same as her father's. Hayden was . . . a chameleon.

Her breath caught. He had all sorts of information she needed, but not now. Because more important than even the answers he held was Holiday's life. Then her gaze shifted back to his sofa, and she realized he did have one thing she needed.

She snagged his phone and lit out as she heard him protest.

• • •

Kylie flew off his porch. The sunrise had painted the horizon a bright color, not that she took the time to enjoy the view. She held the phone up and realized the problem. She still couldn't remember Burnett's number. So she dialed Della.

Della didn't answer, damn it.

Kylie left a message. She told her what she suspected—that Collin Warren had Holiday and that she was looking for him now. She didn't slow down, didn't stop until she stood in front of Collin's cabin. She listened. Not a sound echoed from inside. She had to see for herself. She started up the porch steps when she heard quiet footfalls sound behind her.

Heart stopping, Kylie swung around, expecting Collin, but found Fredericka instead.

"What are you doing sneaking around?" the were asked.

Kylie didn't have time to chat, so she turned around and went to check out Collin's cabin. The door was locked, so she simply crashed it in. She'd done it at Hayden's cabin, what was one more?

Fredericka's gasp sounded behind her. Kylie ignored it.

She went into Collin's bedroom, looking for anything that might help her find Holiday.

"What's going on?" Fredericka asked, following her into the room.

"Just leave. I don't have time for pettiness." She opened the drawer and yanked everything out.

"What's going on?" Fredericka asked again.

Kylie sighed. "Holiday's missing and I think this creep took her."

"Shit!" Fredericka said. "I knew he was weird."

Kylie went to leave.

"Wait," Fredericka said. "I followed him a couple of days ago. He went to some old cabin in that park next door."

"Where?" Kylie roared; every instinct in her seemed to be turned on.

"I'll . . . show you." She held up her hands as if half frightened.

They ran into the woods. Kylie's patience was pushed when she had to slow down for Fredericka, but Kylie held her tongue. Normally, she wouldn't have trusted the were to spit on her if she was on fire, but her gut said the girl wasn't pulling any tricks now. No doubt Fredericka knew Holiday had gone to extra lengths to get her to Shadow Falls, and to keep her here.

They came upon the property gate. Kylie jumped without even trying. Fredericka barely made it and landed hard on the other side.

Kylie hesitated and looked back.

"I'm fine," the were growled, and bounced onto her feet.

I didn't ask. Kylie bit her tongue. They started to bolt again when Hayden's phone rang. Kylie pulled it out of her pocket and saw Burnett's name. Obviously, Della had given him this number.

"Where the hell are you?" Burnett barked. "And why do you have Hayden Yates's phone?"

Kylie and Fredericka arrived at the cabin before Burnett. But he'd said he was on his way, which meant he would be there soon. Weeds and young trees grew around the structure as if someone had forgotten it existed. The sounds of the night suddenly went silent. Burnett must be close by.

He'd ordered them to wait before moving into the cabin. But Kylie heard someone inside. She listened; God help her, she only heard one person breathing. Fear stole her next breath. Her blood fizzed so strong, it almost burned.

Protect Holiday. Protect Holiday. The words echoed in her head like a litany.

She motioned for Fredericka to stand back. The girl's eyes filled with rebellion. Kylie didn't have time to argue. She stormed into the building; the door splintered, the walls wobbled.

Collin Warren jumped up from the floor. At his feet lay Holiday. A very still, very dead Holiday.

Chapter Thirty-six

Fear filled Collin's eyes when he saw Kylie, while pure evil seemed to surround him.

Kylie picked up Collin Warren and tossed him across the cabin. She heard his body hit the log walls with a loud, cracking thud. The air gushing out of his lungs sounded in the room, but she didn't see him land.

She heard a scuffle happening behind her. Fredericka screamed. Kylie ignored it.

On her knees beside Holiday, Kylie removed the rope from around her throat.

"Is she dead?" Kylie heard Fredericka ask. The question floated in the room—unanswered.

Kylie's gaze stayed locked on Holiday. Kylie's heart stayed locked on the fact that she'd tried to save Ellie and failed—tried to save Roberto and failed then, too.

Burnett's footsteps sounded in the cabin; she heard him let out a sound of pure anguish. He knew. He knew Holiday was dead.

Kylie still didn't look up. Everything she had—everything she wanted to believe in—stayed focused on Holiday. This couldn't be happening. Not Holiday.

"No!" Kylie screamed.

Not Holiday, who had always been there for Kylie, always listened, always cared. Memories of them together filled her mind. Memories of them laughing, sitting side by side at the falls, even eating ice cream while talking about heartaches and boys. How many times had Holiday offered Kylie a warm, comforting touch?

"You can't go," Kylie said with a half sob. Tears rolled down her cheeks and landed on Holiday's pale face. Kylie ran her hands over Holiday's swollen, bruised throat.

When Kylie didn't feel her hands heat up, she closed her eyes and prayed. *Let me save her. You gave me this power, now let me use it. I'll pay whatever price it takes, even if it's my own life. Do you hear me? My life for hers!*

A ball of warmth formed in her chest and then slowly spread to her hands. Her hands tingled and then turned hot and then hotter still. Holiday's body felt so cold, so lifeless under Kylie's palms, but she didn't stop. She couldn't.

"She's glowing again," Fredericka's voice sounded in the distance.

But even as Kylie's light filled the small room, Holiday didn't respond. Another somber, grieving sound came from Burnett. It was the last sound Kylie heard before her vision went black.

Darkness surrounded Kylie. Exhaustion pulled at her mind. Where was she? Why did she feel so depleted? So dead?

She tried to open her eyes, but the effort felt too much. *Wake up! Wake up!* a part of her brain demanded. The feeling of urgency filled her chest and she fought to push the cobwebs from her mind.

As the last few clouds of confusion and exhaustion were cleared, she came to. She was in someone's arms, someone who ran. Kylie's body jolted up and down with the footfalls. She forced her eyes open and looked up at . . . Fredericka?

What was . . . ?

"Put me down," Kylie demanded.

"Burnett said to carry you," Fredericka bit out. "Believe me, I don't like it, either."

"Put me down!" Kylie demanded, and the she-wolf came to a sudden stop and dropped her none too gently on the ground. The feel of her butt hitting the hard ground brought it all back.

Collin Warren had Holiday.

Holiday . . . dead.

Pain filled Kylie's chest.

Bolting to her feet, she saw Burnett, holding a lifeless Holiday in his arms.

Kylie rushed over. "Let me try again!" she begged.

"You already did," Burnett bit out.

"But maybe this time—"

"Kylie! You already saved her," Burnett said. "She's weak, but she's breathing. Now, let Fredericka carry you back to camp so we can get both of you help."

"I'm fine," Kylie insisted.

"You're still glowing, Kylie," Burnett snapped. "And I don't know what that means."

Kylie didn't know either. But she didn't care. She stared at Holiday's chest, waiting to see it shift upward, bringing in oxygen. She held her own breath.

Only when Holiday breathed did Kylie draw air into her hungry lungs.

"Let's go," Burnett muttered. "I have a doctor meeting us at the camp."

Kylie pushed herself to run, but it wasn't nearly as fast as before, and damn if she didn't feel every muscle burn. Not that she was complaining. Holiday was alive and so was she. Nothing else mattered.

Kylie sat in Holiday's living room, silent and still glowing, while the doctor checked Holiday out in the bedroom. Burnett, on his feet, kept a listening ear turned to the door.

All the other students gathered in the dining hall. School had been canceled while everyone waited for news. Kylie wondered if Holiday knew how loved she was. That everyone, even Fredericka, cared.

Everyone except . . . Collin Warren. Questions start flipping through her mind. Kylie looked at Burnett. "What happened to Collin?"

Burnett shook his head.

Kylie's gut knotted. She recalled tossing the man across the small shack, recalled hearing the sound of his lungs give up air. Had his soul given up as well?

She'd said she would kill for Holiday, and she would, but now the thought that she might have taken a life made her want to puke. "Did I . . . ?"

Burnett shook his head. "Fredericka. She said he came at you with a knife. She attacked. They fought. He lost."

Kylie now recalled hearing the struggle, but the idea left her stunned. "Fredericka saved my life?" *Oh, hell.* She didn't want to be indebted to someone who hated her. Then she couldn't help but wonder why she'd done it. She could have let Collin kill her.

Burnett stared at Kylie as if reading her mind. "She comes off as a real bitch, but I don't think she's as bad as she lets people believe." He hesitated. "That happens when you have a rough upbringing. People think the worst of you and it just gets easier to let them think it than to try to prove them differently." He looked back at the bedroom door. "Holiday believed she was salvageable."

So did Lucas. Kylie sat there and chewed on her feelings. About Fredericka, then about Lucas. She missed him. Wished he was here.

Then she reheard Burnett's words and picked up on the personal reference in his tone. *That happens when you have a rough upbringing.* A piece of the puzzle of who Burnett was suddenly fell into place. She didn't know why it felt important but it did. She looked up at him. "You were raised in a foster home with Perry, weren't you?"

Burnett's gaze stayed fixed on the door. "She's going to be okay." A smile brightened his eyes. "The doctor, he just said she was going to be okay." He reached back with both hands and laced his fingers behind his neck. When he glanced at Kylie, he was still smiling. "Yeah. I was raised in foster care. Why? You thinking that's why I'm a mean bastard? Because of my rough upbringing?"

Hearing the humor and relief in his voice, she smiled. She knew if he weren't so relieved by the doctor's news, he'd probably be pissed that Kylie figured it out. Then the opportunity occurred to her. "No, but I'm thinking that's why it might be so hard for you to tell Holiday how you feel. To admit that you love her. And I think she really needs to hear that."

His eyebrows arched. "I'm not the one who's been pushing the other away."

"But you haven't told her how you feel, either. And you gotta trust me on this. A woman needs to hear that."

A few minutes passed in silence; she knew Burnett was thinking about what she said, and that felt good. But then the vamp looked back at her with questions in his eyes. "How did Hayden Yates know about Collin Warren?"

Kylie chose her words carefully. She hadn't told Burnett that Hayden was a chameleon and wasn't sure if she should.

"When I went to his cabin, he'd been out running. I accused him of being involved. He denied it. He said he'd seen Collin out and the man looked suspicious."

Burnett digested what she'd said. "Supposedly, Collin's always been socially flawed but no one saw the evilness in him until now." Burnett paused again. "How did you end up with Hayden's phone?"

"I'd forgotten mine when I left. So I . . . confiscated his." She shrugged.

"Did you know he left a message with me, saying he had a family emergency and had to leave for a few days?"

Kylie tried not to let her disappointment show. "No, I didn't know that."

"Do you still think he's involved?" Burnett asked. "If you do, I'll bring his ass back here now."

"No," Kylie answered honestly. "I was wrong. He didn't have anything to do with Holiday. If anything . . . he helped save her."

Burnett studied her. "And you don't see it as suspicious his leaving right now?"

"Maybe a little," Kylie said, so she wouldn't get caught in a lie. "But I'm sure he didn't have anything to do with Holiday's abduction."

"I'm still questioning him when he gets back," Burnett said.

Me too. Kylie shook her head. *If he comes back.* Her heart sank.

Then she recalled the phone again, still tucked in her pocket. Hayden Yates had to be working for her grandfather. And if so, he was probably in contact with Hayden. That meant she might have her grandfather's number in the phone.

If her grandfather hadn't changed his number again.

Thirty minutes later, after Burnett had visited Holiday, Kylie moved into the bedroom. Holiday, her red hair looking redder against the white sheets, looked pale, but alive. The bruise on her throat hadn't gone away.

She touched her throat and motioned for Kylie to hand her the water on her bedside table.

"You brought me back." Holiday's voice sounded raw, painfully raw.

"But I didn't heal you all the way." Kylie's throat hurt hearing Holiday talk. "Do you want me to see if I can—?"

Holiday shook her head. "I think you've done enough. You look worn out."

Kylie felt worn out, but not so much that she couldn't try. "I could—"

"No. I'll heal." Holiday looked concerned. "You haven't stopped glowing."

"I know," Kylie said. "But it'll go away, right?"

Holiday nodded but didn't look confident. Then she motioned for Kylie to sit in the chair beside the bed. "I got to see Hannah before she passed over. Right as I was dying, everything slowed down and she came to me. We talked. We made amends." Tears brightened Holiday's green eyes. "None of this would have happened if not for you. Thank you. I know the cost you have to pay, and I promise to live my life so it won't cost you even the tiniest piece of your soul."

Kylie took her hand and squeezed. "I don't think you've ever lived it any other way."

"I can be better." Holiday swallowed. "Nothing like dying to show you how to live."

Kylie smiled. "I hope in that message, you're talking about Burnett."

Holiday grinned. "The stupid vamp just asked me to marry him. Here, now? As if looking like I just died is how I wanted to be proposed to."

Joy did a lap around Kylie's heart. "And you said?"

Holiday took a sip of water. "I asked him if we couldn't just live together in sin."

Kylie frowned, but then she saw something in Holiday's eyes. "And?"

"He told me it wouldn't be a good example to our students. So . . . I agreed to marry him." She pushed a hand against her forehead. "Dear God, what am I getting myself into? He's not an easy man to deal with."

"I can hear you," Burnett called out from the other room, a chuckle sounding in his voice.

Holiday rolled her eyes.

Kylie squeezed Holiday's hand tighter. "He loves you," she whispered.

"Yeah, that's what he said." She sank deeper into her pillow, looking exhausted, but she also looked happy.

A sense of rightness filled Kylie's chest. She'd done it. Or at least, she'd helped do it. Burnett and Holiday were getting together.

She couldn't help but wonder if she and Lucas would have the same luck.

Holiday stared up at the ceiling for a second. "I also saw your grandmother, Kylie."

"Nana?" Kylie asked. "What did she say?"

"No, not Nana, the other one. Heidi."

Kylie saw something almost sad in Holiday's eyes. "What did she say?"

"Just to say hello." Holiday sighed.

Something told Kylie there was more. What was it that Holiday didn't want to tell? Kylie almost asked, but when Holiday's eyes fluttered closed, Kylie realized now wasn't the time to push. Later, she thought, and reached down and touched Hayden's phone in her pocket. Later.

• • •

It was after lunch before Kylie could sneak away to her bedroom. She pulled out Hayden's phone and searched for her grandfather's number. Unfortunately, there were no names listed. Just numbers. Three had been called the most. Kylie sat down on the edge of her bed and called the first.

She held her breath while it rang.

A woman answered. "About time you called," the voice said.

"Who is this?" Kylie asked, unsure how to approach the call.

"This is . . . Casey. Who are you?"

"I . . ."

"What are you doing with Hayden's phone?"

"I . . ."

"Damn that bastard! He said he wasn't seeing anyone else. Tell him I said to go to hell! He wasn't that good in bed anyway, as I'm sure you probably know." The line went dead.

"Uh-oh." Kylie considered calling back and trying to explain, but what would she say? *I'm not his girlfriend, just someone who stole his phone after accusing him of being a serial killer.* That might complicate matters even worse. Best to let him handle it on his own.

"Sorry, Hayden," Kylie muttered.

Before Kylie called the next number, the phone dinged with an incoming text. She debated over reading it, thinking it might be from his pissed-off girlfriend. Then she saw it wasn't from that number. She might be invading his privacy, but after stealing his phone, what was one more sin?

It took a second to figure out the phone's features to display the message.

But she was so damn glad she did.

Chapter Thirty-seven

The message wasn't for Hayden. It was from him.

You're answering my messages? Hayden

Kylie typed back. *Only because I hoped it was either you or my . . .* She paused. Should she let him know she assumed he was with her grandfather? She didn't see any advantage to playing dumb. . . . *my grandfather.* She tapped her fingers on the phone waiting for a reply.

The phone dinged. *What did you tell the others?*

She decided to be honest. *Only that you helped save Holiday's life. You can come back.*

She waited for him to respond. When he didn't do it quickly, she wrote, *Sorry I suspected you.*

He replied: *If you did the right thing and came to live where you belonged, I wouldn't have to return.*

Kylie considered her answer.

I belong at Shadow Falls.

She no sooner finished typing the words than her reflection in the dresser mirror caught her attention. She hadn't stopped glowing yet. How long could she continue to believe she belonged here when everything pointed to the fact that she was different? Different even from all the other supernaturals.

Her chest swelled again at the thought of leaving. She rejected it. But what was going to happen in two weeks when her mom was expecting to pick her up for parents' weekend? How would she explain the fact that she was freaking brighter than a fifty-watt bulb?

The phone pinged again. *It's not safe for you to stay there.*

Holiday and Burnett won't let the FRU do anything.

It's not just the FRU. You were right in what you told your grand-father. There's an underground rogue gang after you.

Swallowing a knot in her throat, she texted, *Is my grandfather's number in the phone?*

It took a few minutes for him to get back. But he did. *Yes.*

She typed in. *Thank you.* And hit send. Then remembering, she sent one more message. *Call your girlfriend. I might have upset her.*

Her grandfather answered the next number she dialed. And he didn't bother with formalities. Hayden had obviously told him to expect her call.

"I sent him because I was concerned for your safety," her grand-father said, his voice just an octave lower than her father's.

"I'm not upset," Kylie said. "Although I wish someone would have told me."

"You need to come with us, Kylie. It's not safe. You were right about the underground rogue. I don't trust the FRU not to harm you. How can I trust them to keep you safe from others?"

"Please," Kylie said. "You don't understand what you're asking." Tears filled her eyes. "I . . . This is home to me. Burnett's not like the FRU you remember. And Holiday . . . she took me in. Both of them have protected me." Her throat grew tight. "People have died here saving my life. These people you don't trust are my family." Her voice shook and she swiped the tears from her cheeks.

"*We* are your family."

"I can't leave," Kylie said.

There was a long pause. "I will send Hayden back if you offer your word that you have not told the others."

"I haven't told anyone." Silence fell again, then she blurted out, "I'm glowing. How do I stop it?"

"Glowing?" he asked, and paused as if in thought. "You have the gift of healing?"

"Yes," she answered.

"I'm assuming you used it."

"I . . . brought someone back to life."

He didn't speak for a few seconds. "Your gifts are indeed amazing."

"But how do I stop it?" She hadn't been fishing for compliments.

"You must release the energy you drew inside you to complete the healing."

"How?" Kylie asked.

"Meditate."

"I'm not good at meditation." She bit down on her lip.

"Then you'd better learn. And fast." He exhaled. "Kylie, if other gangs learn just how gifted you really are, you'll be a commodity. They will either want you working for them, or they'll want you dead. It won't be just one gang coming after you."

His warning rang in her ears. *Great. That's all she needed.*

"I will send Hayden back," he went on, "but think carefully on this, my child. I deserve to get to know my only grandchild."

Monday morning Kylie sat in the dining hall while everyone stared. She wasn't glowing anymore. Her internal bulb had blown sometime during the night.

She'd stayed in her room all weekend and meditated, and slept.

Obviously, bringing someone back to life took it out of you. Holiday and Burnett had dropped by with food, TLC, and news that all the bodies of the girls has been turned over to their families. Both Burnett and Holiday were now glowing, but it was a natural glow. They were in love.

That only made Kylie miss Lucas even more.

Derek had called twice just to say he was thinking about her. Lucas hadn't. She didn't even know if he was aware of what had happened. Still, his silence was hard to take.

Helen and Jonathon had dropped by. And Miranda, Perry, and Della had checked on her almost every hour. Even during the night, they'd crack open the door and peer at her. Of course, that could be because she looked really cool glowing in the dark. Hell, they could have sold tickets to the other campers for a dollar a peek. Not that they would. They were her friends.

Kylie stared down at her runny eggs and frowned as she felt all eyes in the dining hall on her.

Nope, right now, glowing wasn't the problem. It was her pattern. She'd changed again. She was finally a werewolf and Lucas wasn't around to enjoy it. And neither was Socks. Her cat hadn't come out from under the bed all morning. He made his prejudices known. Just as clear as the other werewolves here at the camp. Not one of them had come to say hello, or go to hell.

"You hanging in there?" Della asked.

"Like a pro," Kylie answered, and looked up to see Hayden Yates walk into the dining hall. Her heart did a little dance. He was back. Relief at knowing she wasn't completely alone washed over her.

We are your family. Her grandfather's words sliced through her.

"You still can't lie worth a damn," Della said.

Kylie looked away from Hayden before anyone guessed they shared secrets.

Della was right. She'd lied. She wasn't hanging in there like a pro. More like by a thread. She was confused, scared, and worried. She might have stopped glowing, but what was next? What freaky thing would she be calling her grandfather or running to Hayden to help her fix? And if she really belonged at Shadow Falls, why did Hayden's presence bring her so much comfort?

"Let's get this show on the road," Chris, the Meet Your Campmate leader, announced after breakfast. Kylie stood outside beside Della. She fought the need to fan herself. Her sudden increase in her body temperature would take getting used to.

"And first on our list of names is none other than our brand-new were." Chris's gaze shot to Kylie.

Kylie's breath caught. The first people announced were generally the ones someone had paid in blood for Chris to arrange. Swallowing, her gaze shot to Derek. But he stared at Chris in concern.

"Kylie, you get the pleasure of Fredericka's company."

Oh, great. The were had saved her life only to kill her later.

"I can follow you if you want," Della whispered, her eyes bright.

Kylie shook her head, tired of always being under someone else's protection. "No."

Fredericka walked up. "You wanna walk to the lake?"

"Sure," Kylie answered. *Why not? The lake would be a nice place to die.*

"I'll see you later." Della's tone came with all kinds of warnings for Fredericka.

As they started walking, neither Kylie nor Fredericka talked. Kylie listened, but amazingly, she barely heard their footsteps. The ability to move in silence must be part of being were. Her mind chewed on what Fredericka really wanted.

Or it did until her friendly blue jay showed up and did a song and dance right in front of them.

Fredericka frowned. Kylie shooed the bird away. "Go!"

As they continued on, Kylie did some thinking. She didn't believe the she-wolf really wanted to kill her. Then again, hadn't she already tried once? Putting a lion in Kylie's bedroom several months back hadn't been an act of kindness. But if the girl really planned on murder, would she have let the whole camp know they were together?

Then another thought suddenly hit. Was Fredericka pissed that Kylie hadn't said thank you for saving her life?

She'd planned on doing it. She really had. But she'd spent all her energy on stopping herself from glowing this weekend. Nevertheless, she should have done it first thing this morning. Was it too late?

Better late than never.

"Burnett told me you saved my life," Kylie said. "I should say thank you."

Fredericka's dark black hair swung loose around her shoulders. She was at least three inches taller than Kylie, and probably outweighed her by twenty pounds. Not that Kylie was seriously frightened anymore.

"I probably did it more for Holiday than you," the were said.

Probably? "I figured that," Kylie said, "but thanks anyway."

Fredericka nodded and remained quiet for the next few minutes. Kylie hated the tense silence. "Did you pay blood to get Chris to match us up?"

The were nodded. "Three pints. He said since he might get in trouble for pairing up enemies, I had to pay more."

"That's a lot of blood," Kylie said, when she couldn't think of anything else to say. Then the thought of blood had her remembering how she'd felt when she thought she'd killed Collin Warren. Fredericka had to feel the same, didn't she? Kylie's gratitude suddenly grew. "I'm sorry that . . . you had to . . . ki—Do it."

"It was nothing." She glanced at Kylie. "I've killed before."

Kylie couldn't swear on it, but something told her that if she'd been able to hear the girl's heartbeat, it would have told a different story.

"It still can't be easy," Kylie said.

"I'm over it," she snapped, but her tone said she wasn't.

And I'm still sorry.

More silence hung in the air. Fredericka finally spoke again. "You were wrong to sic your skunk on me."

"I didn't sic him on you," Kylie said, being honest. "You attacked him."

"It still wasn't nice," she said, and growled.

"Neither was putting a lion in my room." There, Kylie had thrown that bone out for them to chew on.

"I guess so." Fredericka looked away, but not quick enough.

Kylie saw the truth. "You didn't do it." She shook her head. "Why did you lie and say you did?"

She didn't answer for a long time. "I heard rumors that you thought I did it. I figured, why not let you believe it? I didn't like you."

"And now?" Kylie asked, still wondering why the were had paid three pints of blood to have an hour with her.

"Still don't like you," she said matter-of-factly. "But after I saw what you did for Holiday, I don't hate you as much."

"Well, there's a compliment I'll savor," Kylie said, letting a little humor slip into her voice. Fredericka didn't respond.

They arrived at the lake, and the girl stood there and looked out at the water. "I love Lucas," she confessed.

Kylie inhaled and tried to figure out how to play her cards now. Honesty seemed the only way. "So do I."

The were looked at Kylie, anguish filling the girl's eyes. "I know. That's why I wanted to talk to you. While I don't like you, I like *her* even less. And at least I know he cares about you. Even before you showed up here, he'd mentioned you to me. I was jealous of you even then."

Kylie shook her head, trying to play catch-up with Fredericka's conversation. "I'm not following you."

"I'm talking about Monique. I know he's told you that he can get out of it. But I'm not sure he can. I don't think you should let him do it."

"I'm still not following you," Kylie said, but she already had a feeling she didn't like what Fredericka had to say.

Fredericka just stared. "Shit. He didn't tell you? He said he did and you understood. That damn dog lied to me."

Frustration welled up inside Kylie. "Lied about what?"

"Lucas's betrothal ceremony is tonight."

Fredericka's words bounced around Kylie's head. "His what? He's . . . getting married?"

"Engaged, but with weres when you get betrothed, it's written in stone. He thinks he can get out of it, but I don't buy it. You don't just change your mind. And she's a complete bitch. If he goes through with this, he'll be stuck with her for the rest of his life."

"No!" Denial shot through Kylie and anger welled up inside her. "You're lying. You just want to start trouble. You'll do anything to break Lucas and me up."

"You bitch." Fredericka growled. "I'm trying to help and this is what I get? Yes, I've tried everything to break you up. It didn't work. But I'm not lying." She pulled an envelope from her pocket. A small envelope, like an invitation. "If you don't believe me, go see for yourself." She stepped away, and then turned back. "Just make sure you keep your were pattern on, or someone will rip your heart out before they ask questions."

• • •

Kylie didn't want to believe Fredericka. More than anything in the world, Kylie wanted this to be just another one of the were's tricks to come between her and Lucas. Yet the girl was right about one thing: Kylie had to see it for herself.

The ceremony was taking place at another state park around five miles from there. As a were, Kylie could make that run fairly quickly. All day, she considered whether or not to tell Holiday and Burnett, but decided she'd rather ask for forgiveness than for permission. And speaking of forgiveness . . . She swore if Fredericka was lying, she'd never forgive her, never trust her again.

But if she wasn't lying . . . Kylie wasn't sure she'd ever forgive Lucas.

The ceremony was supposedly happening at midnight. Which made it easy to get away.

Kylie tiptoed out of her room. Della yanked open her bedroom door.

Easier to get away, but not easy.

"Where are you going?" Della snapped, her gaze moving up and down on Kylie. "And all dressed up?"

Kylie didn't know what one was supposed to wear to a betrothal, but her black dress and low black pumps would have to do.

"I need to go somewhere," Kylie said, stating the vague truth. She hadn't told Della or Miranda about this. At first, Kylie thought it was because it just hurt too much. Then she thought it was because they'd try to talk her out of going. Right now, she realized it was because she was worried they might say, "I told you so."

They hadn't been pro-Lucas lately.

Not that Kylie totally believed it yet. But she obviously believed it enough to sneak out of Shadow Falls to find out. But how could she not be suspicious? Lucas never told her anything. And damn, that hurt.

"You're meeting your grandfather?" Della asked, studying Kylie with suspicion.

"No," Kylie said.

Della frowned. "You've been acting weird since you walked off with Fredericka."

"I need to go," Kylie said.

"I'll come with you."

"No," Kylie pleaded. She needed to do this alone.

Della's chest puffed out. "Then tell me where you're going."

"You're not my shadow anymore," Kylie countered.

Della's scowled. "No, I'm your friend."

The honest emotion in Della's voice pulled at Kylie's heart. "Look, I'm going to try to meet up with Lucas." It was the truth—or a form of it.

"I thought you hadn't heard from him," Della said.

"Fredericka told me where he was."

Della made a face. "You trust her wolf ass?"

"Not really," Kylie said. "But I'm going anyway, and as your friend, I'm asking you not to stand in my way."

"I don't like it," Della said.

Kylie paused in thought, trying to find a way to get Della to understand. "I don't like that you're doing work for the FRU, but I respect your wishes."

Della frowned. "But I'm not doing it alone."

Yeah, Della was going with Steve, not that she was thrilled with it, but that wasn't the point. Convincing Della to let Kylie go was what mattered. Right or wrong, finding out the truth about Lucas once and for all felt crucial. She had admitted to loving him; now she needed to know if she'd given her heart away foolishly.

It took some time, but Della backed down.

And ten minutes later, when Kylie jumped over the fence leaving Shadow Falls property, she knew Burnett might come running.

It was another chance she took. However, since she suspected that several of the weres might be attending the ceremony—if there really was a ceremony—she hoped Burnett would assume she was one of them. Then again, she *was* one of them, she reminded herself.

As Kylie ran, she felt an odd kind of power flow through her. Different than the strength that came with being vampire. The way her limbs moved seemed less human. The power of a wolf, she supposed.

Her chest tightened, remembering Lucas telling her how he wanted to run with her as a wolf. *Please, please let Fredericka be wrong.*

Trying not to break all her promises to Burnett, Kylie avoided the woods whenever possible. But as she drew near the park, she wasn't going to have any other option. As she moved in a lithe run, her gaze kept shifting to the moon. She felt it calling her, like water to a person left in the sun too long.

When she entered the line of trees, the darkness grew blacker. The moon was no longer visible through thick foliage. The night air was warm, almost too warm. She felt a sense of danger sting her skin.

Ignoring it, she kept running. She didn't stop. Not even when she realized she wasn't alone.

Chapter Thirty-eight

The cold finally started to impair Kylie's speed and she glanced over to see who the spirit was keeping pace at her side.

The ghost, a woman, the one who appeared in the classroom right before the vision, moved with powerful strokes. Her white gown flowed around her, and her long brown hair danced in the wind.

With Kylie's attention on the spirit, her foot caught on a root and she tumbled down onto the earth—hard—landing facedown.

Pushing up with her arms, breathing in the scent of moist dirt below her, she stared at the spirit looming over her. "Who are you?"

"I'm not important. You are." She held out her hands and instantly a long, bloody sword appeared. *"You must kill him."*

Kylie got to her feet and stared at the spirit's bloody hands; red liquid flowed onto the sword, then dripped to the ground. One slow drop at a time.

For the first time, Kylie understood a symbol connected with the spirit world. This ghost had blood on her hands. And now she wanted Kylie to do her bidding.

Drawing herself to her full height, Kylie spoke in her mind, *I don't know what you heard, but I don't . . . I haven't killed anyone, and I'd kind of like to keep it that way.*

She stared at Kylie with gray, dead eyes that held no emotion, no soul. Fear raced up Kylie's spine. Something about this spirit was different from the others. Something scary.

"Then you, too, will die," the ghost said as if it didn't really matter. Without warning, the spirit faded. But the spot where she'd stood was coated with ice. Dark, black ice.

"Couldn't you have told me that first?" Kylie muttered, and then inhaled. "No!" She fisted her hands. "I'm not going to think about this now."

Her heart pounded in her chest and she commenced running, running to Lucas, or rather, to the truth about Lucas.

She remembered the last time he'd kissed her, the way he'd held her, the way she'd felt so loved. Fredericka was lying. She had to be lying.

A few minutes later, Kylie sensed others around her.

Other wolves.

She wasn't sure how she knew, she just did. Not wanting to draw attention to herself, she stopped running and started walking. Hoping to hide the windblown look, she pulled the band from around her wrist and put up her hair.

As she moved closer to the park, she heard voices. Happy voices. She thought she recognized Will's voice. She stopped beside a tree so as not to cross paths with him or any other of the Shadow Falls campers. The last thing she wanted was to be recognized.

Only when Kylie couldn't hear anyone moving around her did she continue on. When she left the line of trees, she saw the crowd, standing in rows. A hundred or more wolves gathered together. A few in the back line turned and looked at her. Thank goodness they weren't from Shadow Falls.

Fredericka's warning rang in her ears. *Just make sure you keep your were pattern on or someone will rip your heart out before they ask questions.*

She felt a few of the bystanders checking her pattern and she prayed it was still were. Her breath hitched in her lungs until they turned around as if content she was one of them.

But Kylie didn't feel as if she belonged. Her heart ached at knowing Fredericka hadn't been lying. She almost left, but stopped herself. Maybe this wasn't even about Lucas. Maybe Fredericka sent her here hoping she'd see the crowd and believe the lie.

Stiffening her spine, she moved in and stood in the last row. Obviously weres didn't need to sit down, because no seats were provided. Her view of the front was blocked, but that meant people up front couldn't see her, either.

A voice suddenly started speaking, welcoming everyone here. Kylie's chest ached when she recognized the deep tenor.

Not Lucas, but his dad.

Her chest started to burn with the idea of Lucas getting engaged to someone else.

"Tonight I present to you my son and his bride-to-be," Lucas's father said. "You will witness their vows, their promise to each other."

Kylie closed her eyes. As betrayal filled her chest, music filled the dark night. The slow bell-like music was unlike anything Kylie had ever heard.

A young woman, dark hair pinned up with flowers, wearing a long black evening gown, walked down the aisle. The attendees oohed and ahhed over her beauty. Even Kylie couldn't deny it.

The crowd in front of her shifted, and Kylie saw Lucas's father. Standing beside him was . . . Lucas. The air in her lungs shuddered. He wore a dark gray tux that fit his hard frame just perfectly. Tears stung her eyes when she saw him reach out and take his future bride's hands.

The crowd shifted again, and she lost the view, but she could still hear. Words were spoken.

Vows.

Promises.

Lucas Parker gave his soul to Monique. *His soul.*

The sound of Lucas's voice cut into Kylie like a dull knife. She wanted to run, to escape, but to leave now would draw attention.

She waited. Her breath held, and she kept staring directly in front of her. The crowd shifted, and the view opened up again. Not a sound filled the night as Lucas pulled the girl into his arms and kissed her. Kissed her like he'd kissed Kylie.

Her breath caught. Anger and betrayal filled her.

She swung around to escape; not realizing another line had formed behind her, she slammed into someone.

"Sorry," she muttered.

"Kylie?" She heard someone say her name behind her.

She tried to dart around, but suddenly the crowd seemed to close in as everyone started applauding, cheering on the kiss.

"Excuse me," she said, pushing through another line of weres.

"Kylie?"

She heard her name again. And this time, she glanced back and saw Clara moving in.

She darted though the crowd, only to land in the midst of another close-knit group of weres. She looked back one more time. Lucas had his arms around the woman. He looked happy. Genuinely happy.

More than anything, Kylie wanted to disappear, to vanish. Then she realized she could disappear. She wished it, wished it with all her heart. Clara charged through the crowd, stopping beside Kylie. The girl looked around . . . and looked right through Kylie.

"Did you see the blonde that was here just a second ago?" Clara asked.

Kylie inhaled and left. Now, merely a wisp in the air, she took off running.

She didn't look back again. She couldn't.

She was crying when she entered the woods, crying when she left them.

Perhaps this was fate, she told herself. Because now she knew the right thing to do.

When she jumped the fence back into Shadow Falls, she didn't go to her cabin, she went to Hayden's. She didn't know if she was visible until he opened the door and stared at her. At her, not through her.

"What happened?" he asked, sounding urgent.

"Tomorrow." She forced the words through her tight throat. "Tomorrow I'll leave."

He ran a hand a through his mussed hair, sleep still filling his eyes. "We could go now. It would be easier."

"No." She shook her head. "I have to say good-bye."

He frowned. "They won't let you go."

She inhaled a breath of resolve. "They can't stop me."

When she got to her cabin and saw who waited on the front porch, her heart stopped.

She started to run away, but realized running wouldn't accomplish anything.

He still wore the tux, but he'd unbuttoned his shirt and the bow tie was gone. When his blue gaze met hers, regret filled his eyes.

She moved up the steps, and he studied her every move. He could probably tell she'd been crying, but she refused to cry in front of him now.

"Go back, Lucas," she said. "You're missing your own party."

"Don't do this," he growled. "I told you I was doing what I had to, that it didn't mean anything. It doesn't mean anything."

It sure looked as if it meant something. "Well, it should have meant something." *You gave her your soul.* She waved him away from the door. "I'm tired, do you mind?"

"Damn it, Kylie. As soon as I'm on the Council, I'll call off the engagement. I had to do this before my dad would give me his approval for the position. You said you understood."

She bit down on her lip. "How long have you been seeing her?"

He closed his eyes. "Dad's had it planned for a few months. He's been bringing her around, but I haven't—"

"Stop!" She shook her head. "Of all the things I considered you were hiding from me, I never imagined this."

"Try to see this from my point of view," he pleaded.

"I do see it," she said, and God help her, but there was some truth to her words. "You did what you had to do. As hard as it is, I understand that." *Lucas belonged with his pack, his people.*

And so did she.

He reached for her. She stepped back. She couldn't let him touch her. It would hurt too much. She held out her hand. "No."

He shook his head. "Please, don't do this. Damn it!" He swung his fist, closed his eyes and when he opened them, he looked at her. Right at her. "I love you."

Now he told her. Now! She lifted her chin. "I think you vowed your love and soul to Monique tonight."

She darted around him, entered the cabin, and shut him out. Then, leaning against the cold door, she wrapped her arms around herself. Her heart felt swollen, inflamed.

Don't ever fall in love, princess. It hurts too much. Her stepfather's words whispered through her broken heart. He'd been so damn right.

When she heard Lucas leaving, her breath caught.

"He's a piece of wolf shit," Della roared. Kylie looked up. Miranda stood beside Della in the kitchen. Had they heard everything? More tears filled her eyes.

"Sit down." Miranda pulled a chair out. "I'll get you some ice cream."

"No . . . not now." Kylie didn't have any strength to explain or to even talk.

"Tomorrow." She went into her room. Socks looked out at her from under the bed, and then disappeared. Even her cat betrayed her. It was the last straw. Kylie dropped on the bed and cried herself to sleep.

Not that she stayed asleep for long. At four in the morning, Kylie knocked on Miranda's door. "I need to talk to you."

Della had already gotten up and stood by the kitchen table, staring sleepy-eyed and suspicious at Kylie.

When Miranda came out, wearing her duck slippers, she pushed a curtain of hair from her face. "What time is it?"

"Early," Kylie said. "I'm sorry, but . . . I have to talk to both of you." *Make it short and sweet. Short and sweet.* She'd told herself all morning.

She'd tried talking herself out of this, but she couldn't. Leaving Shadow Falls was the right thing to do. But the right thing didn't always feel right. Coming to Shadow Falls had felt wrong, yet it had turned out to be a step toward finding the truth. This was just another step—a needed step.

Someday, Kylie hoped her choices could be made by what she wanted, and not by what she needed. But that time hadn't arrived yet.

"No," Della said.

"No, what?" Miranda asked.

"She's going to tell us she's leaving." Della's eyes filled with emotion.

"No, she's not," Miranda smarted back.

Short and sweet, Kylie thought again. "Della's right. I need to go live with my grandfather for a while. Not forever. I'll be back." God, she hoped so.

Miranda stared, her expression one of disbelief. "You can't do that. What will your mother say?"

"I haven't figured that out. But I will. I just need you guys to understand, and not be mad. And . . ." Tears filled her eyes. "And take care of Socks because he doesn't want to . . . go with me."

"You're leaving us," Miranda said. "You can't leave us. We're roommates, we're best friends."

Della stood there, stoic, tears glistening in her dark eyes, and she swiped away every drip of moisture that slipped from her lashes.

Kylie went to hug Miranda first. The witch started crying and Kylie's heart hurt so much she couldn't breathe. When Kylie turned to Della, the girl held up one hand. Anger flashed in her eyes.

"Oh, hell no," Della screamed. "You're freaking leaving us. I don't hug people who walk out on me." The vamp stormed back into her bedroom. Kylie felt the door slam all the way to her soul and it hurt so damn bad.

She walked into her room, picked up her suitcase, and left, before it got harder. Inside, Kylie felt raw. Sooner or later, it would stop hurting, she told herself.

Derek stood outside her cabin. He looked as if he'd woken up, pulled clothes on without thinking, and came running. His jeans weren't snapped, his shirt unbuttoned.

She wasn't sure how he knew, but he did. She saw it in his green eyes.

"Why?" he asked when she walked up to him.

"Because I have to figure things out."

"But you've already figured a lot out while you've been here."

"I know," Kylie said. "But it's time to take the next step."

He didn't try to talk her out of it. He didn't speak on the walk to the office. But she felt him reading her every emotion. When they arrived at the office, she looked back at him. For some reason she recalled the first time she'd seen him—sitting in the back of the bus, not very happy to be there.

She dropped the suitcase and hugged him. Tight. They had something special. She wasn't sure what it was, or if it should have been more, but she knew she cared about him. Probably always would.

He touched her cheek. He didn't say anything, but that touch said so much. He still loved her.

She picked up her suitcase and walked up on the porch. She left her suitcase by the door, then looked out toward the exit. She'd called Hayden earlier and told him to meet her at four thirty. She suspected he was already here. He didn't seem like the kind of guy who'd be late.

"Holiday." Kylie called out her name when she walked in.

"In the office," Holiday called back. "I just poured you a cup of coffee."

Kylie moved to the door. Holiday sat at her desk, her red hair hanging loose. She looked . . . happy. She wore her love for Burnett very well.

"You're up early . . . again," Holiday said.

Two cups of coffee waited on the desk. Had Holiday known she'd be here? Kylie went and sat in the chair. "How—?"

"Lucas came by late last night," the camp leader confessed.

Kylie swallowed. *Short and sweet.* She didn't want to talk about Lucas right now. "I have to go live with my grandfather for a while. Just until I figure out who I am."

Desperation entered Holiday's gaze. "You can't . . ."

Emotion lumped in Kylie's throat. "I need to figure this out."

"We can figure it out together," Holiday said, but her expression was one of sad acceptance. And it wasn't like Holiday not to fight harder. Unless . . .

Kylie remembered that when Holiday died, she'd spoken with Heidi, Kylie's grandmother. "She told you I had to go, didn't she?" When confusion filled Holiday's eyes, Kylie explained, "Heidi, she told you about this."

"No, not . . ." She paused. "She said I shouldn't stop you from making your own choices."

"And this is my choice." *Damn, it hurt to say that.* "I'll be back. You know that."

Holiday pressed her open palms on the desk. "What am I going to tell your parents?"

Kylie paused. "I'll figure it out and call you."

Holiday exhaled. "Burnett is going to be so furious."

"I know. That's why I was hoping you'd just tell him about this. I don't think I could face him right now."

"I don't like this." Holiday's voice sound so tight.

Tears filled Kylie's eyes and she stood up. "Della wouldn't hug me good-bye. Please don't say you won't."

Holiday bolted up. "I'll hug you for me and Della. And Burnett."

The embrace lasted for several long seconds. "I love you," Holiday said. "And I expect a phone call from you this evening. And every day. Every morning and night."

Kylie nodded. "Thank you for not fighting me on this."

Holiday put a hand on each side of Kylie's face. "Don't think I don't want to."

"But you know it's the right thing?" Kylie asked, hating that she needed a little more confirmation. But damn, should doing the right thing feel so wrong?

Holiday inhaled. "I don't know if it's right. I won't stop you." She frowned. "But I will say this. If this is about what happened with Lucas—"

Kylie inhaled. "This isn't just about him." And it wasn't. He was just the proverbial straw that brought the camel to its knotty knees.

Holiday sighed. "Sometimes, when we're hurting, we make choices we wouldn't normally make."

Kylie shook her head. "Remember how my dad told me that we would work out these things together? I think by 'we' he meant chameleons."

Holiday frowned. "You don't know that's what he meant. You thought he was telling you that you were going to die. Maybe if we went to the falls you might—"

"No, this is right," Kylie said, and there was a part of her that believed it.

Holiday exhaled, her breath shaky. "Then I have to let you go, even if I don't agree."

They hugged again. *Short and sweet.* Kylie walked out.

The dad-blasted blue jay swooped in. More tears filled Kylie's eyes. "Go," she told the bird. "It's time to leave the nest. For both of us."

Turning, she spotted Hayden waiting by the gate. She picked up her suitcase, the same one she'd brought with her to Shadow Falls last June. She started walking and got a few feet from the gate when a sudden whisk of wind, a familiar whisk, flashed past, then stopped.

Della's arms embraced her. "Promise me you'll get your wolf ass back here soon. Promise me, damn it!"

Tears filled Kylie's eyes and she held on to Della extra tight, the way only really good friends do. "I promise," Kylie said. "I promise."

It was a promise Kylie intended to keep, too. Della, obviously another believer in short and sweet, flashed away. Kylie looked back one more time. She saw a crying Miranda with Perry running up from the path into the main clearing; she stopped and just waved. Kylie knew that Miranda had helped convince Della to come. Dear God, she was going to miss her roommates.

Then Kylie's gaze shifted to the office porch. Holiday stood there. But not alone. Burnett stood by her side. Even from this distance, she saw his disapproval, but she also saw how his arm tenderly circled Holiday's waist. A warmth filled Kylie's chest; she'd played a small part in helping that happen. And somehow she sensed that had been part of her destiny.

Suddenly she saw Derek standing to the side of the office. He met her gaze and smiled.

If she wasn't hurting so much, she would have smiled back. Right before she went to turn away, she felt another presence. Felt it, didn't see. Somewhere behind the first line of trees, a certain blue-eyed were watched. He was hurting, but so was she.

She turned toward the gate. Hayden had come closer. "You ready?" he asked.

No, her heart said, but her head said yes. She didn't know what awaited her at her grandfather's, but nothing, nothing would take the place of Shadow Falls.

"It's hard to say good-bye," Hayden said.

"I'll be back," Kylie said. "I swear I will."

And she wanted to believe that more than anything, too.

*Love will be won, powers will be revealed, and
one final choice will be made . . .*

Don't miss the explosive final installment of C. C. Hunter's
New York Times *bestselling Shadow Falls series*

Chosen at Nightfall

Coming from St. Martin's Griffin in Spring 2013